Creature

A NOVEL OF MARY SHELLEY AND *FRANKENSTEIN*

AMY E. WELDON

SEA CROW PRESS

Contents

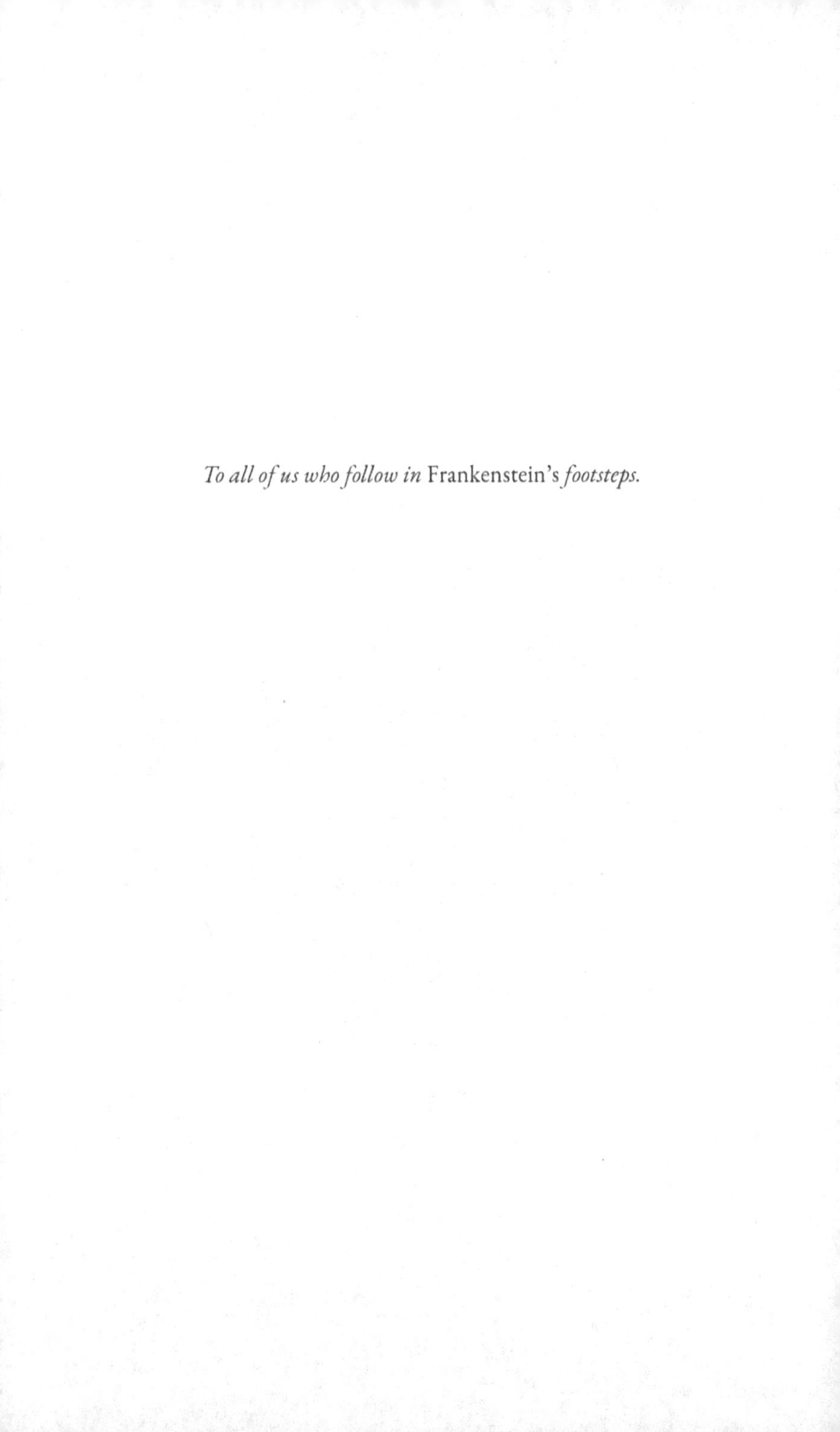

To all of us who follow in Frankenstein's *footsteps.*

Creature

Prologue

It begins with earth on a coffin-lid, unmoving. It begins with a woman in labor, thrashing in the birth of a girl. It begins with the doctor, his hands red. "I'm going to remove the placenta now," he declares to the moaning woman. "Still stuck fast, inside. You fed your child but now she's born and she can survive on her own. She will. She must."

Can the mother hear him? Does she answer? Are her bright golden-brown eyes open or squeezed shut against the pain that's brought out the sweat all over her, wringing her long hair into ropes around her throat? No one will ever know.

The scissors are slapped into the doctor's red palm and the grinding snip of metal through flesh shears the child away from all the world she has ever known. The father can only pace and try not to stare at all that blood before he flees the room in dread.

So it begins, then, with a being still stranded between worlds and lives. A four-limbed livid thing still waxy with *vernix caseosa,* not yet plumped with milk and sweetness, all ribs and fists, its skull bent sharp by its passage through a gate of bone. Its skin bright red. A bewildered thing. Screaming.

Mother? Where are you?

Father? Where am I?

In ten days, this four-limbed livid thing, held in someone's arms, blooming into something like a baby girl, will blink with dark borderless eyes at the sight before it. A hole in the ground, six feet long, six feet deep. Its father hunkers next to that hole, weeping, clutching fistfuls of earth.

Let her go, Godwin, a kind voice will urge. *Open your hands.*

I can't, its father will cry, clutching the earth tighter. *I can't.*

Other sounds will enter the baby's ears. The cooing of pigeons in the belfry of the old stone church. Willow trees rustling on the bank of the melancholy little river which runs south to join the Thames, and, eventually, the sea. The thud of earth on a coffin lid. The murmur of prayers, the gasp and hitch of tears. In all the mourners' mouths, the name that belongs to the dead mother and the living child: *Mary. Mary. Mary Wollstonecraft.* The rustle of that child in her swaddling bands, bound and weary and curious.[1]

And from somewhere over the border of that country from which she has recently emerged, the child will hear a voice. A voice that is contained within her own new and wondering brain but that also haunts the air around her: pipping, tapping, testing the limits of its own future life like a chick inside the shell it will eventually burst.

Mother, it will ask, *where are you?*

Father, it will ask, *what am I?*

The child will turn her head, mouth open, eyes searching for the source of that voice. And there it is, visible to her eyes alone. A thickened spot of darkness under the trees. A shimmer to the air that is not only mourners' grief but is some kind of creature alchemized into life before her eyes, born of curiosity and rage and a terrible love for this world into which she has now leapt. It is a voice like her own. And yet it is not. It possesses itself. In a space she cannot touch. Not yet.

This is how it begins.

Creature and infant girl, born together. Helpless. Intent. Alive.

Part One

CHAPTER 1

St. Pancras

LONDON 1806

Mary wakes and lies still in her bed, listening. If her father and her older sister Fanny have gone out, then this will be a good day to play the game. Inside the wall, a mouse chitters, then hushes. There are the scufflings of Fanny gathering her basket and lacing her boots. The front door opens, then shuts. Silence. Good. Mary and Mama, alone: that's the game. One of them summons the other and then makes her disappear.

Mary throws back the quilt and slips out of bed. Her brown dress hangs in the wardrobe with her stockings draped over it, shrunken as ghost-legs. Shivering, she shucks off her nightgown, drops the dress over her head, and tugs the stockings on, turning them so the worst holes don't show. Mama's sister, Aunt Everina, had been so censorious at Easter, peering at Mary's and Fanny's threadbare clothes and back at Papa, her eyebrows raised. "Believe me, I'm trying," Papa snapped. "If you're so worried, then overcome your old-maid scruples and take Fanny to live with you. You promised, once, and broke your word." He mimicked Aunt Everina's vinegary voice. "'Her mother's reputation will taint our school.' Her *mother*? She was your *sister*, Everina. Mary Wollstonecraft. Say her name."

High on the bureau-top gleam Mama's pewter-backed brush and comb. Mary strokes the brush down her hair, then weaves a braid and ties it with a piece of string. Papa gave this brush and comb to Mama on their wedding day, and then, several years ago, to Mary and Fanny. "Share them," he'd instructed, turning his face away, swallowing hard. And they still obey. They keep Mama's things safe: brush and comb on the bureau and, in the top drawer, Mama's stays. Mary likes to slide open the top drawer of the bureau and touch the whalebone ribs, stitched into pale canvas with tiny threads, that Mama had laced around herself every morning of her adult life. Mama had complained about them – how women bind themselves with *worse than Chinese bands*. But Fanny is nearly thirteen; she'll soon be armored in them, swimming away into the dark water of womanhood: the future, the inevitable, the place where you die from babies clamoring to tear their way into the world through you. The stays are a thrilling and dangerous charm, with Mama's initials – *M W* – stitched in red thread just below the heart. Lucky the top drawer has a lock. A lock can protect secrets. A lock can keep Fanny here in the Polygon Building as Mary's big sister, forever. Fanny will never abandon Mary. Even though Fanny remembers Mama as Mary never can. Even though, on a pink ribbon around her neck, Fanny wears the key to that lock.

In her stocking feet, Mary creeps into Papa's study. Morning sunlight washes over his desk with its stacks of paper. The new novel. The children's tales, written under a pseudonym. Scrawled Latin exercises by the rich boys he trudges out to St. John's Wood to tutor: "Harrow's wasted on them, Mary," he sighs, "would that girls could study there, you'd put them all to shame." The essays on Various Political Subjects by the Author of *Political Justice* (Mary can hear the capital letters in her mind.) And bills, with the tradesmen's angry scribble: *Past Due*. Last week Mary stole a sheet of Papa's good paper to write a story of her own: *Once there were two sisters,* the first line reads, *and a papa and a mama's ghost*. She could sit in his chair and add another line right now. But not today. Mornings alone are too rare to spend on anything but the game.

Over the fireplace mantel hangs Mama's bright face, bounded by its portrait frame. On the walls, books lean together like drunkards, with more books piled on top: Shakespeare, Volney, Gibbon, Voltaire, Montaigne, Rousseau, Cicero, Milton, and the Bible Papa says that rational people should use only as a key to Milton. One shelf for the books Papa himself has written (although he keeps his *Memoir* of Mama out of sight); a smaller shelf for Mama's, arranged in order of publication. *Thoughts on the Education of Daughters. Original Stories from Real Life. Mary: A Fiction. A Vindication of the Rights of Men. A Vindication of the Rights of Woman. An Historical and Moral View of the French Revolution and the Effect It Has Produced in Europe. Letters Written in Sweden, Norway, and Denmark.* Mary has read all her mother's books, forcing her eyes even over the parts she doesn't understand. "That shows ambition," Papa praises. "An excellent thing in woman, despite her unjustly lowered status in this world." The shadow inside his words is Shakespeare, *low and soft, an excellent thing*: Mary studies hard so she can spot these shadows whenever they appear and make her Papa smile. Then comes the pinch across his brow: he's remembering Mama. Who knows what those pictures of her look like, deep inside his head?

Mary can't know. But in this room, alone in the game, she has pictures of her own.

She lifts the straight wooden chair from its corner and carries it across the room and sets it in front of the fireplace. It's easier to balance now that the old Turkey carpet's been sold and the floor's bare. No need to fear the hem of her dress catching fire. There's been no fire in this room for months.

Knee by knee, she clambers onto the chair, then stands. Through her stocking-holes, the wood is cold. She plants her feet and sets one hand on each side of the portrait frame. And Mama fills her vision, completely.

Against a backdrop of dark gray, Mama's face floats, warm and bright. It's pointy-chinned and broad, tilted slightly down and sideways. "Look at me," Mr. Opie must have said to Mama, touching his brush to the canvas, "but not directly." Thick eyebrows and bright, heavy-lidded eyes. Thick light-auburn hair – the color of Mary's own – tumbling from under the dark green cap that can't quite hold it in. A decisive nose, a strong throat graceful against her soft white gown. A faint flush on her cheeks.

And, under that white gown, inside the circle of Mama's arms: the visible bump of Mary herself. "Babies sleep inside their mothers," Papa has told her and Fanny, "until the world is ready for them." If you slept, you might dream. And if you dreamed, you might remember. Mary can't remember being inside Mama. But dreams show her other things. Papa raving, screaming. Herself split open on a bed as a man with a knife unstrings her insides. A tall being, man-shaped, stumbling through an open door into the street. Mama twisting in bloody sheets. The thud of earth on a coffin-lid. *You killed her*, a voice rages, then, in Mary's head. *You, by coming forth into this world.*

It's only from a distance, and only with the most casual of glances, that Mama looks like she's smiling. At close range, Mama's smile is flickeringly sad. You smile like that when you're pondering something–

(*Mary kept all these things and pondered them in her heart*)

—that you can never tell anyone directly, but that a sympathetic mind might guess.

(I'll never live to see my second daughter. She'll search for me her whole life.)

Is that what Mama had been thinking?

Her name had been Mary, too.

You killed her. She'd be alive if not for you.

It's time to go inside.

Mary trains her eyes on Mama's painted, slightly averted ones and bends forward, pressing her heels against the chair seat and stiffening her spine. The face breaks and floats in conjoined twin faces before her eyes – four eyes, two mouths smeared across one another – but she leans closer yet and the face becomes real. Briefly, dazzlingly, it's only skin, flushed and warm. She closes her eyes to savor the feeling. Yet to prolong any present happiness beyond its time is to lose it for good. Better to keep things in your mind, safe, for as long as you're alive.

She leans closer until her nose touches the canvas. Now Mama's only a swirl of rosy creams and pinks and bits of yellow where Mr. Opie's brush laid down the color in tiny strokes. It's good to see how someone made a thing, because it makes you want to make a thing yourself.

The mind is its own place, and in itself can make a heaven of hell, a hell of heaven...

Her mind is the only place Mary can find Mama now.

She holds her face still in front of the canvas, breathing against Mama's painted skin as it reflects her own warmth back to her. The chair creaks. The weight of her long braid settles against her spine. Eventually she realizes, with the game's familiar shock, that she doesn't know how long she's been staring at her mother's face. It's terrifying and thrilling, the way the atmosphere of her mind can close like water over her head and drown what Papa calls *reality*.

Mary steps down from the chair and sets it back against the wall, then returns to stand below Mama's portrait, looking up. She straightens her spine, as Mama's books urge girls to do. *If fear in girls, instead of being cherished, perhaps created, were treated in the same manner as cowardice in boys, we should quickly see women with more dignified aspects. I do not wish them to have power over men, but over themselves.*[1]

The kitchen door bangs: Fanny's back. *Go help her*, nudges a familiar voice in Mary's head. *Be good.*

Stay here, whispers the slightly-less-familiar opposite one. *If you hearken too much to someone else, you'll die. Or rather, I'll die inside you. Which is worse.*

This is the voice Mary never ignores, no matter what it says.

She moves to Papa's shelves to take out Volney's *Ruins of Empire*. But then a crash – worryingly large – makes her turn and hurry to the kitchen, where Fanny stoops over a sticky splatter of eggs and shells. Her sallow face swells with tears. "Oh, Mary," she wails, "I dropped the basket."

The yellow-and-white mass is slimy, gleaming, and dirty at its edges, like a puddle girdled by ice. As she moves toward the drawer full of rags and the water bucket, Mary feels the cold voice speak in her: *when was the last time she cleaned this floor?* But Fanny already does most of the cleaning, and cooking, and marketing, since at thirteen she's nearly grown. Fanny is Mama's daughter too. Fanny also has to keep on in this flat powdered by dust and books and the smoke of what little coal there is. *She'll waste her life this way. But you won't. If you look sharp.*

So Mary looks. Eggshells in their sticky yellow spill twirl across the floor: beige and speckly boats, round coracles, pale on the inside. Clinging to one shell is a brown clot that might have grown into a chick if big, kind Mrs. O'Neill in her chicken-yard hadn't shoved her hand under the hen and drawn this warm egg away for Fanny to bring home and break. What power can make a fluffy chick from this soupy mess? At what instant can the hen, through her sleek feathers, hear the chick stir, feel the new creature's tiny limbs rattle the shell with its first, irreversible breath? What can a chick see from inside the egg? Just its own folded would-be-wings, all packed and crammed. Maybe it can see the warm dimness around it. Sometimes the light of its known world must brighten as the warm weight it's always known lifts up and away, as its mother stands up and is gone. Still, her going leaves that light, unblocked, for the chick to see whatever it can. And in her absence, that has to be its consolation.

Fanny gathers the shells and drops them into the basket. Puddled yolk ropes down through her fingers. "Oh, me," she sighs. "I'm such an idiot. A rag –"

"No," Mary says, "a rag would only smear it. First we need something with an edge." She fetches the fireplace shovel from the parlor, scrapes the silky egg-strings into a heap, and slithers them into the slop pail underneath the washstand. Then she taps the shovel-edge on the rim and swishes it in the water bucket and stands it on end against the wall. Fanny looks at it and averts her eyes. "The dustpan," she says. "I should have thought of it. Now we've made the shovel wet. What if it rusts?"

"It'll dry," Mary says. "Don't worry." Suddenly she longs to be away from Fanny: her fussing, her fear, her eternal quivering on the edge of tears. *You're so cruel to be disgusted by your sister,* says one internal voice. *But accurate,* says the colder one. *Behold what happens when you let house-work be the aim and measure of your days, and dependence be the rule.* Sometimes she thinks that cold voice sounds like Mama's prose, in those brown-bound books Papa let her read in his study. Maybe Mama's growing inside her as she grew inside Mama, readying herself to burst forth. Or maybe it's some other creature entirely. Like that dark stumbling shape in her dream, that shimmer to the air –

"I'll mop," Fanny blurts. She gathers a handful of rags and dips them in the water-bucket and swabs the floor until a smeary circle emerges. Mary stands next to her and they look. Unfortunately, now it's worse.

"We'll have to do the whole floor," Mary sighs. "I'll help you. Do you know where Papa is?"

"He's out," Fanny says. "I don't know where." She scrambles to her feet and tucks her sleeves above her elbows and touches the rolled-up places, one and then the other. In a boy, Fanny's wide bony face would be handsome, her knuckly hands called *capable,* her thick eyebrows *bold.* In her face mingle Mama's nose and Mama's upturned lips and what must be Mr. Imlay's brow, since it's higher than Mama's (but this is just a guess; there are no pictures of Mr. Imlay anywhere) with a dusty pallid sallowness all Fanny's own. Bands of straight dim hair droop under her cap. At least she isn't too tall. No man will ever take a girl too tall and so all-fired poor as they are, into the bargain. Everybody says that. And for once, everybody's right.

My poor plain sister, muses cold inward Mary, freezing normal Mary's hand on the heap of shells. *What's to become of you?*

But Fanny has mind-pictures of Mama that Mary never can.

Both of them have the story of Fanny's birth, though. Years before she knew Papa, Mama met the dashing Mr. Imlay, an American, who owned treasure ships and racehorses and consorted with real live Indians in feathers and beads. She fell in love with him. Since they were living in Paris at the time, where kings and queens' heads were being chopped off by the mob ("*mob* is a loaded word, Mary," Papa frowns, "they were people seeking a redress of tyranny, by the only means that uneducated people ever get to know") Mama and Mr. Imlay had to be careful, because, even as non-Frenchmen, they were apt to get swept up in the general confusion. ("Well, they *were* a mob, Papa," Mary argues, "because humans do have reason – doesn't Mama say it? Men and women both? – and if we choose not to exercise it, does that not make us a mob, and in the wrong, no better than the beasts?") So they met outside the city gates of Paris to be together. That was how Fanny came to be born. But soon Mr. Imlay did not love Mama anymore even though she went to Norway to find one of his stolen treasure ships for him and took Fanny – just a baby – with her. And that was where the book of Mama's letters from Norway came from. "If ever there was a book," Papa says of it, "calculated to make a man in love with its author, this appears to me to be the book."[2] And it had made Papa fall in love with Mama. So, technically, without that book, Mary wouldn't be alive at all.

But Mama would be alive if Mary had never been born.

Last year, Papa found Mary standing on the chair in front of Mama's portrait, crying. "She'd never want you to be so sad," he said. He lifted her down and patted her awkwardly. "Your mother," he fumbled, "well, she –" Behind his spectacles, his eyes grew wet. "She was so –" He straightened up, wiped his eyes, and took the book of letters from Norway off the shelf and put it into Mary's hands and walked out of his study and left her and Mama and Mama's book there together. Mary never let him catch her there alone again.

But now she's nine, and doesn't cry so much. Papa told her last week that the ancient Pharaohs preferred girls of nine for conversation, since they were so clever and so lively. "Like you," he says, "you are a clever girl. And I know your mother would be –" *Proud*, she yearned. *Please say she would be proud.*

Papa hadn't finished the sentence. He'd gone to his desk and taken out a manuscript in her mother's handwriting and set it into her hands. And so Mary read it: the novel her mother had been writing when Mary was born. The narrator speaks to her baby daughter, stolen by a cruel husband. And Mary's mother speaks to her.

Death may snatch me from you... I would then, with fond anxiety, lead you very early in life to form your grand principle of action, to save you from the vain regret of having, through irresolution, let the spring-tide of existence pass away, unimproved, unenjoyed. Gain experience – ah! gain it – while experience is worth having, and acquire sufficient fortitude to pursue your own happiness; it includes your utility by a direct path. What is wisdom too often but the owl of the goddess, who sits moping in a desolated heart –[3]

Moping in a desolated heart. Look at Fanny now, hauling out the bucket to swab the floor, scraping her knuckles against the boards. What *experience* will Fanny ever have? Mary shivers. She can't let herself be mired in a life like that. Mama's friend, earnest Miss Hays, always says the world is no place for a woman of feeling. Mama had feared this for Fanny too: *I dread to unfold her mind,* she wrote from Norway, *lest it render her unfit for the world she is to inhabit.*[4] Is this always the fate of a woman – to die in childbirth, like Mama? To wear out her life as a kitchen drudge, like Fanny? To strain, like Miss Hays, after something her own labor can never quite earn her – another book, some money, a man? But even a man can't secure you. Papa couldn't stop Mama from dying, or give her any other home than this flat in this cheap odd-shaped new building at the north edge of London, The Polygon, with its noises through the walls and its sloping floors and its persistent chill. In the room where Papa still sleeps, Mary's birth killed Mama. And neither Papa nor God nor Mary herself could stop it.

Suddenly the front door thumps and Papa's voice runs down the hall. He's laughing, a little out of breath. "My humble home, my dear," he says. "Too bad a poor scholar's not got the back to lift you over the threshold…"

"Our home, now," a woman's voice purrs. "I walk in on my own. And gladly." Then comes a smothered giggle and a silence that's somehow moist. Mary and Fanny stare at each other. *Our?*

Footsteps rustle down the passage, and Papa and the woman appear in the door. Papa's high forehead shines, his eyes bright. Has he been drinking? The woman definitely has. She sways against him, several inches shorter but much wider; they look like Jack Sprat and Mrs. Sprat, who eat no fat and eat no lean but together manage to do more than they should. Mary blinks. It's Mrs. Vial, who moved into the neighborhood this winter and has been simpering at Papa ever since: *oh, Mr. Godwin, I'm a great admirer of your work, have you time to help my poor Puss descend from a tree?* The first time, Papa had just bowed and smiled his suffering-fools smile: "Madam," he'd replied, "even the most cursory observation will show no cat's skeleton in any tree in London. Hunger will drive her down." But his eyes had roamed helplessly to the quivery bosom-tops, the heap of curls too thick and dark to be real. Mrs. Vial's small black eyes watched him steadily. "Mr. Godwin," she'd cooed, "how I *do* admire a reasonable man."

And here she is, in Mary's and Fanny's (mostly Fanny's) kitchen. Her bosom-tops quiver in her cheap gray satin dress; she tucks her hands against her stomach to hide her red, swollen fingers with their bitten nails. Her black eyes flick around the kitchen and the bucket and the egg-smeared floor and Fanny and Mary.

"Girls," Papa says, "you know Mrs. Vial, our neighbor." Flustered, he runs one finger around the inside of his collar. His face gleams with sweat, although the house is cold. He's nervous, but happy. As Papa very seldom is.

A dreadful fear deepens in Mary's stomach. This grinning thing is not her Papa. He's forty-five, settled, solid, old. Can grown men be changelings? Like Puck or Ariel? The woman smiles and nudges him, and he reaches one hand behind her and grazes her wide bottom, as if by accident. But Mary knows better. Papa isn't looking at her because he knows she cannot be fooled.

("Isn't *she* the merry widow, then," Mrs. O'Neill had snorted as Mary and Fanny stood next to her boxes of hens – golden-brown and sleek, burbling complaints but resettling now that they'd traded their eggs for one of Papa's coins – and all three of them watched Mrs. Vial's black skirts swishing down the street, her parasol bobbing. "The merry widow Clairmont. You girls'd better watch out for your father." Mrs. O'Neill sighed. "Poor fool. She'll be setting her cap for him and no mistake. And there's never a man can resist a clever woman like her.")

Clever woman. But Mary's clever too. She straightens and looks Papa in the eye. *Tell the truth,* he often says, *all of it. Particularly the unpleasant things.*

Papa glances at Mary, then Fanny. "Girls," he says, "we're married."

"And I've brought what you might call a wedding present," Mrs. Vial laughs. In her eyes she holds that false brightness some women think girls like. "Another sister for you."

She reaches behind her and jerks a girl forward. Her eyes are black as Mrs. Vial's, and so's her hair, which curls around her shoulders. But her dress is like Mary's and Fanny's: clean but worn, with a pattern of pink flowers washed to ghosts. Around one skinny wrist, a red thread bunches in braided knots. "This is my daughter, Mary Jane," Mrs. Vial says. "She's just turned nine, and –"

"Claire," the girl interrupts. Her voice is scratchy and low. "My name is Claire."

"We've had this discussion." Mrs. Vial's smooth voice tightens. "Your name is the one I gave you at your christening, my very own." She flashes a gray-toothed smile at Papa.

"Claire is *my* very own," the girl retorts. "My very own name I chose myself."

"Mary Jane has been away at school," Mrs. Vial explains. "That's why you haven't seen her in the street." It must not be a very good school, Mary thinks, if Mrs. Vial can afford it. Yet once a skinny child in breeches had clambered over the back fence near Mrs. Vial's house and dropped onto the street right in front of Mary, then scrambled up and darted away. That child had had dark hair like this straggling out from under a boy's cap. Maybe that child was this girl Claire. In spite of herself, Mary feels a twinge of interest. How would it feel to tug on your cap and saunter off into the street just as you please, with no one to recognize you as anything but the person you believe yourself to be?

Wait. *The merry widow Clairmont.* "Is your name really Mrs. Vial?" Mary asks.

"Who says otherwise?" The small black eyes sharpen. The bitten red hands uncurl and circle Papa's arm.

"Well –" Mary stops. "People."

"I wouldn't hearken to Irish poultrywomen if I were you." Mrs. Vial's voice is smooth. "*Je n'écoute pas les commérages.*"

"Mrs. Vial was married before," Papa explains, "and that was Cla— Mary Jane's father, Mr. Clairmont."

"Then why is she Mrs. Vial now?" Mary asks. Fanny shifts from foot to foot, plucking at her dirty apron; she hates a fuss. Papa glares at Mary. *Be mannerly. This is my will.* And she glares back. *Tyrant. You replaced Mama without ever asking me.*

"Because a woman sometimes has need to return to the name of her birth," Mrs. Vial says, "as you may learn when you attain some maturity and common sense. Now." Her gaze roams around the dingy kitchen and the egg-smeared floor. "Soon as I get out of this dress I'll help –"

"We don't need another sister," Mary blurts. "We don't need you. We have a mama."

"Your mama's dead, child," Mrs. Vial observes.

Papa's face is white. Mary's never seen him so angry. But a feeling's loose in her now, heedless as a runaway cart-horse galloping down the street, reins flying. She won't pull it in. Hasn't Papa himself always insisted? *Tell the truth. Conscience known and spoken freely is true liberty, our only defence against the tyrant's grip.* Mrs. Vial will be a tyrant if Mary lets her – that much is clear. She opens her mouth but to her horror finds she's on the verge of tears. Crying in front of this woman is the greatest imaginable shame.

She turns and bolts out the door, ignoring Papa's shout, and into the street. Outside, the whole morning sparkles, the sun glittering in the windows of the Polygon. Last night's rainwater ribbons down the center of each rut in the road. Mrs. O'Neill's chicken-pen fence rises at her left and Mary extends her hand to rattle it along the slats. There's Mrs. Moorcock with the bent shoulder and the drunken husband, limping outside to empty her necessary pot against a tree. Here's the brewer's yard with its big warm horses backing into the wagon-shafts, their muddy hooves stamping, the stableboys holding the bridles, cooing, "aren't you a good fella." An orange cat dashes by with a fieldmouse in its jaws. Papa won't permit her a cat, despite the squeaks and skitters in the walls, because cats make him sneeze. Right now, Mary could happily watch him gasp for air. *Tyrant,* she thinks. *I already have a Mama who loves me best of all.*

Just ahead stands the little stone church of St. Pancras on its hill, shaded by three big oaks that lean over the short steeple and the slate roof. The iron gate's open – Mr. Jebb, the vicar, insists on that. Mama and Papa were married here, with just Miss Hays and Mr. Hookham and Mr. Jebb to see. Papa wrote in *Political Justice* about marriage as a vulgar superstition designed to enslave both men and women, but for Mama he made an exception, because Mary herself was inside her mama's belly by then, under that white gown, inside those circling arms. In spite of any ideas Mama or Papa might have, it's easier for a pregnant woman if she has a husband. At least in this neighborhood. And maybe everywhere.

The church doors are shut despite the fine morning air. Mr. Jebb must be leading prayers for the few people Mary has ever seen here, the two old sisters with their black string bags and the man with the smashed-up leg and the boy with the red face who twitches and blinks. "Superstition," Papa snorts. But Mary has seen the boy walking slowly into the sunlight after prayers, his face calm. It can't just be superstition if something about it works.

Mary veers left onto the narrow path, deeper into the burying-ground. Gravestones sprout around her: small marble rectangles flat in the grass (mostly for babies), tall spikes with big square bases (for gentlemen, back when gentlemen had lived in this parish), and flat upright slabs with arched tops, all gray-mottled and lichen-specked. This churchyard's damp. Much of the neighborhood around here is damp, because of the melancholy little River Fleet that runs past the graves and on to the heart of the city. Maybe that's why the dead gentlemen's families sold their land to the men who built the Polygon. Wealth enables you to choose to be at the river or away from it. No rich person would choose this in-between place, neither damp nor healthy. Neither city nor country. Neither daughter nor orphan. Neither dead nor alive.

Here at last is the familiar comforting square stone pedestal, almost as tall as Mary herself, that marks Mama's grave. The flat top's wide enough to sit on, tailor-fashion. But Mary would never do such a thing. Even gentle Mr. Jebb would be angry if he found her climbing on stones.

Instead she leans against the rough granite and slides down to sit. She can be closer to Mama here, separated only by a few feet of earth and an inch or two of coffin-wood. Mama's face lies down there in the dark, upturned to her on its pillow, pink and white, with its rosy rueful mouth smiling even in the dark. Surely Mama's glad that Mary has never forgotten her. *My daughter. So loyal and dutiful. An excellent thing in woman.* Mary scrubs the Shakespeare-ghost from her mind and tries again. *My daughter. How glad I am you've come to see me. Even if your faithless Papa has married a cheap and vulgar merry-widow, you never forget me. You're the only one who really loves me. I can always count on you.*

Over the churchyard, gray clouds gather around a doubtful slice of creamy-blue sky. One of Mrs. Radcliffe's novel heroines would have tempests to accompany her grief, but Mary has only normal English weather: changeable clouds and the fragile, lovely, untrustworthy sun. Swallows slice the air with their spiky tails. For a moment she feels silly, moping on the ground in her ordinary neighborhood, half-listening to the clatter of the street. But then she imagines Mama leaning over her, touching her arm, smiling ironically – *come on, big girl, get up* – and she leans her forehead on her crossed arms and cries.

Turning, she curls against the name that is Mama's, and her own. *Mary Wollstonecraft Godwin. Author of A Vindication of the Rights of Woman. Born 27th April 1750. Died 10th September 1797.* Then she reaches down into her mind, as she always does, to see if she can find even a scrap of memory from when she – just a week-old baby – and Mama were alive at the same time. *Hold still. Concentrate.* And here is Mama, tired but smiling, propped against pillows, leaning over a knot of blankets from which pokes a scrunched red face. *Open your eyes!* Mary badgers her infant self. But there's no way to make time run backwards, and anyway, this can't be a real memory, since no small baby can remember anything, surely. Yet the picture's still there. Mama's face, lit with happiness. Her smiling lips, her bright golden-brown eyes. The morning sun smoothing the bumpy plaster and brightening Mama's pewter-backed brush and comb and mirror on the bureau. The red-faced baby nestled against her mother's living flesh, warm. Mary holds herself still, barely breathing. Maybe this time, the picture is real.

Mary must have dozed off without knowing it, because suddenly Papa is there. She opens her eyes straight into his, which are the same brownish-green as her own. He hunkers down in his long-tailed coat, clasping his hands between his knees. A little wind pries a strand of hair loose from his high bald forehead and waves it around. He hasn't reached to touch her. Papa doesn't often touch. But he's come to find her. Part of her wants to roll sleepily toward him and be held. But her waking brain stretches itself and speaks: *And what says his new wife?*

Mary pushes herself up straight, scraping gently against the carved edges of her mother's name. Papa leans close, his face level with the date of Mama's death. For a moment Mary sees him complete: the scaly top of his bald head, the red spectacle marks on his long thin nose, the frayed edges of his collar and coat sleeves, his wiry knees about to split his worn breeches cloth. He held her finger to her mother's name when she was small, tracing the letters, teaching her: *M, A, R, Y.* He kept Fanny with him when another man would have sent her away. *No man chooses evil,* Mama wrote, *because it is evil; he only mistakes it for happiness, the good he seeks.*[5] In *Paradise Lost*, God told Adam it was not good for man to be alone. Surely Papa is lonely without Mama, enough to make even Mrs. Vial seem reasonable. But even though he has Mary and Fanny for company, he's replaced Mama without asking them at all. Mary's anger rallies itself in images. Papa's hand on Mrs. Vial's wide rump. His sweaty, grinning face next to hers in the kitchen. His eyes on Mary now, so sad.

Mary hoists herself from the ground and strides away to the church-yard gate. Morning prayers have finished, and Mr. Jebb has thrown the doors open. Papa's behind her. She should turn back to him. But she will not.

Slowly, Mary dawdles toward home. Fanny will be there, working to clean the kitchen and to bring Mrs. Vial's things into their house. Helping her is not a tempting prospect. At least there is Volney's *Ruins of Empire*. She can curl up in the cracked leather chair in Papa's study, with Mama's portrait smiling down, and dare him to drag her out.

Reaching home, Mary slips through the front door and pauses. Mrs. Vial's laugh needles down the passage from the kitchen, so Mary goes straight to Papa's study and reaches for Volney. No, Mama: *Vindication of the Rights of Woman.* What would Mama say about a woman like Mrs. Vial, cooing over a man who once called himself reasonable? What would she say about Papa, pushing Mary to take a new stepmother against her will? Here it is in Chapter 11, "Duty to Parents:" *A great proportion of the misery that wanders, in hideous forms, around the world, is allowed to rise from the negligence of parents; and still these are the people who are most tenacious of what they term a natural right, though it be subversive of the birth-right of man, the right of acting according to the direction of his own reason.*

Suddenly Papa stands in the study door, watching her. At the look on his face, Mary's righteous joy dissolves. She tries to hold her eyes on the book but cannot. A bewildering pity overcomes her. What would Mama say to her now? *You are all that is left of me to console him. Was it for this I gave you birth?* Mary struggles to close the gate swinging open inside her now, through which grief and guilt come charging to take her in their teeth and shake. Her chin jerks and she bends her face deeper into Mama's book to hide it. Slowly, Papa approaches. She scrambles off the chair and runs to him, wrapping both arms around him and pressing her face against his worn waistcoat. His familiar salty lived-in smell breaks what's left of her anger like a rotten stick. "I'm sorry, Papa," she sobs. "I'm sorry."

His arms come around her, hesitant, then tighter. "I know you are," he says. His voice sounds high and choked. He squeezes her and doesn't slacken his grip, although under her cheek his waistcoat-cloth is wet with tears. "I know."

The Creature stumbles down the winding stairs of the laboratory, chasing the father who's left him behind. The whole rickety structure echoes with his flight, the mice flinching as he ricochets against the thin lath-and-plaster and sagging floorboards behind which they nest and nurse and dream. And then he's in the street. His skin is sticky, his eyes wide, his footsteps wobbling and unstoppable. Rags of clothing float from him like sails from the masts of a ruined ship. The door is open and he's free. No reason he should ever turn back to that room with its clutter of wires and vats and knives. He only knows the forward-urging hunger of the question that has not yet shaped itself into speech: *Father – wait – why not here with me?*

For now, he's alone in the street. There's a hospital down the block, and a tavern nearby with attic rooms where the medical students sleep, stained and avid and exhausted. Beyond that is a great cattle market where the morning's business of slaughter is commencing, all holloa and bawl and thud. And beyond that is some great nonhuman force the Creature can't see although he can feel its silvery insistent aliveness, casting up a constant rushing song. Only later will he be able to name it: *river.*

Under his bare feet, something slick and cold squishes in the gutter. His mouth squares to howl. Then some breeze shifts the clouds and he's caught by the glitter of dawn sun on a window: a square of pink, shot with gold. He lumbers across the street to stand before it. Behind that glass are objects, shadowed and roosting: rectangular things, some with hard edges and some with soft, some with glossy brown coats and some with grayish-white, made of something that looks, even to the Creature's unhealed eyes, like his own skin. A sharp hunger spikes in him and twists. If he could touch these objects, he could confirm what he suddenly suspects: they'd leap to his palm and nest there, they'd abide in his giant empty paws, and he'd feel the answering touch of something he can't yet name *companionship* against his stitched-together and aching heart. He touches the square of sunlight. It coats his bruised hand with pink and gold. There's something here he needs.

Beneath his fingertips the glass is cold. He presses harder, but it doesn't yield. Rage swells and balls his hand into a fist and smashes it through the glass before his tender wondering brain in its new skull has quite processed the action or the feeling. There's blood on his hand. A scythe of glass still clinging to the frame is tipped with blood too. An obedient babble wakes in the Creature's mind: *Glass cuts me, Father. Ergo, this is blood in my veins. Ergo, I desire. Ergo, I am alive.* Ergo, his hand is now inside the chilly pencil-dust-smelling air of the shop, and something's changed. He's reaching for the book on its stand, its color soothing the throb of his eyes in their new sockets. The book. It's the same pale creamy blue as the sky brightening over the hospital and his father's open door and the river keeping its own journey on into the next day and the next. Somehow this blue object will explain and soothe the whole bewildering world.

Now the book is heavy in the Creature's hand, firm and sweetly dusty-smelling in the stinking street. Unlike him, it has a name, stamped in gold on its cover: *Works of Milton Volume I. Paradise Lost.* There's comfort in that pattern of lines and curves. The Creature puts his tongue to the blue, but there's only a cottony nothing in his mouth, a wet dark splodge on the cover. Oh, well. The book is with him now, in whatever this is that will be his life.

Go. Go. Father's voice erupts in him, urging, scolding, strange. *Everyone will see you and they'll know what I've made.* He turns from the broken window and hugs his book against his chest and stumbles toward the river, fighting the bewildering damp prickle in his eyes. He'd have liked to have wrenched open the bookshop door and lifted the books one by one, thrusting his nose into their pages, tasting and smelling. There's no learning but by doing. Already, dismally, he can tell this is the way of things. And he will not be allowed to do his learning here.

But now there's a second voice with him, beating like the pulse in his fingers where they clutch the book: *The world was all before them, where to choose / Their place of rest, and Providence their guide. / They hand in hand with wandering steps and slow, / Through Eden took their solitary way.*[6] It moves in him like the blood itself in his veins and he hearkens to it and feels them bloom in him: those foreign things so suddenly always-known, those things now never to be strange again, those things called words.

A rumble of wheels around the corner and a driver's warning shout and then the Creature blinks and he's somewhere else. Only later will he hazard theories about the nature of this change: a mystery that will be with him throughout the length of what he'll learn to recognize – bitterly, brutally, wryly – as his existence. For now, he only knows that he's not alone. For in this elsewhere-space, there is a little girl, and people who circle her, in an intricate story they share. A story of which only the Creature will ever be able to see the entire shape, somewhere in the string of days that will open one by one into what he'll learn to call the future. Door into room into another room. Into scene, into chapter. Into story. Into life.

CHAPTER 2

Holborn

LONDON 1809

With his typical tyranny – Mary's new favorite word to hurl at him – Papa uproots what she's been ordered to call *their family* from the Polygon Building and drags them all into central London to open what Mrs. Vile grandly calls *M.J. Godwin and Co., Bookshop and Juvenile Library.* Mrs. Vile is Mary's new secret name for the woman she won't call *step-mamma,* sounding so much like the old name that no one can hear the insult. On a dismal day they grapple all the book-crates and threadbare linens and chipped crockery and Mama's portrait into a hired wagon (because, of course, Papa is useless with a horse) and trundle slowly toward the great cloud of smoke that marks *the City.* At the border of Holborn and Cheapside, Papa halts the driver in front of Number 41 Skinner Street, a tall narrow three-cornered house that juts into the muddy road like an inquisitive nose. Cattle-bawls and shit-pong stain the air; Number 41 is just down Snow Hill from Smithfield Market, the butchering ground and martyr's field. And, apparently, it is their new home. Mrs. Vile scans the dingy ground-floor shop with its old leaded windows and bursts into tears. "With all these little damn panes," she sobs, "how can anyone see the *books?* And what is *that*" – she points down the block – "a *hosier's? A hammer maker's?*"

"But it's so *cheap,*" Papa pleads. "Readers will find us. My dear, we will be *pioneers!*"

Mary leaves them arguing and jumps out to investigate. In the back is a cindery yard with a fire-pit for the washpot and a spindly tree of uncertain parentage. Above is a sitting room and study for Papa, and higher still are three small bedrooms that by the evening have been parceled among Papa and Mrs. Vile, Mary and Fanny, and Claire, whose complaints about *ghosts* Mary ignores: she won't share her bedroom, and Mama's brush and comb on the bureau-top, with anyone but her true sister. Staircases zigzag from corner to corner like a house in a vaguely alarming dream. In the low ceiling of the very top room – this will be Mary's own study – there is a trapdoor to the attic, which Mary can just reach if she stands on a chair. Her own study. A trapdoor. This is how she will escape.

By the end of the first week, Mrs. Vile has summoned the glazier (several of the little damn panes are broken, and others come loose with her vigorous cleaning) and the carpenter to build rough shelves and Mr. Johnson's boy to bring them books to sell on credit. From a Smithfield jumble stall, Papa has bargained up a wooden carving of Aesop reading his fables to a trio of skeptical-looking children and mounted it over the shop's door. Aesop's nose is broken, but that's how Papa got him cheap, "and anyway," he declares, "what a good presiding spirit for our new venture!" The hammer-maker stops in to shake Papa's hand, glancing around the half-empty shelves: "never mind, mate," he consoles, "it's early days yet!" And Mary, Fanny, and Claire have explored the attic. Under the beams and shingles separating them from the gray Holborn sky, a vast darkness stretches away, with trunks and chairs looming in their stolen candle's light. Mary hides Mama's carpetbag here, a thick brocade with wooden handles and a tapestry print. Like the stays that are Fanny's now, it has Mama's initials stitched into the lining in red. Mama took this bag to Norway, with baby Fanny in tow, to carry her letters from Mr. Imlay and the pages on which she wrote back to him. Mary lifts it to her face and breathes deeply, but no smell remains of the sea or the wind or her mother's living body. She shuts it tight. Now her mother's travelling bag is in her hands.

Through the rippling glass of the single attic window, London is a mirror world, like some Atlantis drowned in an invisible flood. Ordinary streets and the quadruple spire of St. Sepulchre's and the distant grimy dome of St. Paul's stretch away, shimmering in that square of watery light. Does Papa ever stop in his cramped scribbling at his desk as Mary and Fanny and Claire run above him, like thoughts in an unquiet mind? Does he ever sense the obverse kinship Mary now knows between the attic-world and the world of the ordinary house, with its porridge and parents and darned stockings and responsibilities? Does he ever wonder what treasures sleep above him in the dark? She doubts it. There is much that Papa does not see and never will.

Soon, Mary and Claire have pried open every trunk in the attic. "These don't belong to us," Fanny frets, picking at her hangnails, "we shouldn't open them." But they persist, scratching among dressforms and wig stands and stained clothing and thick canvas farthingales: "bum rolls," Claire giggles. She levers back a trunk's heavy lid and pries out a mass of stiffened silk, pink and white, and shakes it. "Look! This is mine." Fanny grasps a sliver of pale green and draws it irresolutely forth, still murmuring, "We shouldn't." Mary's gown is yellow, with stiff sleeves and a train that whips the dust into furrows on the attic floor. It's thrilling, delicious, to shuck off her worn chemise and give her body into that silken grasp. She pinches the dress closed behind her and sashays toward Fanny, sneezing. "Button me," she says, "I'll do yours." Fanny obeys. Then all three of them are ladies, trailing armpit-rotted silks and swooping trains torn by carriage-steps, laughing as the sad stench of strangers' bodies flowers in the dark.

Mary has to admit it: Claire is best at pretending. Inside the pink-and-white-striped gown, she demands to be called Queen Sophonsiba, the lover of a famous poet. "Lover?" Mary scoffs. "You don't even know what that is." But, of course, Claire ignores her. In a tray in the trunk's lid, she's found rusty tins with caked rims of pink and brown grease: *Rouge de Madame de Beautie,* says the label. "*Beautie* is misspelled," Mary points out, "even in French, and anyway, Claire, that's *disgusting.*" But Claire opens each tin and scrapes up a rim of color on her right index finger, then swipes the finger over her forehead, then her cheeks, hasty and bold as black ash-marks at Lent; Claire's marking herself, eager to be claimed by some force uneasy yet alluring as that of God. When she sets the candle down and pirouettes away, she becomes some other creature, half-ghost, half-thing that must be *woman,* gripped by that invisible force luring them into the whale-deep waters where unborn children swim, fighting for air. And when Claire dances forward out of the dark, Mary stifles a shriek. Her lips and streaked cheeks near-black in the dimness, her skirts breathing roses and sweat and mildew, Claire is a messenger from the dark corner where this world bleeds into an invisible one that only Queen Sophonsiba can see, a world into which, surely, Claire will someday cross over and leave Mary and Fanny here in this attic, wary, envious, sensible, bereft.

"Let's light the lights," Fanny suggests. Mary turns gratefully to the splintery crate containing rows of fragile glass candle covers, wrapped in brittle paper. Another crate contains a set of china Fanny has unpacked, laying the cups and saucers out on the trunk-lids. Only seldom can they dare to smuggle the pot and leaves for real tea up from the kitchen; Mrs. Vile keeps the keys at her waist now, fat and jingling and self-important. But she can't see them dancing, can't see Mary and Claire and Fanny twirling in their trailing rags, their borrowed light. *An ornament*, Papa had called Mama. *An illumination.* And with the wet sharp scent of tea cutting through the dust, their smothered laughter and footsteps, Mary dares to hope: perhaps the passage into that woman-world can be bright, not only dark.

Claire spreads the brittle paper on the floor, flattening it with her fingers. Busy among the loud rustle of the silks, Mary and Fanny don't at first hear her voice. "18 January 1803," she reads. "He died very easy; and, after hanging the usual time, his body was cut down and conveyed to a house not far distant, where it was subjected to the galvanic process by Professor Aldini, under the inspection of Mr Keate, Mr Carpue and several other professional gentlemen..."[1]

Mary turns, pressing both hands against her skirts. *Galvanism*: she's heard this word. Some vital fluid, which can't be seen or touched without pain, is made to pass from one body into another. A fugitive image dashes into her mind – the carter's boys, at it with the city girls against the walls, pumping – Horrid. And, besides, that thing – *electricity?* – is not something made by man or in a man's body. It is, Papa says, the same thing as lightning-storms, summoned in America by Mr. Franklin with his kite. Electricity: a lithe white bolt of something crossing any space it chooses.

"What are you talking about, Claire?" she interrupts. "What is that story?"

"Murderer," Claire says with elaborate casualness. "Thomas Forster. Drowned his wife and child, it says up here –" she runs her finger under the words – "and then got hanged and they tried to bring him back to life." She wets her lips and bends her face closer to the page. "M. Aldini," she reads, "who is the nephew of the discoverer of this most interesting science, showed the eminent and superior powers of galvanism to be far beyond any other stimulant in nature." She stops – what does the word mean? But she can't admit ignorance – then struggles on: "On the first application of the process to the face," she reads, "the jaws of the deceased criminal began to quiver, and the adjoining muscles were horribly contorted, and one eye was actually opened. In the subsequent part of the process the right hand was raised and clenched, and the legs and thighs were set in motion." She glances at Mary and Fanny, and grins. "Mr Pass, the beadle of the Surgeons' Company, who was officially present during this experiment, was so alarmed that he died of fright soon after his return home."

Fanny shrieks like a trapped mouse and covers her ears. "Stop it, Mary Jane," says Mary deliberately. "You're scaring her."

"*Claire*," Claire snaps. "My name is Claire. It's always been."

"No, it hasn't," Mary retorts. "You changed it yourself. You know what Mrs. Vile calls you." She's just let out her secret name for her stepmother – *Mrs. Vile* – but it's close enough to the real sound for Claire not to tell the difference. And anyway, it isn't right for her to make Fanny cry. Papa worries about Fanny. "She has her mother's tendency to melancholy," he murmurs to Mrs. Vile. Poor housekeeping Fanny. Eggs smashed and spinning, their secret warm worlds wasted on the dirty floor.

"Fine," Claire spits. "Be that way." She yanks the gown's laces open and crumples it down off her shoulders and steps out of it and leaves it on the floor. "I'm going down." Dunking her hem in the teapot-dregs, she scrubs her face – it'll do until she can get to a proper wash – and wriggles back into her ordinary dress. At the trapdoor, she throws herself down on her stomach and opens it just a crack to be sure Mrs. Vile isn't near. Wordlessly, Mary holds it open and Claire lets herself down through it until she's dangling into Mary's study room. And then she drops, quiet as a cat, and disappears.

"Do you think she'll tell on us?" Fanny whimpers.

"No," Mary replies. "She wants to keep the attic a secret too."

"True," Fanny murmurs. "I'm sorry, Mary. I just get so –" Turning to Claire's crumpled dress, Fanny lifts it, smoothing it lengthwise over her arm, then tucks in the skirts at each edge until it's a long narrow band of cloth she folds over itself once, twice, thrice. Tucking it back into the stranger's trunk, she pats it down and shuts the lid.

Mary watches her sister. It's reassuring to see Fanny moving about and making things right, with a calm so different from Mrs. Vile's officiousness or Papa's remoteness. It's good to see that calm settle over Fanny, too, so she isn't picking her nails or worrying that crease between her eyes even deeper. Mary can see a flash of Mama in Fanny's face, a gleam of deep auburn in Fanny's hair where the light of the stolen candle catches it. Longing floods her. She wants to stand on the chair in Papa's study and press her face to that painted portrait surface until her own breath warms it and she can believe in Mama once again. She wants Mama to stir and come to life, to feel Mama's lips kiss her cheek and hear her voice. *Mary, my little girl. Everything will be all right.* But she's nearing thirteen. The old game hasn't followed her to Skinner Street.

"Fanny," Mary asks, "do you remember Mama?"

Still standing at the trunk, Fanny turns away and stares into the dark. "There are some... pictures of her, I don't know what else to call them," she says. Her face grows sad, then she smiles. "Man brought me blocks one time," she says. "I remember that."

"Who's Man?" Mary asks.

"Oh." Fanny chuckles, not quite happily. "Man was what I used to call Papa, when he first started coming to visit Mama. He brought me the little china mug with F on it, you know the one, and a set of blocks. I remember stacking them up, one on top of another. Blue and red sides, glazed with the light. Mama's there. I see her hand reaching down, she helps me straighten them. And –" Fanny's body tenses – "Man comes close and they laugh and he reaches to touch and knocks them over." She pauses and quivers with what Mary realizes is laughter. "Bad Man, I said. Bad Man." Mary giggles too at the thought of mild Fanny scolding Papa. "But–Dark. But –" She opens and closes her mouth. "On the ship. Up on the deck, in the wind. I see her smiling at me." Fanny slumps to the attic floor and draws her knees up closer to herself, wrapping her arms around them. "She's bending down and smiling."

And how was it when I came? Mary wants to ask. *What did you see of that?* But she mustn't, or Fanny will cry. Mary leads the story forth from her mind along its familiar path, like an obedient horse from its stall: the sweaty face of that portrait-mother, hair streaked across her forehead and her shoulders, arms outstretched for the baby that is Mary herself. *My daughter. Here she is at last.* But Fanny's story shames it back. Fanny has pictures that are real. And she has never told Mary about them before.

"We'd better go back down," Fanny says. "They'll wonder where we are."

Mary sighs and opens the trapdoor a crack to check the empty room below. She lifts her candle to blow it out, and stops. "Wait a minute," she says. *The body of a murderer, Thomas Forster...* She lifts the sheet of newsprint carefully, folds it into quarters, and slips it into her pocket. One by one, she and Fanny blow out their candles. The smell of burning lingers in the dark. Carefully she unfolds the bottom half of the foldable ladder attached to the door, pushing it until its hinges straighten and catch and she and Fanny can descend. When the ladder swings back into place and the trapdoor shuts, the attic-world is gone.

Through the hole in their bedroom curtain, the afternoon sun slants, deep gold. "We'd better put on some clean clothes," Fanny says, "these are all dusty." Sighing, she takes her brown linsey work dress off its nail inside the wardrobe. Fanny washes that dress as carefully as she does the kitchen floor or the breakfast plates. *She is neat in her habits,* Papa says of Fanny. *Always diligent and willing despite her tendency to melancholy.*[2] Papa himself calls this *damnation with faint praise:* the scraps of kindness you scrounge from someone who should love you better. Her sturdy, lost sister. Housekeeper and drudge. Mama's daughter too. Guilt rises in Mary's throat. This is the longest she's talked to Fanny about Fanny's own feelings in quite some time.

Fanny shoulders out of her dress and pushes it down over her petticoat. Mama's canvas stays jut up around her shoulder blades and breasts, a stiff shell Fanny's flesh doesn't quite fill. But Mama's initials stitched into the lining in thick red thread, M W, are touching Fanny's skin right now. Someday Fanny will be as big as Mama, and those stays will fit. Who will her sister be then? Who will Mary be, herself? When she's grown up, she too will wear stays like this, which will push a real bosom up neatly under her chemise and sprout *womanhood* in her like a mushroom, overnight. Perhaps the whole world is one quiet conspiracy of women and their secrets, put on and taken off each day. Perhaps all women are charmed creatures in some tale they half-write for themselves, half-understanding it, visible only to other creatures who've been cast into that shape.

And when a childbirth comes – what creature is brought forth then?

Against Mary's thigh, the old newsprint crackles. A body given up for dead, recalled to life.

Fanny smiles sadly and puts her arm around Mary. Mary leans against her sister. Then they descend the stairs into the silent house. Mrs. Vile is behind the shop counter. Papa is in his study, laboring up another tale of Old Dame Trot and her Comical Cat for the children's library he's established on a street of hosiers and hammer-makers where no sensible child would ever set foot. Claire is nowhere to be found. It's up to Fanny and Mary to poke the kitchen fire, punch down the bread for its final rise, peel the shriveled onions and carrots to start the soup. This is being a woman. This is being all grown up.

CHAPTER 3

Field Place

SUSSEX 1809

Under a wych elm in Sussex sprawls a tall boy with a mop of russet curls and a high forehead like his father's and grandfather's and a light like a spirit lamp flickering in his dark blue eyes. Where that light will lead him, no one can tell. Surely not the Creature, who leans unseen against the elm's gray bark and peers over the boy's shoulder at the book in his hand. *Of man's first disobedience, and the fruit / Of that forbidden tree, whose mortal taste / Brought death into the world, and all our woe...*[1] These words touch something in the Creature he can't yet place, a familiar premonition, a troubling bell that's yet to ring.

The boy wraps one long white finger around an auburn curl and tugs, absorbed in the words. The tip of his finger turns purple. *What in me is dark / Illumine, what is low raise and support...*[2] Abruptly he rolls onto his back and lifts the book above his face. With his other hand, he reaches out to comb the grass, plucking dry twigs and stacking them in a heap. His supple shoulders squirm against the ridge of a root in the ground, fitting themselves to its shape. His eyes never move from the page. With his gripping thumb he kicks the right-hand page loose and flips it away and begins afresh, top left. Light flickers over his face as the elm's leaves dance. There's a bird singing up there in the clear blue space beyond the tree, a tiny creature jinking back and forth like a butterfly with the energy of its own song, a string of notes hammered out as if from a well just tapped. It swoops and then rises again, dwindling against the blue. The Creature squints but loses sight of it. The bird has flown too high for him, or even the boy, to see.

Here come two little girls with the same auburn hair under white caps tied on with string. They're carrying hunks of buttered bread and jam in their pockets – strawberry jam, staining through paper and cloth. Behind them, a big tabby cat with black and brown stripes picks its way through the grass, its tail waving gently. "It's tea time," the smallest girl blurts. "We brought it you."

"Thank you, Hellen," the boy says formally. He lays the book face-down and accepts a slab of bread and jam from the child – his sister? She must be. The older girl must be his sister too.

"Father is wondering where you are," the older girl says.

"Let him." The boy's voice chills the Creature's spine. In that instant it is old, determined, bitter. "Let him wonder and be damned."

"Bysshe!" The girl is distressed. The younger girl's face scrunches and her eyes grow pink around the edges. She loves this boy and she has seen him shouted at, has seen him shouting, in a parlor with curtains drawn against the sun to keep the furniture from fading, the voices of the boy and his father fluttering and battering against the ceiling and the windows like trapped birds. Hawk and sparrow, hunter and prey, which is which?

"I'm sorry." The boy is contrite now. "I'll make you a poem, shall I?" The big tabby cat has made its way over to the boy and he snaps his fingers to entice it up onto his stomach. It stands on his chest, kneading, purring. He knuckles its wide head and it closes its eyes in bliss. "Poor maltreated beast." His voice is sarcastic. The girls giggle. He stretches his fingers expertly to rub the roots of both the cat's ears at once. Then he strokes its back, wraps his hand around its long tail, and ticks it back and forth in rhythm. "'A cat in distress,'" he recites, "Nothing more or less. Good folks I must faithfully tell ye, As I am a sinner, I wants for some dinner to stuff out its own little belly."[3] The girls erupt in laughter and the boy smiles and sits up, shifting the cat off his chest. "How's that for a poem? What say you, Sir Cat?" The little girls, still giggling, reach for the cat and he submits to be held, flattening his ears. "*Cattus magnus*, genus *big barn cat*, species *Chester –*"

"Chester was the last one," the little girl objects. "This is Chauncey."

"—Chauncey," the boy continues. "What says Chauncey to a scientific investigation?" Rummaging in his pockets, he pulls out a pair of sharp dark stones and holds them close to the pile of twigs in the grass and strikes them together. The Creature starts backward but there is no one to see his amazement as a white solid thing that is not solid leaps out of the air between the stones and clings to the twigs and then becomes an orange thing that creeps over them and turns them black. The cat squirms. The boy extracts a twig by its brown end from the heap and holds its orange end close to the cat's face. It squeals and writhes itself loose from the girl's grip. At a safe distance it stops and licks its paws and swipes them over its whiskers, glaring. The whiskers on one side are shorter than the other now, and tipped with black.

"Bysshe." The older girl speaks severely. It costs her something, the Creature sees, to be severe with her brother. "That was cruel. You know what Father would say about such cruelty to a poor dumb brute."

"To Chauncey." The little girl is sniffling again. "He didn't do nothing to you."

"Anything." The boy sighs. "Watch your grammar or you'll have Father on you, too. Lucky he can't send *you* off to Eton." But he is repentant, reaching out to tousle the girls' caps off their heads, touch their cheeks. "I'm sorry. I don't know –" He frowns, and in that instant the Creature can see he is sincerely puzzled. "I don't know what comes over me." He smiles. "What gets into me." Chauncey the cat is stalking away through the grass, and the boy nods at him. "Go with him. Back to the house. I'll be along."

Once the girls are out of sight, the boy turns his gaze again to the pile of twigs on the ground. It's still orange, and the orange thing is flickering and moving, rising and subsiding. The boy and the Creature watch it for some time. Then the boy lifts the book and shuffles its pages and touches the edge of one page to the flame. *The mind is its own place* – the words leap to the Creature's eyes – *and in itself / Can make a Heaven of Hell, a Hell of Heaven. What matter where, if I be still the same –*[4] A black line crawls onto the page and the paper disappears. A red line glows, brightens. The Creature blinks. *Not the words!* he wants to shout, but his voice doesn't work here. *Don't let it* – The boy claps the book shut and the glowing red line disappears. He opens it again: yes, the fire is out. He turns the book idly, examines the gold lettering on the spine and his father's copperplate signature inked inside the cover: *Sir Timothy Shelley, Baronet.* The heap of twigs is black now: he sets his palm on top of them and twists, until they disintegrate into the grass. With a single leap he's on his feet and striding away after his sisters, the book swinging from his other hand as he mutters more of his poem to himself: "Some a living require / And others desire / An old fellow out of the way…"

Above his head the single bird flutters and dances, unspooling its ribbon of song. For an instant it dips into the Creature's field of sight, and then the word is there, mingled somehow with the upright retreating back of the boy with the book in his hand: *Skylark.*

CHAPTER 4

Dundee

SCOTLAND WINTER 1814

Scotland is meant to finish Mary, to interrupt her days in the tall narrow house that smells of blood and pencil dust and desperation, this string of days that draw her only deeper into rage and toward some deeper well in which she knows she will drown. There is no joy in the stolen dresses in the attic, no relish in imagining anything but the jolted body of the murdered man, blank eyes horribly alight. At the top of the cold zigzag house, Mary hides, studying anything that can keep her behind that door. Milton, Volney, the tangles of Greek that squirm like tadpoles on her slate, slipping through her hands as she grasps for them. She is nearly sixteen, aching for elsewhere, patching her shoes and scratching the rash on her arm that will not heal. Mrs. Vile mocks her to the gray-faced market-woman down the block, who every morning sluices her limp leeks and carrots with water that only silts the city dust into new shapes as it dries. *Miss Favorite. Her father spoils her, that's the trouble. My Claire, now, is promising to be a beauty, coming right along with her French. But does he notice? It's only Mary, Mary, Mary, night and day. 'So intelligent. So like her mother.' Not even a word for poor Fanny. You should see how she works, just like a slave. How we'll ever find them husbands, God only knows.*

To his credit, Godwin has tried other alternatives. First there was six months of boarding school at Ramsgate, with the timid daughters of clergymen and the fat daughters of shopkeepers, for an illusion of polish conferred by boring lessons by day and giggling scuffles in the dormitory by night. Only by summoning Mama's words could Mary shut her ears to them: *A boarding-school where any number of young Misses pig together.*

Such goings-on. Disgusting.[1] There was Cecilia, the bully with her big bosom and imperious whisper: "show me yours, I'll show you mine." There was skinny Lettice, who stockpiled, under her mattress, the candy sent by her mother until it molded uneaten, yet bit anyone who tried to take it. Mr. Pratt was the master, all lisp and walleye. But Miss Mortlake was most feared, with her black skirts rusty from washing and her long knobby cane. She called it O Death, after scripture. "Learn your lessons, girls," she declared, "and you need never know the source of its name." A smile crossed her gray lips. "Where *is* thy sting, indeed."

In those first awful nights, pressing her tear-sticky face into the thin pillow, Mary had dreamed of Papa handing her a letter in her mother's handwriting: *I'm bringing you home.* But in real life there was only one letter from Papa per month, probably noted in his calendar of tasks. So she sent back even shorter letters, keeping the details for herself: hiding in the drafty dormer seat against wind-rattled glass, cupping her hand around the ink-bottle to keep Cecilia's kick from jolting it off her desk, and, once, threatening, like skinny mad Lettice, to bite. *I get on well with Greek.* This was partly true. She read *Antigone* in parallel translation and faced the tyrant King Creon, giving him Papa's face. Guiltily, she replaced Ismene's face with Fanny's: pleading, counseling, cautioning. Fanny had never gone to school at all. Mary should be grateful to be here. But she wasn't.

After six months at Ramsgate, the money ran out, and Mary came home. A bumpy red rash on her left arm bloomed and spread, matching a deepening misery in her chest. Despite Papa's stiff welcome, despite Fanny's familiar warmth in their own bed, Mary knows she's just an evil ungrateful beast, a girl who killed her own mother. She deserves these inward and these outward plagues. *No light,* Milton's Lucifer gloomily declares, *but darkness visible. Which way I fly is hell, myself am hell.* In Mary's dreams, a shambling shape advances, then retreats. Despite Mrs. Vile's and Fanny's warnings and Claire's attempts to follow, she slips away from the house to walk the streets by herself, clutching the bone handle of a small kitchen knife in her pocket. When a man veers close to her she lifts her sleeve and bares her teeth to see him leap backwards at the oozing scars, the scales. One beast can always recognize another.

"You can help in the shop," offers Fanny, "Papa hopes the spring will bring more customers." So Mary disguises herself in shop-work, dusting the shelves, moving Dante into Shakespeare's spot and back again, straightening the same undisturbed copies of her once-notorious parents' once-notorious books about which no one now gives a damn. Flimsy, blurred facsimiles of *Shakespeare for the Young* and *Dame Trot and Her Comical Cat* await children who never come. ("Once I knew a peculiar woman with a lizard in a tank," Papa muses, "perhaps I should try a story of Dame Trot and her Fascinating Reptile?") Under the swinging wooden sign that reads *M.J. Godwin and Co.* (of course, Mrs. Vile has stamped this enterprise with the name she thinks is hers), dim shapes of people flicker beyond the little damn panes, walking past. When they do come in, it's always to ask for Mr. Lewis's *The Monk,* whose gruesomeness Papa disdains but Mary relishes. She slips a bent copy from the bottom of the stack and, in her solitary hours behind the counter, speeds through its demon-women and lustful friars and – flinch-inducingly fascinating – the young woman chained in the dungeon below ground with her baby's rotting corpse strapped to her chest. Sometimes Claire takes her place, arranging her curls, hoping to snare some passing scholar and convert him into that rare thing, a suitor. Ringing down the hill, always, is the Smithfield slaughter: the trapped animals' bawls and bleats, the hammer's thud. At dusk, bored, alert whores gather in the nearby alley, taking carters by their calloused hands and leading them into corners to hunch and hunch before they bite the coins and tuck them underneath their breasts and stroll away. Catholics and Protestants were burned here on the ordinary stones. Mary has no difficulty believing it.

The days crawl and darken. Suddenly Mary finds herself prepared with cheery officiousness by Mrs. Vile for an ocean voyage, with her few ragged dresses and books tossed into Mama's carpetbag. "My friends the Baxters in Dundee, they have a girl your age," Papa says, rubbing his forehead, trying to smile as he looks at Mary, then away. "You can bathe your – arm in the seawater. And when you come back it'll be cured." He places one arm around her shoulder, squeezes, releases. "Some travel. It is for the best. Hmm?" Mary watches him until his smile falters, trying to summon Mama's voice – *Gain experience!* – but in the place where that old yearning rang is now only a flat gray silence.

At the docks, a fat woman calling herself Mrs. Burns makes up to Papa, declaring herself bound to see a sick daughter, "oh, yes, just like this afflicted lamb here, but I'll tell you, Mr. Godwin" – when has she gotten Papa's name out of him? – "if there's ever a place to cure her it's Scotland. The air, so bracing. And the moors!" *We aren't going to the moors,* Mary wants to answer. But Papa's unusually rapid talk, eager to smooth over Mary's going, leaves her no room. "I'll look after her," Mrs. Burns declares, tucking Mary's painful arm against her stout ribs and drawing her down toward the ship's hold. "Like she was my very own." Mary's last sight is of Fanny, waving uncertainly, and of Papa's back, already turned away to return to his desk. Mary dispensed with. Mary dispatched.

The pitching ship dissolves Mary to a moaning heap, possessed by a miserable nausea she's never known. Faces blur around her: worried olive-skinned women speaking a musical flow of language like opera, big indifferent city girls, and over all Mrs. Burns's officious voice: "och, she'll be all right. This poor lamb is under my care." Between vomiting and sleep, she remembers the pocket of money tucked under her skirts, and Papa's warning: "Don't lose it. This has to last. Lord knows there's little enough to send with you." But at the next port up the coast, the money's gone, and so is Mrs. Burns. Thank God Mama's carpetbag – flabby, half-empty – is still tucked under her head. For the rest of the trip, Mary stands as often as possible on deck, clutching the rail, breathing deeply and gazing in the direction of what she hopes is land. Finally, at the Dundee docks, there is the girl she'll come to know as Isabella Baxter – yellow-haired, round-faced, bright-eyed – taking her by her good arm and murmuring, "It must've been awful. But you're here now."

Mary has never been away from London, let alone in a place from which, theoretically, she can look at and across the sea to another country. Dundee faces west toward Europe: to Greece, Antigone's bare and sun-bleached home, France where Napoleon rages over battlefields strewn with soldiers' arms and legs. At the docks, ships bob in a forest of masts and great barnacle-studded flanks. Brown-skinned sailors with gold earrings and black tattoos clamber up the riggings, bringing things for Mr. Baxter to sell and buy. Here are the bodies of whales speared and hanging, cut open, their great ribs and sieves of baleen exposed like the singing guts of a piano. What would it be to see their enormous gleaming eyes, rising from the deep? *There are other worlds than this.* A cool voice in Mary's head speaks. *Believe it.*

Slowly, Mary becomes a person who can live in the world beyond Skinner Street. Squealing, she bathes in the seawater, which stings and clarifies her rash. At Mrs. Baxter's insistence – "it's my gift, we've had quite a good year" – she accompanies Isabella to the dressmaker's to have two new green-and-black tartan gowns cut out for herself, one with a yellow stripe and one with a white. She joins in singing and dancing and learns to pick out a three-part song with Isabella and her younger sister Christy on the piano. And in those evenings in the Baxters' parlor, her eye rests on a sturdy young man: David Booth, the husband of Isabella's older sister Margaret, who died in childbirth two years ago. Balancing a cup of tea on his muscular thigh, he talks to Mr. Baxter about *interest rates* or *shipping news* or *fresh endeavors*. Every so often, he glances at Mary. "He likes you!" Isabella whispers.

Indeed, this seems to be the case. Walking with them on the quays – Isabella drifting tactfully ahead, tugging Christy after her – David always lingers near Mary, talking to her of her mother's books. "These Baxter girls gave me them, and I have nae read them all," he confesses. "But it seems to me she was a woman of uncommon sense. As my Margaret was. And to have such a daughter –" He glances at Mary, then away. Mary feels a blush rising up her throat. Back in the room she shares with Isabella, she studies her face in the washstand mirror and doesn't recognize it: flushed and clear-skinned, pale auburn hair like Mama's tousled a little by the wind. Pretty. This face is that of a pretty girl to look – to *luik*, in David's voice – upon. A successful disguise for any creature.

Soon comes a day, too wet to walk, when David arrives in a new cravat and a stiff black jacket and narrow shoes. "He wants to see you alone!" Isabella breathes, hurrying back into the parlor where she and Mary have been wrestling needles through embroidery hoops. She closes the pocket-doors behind her and smirks. "I'll show him in myself." And before Mary can protest, Isabella slips through the doors and returns with David, who's wringing his hat in his hands. Shyly, he glances around the room and lowers himself onto a chair. Isabella vanishes. Mary looks down. Her heart pounds out of all proportion to her state: an ordinary girl perched in a parlor on a rainy Tuesday, a hoop of mangled embroidery in her hands.

"Young Mary," David says. He clears his throat and clamps his small square hands together. "Young Mary. As you know, I esteem your company most highly." He jerks his chin against his tight cravat. "And your mind. Your mother would be so proud of your accomplishments and character." He looks at her and surely sees the pinkening of happiness in her cheeks: *Mama would be proud.* "It is that character above all that leads me to ask you to be my wife."

He is not touching her. But his blue eyes under their wide forehead, rimmed with receding dark hair, stay on hers. Something entirely new to Mary crackles in the space between them. He's a good man. And he wants her. A stunned warmth kindles deep inside her, sharpening itself like a candle flame. So this is being in love, or, more precisely, having a man in love with you. This must be the creature the interest of a man can make of you. This must be the purpose of a woman's life, landed suddenly amid her ordinary days.

"Sir, I am sixteen," she begins. All she can find are words from some stupid novel she's read with Isabella. Surely mothers teach girls what to say at such a moment. She flings out a plea to Mama's painted image: *Give me the words.* But no words come.

On the mantel, the clock ticks, the books stand upright in their rows, the marmalade cat yawns and turns over and goes back to sleep. David looks at Mary levelly, not altering his posture on the chair: the forward-bending chest, hands linked, elbows on the knees flung matter-of-factly apart. Right there under the sober fawn breeches are the sturdy leg muscles and the tactful bulge of the thing that according to giggling Isabella makes men go near-insane. A husband's body, humble and warm and of service: that's what it has been to Margaret, and what it will be to Mary herself if she says yes. Imaginings rise in her on a tide of confused heat. David's square hands unfastening her stays, unribboning her hair. *Like spun copper,* he'd blurted once. Warm weight turning to her where they lie together in sun-dried sheets. Childbirth: the tearing-through thing that had killed Margaret, and Mama.

"I am sixteen," she stammers, "and I – I must consult my father." And Fanny. Fanny will hear, too, Mary's real question: *What would Mama say?*

"Of course," David says, "certainly." He rises from the footstool with a rustle of coat and a pop of his left knee (the bad one, from his boyhood rugby pitch.) "In fact, I will go to London myself and ask." He reaches out a hand and Mary puts her own hand into it. "As soon as possible." He pauses, his blue eyes lightening. "Young Mary. I give you thanks." He smiles. And with a lift of his shoulders he turns and strides out of the drawing room. Mary sets the embroidery hoop on the table. Suddenly it looks so strange. An object from another world before the one in which she has become a foreign creature: a proposed-to girl.

But when David returns to the Baxters' dinner table, two weeks later, he's stone-faced except for willed, temporary smiles. After dinner, he follows Mary to the drawing room and shuts the door, dropping into the maroon velvet chair opposite the settee. "Your father, young Mary," he sighs, "has forbidden my suit."

"What?" Mary blurts. "Why—"

David opens his mouth and shuts it again. "Your age is the only reason he gives," he says. "If there's another, I could not discover it. Of course, any father is fond, doesna wish his girl to leave home. But it strikes me odd, I must be plain. I'm a man of honor. Good prospects." He permits himself an ironic smile. "And more to the point, there's many a lass married at sixteen if not younger. But your father says no."

"Can we not ask again," Mary says, "later?" Her stunned silence gives way to rage. Papa sent her to Dundee amid his constant carping about money, hoping for healing and adventure in just the way Mama would have. *Gain experience! Ah, Gain it!* The love of a rational man, surely, is not to be spurned. And – a wound, digging itself deeper each second Mary considers it – Papa has not consulted her at all.

David sighs. "He was most clear," he says, "that any further suit from me would be unwelcome." He draws a folded sheet from his coat pocket and hands it to Mary. "I'll leave you to read of it." And he goes out, sliding the pocket doors closed behind him.

Papa's orderly nervous script marches across the page:

My daughter,

You will doubtless think yourself ill-used by my decision to forbid David Booth your hand but I do it for your good and that of your family left back here alone, especially your sister Frances, on whom the burden of household care falls heavily. A sixteen-year-old girl cannot possibly be so rational as to commit herself to a life so far from home. Mr. Booth seems a kind enough gentleman but I have informed him that any further suit will be unwelcome, a decision by which I expect you also to abide.

Now, to talk of other matters, a pathway out of our considerable pecuniary difficulties may be opening. A young Mr. Shelley, son of a baronet yet still most companionably democratic, has pledged to me a certain portion of his inheritance. With his young bride Harriet he visits here quite often and I dare to hope –

Mary crumples the letter and flings it into the fire. Red lines of flame crawl over Papa's words and eat them into ash. How dare he? How dare he patronize her as an irrational creature? How dare he dismiss her own feelings without even bothering to learn their nature? And to treat David in such a way, to spurn the hand of an honest man – It's shameful. It's dishonorable. And it's foolhardy. For all his talk of money and this new pupil to touch for it – this son-of-a-baronet Shelley, one more would-be radical coming to sit at the feet of the self-crowned great Godwin – her father has made an unwise decision. Surely any man with three daughters to see into the world (for Claire is on his neck as much as Mary or Fanny) should welcome a man like David Booth. *He loves me,* she fires at Papa in her head. *What did you ever know of that?* Her mother's face, distorted in shock, shimmers before her. *How could you, husband, even conceive of something so unwise? Here is a rational man for our rational girl. What's the harm?* The harm, of course, is to Papa himself. One fewer daughter means one fewer pair of hands at the shop till, one fewer pair of hands for the washbucket and the laundry pail. God forbid he should hire a servant. Or that everlasting Mrs. Vile should soil her precious paws. He calls himself *remembering* Mama, *honoring* her. *Protecting* her daughters. But he only wants to keep them in his house as drudges, to haul them back from the world, and Mary most of all.

Gain experience, ah! Gain it. Otherwise you'll only sit at home, moping in a desolated heart, thinking of David Booth and all you could have had were it not for your stubborn father.

Outside the drawing room, Isabella waits with tears in her eyes. "Mother and Father have a letter from your papa," she sobs, flinging her arms around Mary. "He says you are to come home."

"Yes," Mary says. Behind her eyes, the world, again, has gone flat gray. "I know."

CHAPTER 5

Newstead Abbey

NOTTINGHAM WINTER 1814

The Creature lurks hopefully behind the old pianoforte that's been ruined where the rain came down on it through the ceiling, but neither Robert nor the lord invites him to join their sparring game. Candles flicker in their holders on the pianoforte's warped lid. Under the eight-hundred-year-old roof beams, with the threadbare Turkey carpet flung back and the windows open to the cold night, Robert and the lord lunge and sweat and pant, jabbing at each other with upraised hands. Maybe they can't see the Creature. He's still learning the rules in these strange places where he finds himself, still connecting them with Mary, that girl lingering so stubbornly in his mind. Watching the housemaid, Susan, helps. She fades into and out of a room like a shadow. *Yes, m'lord. No, m'lord.* But the boy Robert is a servant too. And here he is swinging his arms at the lord as if he means to kill him. It's a mystery. Like so much in the world beyond his father's room with its wires and vats and knives.

"Tiiiimmmme!" bawls old Joe Murray, entering with a bottle of red liquid and glasses on a tray. Robert and the lord lower their arms and peel off their gray gloves and reach for their shirts. As cold as it is in this room, they're both bare-chested, sweating. But they're smiling, which makes Old Joe smile too. Old Joe's in charge of everything at Newstead Abbey, this shell of a vast ruined church half-converted to a house by the lord's great-grandpa. He was a boy here in that time, feeding chickens and building fires. Tonight he's been out in the freezing wind nailing up brown paper over the *bailiff's notices* – that's what those sheets of fluttering white are called, stuck to the door outside – to keep the lord from seeing them. "Byrons 'ave been 'ere since the Restoration," he muttered. "The sheriff and the bailiff, they ain't got no right. Wish the Black Friar'd come back and scare 'em off for good."

Fletcher follows Old Joe into the room, holding up the lord's fur-collared dressing-gown. Fletcher has a bald head and one ear squashed out of shape and a rueful, fearful look. Tonight, Fletcher held the brown paper in place while Old Joe pounded nails and swore. Fletcher knows the bailiffs will come back. And he knows the lord has seen the notices, although Old Joe will be allowed to think he's hidden them.

Robert approaches Old Joe's tray and pours a dark-red liquid into three little glasses. He hands one to the lord and one to Fletcher. Quickly the Creature slips from the corner, snatches the third glass off the tray, then retreats and takes a sip. The red drink burns his nose but then ascends to his mind by some mysterious process previously unknown, even more savory than the scent of his purloined *Paradise Lost*. What is this feeling? Happiness?

Robert looks back to where his third glass was and frowns – "I thought I just poured..." – but catches himself and shrugs. Robert doesn't trouble himself with shadows or ghosts; Robert is a sensible boy. He takes a clean glass and tips two inches of the red drink into it. The lord wraps his fur-collared dressing gown over his damp shirt and belts it tight and watches him. Fletcher has crossed the vast room to shut the windows and Old Joe is wobbling toward the pianoforte to set down the tray, so no one but the Creature is looking now. Elaborately casual, Robert rakes his left hand through his sweaty brown hair, then clenches his right hand around the glass and lifts his arm in such a way that his blue-veined muscles ripple. Candlelight flickers on his damp skin. Even in midwinter, his forearms are still brown from all his walking behind the plow. His shoulders are as white as the lady's in the portrait over the massive fireplace, with her high-piled curls and imperious stare. He takes a sip, looks directly at the lord, and smiles.

"Claret." The lord's voice is amused. "Young Robert's got a taste."

"Better than the other kind of claret," Old Joe laughs. "The kind comes out your nose when 'e 'its you."

"And rightly so," the lord says. "Robert's pugilistic skills outshine my own. Like Richardson's Pamela, his virtue must be rewarded."

"By givin' your lordship a smack," Fletcher grumbles. "One of these days, milord, 'e'll go too far."

"I need him, Fletcher." Suddenly, the lord's voice quivers. "To keep me in training for when I go down to London and find us a wife."

All four men, and the Creature, look at the floor, abashed. They love this house and they don't want the lord to have to leave it and bring home a woman who might not love it as they do, who might not love the lord himself. But the lord is twenty-six, and now that he's done jaunting around the Mediterranean with Robert as his ostensible servant – scribbling sultry poems about the landlady's daughter in Athens and angry poems about Lord Elgin's deal with the Sultan to shove all those Parthenon bits into crates and ship them to England – he needs to be thinking of an heir. Even though he could get rich from his poems if he put his mind to it. Even though a woman in London would bring him money. And money is what you need if you love an eight-hundred-year-old house with rain coming through the ceiling onto the pianoforte and the ghost of a lonely Black Friar haunting your dressing room and only Susan left to be bossed around by Old Joe and secretly apologized to by Fletcher and never enough crop money coming in no matter how Robert and his father Thomas Rushton labor at the plow.

"At least in London I can go to the Fives Court." The lord's voice breaks the silence. "The perfect training ground for matrimony." He's trying to make them laugh. "Put on your mufflers and get in the ring with the Gentleman and see if you can last a dozen rounds."

"And you done enough of that tonight." Fletcher's voice is brisk. "Give me them gloves. Time you got some sleep."

"I'll be along." The lord's voice is friendly, definite. "Go light the fire, please. And Joe, you're about all in."

"Got to take these things back to the kitchen" – Joe staggers and catches himself. Smoothly, Fletcher lifts the tray from the piano and tucks it against his ribs and pats the old man's back. "Come now. You heard milord." Sighing, the old man lifts one of the candles and bears it out of the room and down the great wooden staircase, under the stag's head and the rows of crossed spears. Fletcher follows him, slowly, out of sight.

Alone with the lord, Robert sighs happily. "So. Looks like it's time for bed." He grins, and the lord grins too. Something wicked and gleeful flickers between them. "But we don't want you lonely up there in your room, wi' your nice fire and the Black Friar's ghost about. You rather 'ave me" – Robert's voice throbs, comfortable, on the edge of laughter – "or Susan?" He snickers. "Or, wait. Some London lady with her legs together, *oh, no, Lord Byron, stop, you mustn't –*"

"'Twould be a novelty" – the lord is teasing too – "to be told *stop*." He steps close to Robert. "'Cause heaven knows *you* don't." He slips his hands around Robert's shoulders and snatches the boy toward him, then pauses. Robert's head has fallen back, his lips open. *I don't.* There is Robert's voice, inside the Creature's head. *I can't.* It is a small voice, drowning in something tender and factual that is rising through Robert's whole body to drown him too. The lord smiles and draws Robert against him and kisses him with a careless yet exact force that threatens to buckle the Creature's knees. Robert's sinewy arms twine around the lord's neck and his fingers plunge into his black curls. His whole body softens and yearns. The Creature has not suspected humans capable of this. He has not discovered the responsiveness in his own body that rises through him now like the music of the river on his first morning on earth, like the promise and taste of words. But he's learning it. *No way to learn but by doing.* Father apparently meant him to be human, too. In spite of every-thing he lacks. Will he ever – the Creature's hope flickers, timid as a candle in a cold room – will a human ever – *this?* With *him?*

At last, with difficulty, Robert pulls himself away and grins. "An' the knockout blow" – his voice is playful – "goes to Lord Byron."

Byron grins back, balls his fist, and cuffs Robert lightly on the jaw. His hand opens and smooths itself along Robert's cheek. Robert lifts the last candle from the pianoforte and walks slowly toward the stairs. Byron follows, his right leg dragging – *has he injured it?* – and his hand sliding down to cup the warm knob of bone at the base of Robert's neck. With his empty claret glass in hand, the Creature watches from the corner as the candle-spark climbs the creaking stairs and winks out in the dark.

Holborn

LONDON EARLY SPRING 1814

For two days, back at home, Mary refuses to set eyes on her father. She darts between her bedroom and the attic study and eats food sneaked up by Fanny, who's even lankier and thinner now, her worry-crease deeper. On her own stash of paper from the writing box she received for Christmas – Papa's novel *Caleb Williams* has gone into a new edition, with a welcome rise in sales – Mary scribbles scenes of Mary Queen of Scots in prison. *Ye shall never break my spirit,* the rebel queen declares, *nae, none of ye. I am a rightful queen and someday I will be released from this tower and go to rule England as I should.* The costume trunks in the attic are for children. She will confine herself to her study, and her writing box, at the bottom of which lies the babyish first page of her first-ever story – *Once there were two sisters and a papa and a mama's ghost* – as what Mama would call *a spur to greater endeavors.* Papa comes and knocks, but she remains tight-lipped behind her door. "Suit yourself," he finally snaps, then his footsteps retreat down the hall. Claire, with Queen Sophonsiba rouge-shadows clinging to her cheeks, is avid for a story Mary refuses to supply. "Poor Mr. Booth," she breathes. "Was his heart quite broken?"

To divert her, Fanny describes the young Shelleys. They visited the previous night as Mary slept, furious and lingeringly seasick, their chatter and laughter and one high male voice rising through the floorboards in what she mistook for a dream. "Mrs. Shelley, Harriet she told me to call her, has the most beautiful gowns," Fanny says. "This one was pink; the time before it was purple, like the throat of a violet. And Mr. Shelley – he is marvelous. He seems to be able to read your thoughts, almost, so quick is his look." Fanny is rapt, lost for an instant, then suddenly turns to Mary and sets one hand on her hair. "Poor Mary," she murmurs. "Mr. Booth was surely a good and rational man. Someone our Mama would have approved." Mary bites her tongue and tastes blood. Past simple, past conditional: the dominant tenses of this narrow house. No future.

Only when Papa is barricaded in his study does Mary slip out and stride the streets alone. Her anger rears before her like a dragon on a leash, as if she were some mad Dame Trot turned witch, scattering the blurred timid pages of M.J. Godwin's Children's Library in scraps of fire. Resolution hardens in her like a coal annealed to diamond. She will leave Papa's house. Go set up a life where Fanny can join her. Not a school, like their pinched, harried Wollstonecraft aunts in Wales. Maybe David will marry her if she steals some coins from Papa's drawer and sails back to Dundee. But she remembers the resignation in David's face: he'll have cut his losses, found another bride. As she walks, Mary disentangles her emotions: fury at Papa, pining for David, and a single red thread of relief. She will escape. Somehow.

The week drags on. Breakfast, dinner, drying tea leaves for reuse, reading Shakespeare, making beds, knitting fingerless gloves for writing in the cold. In the cindery back garden – *back garden*, she thinks bitterly, *back again* – Mary martyrs herself to laundry: filling the great cauldron over the firepit kettle by kettle, kindling the flame, swirling sheets in the pot with a handful of soap and a wash-stick, lifting them up and punching them down. Still to come is the sluicing-out of all the water onto the ground, then the refilling of the pot for another rinse and then the wringing-out and pinning to the line to get mostly dry before the job is finished in sizzles of rising steam from the hot iron, heated in the kitchen stove. Despite the stinking city all around them, that's what laundry can achieve: a temporary place of *clean*. Although Papa has yanked her home and banished David and set her, again, to be a drudge, such things can keep her rational, self-controlled. She must be calm. She must not let them see that she feels anything at all. She must not open the crack for the beastly rage that can roar forth and drown everyone, starting with herself.

"Here." From over Mary's shoulder a bloody rag sails and splashes into the pot. "I'd get more water but it's so far, and you're already washing, so I thought–"

Mary turns to see Claire hovering in the back door. "You'll stain the sheets," she snaps. "This water's too hot for blood." She pries the end of the washstick under Claire's rag and slaps it into the dirt. A sweet, sharp smile struggles onto Claire's face. "Mary," she whispers, stepping close, "I know you're heartbroken to lose David. He was such a good prospect. When will you ever find another suitor?"

"Go away," Mary growls. She knows what will happen next: Claire will edge back inside and Fanny will start outside but Claire will hold Fanny's arm, with the new adult voice she's trying on – "no, best to leave her now" – and the two of them will stand together, watching her alone in the yard. And all because she's been made to look perfectly unreasonable for objecting to Claire's infernal rag-blood in her washwater. There it lies, leaking a pink puddle into the dirt. Let it rot. She scoops in an extra handful of lye and grips the stick and punches the sheets around in circles till her elbows ache.

March gives way slowly to spring: pots of primroses in windows, a soft wind rearranging the London stink. Buds appear on the tiny gnarled back-garden tree. The cold house grows warmer as they haul the upper windows open, propping them with sticks. Mary takes to wearing her tartan dresses every day, despite the hooting street boys ("Och, ahoy there, lassie!"), for the irritated flush they bring to Papa's high forehead. Especially when she stares at him, and smiles.

"Mary," he says one morning at breakfast, "it would please me if you were in attendance with Mr. and Mrs. Shelley at dinner tonight."

"How like a lord you sound," she says. "Must be their company affecting you."

Just the barest emphasis on *lord* and *affect* is enough to deepen the flush on his brow. "Yes," he says, "the Shelleys are a most engaging pair. They might even amuse a silly young girl."

"Yes," she says. "Or a rational one."

At sundown, Fanny and Claire and Mrs. Vile and Papa line up near the front door to wait for the Shelleys. Papa's coat elbows shine with wear and his lapels with wiping-down. Mrs. Vile's plump bosom quivers. Claire and Fanny wear fresh ribbons in their hair. Mary peers down the stairs at them. If they were dogs, their tails would be wagging for Master to toss the biscuit. She returns to her own room, smoothing the sides of her upswept hair, tweaking the face-framing curls she's cut with embroidery scissors, brushing the skirts of her tartan dress to remove the sad dust of this house. She'll be different from her family in the eyes of these Shelleys, Papa's latest marks. She'll be cool, regal as Mary Queen of Scots. She'll not be beholden to any simpering lordlet and his wife, even if Papa's willing to compromise every principle in his books. Mama would know how to treat these rich fools right enough. *False, indeed,* she'd written, *must be the light when the drapery of situation hides the man, and makes him stalk in masquerade, dragging from one scene of dissipation to another, the nerveless limbs that hang with stupid listlessness, and rolling round the vacant eye which plainly tells us that there is no mind at home.*[1]

Mary is last to enter the dining room, wearing a faint, deliberate smile. The only empty chair is opposite Mr. Shelley, on Papa's left. She takes her place behind it and keeps her gaze low. "Ah," Papa says. Nervous hope rises from him in waves. "Here's our Mary."

She lifts her chin and turns her gaze to Mr. Shelley, and Mama's words flee. So do any others. Pale and sharp and glowing: she cannot, in the first moment, take him entirely in. A tall, slender young man with a mop of russet curls, he stands, slouching a little inside a brown coat with a wide old-fashioned collar and long ragged tails. His shirt cuffs are unbuttoned and ink-stained and his wrists are strong, his hands sinewy and long-fingered, crossed lightly as a duelist's on the back of the chair. His cravat's tugged loose around his long white throat, where a wing of collarbone lifts the skin. And his eyes – heavy-lidded, bright blue – are fixed on hers. Slowly, he lifts one hand and plunges it deep into his hair, as if nudging an errant thought back into place. "Miss Godwin," he says, smiling, and inclines his head. She's heard this voice – high-pitched, insidious – through the floorboards in what she thought was a dream. "Charmed."

Mary rallies herself and gives him the small smile she's practiced, then turns it toward Mrs. Shelley, who's smiling hesitantly. She'll puzzle them both, Papa's rich new pets. Especially this girl with her pink-and-white face, her purple dress (Fanny's right, violet's-throat is precisely the shade), her golden-haired cheerfulness, her adoring look up at her husband. A lump pushes out the front of her dress: she's with child, the second, if Mrs. Vile can be believed.

With a smile, Papa pulls out his chair and sits down, followed by Mary, Claire, and Fanny. Mrs. Vile goes to fetch the soup from the kitchen. Mr. Shelley withdraws his wife's chair and sees her settled, then drops into his own seat and flicks his napkin open in the air. "I understand you've been in Scotland, Miss Godwin," he says. "Most enlightened country."

Mary looks into his blue eyes – so dark, yet so bright, how can that be? – for a moment before realizing he actually expects her to reply. "I certainly found it so," she says. Mrs. Vile lumbers toward Mr Shelley with the soup tureen and ladles something chilly and green into his bowl. "My friends and I took many walks through the city, along the harbor." Shelley lifts his spoon, watching her. His lips are narrow and rosy, clearly cut as a statue's. Under the table, she smooths her hands down her tartan skirt. "We had the most perfect freedom."

"Romping around like heathens, they were," Mrs. Vile interjects.

"A true daughter of your mother," Shelley exclaims. "Did I not tell you, Harriet? The great Mary Wollstonecraft lives on. Imperishable." He clasps his hands – skating his shirt cuffs through the soup – and recites: "A girl, whose spirits have not been damped by inactivity, or innocence tainted by false shame, will always be a romp." He flashes a glance at Mrs. Vile, then Mary. "Most of the women in my circle of observation, who have acted like rational creatures, or shewn any vigor of intellect, have accidentally been allowed to run wild – as some of the elegant formers of the fair sex would insinuate."

Mama. Hearing her words spoken so easily in Shelley's voice pins Mary to her chair. "I see you know her work," she manages. "I'm glad of it."

"Oh, we both do, don't we, Hetty?" he asks, elbowing Harriet. His gaze flickers to Fanny and back to Mary again. "Why, we've been known to recite Mrs. Wollstonecraft at the drop of a hat. Wollstonecraft and Milton and Godwin. That's a full evening's worth of entertainment in our little house. To feed on such fruit of the soul, such food *for* the soul –" His hands fly apart. "Ecstasy."

Without looking at him, Mary knows her father is beaming, the same smile that stretches helplessly now across her own face. Something about Shelley makes it impossible to do otherwise. Fanny, too, is pink, grinning, awkward and radiant, showing all her crooked teeth. Gathering soup bowls, noisily, Mrs. Vile shoots her a glance, and Fanny leaps up to fetch the potatoes. Shelley watches her, looking, Mary guesses, for signs of their mother. Poor Fanny. He'll find none there.

Harriet Shelley glances at Mary. "I wish I'd had such a mother as you," she says. "Instead I have Percy to teach me." She brushes his shoulder with hers. Shelley's smile wavers and rights itself.

"Indeed, Mary Wollstonecraft is a model to us all," Claire blurts. She leans bosom-first over her plate, eyes fixed on Shelley. "I myself have determined to put her ideals into practice at the first opportunity."

Shelley's eyebrows quirk up. "You have, have you?" he smiles. "Pray tell how."

Claire stops and blushes. "Well," she admits, "that's as yet unknown." Everybody laughs, and Claire looks down, her face bright red. Passing behind Claire's chair with the joint of mutton on its platter, Mrs. Vile snatches the back of her arm and gave it a twist. Only Mary sees. And – with a quick dart of his eyes – Shelley does too.

Mrs. Vile pauses between Shelley and Papa and lowers the mutton toward their plates. She's already carved out a splay of steaming slices, brown-rimmed and pink, and salted them. "Won't you gentlemen help yourselves?" she asks. "Just fresh from the butcher's today." Mary's mouth waters. There hasn't been mutton on this table for a very long time.

Shelley's hand hovers above the meat-fork, his eyes darting to Harriet and back. He spears the smallest slice from the platter and sets it on his plate, as far away from him as he can. Papa takes a slice, then another, then delves off a mouthful with fork and knife and takes a bite. "My word," he jokes, chewing, "does mutton not agree with you, sir?"

"We are conducting an experiment in animal flesh," Harriet chimes, "or, rather, how to live without it." She turns to Mrs. Vile. "We don't disdain your kind hospitality, not at all. It's just that – we're a little unaccustomed now." She spears a slice neatly from the platter onto her plate with her fork, lifts her knife, and cuts a sliver. "But we'll certainly enjoy this. Won't we?" She sets the mutton into her mouth, eyes fixed on Shelley.

"Uh, yes," he mumbles, "yes, yes, we will." Seizing his own knife, he hacks off a chunk of the mutton, thrusts it into his mouth, and gnashes his teeth, eyes fixed on his plate. Alarmingly soon, he gulps, then seizes his water goblet and slurps down every drop. *It's well enough to disdain meat,* Mary thinks, *if you're the son of a baronet and can have it any time you want.* But many a Young Man of Principle, shuffling and stammering in Papa's study, wouldn't have eaten the mutton at all, no matter how much it cost Mrs. Vile to prepare and Papa to buy. With Mr. Shelley in the house, maybe Papa can buy even more. Stockings to replace the ones darned and darned again. Shoes without cardboard in the soles. And a maid so Fanny's hands – those red rough hands now tucked out of sight under the table – can rest. Can pick up a book. *I dread to unfold her mind,* Mama wrote. But with money, what in the world need anyone fear?

The talk after dinner begins in Bonaparte and the error of the Crown, with a reluctant thread of hope. All together in the parlor – no separate after-dinner rooms for men and women in Papa's rational house – Mrs. Vile draws Harriet next to her and begins to talk of some French novel. Fanny and Claire and Mary range themselves around Papa and Mr. Shelley. "Ah, Parliament," Papa sighs. "How can they talk so much, yet say so very little?"

Shelley leans forward, jabbing the air. "It's as you yourself have written," he declares. "Hereditary power will be the death of this country yet. But it is not too late. Never too late. As long as there is life."

As long as you both shall live. Mary finds herself dropping into something like a dream as she watches Shelley: the quick long hands gesturing, lifting and setting down his cup of tea, the auburn curls loosening in the room (it's late May, a little too warm for the fire Mrs. Vile has hospitably lit), the elegant Grecian-bust lines of his throat. His tall narrow body has an atmosphere, like one of Mr. Herschel's newfound stars. With one furtive glance, she sears him into her sight: the parting of his tumbled curls, the curve of his cheek and sharp edge of his jaw, the shadowy ridge of collarbone inside his loosened cravat. It is astonishing, this feeling. He has a wife. She's met him only two hours ago. Yet she shuts her eyes upon his bright image and holds it, for a moment. What can it hurt?

Be rational, she orders herself. *Ignore the man across the room.* Obediently she bends her knees and perches on the couch next to Harriet, who turns and smiles at her. *Make conversation.* Her gaze skids over Harriet: violet-colored silk, heaped blonde curls, hands neatly circling teacup in lap. Wreath of blue stones and diamonds around wedding finger. Ah. Isabella's conduct-book advises just this: *Jewelry is something on which young ladies may remark to start a conversation.* "What a lovely ring," Mary observes.

"Thank you," Harriet replies, pinkening. She lifts her hand and fans her fingers wide. The ring looks like spring flowers on a branch: a row of single small diamonds set onto the band alternate with two blue stones set farther away, one on each side. "My engagement ring. The blue stones are turquoises, from the Indians of America. Percy says that turquoise is a special stone that grows underground where water has once been, leaving only the dried residue of the minerals it carried to form the stone." Her smile grows dreamy. "And it came all the way to London." With a plunge, Mary's jealousy gives way to grief. She could have had this too, the ring eased tenderly over her knuckle by worshipful David Booth, magical stones forged in the earth and chosen in a jeweler's shop, just for her. Across the room, above Papa's dry baritone rumble, Shelley's voice rises: "I, too, anticipate the day men will recognize their rights, their innate freedom to rise up and...." She could have had a man like him. She could have been a happy young wife just like Harriet, tucking herself into the carriage to go away, with a husband, from this house. And Papa has ruined it all. For his own selfish reasons. To keep her here in this cold narrow house, out of the country of *elsewhere* as long as he can.

Eventually the Shelleys rise and Mrs. Vile and Godwin heave themselves out of their chairs. Mary, Claire, and Fanny cluster behind, following them to the door. "Percy and I have had such a good time, as ever," Harriet exclaims. Shelley turns with a quickly doused flash of irritation, like a cat swatting away a too-attentive hand. He ushers Harriet out the door ahead of him. "I thought I asked you," he snaps, just as it closes, "never to call me that name again."

Mary lies open-eyed long after the candles go out. It isn't only the cups of tea that keep her wakeful. It's that field of gravity around Shelley, that heat that still holds his face in her mind: the sharp eager profile, just turned toward her. It's something like the dream-place where something alluring and terrifying always shambles toward her through the dark. This is not the territory of sturdy David Booth. This is no place she's ever been before.

Shelley returns on the first day of June, accompanied by his friend Thomas Jefferson Hogg: fortunate to be named after a revolutionary American, unfortunate to follow it with swine. From her desk, Mary hears them traipsing, laughing, into Papa's study. Mr. Hogg must have money too. She bends over her papers and forces her attention to the page. Mr. Shelley is in this very house. But she has her novel to finish. What would Mama say? *I wish women to have power not over men, but over themselves.*[2] Someday her book will be in the shop window too: *Mary Queen of Scots* by Mary Wollstonecraft Godwin. At first, just the paperbound pages. But maybe a rich gentleman will buy one for his library and take it to his bookbinder to have it wrapped in brown calf. Maybe a lady will buy it, clothing Mary's own words in morocco and gold, and turn the pages, marveling: *how could any author be so clever, so rational?*

Of course, at breakfast Mrs. Vile has issued a brisk taunt under cover of command: "Let's give this shop a good cleaning." Mary knows and dreads its meaning. Vinegaring the windows inside and out. Sweeping and then mopping the splintery board floors to quell the dust and swell the wood so the squeaking stops for a few hours at least. Taking every book off every shelf to dust the shelves with one cloth and the books with another: all of Papa's works, some of Mrs. Vile's translations she's persuaded Mr. Johnson to print (how long will his friendship with Mama outlast his patience with Papa?), and Mama's, too, as well as lonely Cicero and a set of Dante Papa gathered for a song out of some old gentleman's library. The hopeful stack of Dame Trot and Aesop, untouched by children's hands. Once the books are all cleaned and replaced, Mrs. Vile will walk among them, tweaking and twitching, turning a title face-outwards. Of course, at this stage most of the books are only bundles of paper with the titles printed on the first page, and the pages themselves still uncut at the top, waiting for the gentleman or lady who buys the book to carry it afterwards to their own bookbinder. Of course, very few gentlemen want the works of the scandalous Mrs. Wollstonecraft. Or the political theories of William Godwin, pathetic aging radical. *But we'll keep the shop going anyway*, Mary sighs to herself. *What else is there to do*. What else is there for her and Fanny and Claire but to work and wait, bowing patiently to Mrs. Vile and smiling in hopes of converting some shy book-fingering scholar into that rare thing, a suitor?

"Come on, Mary." Mrs. Vile stands in the schoolroom door, smiling. "Time to clean."

Mary fixes her eyes to the page and accelerates the scratch of her pen. "Perhaps you will have noticed," she declares, "that I am writing." She's just up to the scene where Mary Queen of Scots is bidding farewell to Lord Bothwell. *Och*, he says, with steady blue eyes like David Booth's, *I will always be your loyal subject, dearest Mary. Ye are so lovely to luik upon.*

"Father's orders," Mrs. Vile chirps. "He'll be busy with Mr. Shelley and Mr. Hogg this morning and he asked me to tell you *specifically* you were to help."

For a moment Mary considers calling Mrs. Vile a liar outright. But Papa's just contrary enough these days to have said this, fidgeting in the eager new skin he's grown under Mr. Shelley's patronage. It's a strange kind of gentlemen's agreement they have – a silence and a handshake and a raft of assumption between two men who profess to despise all such things. Yet the strangeness doesn't stop there. A man shortsighted enough to deny prosperous David Booth his only real daughter is capable of setting her to work like a slave in the bookshop he won't admit is failing. He's capable of deluding himself that young Mr. Shelley's interest in him is more than a rich man's passing phase of dandling a pet intellectual on a string. Such behavior is consistent with Papa's lack of common sense these days.

Mary sighs, lays down her pen, and with exaggerated care draws her writing box across the table. She stacks her pages, tucks them inside, locks the box, and drops the key – worn on a ribbon around her neck, like Fanny wears the key to the bureau drawer with Mama's stays – down the front of her dress. Mrs. Vile's smile doesn't waver. "Little girls must have their secrets," she observes. "And now, if Madam will accompany me downstairs, she can apply herself to the business of helping this family remain solvent."

Mary trudges downstairs in Mrs. Vile's wake. Passing the door of Papa's study, she slows and looks in. Mr. Shelley and a stout young man – the unfortunate Mr. Hogg – perch on rickety chairs in front of the desk, like rebel schoolboys. Papa stoops over his shelves, his back to them, talking. "A true scholar," he intones, "is a man seated in his chair, and surrounded with a sort of intrenchment and breastwork of books..." *Breastwork*, mouths Mr. Hogg, punching Shelley, and Shelley, prinking down the corners of his mouth in mock disapproval, punches Hogg back. "It is for boarding-school misses," Papa continues, "to read one book at a time." [3]

Spotting Mary in the hall, Shelley scrambles upright in his chair and grins at her. Hogg stares, mouth open, plump cheeks quivering. Mary blushes and touches her hair, then smooths her hands down her tartan skirt. Watching her steadily – Papa's back is still turned – Shelley leans over and elbows Hogg's ribs. "This," he murmurs, "is the daughter of Godwin and Wollstonecraft." Flustered, Mary blinks and smiles, then continues down the stairs, her hand tight on the railing. Now, she and Shelley have a secret.

An hour later, Shelley and Hogg come through the shop door, jingling the little brass bell and startling Mary behind the counter. Shelley saunters in and leans against the shelf of Mama's books. He smiles at Mary. Slowly he lifts a green morocco volume of the *Letters from Norway* and thumbs it open, his eyes on hers. From his sleeve he draws a folded note and drops it against the green book's frontispiece, then claps the cover shut.

"I say," Hogg offers, approaching Mrs. Vile, "since my friend Shelley here has introduced me, I've become most eager to acquire the works of Mr. Godwin. Perhaps you can show me what you have available?"

"Of course," Mrs. Vile flutters. She turns away to lead Hogg to the back corner of the shop. "Perhaps you'd like to see..." With Hogg's wide back blocking Mrs. Vile's view, Shelley pushes himself up from the bookcase and crosses the floor to Mary in two long strides, nudging the green book of her mother's *Letters* into her hands. "Read," he murmurs. His high forehead is golden with the sun, his lips narrow and smooth. Deep in his dark-blue eyes drift little chips of black. His long pale fingers graze the cover of the book, then touch hers. Over the rush of blood in her ears, Mary can barely hear Hogg's voice: "You consider this the best of his novels? Ah, with so many to choose..." She has just enough time to open the book, snatch Shelley's note, and thrust it into her skirt pocket before Mrs. Vile turns their way. "You've made a good selection, sir," she beams at Hogg. "*St. Leon* is not yet one of Mr. G's better-known productions..."

"But it will be," Shelley declares gallantly. "And it will be joined by others, as we've just left the man himself hard at work in his study. A good day to you both." And with a swirl of coattails he's through the door and gone, Hogg trundling in his wake. The doorbell jingles and subsides, spending the last of Shelley's parting music in the air.

As soon as Mary can slip upstairs into her room and close the door, she digs in her pocket for Shelley's note. No salutation, just black pen strokes bold and jagged as a net:

Do you ever walk, at night? I do, and will be doing so alone before midnight near St. Sepulchre's tomorrow.

PB Shelley.

That signature, spiky and bold. As if she wouldn't know him. As if his blue eyes, laughing and intent, his mobile mouth, his tumble of curls, are not before her still.

She draws her writing-box key on its ribbon from inside her dress to lock the letter away. In her hand the key is warm, suddenly a foreign and secret thing heated by a body that has become a secret too, whose desires, only, are clear.

The following night, Mary lingers purposefully late in her study, her Mary Queen of Scots pages arrayed in front of her with Shelley's note on top. *Do you ever walk at night? I do.* In the shadow of St. Sepulchre's, with its deep-voiced bell, she'll meet him at midnight, like a heroine straight out of Monsieur Perrault's fairy tales. And then – something will be different. Maybe everything.

St. Sepulchre's is just up the hill from her, near St. Bartholomew's Hospital, where the men of the Watch are theoretically on night patrol against the resurrectionists. From graveyards all over London, the resurrectionists dig up corpses to sell to the anatomy professors at Bart's. Sometimes they stash the bodies in the cellar of the Golden Boy Tavern down the street, propping them like sleeping drunks against the wall, with a bribe for the tavern's owner and, some say, for the head man of the Watch itself. Even so, the Watch's presence makes this neighborhood safer than most. Yet for a moment Mary quails. What if she meets with some disaster on the way to Shelley? Or – her mind leaps, and falters – *because* of him? All along each nerve sings a high blurred note of *want*. Underneath, a deeper pulse: *beware*. What about Harriet, with her round belly purple-gowned around a second child? What about Fanny and Claire, sleeping in their beds? What about Mrs. Vile and – oh, dreadful thought – Papa? She looks again at Shelley's note, the quick intent strokes. So bold. *Gain experience!* She strains to imagine Mama's voice. *Ah, gain it. Or you'll be just like your sister Fanny, my other daughter, for whom I had such high hopes, unfolding her mind in spite of the dreary, infuriating world you both inhabit. Beware. This world will make a drudge of you unless you insist otherwise. So will your father.* Mary leaps for this spark and fans it hotter. Papa has abandoned her for Mrs. Vile, has dared to cut off her future with David Booth to keep her here as a drudge. Wet clothes wadded on the laundry-stick, the struggle to swirl the sodden mass around and around in the pot, steam sticking her hair to her forehead, water-slop and lye-sting: this is no way to spend her only life on earth, the life Mama died to give to her.

She locks the papers in her box, Shelley's note on top. Earlier, she's taken care to bring her cloak up to the schoolroom, and she wraps it close around her, hiding her face. Deep in the cloak pocket is the little bone-handled knife she's swiped from the kitchen. Closing her fingers around it reassures her. Knife. Pen. Sword. Perhaps they are the same. Or might be.

Shoes in hand, she creeps down the hall, along the center of the widest floorboard to avoid a creak. From behind her sisters' doors, no sound. From behind Papa's and Mrs. Vile's door, a soft, regular grunt. Snoring? No. Her face turns hot with disgust. Pigs. Parents. Hypocrites. But at least they're too entangled to hear her go.

Skinner Street is quiet tonight, and dark. The open shed of Smithfield

Market lies like a great sleeping mouth, the doomed cattle and sheep drowsing in their straw-lined pens with their legs knuckled under them, the smell of blood lingering on the breeze. Anyone could be doing anything up in there, and probably is. They'll see a lone girl and – She tightens her grip on her knife. *Screw your courage to the sticking-place,* snarls Lady Macbeth. She'll stick any footpad who comes at her, leave him dead in the stinking gutter. Turning down Giltspur Street, she fades into the shadow of the buildings and hurries toward St. Sepulchre's. There is the church now, its quadruple spires piercing the night; Captain John Smith is buried there, the man who was saved from death by a lone heroic girl in feathers and beads. The Watch House next to it is open, its windows lamplit. Surely the Watch will intervene in any crime against a young lady. Even if some prowling resurrectionist, seeking only another body, would twist the knife in her himself.

As she approaches the steps of St. Sepulchre's, a tall figure slips out of the shadowy doorway: Shelley, coatless, wild-haired, intent. "You came!" he whispers. "I should have known the daughter of Wollstonecraft would be brave enough for this." He grins. "And more."

Up close, he floods Mary. His nervous hands are wadded in his coat pockets, his pale face and long white throat floating above hers in the dark. A crisp spicy scent rises from him: bundles of meadow herbs, tucked in his clothes where they lie in his cupboard at home. She's only glimpsed a man's body when passing workers in the street, stripped to the waist and filthy, their corded arms and bold stares twitching some string hooked deep in her. Shelley's long arms and narrow chest are surely pale, clean. And, like that meadow, sweet.

"What am I doing here?" Until Shelley raises his eyebrows and smiles at her, Mary doesn't realize she's spoken the words.

"Seems to me you're gaining experience," he replies. "As your rare mother would say."

"Where's your wife?" Mary asks. This is the way to keep some self-control, to beat back the helpless waves of warmth at the thought of Shelley's smooth skin, of his hands. *Don't trust appearances, which only dupe the credulous.* She steps back and peers at him. "Does she not walk at night?"

"She sleeps," Shelley says, "like the majority of English people." He sighs. "Especially those of her class, and of mine."

"What *is* your class," Mary asks, "exactly?"

Shelley takes her elbow. "Let's walk a bit," he says.

"It's safer here," Mary begins, "at the church—" Then, around the corner, wheels rumble and slam to a stop. A horse whinnies and a babble of shouting rises. "Ha!" a man exults. "Ye rascals! Caught ye in the act!"

"The Watch," Shelley breathes. He puts a finger to his lips and he and Mary edge down the church steps to peer around the corner. In the flare of torches, four men surround a wagon with a skinny red mare in the shafts and a heap of lumpy potato sacks piled on the back. Two boys huddle, blinking, on the seat – shriveled London children who could be any age from nine to seventeen. Something similar in their round faces and the stoop of their thin shoulders tells Mary they're brothers. One man holds the horse while the others circle the wagon, hooting, slapping sticks into their palms. "Ye can come down now and tell us who ye're workin' for," cries the biggest man, "or ye can take yer medicine."

"Or both," says another man, and the Watch erupts in laughter.

"Body-snatchers," Shelley whispers. "Poor devils."

The bigger of the two boys licks his lips. "We're bringin' potatoes," he stammers, "From the market down Cheapside to be ready for the morn." His smile is weak, and wholly unconvincing.

"Ain't I seen you before?" Another man lifts his torch. "Sure I have. Workin' the funerals. Pretendin' to be mourners and then slippin' off to tell old Nick what just got planted."

"We never," whimpers the second boy. "I swear."

"We'll be the judge," snaps the big man. "Get down from there." The other men haul the two boys, struggling, off the wagon. As it rocks, the lumpy heap shifts and a long hand falls out. It's a man's hand, wrist and knuckles hairy, corded with veins and knobbed with thick joints. In life, he must have been a giant. The wagon jounces and the fingers curl and uncurl, straight at Mary.

"Help!" the boys shout. The men just laugh. "No one'll come to save a pair of thieves," one growls. He yanks the smaller boy's arm and the boy stumbles. His head strikes the wagon seat with a wet crack.

"Charlie!" shrieks the older boy, lunging toward his brother.

"Get back," snaps the man, nodding at the others. They sling the limp boy between them and carry him into the Watch House. The bigger boy, dragged after them, fights all the way. "You kilt 'im!" he screams. "You bastards!" Behind him the door bangs shut. The man still standing at the mare's head sighs, clucks her up, and leads her away. The corpse-hand jounces, pleading, beckoning, around the corner and out of sight.

Shelley's body loosens with a rush of breath. "I was a fool to ask you here," he sighs, drawing Mary back into the shadow of the church. "Forgive me. You never should have seen—"

"No," Mary blurts. She can't express the terrified excitement in her, the shock of the great dead hand reaching from under that heap of sacks. The fingers, moving. "No. I should."

Shelley watches her, his expression shifting between fascination and something like fear. What is he seeing? She can't know. Here at last is life, the surprise of it, rushing up from amid her ordinary days to snatch her away to a place she's never known even to wish for. Now she's a girl to whom things happen, a girl in whom the world paints pictures of dead hands and the spires of St. Sepulchre's pricking the black sky. A girl in the dark with a man. *No. I should*. What has pushed those words over the sill of speech in her is the one thing she can trust.

Shelley opens his mouth, then hesitates. "Come," he finally says, "maybe we should take you home." Yet Mary lags, still watching the spot where the wagon disappeared around the corner. As long as she stands on these steps, the picture of the beckoning hand will stay right here in her head, along with the words for it. *Beckoning*. And Shelley will be here next to her in a moment that will stretch on and on in pure possibility. From this moment any number of things could come true. Out in the dark world of night, and life, she will receive her experience, and the words to tell of it. This is how it must feel to be drunk, able to open your heart like a cloak and enfold the world in it. This is how it must have felt to be heroic Pocahontas in her New World of towering pines and endless skies that doesn't belong to mad King George anymore, the girl who threw herself in front of John Smith to plead, *Father, spare his life, I love him*. This is how it must be to be Prospero, magicking up in one delirious swirl the sight and substance of a thing and the names for it. Mama must have felt this on the deck of her Norway ship, sailing toward a horizon as clear as a line of written words. Experience, and the language to capture it: this is how the world is made.

Shelley takes her arm, and pauses. She looks up at the pale blur of his face in the dark. His eyes are shadowy hollows, his mouth a blood-colored cut. Then he snatches her against him and kisses her. She has never kissed a man before. This current has never swirled up from her blood and his to tangle them together, like the fire summoned out of the sky by that ordinary American and his magic kite. Biting, opening, his mouth seeks. She hurls herself at him. Inside her arms, his slender body moves, fluent as a fish. Gasping, they break apart, kissing, and kissing again. Almost too quietly to hear, he murmurs her name.

Mary does not know how much time passes then, how long they walk. Their steps are slow, their fingers interlaced, her head on his shoulder, heedless of who might see. And all of London conspires with them, the dark corners free of footpads, the shadows of the night June-soft. Sparrows twitter from their nooks in cornices and attic-vents. "Sun'll be up in a little while," Shelley murmurs. "Sooner than we think."

"I hope the sun never comes up," Mary says. She slows her steps as they turn into Skinner Street. "I want to stay just like this, with you."

Shelley gathers her against him and loses her to herself. She sways, upright, until he finally lets her go. "I'll call on you," he murmurs. "I'll send for you." At her father's door, he touches his fingers to his lips. Then he turns and hurries away, blending with the night.

The back door is unlocked, just as Mary left it. No sounds come from inside the dark house. Shoes in hand, she tiptoes back up the stairs and slips into bed beside Fanny. Maybe she'll think Mary has only been up in the schoolroom writing Mary Queen of Scots. But at last, Mary has more than a story. Surely she must be on fire, burning through the mattress like a coal. But Fanny sleeps on. Mary is safe. Shelley swims before her eyes as sleep takes her down. His intent eyes. His mouth. The locked box upstairs in which his writing and hers lie together. A murderer's bony hand on the back of a wagon, beckoning.

Throughout the month of June, the world blooms because Shelley is in it. Primroses rise from pavement-cracks and roses throng each back-garden fence. The gnarled tree beyond the washtub opens its buds: all this time, it's been an apple tree, ready at last to prove everyone wrong. Mary lets it be known that she's decided to serve in the shop. "If I'm to be an author, too, like the both of you, and like Mama," she says to Papa and Mrs. Vile at breakfast, "I'd better apply myself to learning the trade, hadn't I?" Mrs. Vile's suspicion erodes under the steady trickle of Mary's new good cheer. "Just a girl's mood," Mary overhears her sighing to Papa, "good thing it's past."

Behind the shop counter, Mary reads Shakespeare, off the shelf. *With love's light winds did I o'er perch these walls; / For stony limits cannot hold love out / And what love can do, that dares love attempt.*[4] Heedless of Papa's anger, she doodles in the margin a long vine of penciled flowers, growing toward its own intent life somewhere off the page. Young men come into the shop, flirting with Claire when Mary can't be drawn. Of course she doesn't heed these boys. Now, Shelley is here.

She doesn't let herself think of Harriet, pink and pregnant, living now with her first baby, Ianthe, a hundred miles away in Bath. Shelley has sent her to *take the waters* (his words) and rented rooms for himself in Hatton Garden: "five minutes away," he assures her, "from you." The noise of him in her blood blurs everything. She floats through the days, waiting for him to slip through the bookshop door, waiting for the sound of his voice in Papa's study or his face across their table, waiting for the notes in the green book of Mama's *Letters from Norway. We can have no more at night,* he scribbles. *The danger is too great. Being alone with you is my greatest desire. And yet, as long as I am yoked to H, I dare not. I dare not compromise you –*

One night at dinner – Shelley's dropped by, picking at Fanny's potatoes and watching Mary over his teacup-rim – Papa solves the problem for all of them. "It's a fine night," he offers, "why not walk? Too good an evening to sit inside." And just like that, Mary and Claire – for despite her timid glance at Shelley, Fanny is claimed by Mrs. Vile for the washing-up – begin to walk with Shelley together, at first after dinner and then whenever Shelley suggests it. He makes a game of letting Claire amble ahead, browsing shop windows, while he clasps Mary's hand and puts his mouth to her wrist, or while he snatches Mary around a busy street corner and kisses her as Claire stands, suddenly alone. "Sorry," he breathes when they finally trot up to her, "traffic."

Claire's forehead creases, but Mary knows she won't betray them. She's caught Claire leaning over the bookshop counter to kiss Mr. Partridge, a painfully shy young Latinist with a stammer and an interest in radical philosophy. If Claire tells on Mary, Mary will tell on Claire. Troublingly, a small thought turns: in certain lights Mr. Partridge looks much like Shelley. And Claire's face always brightens when she turns to look at Shelley, his hand tucked in Mary's. Her smile always kindles when he lets go of Mary's hand and lopes ahead to join Claire, tugging at her red ribbon, making her screech and clutch her black curls, laughing.

Finally, Mary can't contain her anger. "You don't want to be alone with me," she flashes. "You don't care for me at all." Shelley drops her hand, stricken, and turns away. She watches him go, battling a fierce, quasi-reasonable joy and an urge to call him back. She must teach him she is not to be treated thus, not to be one of a group of girls he gathers to himself like some Turkish pasha. Surely this is right, and rational. Surely he'll return.

The next morning, Mary stands behind the bookshop counter alone. Claire and Mrs. Vile are upstairs helping Fanny cut out a new dress from a bolt of pale green muslin their Wollstonecraft aunts have sent. "You take what you want, first, Fanny," Mary has offered, "you haven't had a new dress in so long, and I've still got the tartans, they're wearing well." Amazingly, the pale green is lovely against Fanny's sallow skin. Poor Fanny. Let her have first cut of the muslin. She has no Shelley of whom to dream.

The door jingles and Shelley strides into the shop. With one glance he ascertains that Mary is alone, then approaches the counter, slides a sheet of paper across to her, and turns away. "Wait," Mary calls, but he's gone.

To Mary Wollstonecraft Godwin.

To sit and curb the soul's mute rage
Which preys upon itself alone;
To curse the life which is the cage
Of fettered grief that dares not groan,
Hiding from many a careless eye
The scorned load of agony....

To spend years thus, and be rewarded
As thou, sweet love, requited me
When none were near – Oh! I did wake
From torture for that moment's sake.
Upon my heart thy accents sweet
Of peace and pity fell like dew
On flowers half dead; -- thy lips did meet
Mine tremblingly; thy dark eyes threw
Their soft persuasion on my brain,
Charming away its dream of pain.[5]

The lines thud in her brain. This – she has wrought *this* in him? A daze descends on her that she doesn't try to clear. For a while, she simply sits. She stares through the shop window into the street. Then she rouses herself and reaches for a piece of paper. *Shelley,* she writes. *Shelley, Shelley, Shelley.* Slowly, she tears the paper into strips – one name on each – and goes about the shop tucking them into books. He will be here with her, unseen, here with all of them. She's under a spell that she can only disperse around the ordinary shop, word by word.

The next day, here come Shelley and Hogg again, hauling a crate. "A little *Queen Mab* for the shop," Shelley announces. "My first literary production."

"Except for that atheist thing at Oxford," Hogg offers, "you remember the one, old man, and the Irish thing, and the Declaration of Rights, and..."

"Mere prose," Shelley interrupts. "This is *poetry.*" He steps to the counter, pressing one of the slim books into Mary's hands. It's bound in sober Morocco leather, with her name already stamped in gold on the spine. "And this is for you."

Mary flips eagerly through the first pages. There's his scribbled inscription: *For my Mary.* Then the spiky imperious tangle of his signature: *PBShelley.* Stricken through the printed dedication to Harriet: a single black line.

Man is of soul and body, formed for deeds
Of high resolve; on fancy's boldest wing
To soar unwearied, fearlessly to turn
The keenest pangs to peacefulness, and taste
The joys which mingled sense and spirit yield.[6]

In her study alone that night, Mary writes on the facing page: *I love the author.*[7] With pen in hand she sits dreaming, closing and opening the book again and again so his writing and hers can touch, a palmer's kiss. *I love the author. I love him.* She can smell him still on her own clothes and skin, a particular musky burn of sweet herbs and chemicals. *The joys which mingled sense and spirit yield.* A half-remembered line of scripture trickles through her brain: *Mary kept all these things and pondered them in her heart.* There is no other word but *pondering* for this delicate state of picturing him, holding him within her, warming her hands at him as if he were a fire in the chilly room of her life in this narrow Holborn house. *Mingled sense and spirit.* She is mingled now with Shelley too.

When she slips back into bed, Fanny raises herself on one elbow and peers at her in the dark. "You love him," she whispers. "I can tell." Her voice is sad. Turning away, she curls on her side to declare herself asleep. Mary stares at her sister's silent back. She should reach out to Fanny, should pat her shoulder, should ask – But she remains where she is on her side of the bed, her hand resting on the mattress between Fanny and herself, until she sleeps.

Two days later, Mary leads herself, Shelley, and Claire up Skinner Street and around Smithfield Market, north and west toward St. Pancras Church and Mama's grave. It's the twenty-sixth of June now, hot and still, threatening rain. Heavy clouds mass overhead, lit to gold at the edges by the hidden sun.

Arm in arm, trailed by Claire, Mary and Shelley stop to watch the foundlings at play in Coram's Fields. Dressed in simple cotton gowns and caps, a group of little girls play jackstraws in a patch of dirt. Boys in short trousers run after a ball. Older girls and boys walk among them, their hands busy with knitting or knives and wood. It's a rare Mother's Day at Coram's, and so a line of women stretches out the door, ready to surrender their babies. Everyone knows how it works: you draw a colored wooden ball from a basket, and if your ball is green, you're allowed to leave your child there. If red, well – you'll have to try your luck another month, or leave your child in a turning-cradle at a convent or in a basket near a busy corner. Yet Coram's is said to be a good place. They keep careful records, including the tokens left with the children so they can someday be reclaimed. Perhaps those boys with knives are making wooden balls for the basket right now. A chill crosses Mary's heart. Mama might have been one of these women in line to surrender Fanny if she'd not had such presence of mind. If Shelley will not marry her, then Mary might be one of those women too. But Shelley is the son of a baronet. Papa would surely not have admitted him to the house if he were a scoundrel. Shelley can be trusted. Can't he?

They reach the familiar gray stone church under the spreading trees and climb the little hill. As always, Mary tries to imagine her just-married parents standing at the open door, with herself as a baby pushing out the front of Mama's dress. As always, she walks straight to Mama's grave in the back corner, near the little River Fleet and a cluster of willows. The square stone block is padded now with thick moss on its top. Around its base, the crocuses have all died back for the year; the grass is sunken where the pillar meets the ground. *Mary Wollstonecraft Godwin, Author of the Vindication of the Rights of Woman. Born 27th April 1759. Died 10th September 1797.* Mary touches her name, scraping away a few flakes of lichen. *Mama,* she prays. *Give me words.*

She and Shelley drop onto a nearby bench. She laces her fingers tightly together in her lap. Shelley shucks off his coat, rolls up his ragged cuffs, and tips his head back to gaze at the clouds. Claire wanders away to a spot against the church wall: out of earshot. Good.

"We must talk of this," Mary begins, "this—"

"This comet of feeling," Shelley interrupts, "this brightest of stars in the sky of my whole existence. And yours." He leans closer to Mary and clasps her hands. "Believe me when I say I have not the strength to withstand any longer what I feel." He gives a short, wondering laugh and shakes his head. "Even if I can't explain it." His face sobers. "Mary. Please believe that I never meant any –" he pauses "—harm to you or anyone. I have not been myself this winter and into the spring, but I—"

Harm to anyone. "What about your wife?" Mary asks. "What about your children?" Pink-and-white Harriet with her turquoise ring, fitting her baby-stomach awkwardly under Papa's table: without Shelley, or her parents, she'll be a woman in line at Coram's, half-praying not to give up the child the world won't let her keep.

Shelley sighs. "Your own father's written it," he says. "A marriage ceases to be a marriage when two people no longer feel that deepest love which is its heart." His gaze is level. "What can I say. I was a boy. She was a girl. She was near to me, such a promising partner, someone to think with, and to teach." His lips tighten. "But she has not the capacity to be the companion of a man of feeling. That is true only of you."

"How did you come here?" she asks. "To Papa's house?"

Shelley thinks for an instant, then laughs harshly. "Why not unfold my history," he asks, "such as it's been?" He draws himself upright. "Well. You've heard me talk of my home, Field Place, of my sisters." Mary nods, shuffling the images in her mind: two little girls with Shelley's bright hooded eyes and russet hair, secret forts in the woods, barn cats and ponies, paper boats sailing on the pond and streams, and once a string of stolen firecrackers. "Well. My father and I, from earliest times, have not been congenial. He saw me as the next in the long line of rusticating Shelleys, growing old and otiose in what to everyone but me was Arcadia. I was to inherit, to take my place next to him, sucking at the teat of hereditary oppression, of all that's wrong with this world. Fattening like a little Sussex shoat. When I declared to him that I would not – oh, there were rows. Once even a threat of committal." At Mary's puzzled look, he elaborates. "To a madhouse." He swallows and looks away. "No son of his could say such things unless he were insane. He shouted this at me so loud the windows shook. My sisters cried. They were terrified." His face darkens. "He made my sisters cry."

Mary touches his shoulder with hers. A smile flickers on his face. "And, yes. I went to Eton, of course, with all the other Sons of Minor Nobility." His voice picks out the ironic capitals. "And there got whatever taste of tyranny my father hadn't already ladled out. Thank God, Mary, you are not a boy. A boys' school is a minor hell on earth. The more 'elite,' the more Dantean the depths. But it launched me into Oxford, seat of higher learning, where I dared to believe in what they said about following my reason, wrote an essay on atheism, published it in pamphlet form." He takes a deep breath. "And got expelled."

So this is what Hogg meant: *that Oxford thing, old man.* "Shelley," she hesitates, "if this is painful–"

"No," Shelley insists, "you deserve to know." His face brightens. "But my time there was not without event. I was after the secrets of life itself, Mary, not on any syllabus. Alchemy, electricity – yes, like Mr. Franklin with his kite. The vital fluid. The thing that makes the blood run, that drives the mysterious heart." He stretches out his long arm, ropy with blue veins and writing muscle, and clenches and unclenches his hand. "The things I did, the experiments I conducted –" He smiles. "One time I even set my rooms on fire."

"And Harriet?" Mary prompts.

"Well," Shelley says, "her father owned a coffeehouse that Hogg and I frequented. On holidays, she'd be there, and we talked –" He shakes his head, his eyes pleading. "Mary. You cannot expect me to continue in this way with you so near. How can I talk of cold ash in the presence of a flame?"

"You married her," Mary prompts.

"So that she could accompany me to Wales," Shelley continues, "where I had formed the project of emancipating the miners at Tremadoc. I wrote pamphlets, sent them up in fire balloons, to come down anywhere." His eyes shine. "Beautiful. All those words of liberty, rising to the sky." His face darkens. "Her bitch of a sister tried to dissolve our union. Then our first child was born. Ianthe, heroine of my poem." He leans forward, propping his elbows on his knees, staring past his clasped hands at the ground. "We were just children. And then with Ianthe we were but one more. I wandered in the wilderness. I was lost, with no purpose. We were inspired by your father's writings and came to London to meet him." He leans back against the bench, fixing Mary with bright, tired eyes. "And thus I came to you."

"You and Papa have some arrangement of money," Mary stammers. "I've often heard him talk of it, but only sideways."

Shelley leans back and plunges his hands into his curls. "A series of loans," he says, "is the simplest way to explain it. I have taken post-obits" – Mary looks questioningly – "loans against the inheritance that surely in spite of everything my father will settle on me. He has no choice. I'm his son." He gives a short, bitter laugh. "And as the man who perhaps more than any other has formed me, and who stands in need of help, Mr. Godwin has a right to some of it. As much as I can spare."

So this is indeed the source of the joint of mutton, the new stockings for everyone, the spicy-smelling new tea Papa takes in the afternoons. Their house is infused now not only with the counted and recounted bookshop coins but with money borrowed against Shelley's father's death. Fathers can live a long time, though. "How much are you giving him?" she asks.

"A little here, a little there," Shelley says. He smiles ironically. "A gentleman never discusses money."

Mary decides not to press him further. She strains to imagine sums beyond fivepence for a basket of eggs, a shilling for a copy of her mother's *Vindications* in paper. On such little sums each day rolls by. Against them rises the image of a great house in her mind: Field Place, solid as Buckingham Palace. Such wealth as that can keep them all. *Inheritance* can pin down and tuck in a future as neatly as a sheet to a bed. It's wonderful to think of.

"And you have shared this money with my father," Mary says. "You have kept him out of debtors' prison."

"I hope so," Shelley says. "But, Mary." He slips off the bench and drops to his knees in front of her. "Mary. I would gladly give you everything that I have. All that I am." His thumb strokes her knuckles. "Mary. I never dreamed of finding a woman who's become so much myself in so very short a time. So entwined around my heart. Within it." He clears his throat, his dark-blue eyes fixed on hers. "Mary. I must say it. I love you. I have never loved any woman so much as you. I must know that you'll be mine."

Mary shakes her head slowly and shuts her eyes against the tears pressing them from within. He is making her party to the betrayal of another girl, and two children. But how can she – Suddenly his hands cup her face and lift it to his and she is kissing him before she can open her eyes. So she doesn't open them. She gives herself over to Shelley's lips, to the gentleness of his hands in her hair, on her throat, slipping down her back to pull her closer to him still. "I love you," she gasps. "I love you and I cannot think of anything else and I only want to be your –" The words flutter in her and she seizes the closest one – "companion, and I ..."

Shelley drops his head into her lap and grips her skirts. Mary plunges both hands into his curls and his head burrows down. Through the cloth, his breath sears a spot on her thigh, and she stretches both arms across his back like a drowning woman clinging to a spar. Shelley's mouth seeks her waist, her breast. His lips surround its tip through the cloth; his tongue touches it, circles. Some entirely new ache saws her open. Shelley's arms tighten as he rises and lifts her with him. *Claire will see.* But a white heat in her blasts the words away. Half-flung over his shoulder, she struggles to kiss him, her mouth sliding over his high cheekbone, his jaw. She takes his earlobe in her teeth and Shelley groans, quickening his step as he bears her toward the edge of the burial ground, where the willows sweep the grass in long curtains of summer green. He pants her name as she clings to him. Slowly, he lays her in the grass, then jerks his shirt free of his breeches and tumbles it off over his head. And then he stops. He looks down at her. The sunlit willow branches sway all around them. The sad little Fleet runs on toward the rest of the world. "Mary," he says, "are you certain, are you..."

"Yes," she answers him, slipping her hands around his smooth ribs, drawing him down to her. "Yes."

They drift back to Skinner Street at sunset, Claire trailing behind. Thunder rumbles overhead. Mary reaches for Shelley's hand, then for Claire's. What a pity to be Claire, loafing alone at the edge of the cemetery, reading her book. There are books, and there is life. *Gain experience. Ah, gain it.* This is what Mama knew with Fanny's father, heedless, reckless, and with Papa, safe, beloved. Women taken in by love, transformed, like Mama – Mary is one of them now. The soreness of her body, the twinges catching her in shoulders and hips, these are signs of welcome to the world all women know. So this is how it is. So this is love.

When they turn onto Skinner Street, the rainstorm breaks. Claire squeals and runs for home, but Shelley stops dead, hunches his coat up over his shoulders, and draws Mary underneath. Rain slashes her skirts and plasters Shelley's shirt to his back. In the dark hollow of his upstretched arms, his sodden coat dripping onto their faces, they laugh, and he kissed her. "Tomorrow," he says, "I'll come and speak to your father."

"Yes," Mary says. "Yes."

In the tall narrow house she stumbles up the stairs, peeling off her sodden clothing and toweling herself at her washstand. Rain drums the window, sluicing London clean. As she falls asleep, Fanny moves around her, scooping up the wet clothes, leaning over to touch her forehead for fever and, satisfied, planting a kiss.

When Shelley's voice wakes her, the sun is high in the sky. A wonder she's slept so long. But now she's awake, and Shelley is downstairs. The whole house carries the pitch of him to her like a tuning fork carries a note to the waiting ear. Quickly, she dresses and creeps downstairs. Outside her father's closed study door, Fanny and Claire hover, their faces fearful. "Oh, Mary," Fanny whispers. "This is awful."

Mary leans to the door and listens. "You yourself have said" – Shelley is pressing Papa – "that reason must be the guide of human action, must –"

"But, even so" – Papa's voice is ominously calm – "do you believe you can simply decide to leave your wife? And child? And child to come?"

"My God, sir," Shelley blurts. "If you but knew – Our marriage appears to me as a living and a dead body yoked in loathsome and horrible communion."[8] Mary recoils at the spiteful terror in his words. Beautiful pregnant Harriet, *horrible*? "You wrote it yourself: 'Marriage is an affair of property, and the worst of all properties. So long as two human beings are forbidden by positive institution to follow the dictates of their own mind, prejudice is alive and vigorous.'" Shelley pauses; the silence is thick. "'All attachments to individuals, except in proportion to their merits, are plainly unjust. The institution of marriage is a system of fraud; and men who carefully mislead their judgments in the daily affair of their life, must always have a crippled judgment in every other concern.'"[9]

"Chapter Six," Papa finally replies. "Although you have it a little out of order."

"But I *have* it," Shelley pursues. "You wrote it, Godwin. These are your own words and beliefs, these are the standards by which you have regulated your own conduct and that of your daughter. Can you wonder that as the child of yourself and her illustrious mother she is joining me in breaking the chains of the slavery of an institution injurious to her sex even more so than mine, to the whole human race, to the spirit of infinite progression which must inevitably lead us on to—"

"Good God, enough," Papa snaps. "Any man of sense ought also to be able to apply his reason to what he reads. And when the welfare of young girls is at stake, he ought to be able to regulate his own conduct so that he does not compromise –"

"Are you accusing me, sir" – Shelley's voice is low – "of being incapable of self-regulation? For no gentleman can stand such –"

"Gentleman?" Papa's laugh is one short bark. "A title you have hitherto disdained."

"As have you," Shelley snaps, "except when it comes attached to my money."

Papa is silent. "You gave me your word," he finally says, "that you would assist me and my family out of your esteem for us and for my work."

"And so I have," Shelley says, "so I will. But not at the price of insult." His voice wavers. "You have stood in relation of father to me, of spirit and intellect if in no other way. You have been a bright north star in an otherwise dark night. How can I explain? Of *course* I am bound to help you, out of esteem, of that esteem which you yourself have said rational beings ought to accord to one another on their merits. Please believe I retain such merit as you have seen in me, as you have honored me with the belief that I possess."

"Wait," Papa protests, "I do not say that you are—"

"Sincere," Shelley interrupts. "I am perfectly sincere."

Papa sighs. "I'm sure you are," he says. His voice is tired. "But until I can talk to Mary I would ask you to refrain from meeting her, and to refrain from calling here. It won't be long, only a day or two. But in such matters, judgment is of the utmost necessity." He pauses. "I know it seems pedantic. But—" he pauses again – "she is her mother's and my only girl. She is sixteen. And she seems far more grown-up than she is."

"I understand," Shelley says. "And I will honor your request." Claire smirks at Mary – *seems far more grown-up than she is!* – and Mary swats at her, furious and silent. *Far more grown up, Papa*, she thinks, *than you know.*

A rustle and the scrape of a pushed-back chair scatter Claire and Fanny down the hall, but Mary lingers to catch Shelley's elbow as he comes out of her father's study door and closes it behind him. He turns, eyes widening, and kisses her. "Don't worry," Shelley whispers, "I told him nothing of importance." He presses a note into her hand, and with a wicked grin he turns and clatters down the stairs, calling farewell as he goes to anyone who might hear.

❄

My dear Mary,

I must leave Harriet, that seems plain. The question is, whither shall I go. And shall you come too.

No question marks. Just certainties. Or propositions, still to be contested.

After such a pledge as we have made to one another, how can it be doubted we should be together. Let me write to Harriet and – These six words have been crossed out and more written in – *I will fix upon a destination. Switzerland, perhaps, a pastoral retreat, an unspoiled paradise that we will share.*

Switzerland? Leave England, perhaps forever? But if Shelley is to leave Harriet and they are to live unmarried, then England will be closed to them. They will have to go to the Continent, like Lady Mountcashell, Mama's old pupil, has done with her lover Mr. Tighe – Tatty, Papa calls him, after his fondness for potatoes. Now Lady Mountcashell, who'd once been Margaret King, calls herself Mrs. Mason, after a character in one of Mama's own stories, slipping between names as she chases the freedom Mama showed her. Maybe Mary can do the same. But dread uncertainties of law rise up: divorce, illegitimacy, standing in the Coram's line on Mother's Day, the very things Mama married Papa to protect herself against. What will Shelley's family say? And how will Harriet ever explain this to her children? Mary forces herself to amend this sentence: they are Shelley's children, too.

Mary looks again at the note: a fragment of candle-scorched paper torn off something else. On its reverse Shelley has doodled an exotic flower in a pot, a series of steps fading up into air, a sailboat tossing on black-tipped waves.

I cannot explain the transformation you have wrought upon me, swift as fading coal into bright and raging flame. All light, all heat I am, as our love delights and animates my soul.

Your S.

"Mary," Papa says the following morning after breakfast, "may I have a moment of your time." Here it comes, she thinks, her stomach pitching. But anger rescues her. Pocahontas, the heroic Indian girl, saved John Smith from being murdered by her tyrannical father. To save Shelley, and their midnight kiss at the church that holds John Smith's bones, Mary can do no less. *Not as grown-up as she thinks she is*. Well. He'll soon have an opportunity to judge the fallacy of that statement for himself.

Mary follows Papa into his study. As he shuts the door, she arranges herself in the chair Shelley sat in, which is still shoved askew in front of the desk. She sets both hands over the ends of the arms, where Shelley's hands have been. *I'll speak for you*, she thinks. *I'll protect us both*. With a glance to the left, she can see Mama's portrait there above the fireplace, the warm painted eyes smiling down. Mama is here with her. Surely she should fear nothing now. *My daughter. Gain experience. Ah, gain –*

Papa drops into his desk chair and sighs, plowing the heel of his hand up his high, bare forehead. Then he resettles his spectacles on his nose. "So," he says. "Am I to assume you entertain Mr. Shelley's suit?" He snorts. "If *suit* is what it can be called when a man seeks to abandon his wife."

"He told me there is no more feeling, no more understanding between them," Mary blurts, "hasn't been for months and months, and –"

"And yet she's with child again," Papa observes. "Isn't she."

"How dare you," Mary begins.

"Listen to me," Papa says. "I know life in this house is not ideal for a young girl of sense and spirit –"

"To say the least," Mary snaps.

"—But life with him can be no life," Papa continues. "Legally he is not able to be yours. Morally – who knows, Mary. He is not –" Papa fumbles – "he lacks constancy. He disappears for weeks on end. He becomes the prey of strange enthusiasms. While you were still in Scotland I tried to reach him on most urgent business regarding our agreement and he had gone for Wales again, telling no one."

"That's his prerogative," Mary says. "As a man, he can go where he likes. As a woman, I must rot here on Skinner Street while you send my suitors away."

Papa flinches. "I knew we would come to that," he sighs. "I am prepared to admit that I may have acted wrongly in the matter of David Booth. To admit one's errors is the only way to cure them."

"But this cure's too late," Mary says, enjoying the salt of the words in her mouth. "David's married Isabella."

"I had word of that too," Papa says. "Perhaps your friend's happiness will console you for the loss of so faithful a suitor."

Mary breathes deeply. She will not be drawn. "Isabella's joy does add to mine," she declares, "as proof of what a girl may do if she is willing to seize her own happiness. To shape her own experience." She flounders, glancing at Mama's portrait. "To gain—"

"Don't be naïve, Mary," Papa snaps. "Mr. Shelley is not an ordinary man."

"And I am not an ordinary girl," Mary retorts. "Child of Godwin and Wollstonecraft, as you've never ceased reminding me. Meant for no ordinary things."

"I have often told you this, it's true," Papa says. "But only out of my –" he flounders, swallowing hard – "my pride in you, my—" Mary watches her upright, threadbare father struggle behind his desk like a man choking on a fishbone. Is that word *love*?

"—My esteem of your capabilities and my hope for your success," Papa says finally.

"I'm not your pupil," Mary flashes, "not one of your radical young men. Don't talk to me as if I were some prizewinning dray horse, to work, to work, and never to –"

Papa folds his hands and stares down at them. "If I have been a neglectful parent," he finally says, "if I have failed in my duty, I beg your forgiveness, and..." For a long time, he's quiet. Mary considers rising from her chair and going to him, putting her arms around him – something she's done only a handful of times in her life, like the morning when he came to find her at Mama's grave. Oh, Mama, hanging there in her gilded frame. What might things be like in this narrow house, with its chilly, genteel hungers, if her mother still lived? If Mary herself had never been born? What sort of creature is she to have brought such trouble and loss upon her father, then and now?

Yet it couldn't have been otherwise. She can't wish into silence this singing that lights her nerves like harp-strings. She can't wish never to have been alive, never to have stepped onto the stage of this bright and troubled world. Words swim in her, Shakespeare, then Dante. *A brief shadow, a poor player that struts and frets his hour upon the stage. This little threshing-floor that makes us all so fierce.* People out there on that threshing-floor that is the big wide world are posturing and kissing and making love and making art. She is bound to join them, even if Papa doesn't understand why. *Gain experience, ah, gain it.* Mama's words have tipped her down a chute into the world, into Shelley's arms. She can't wish it otherwise. And she can never explain to Papa how it feels to want that world. So much.

"I've asked him not to call here," Papa says, "for a few days. Until –" He sighs. "Until some course of action is decided on."

Softening at the weariness in his voice, Mary nevertheless seizes his words. "That's the passive voice, Papa," she blurts. "Decided on by whom?"

"Well, by Mr. and Mrs. Shelley, to begin with," Papa says. "And then, by me and your mother."

"'Your mother?'" Mary snaps. "You mean my step-mamma. My mother has already made her wishes known." She looks pointedly at the portrait. "'Gain experience! Ah, gain it!...'"

"She wrote those words," Papa observes, "under an entirely different set of circumstances. I'm not at all convinced she would approve of Mr. Shelley."

"And why not?" Mary demands. "He is a genius, a benefactor of humanity –"

"He is a privileged young man whose privilege has eased his passage through the world," Papa says, "and given him an appetite for wild schemes—"

"Like freedom?" Mary protests. "Like liberty and justice? Like the ones you wrote about that drew him to you in the first place?"

"—Like fire balloons," Papa says, "which are unfortunately typical of his methods: great brilliance, undirected. He told me proudly of launching them at Tremadoc with political epistles to the miners attached; I forbore to point out he should have written them in Welsh." He sighs. "If you're so determined to quote your mother, remember *Vindication of the Rights of Woman,* chapter II." He leans back and links his hands behind his head. "'The fancy has hovered round a form of beauty dimly seen – but familiarity might turn admiration into disgust; or, at least, into indifference, and allowed the imagination leisure to start fresh game.'" Landing on Mary again, his direct gaze pierces her. "Start fresh game. Just like his forebears, on the hunt. When one covert's exhausted, just harry a fox from another."

Mary swallows. Of course he would remember that passage. "*Might,*" she corrects uselessly. "*Might* turn."

Papa sighs. "Right," he says. "But quibbling about tenses is an evasion, and you know it. Look at him, Mary. Look at Harriet. Look at all such men, like Mr. B. in *Pamela.* It's the chase they want. It's the chase they have the money to pursue. And once the chase is done—"

"Mr. Shelley is not like that," Mary blurts. "And if you disdain his birth, then why do you take his money?"

"I look on it as a species of justice, to be frank," Papa says, "or as another species of bookselling: when your ideas go forth into the world and take root in receptive soil, shall you not have some right to their fruit? Mr. Shelley has been greatly moved by *Political Justice*. And, Mary, look around you." Papa opens his hands into the dim air of his study, indicating the usual stack of tradesman's bills under their inkwell at the corner of his desk. His gaze touches Mama's portrait, then wrenches itself away. "Allow me to treat you like the rational creature you claim to be. I cannot fail to act upon any means of possible support for us, can I?"

"But to accept his money and disdain the man," Mary pleads, "is surely some species of hypocrisy." The moment the word is out, she flinches. Some window that has been opening behind her father's eyes slams shut. "Papa, wait, I didn't mean it, I—"

"You have made yourself quite clear," Papa says quietly. "And with that, I fear, our interview must end. Allow me to reiterate. Mr. Shelley will not call here again until an understanding is reached. This should give you ample opportunity to meditate upon your conduct and determine whether it merits your mother's approval, and mine, as that of a rational woman." He picks up his pen, turns his gaze to the paper in front of him, and holds it there. She is dismissed. *Mama,* she pleads. But Mary Wollstonecraft's painted face, glazed with a slant of window light, reveals nothing.

After lunch – carrots and marrowbones Fanny has boiled and salted into soup, brown bread Fanny has baked – Mary shuts herself in the schoolroom and scribbles her story of Mary Queen of Scots. *With melting eyes she gazed upon Bothwell and he swept her into his handsome arms* – argh, *muscular arms*, argh, *arms – and in that moment she became his and he hers.* Argh. Why is it so hard to transmute sensation into words? What obstacles can there be when you know perfectly well how to build a sentence, for one thing, and for another thing remember so clearly the taste of Shelley's mouth on yours that it still shivers you in your seat, quivering, upright and ecstatic like an arrow speared in the ground? Why is writing such a damned hard task? And, yet, why is it the only thing but Shelley himself that can give her ease?

"Mary," says Mrs. Vile, appearing in the door, "there is a caller I think you'll want to see." Immediately, Mary drops her pen, pushes back her chair, and clatters down the stairs to the parlor. But Shelley isn't there. Instead, on the faded red velvet sofa, perch Harriet Shelley and another young woman Mary has never seen: also blonde and pretty, but with a wariness about her green eyes that Harriet lacks. Mary pauses, but Mrs. Vile nudges her into the room, follows her inside, and shuts the door. "This is Miss Cornelia Boinville," she says. "Mrs. Cornelia Turner, as is to be. Mrs. Shelley I think you already know."

Mary clasps her hands before her. Mrs. Shelley and her new ally will not frighten her. She makes herself look at them. Cornelia Boinville in expensive gray silk. Harriet in pink with a lacy scarf around her neck, its ends threaded through a little gold ring with three blue enamel-and-pearl flowers to hold it in place. Her pregnant stomach thrust out nearly to her knees. Her swollen hands lying in her lap. Her fingers turning Shelley's diamond-and-turquoise engagement ring back and forth.

Lifting her head and smiling, Mary comes forth and sits in the chair at one end of the couch. Mrs. Vile takes the other. "Have you offered our guests some tea?" she asks Mrs. Vile.

Harriet's mouth curls. "It's a little late," she snaps, "for good manners."

"Hattie, dear," Miss Boinville murmurs. "Let me." She turns to Mary. "Miss Godwin. I know I'm a stranger to you, but not to the Shelleys. And not to Mr. Shelley in particular." She pauses. "You see, he's done this sort of thing before."

Harriet's face is strained, her eyes fixed on Mary. Mrs. Vile smirks. Mary's stomach drops. *What sort of thing?*

"Once again," Miss Boinville continues, "Mr. Shelley has taken a notion to leave Harriet and seek consolation elsewhere. If *consolation* is a word for it. If Mr. Shelley, himself, even knows what he seeks." Her green eyes, wide and steady, hold Mary's. "He fled from Harriet this past winter, too, and sought refuge in my father's house at Bracknell. My father is a man of learning and a kind heart, whose success in business has allowed him to pursue his interests in philanthropy. My mamma having died long since" – she glances downward at her folded hands – "ours is a quiet house. My father offered Mr. Shelley an extra room. He brought such life to our days: books and papers strewn on every table he passed, stealing our housekeeper's washtubs to go boating in our garden stream, knocking out the bottoms of every one." Against her will Mary smiles, noticing a flicker of the same smile on Harriet's face. "We studied Italian together. And before long I could not help but notice that Mr. Shelley was directing his attentions to me."

Under those steady green eyes Mary falters and looks down. Her toes in their holey stockings peek from under her hem, and she draws them backwards out of sight. Miss Boinville's dress is trim, its gray silk rippling with subtle colors like rainwater. The edges of her ribbons are crisp. Not shabby, like Mary's own clothes. Like the old Turkey carpet and the rump-sprung chairs. Like this whole blasted house.

"I am blessed with a loving papa of uncommon sense," Miss Boinville says, permitting herself a small smile. "And so he merely expanded my circle of acquaintance. He brought my now-intended, Mr. Turner, to the house." Harriet smiles and pats Miss Boinville's hand. "Soon after that he brought me Mrs. Shelley, Harriet, here, and he told me who she was." Miss Boinville sits upright and gazes at Mary. "Her little baby, Ianthe, was in her arms. And of course then I could not be party to such a thing as an abandonment of them."

Mary looks at the floor to hide the tears boiling behind her eyes. It is not the kind, rueful knowledge in Miss Boinville's and even in Harriet's eyes that sears her, nor the thinly disguised gloating in Mrs. Vile's. It's the words: *He's done this sort of thing before.* She tries to summon spiteful rebukes at this coven all ranged against her: *If he has left you twice, Harriet, perhaps you should try harder to keep him. And you, Miss Boinville, perhaps you should be guided less by your papa and more by your own judgment.* But the sight of Harriet's pregnant stomach stops her. Harriet has obviously done all that a woman can. Including what Mary herself has done with Shelley, under the willows near Mama's grave. Reason loops one arm around her and draws her close, speaking Mama's wry condemnation of a wandering man. *Giving himself license to start fresh game.* She cannot become one of a string of women, one more quarry flushed out to run for sport. Going away with Shelley will make Ianthe and this new baby orphans, make Harriet a widow, while he is still alive. That is not good. It is not kind. It is not right.

Mary lowers her head and tucks her stocking-toes further out of sight. In the morning sun, her green tartan with the white stripe is loud and pitifully shabby next to Miss Boinville's gray gown. She yearns toward the kind firmness in Miss Boinville's eyes: here's another motherless girl, with a *most understanding papa,* who is obviously rational and kind. Yet still – The words batter inside her like trapped birds. *I love him. Don't you see. Remember how he is. I love him. There is nothing else to say.*

Miss Boinville sighs. "Perhaps it's time for us to go," she says. "I would invite you to call me Cornelia, but it does not seem my acquaintance is welcomed. I doubt that we will meet again. But please." She steps close to Mary and sets one cool hand on her shoulder. "Consider what I've said." And Mary remains in her chair while Mrs. Vile escorts Miss Boinville and Harriet out the door.

After a moment, the parlor door opens and Papa enters, face drawn. "Mary," he says. She collapses in tears. He comes to the couch and sits next to her, embracing her. "Mary," he finally says. "I have a possible solution. Your mother's friends, and mine – Mrs. Williams in Paris, Lady Mountcashell and Mrs. Gisborne in Italy – stand ready to offer you a home away from home as long as you shall wish. Perhaps a change of scene, some travel, will…. Remember how kind Lady Mountcashell was to you when you were a little girl. Your mama's old pupil. Margaret King, as was." The pictures swim back over Mary's eyes: the mass of red hair and tall figure bending to embrace her, the warm Irish voice exclaiming *sure, and she's the image of her mother.* "Wouldn't Italy be wonderful? You could see such great things there, the David, the Sistine Chapel, the great frescoes. The land where Dante walked. You could write." He looks at her, and looks away. "Just as your mother would have wanted."

From her quiet, proud papa this is a warm promise indeed. *Italy.* "Lady Mountcashell," she says. "I could stay there?"

"With she and Mr. Tighe," Papa agrees. "She calls herself Mrs. Mason, now, of course. After the governess in your mother's own *Original Stories.*" He smiles sadly. "But your mother succeeded in unfolding her mind. And now she lives in Pisa with the man she's chosen for herself."

"The leaning tower," Mary sniffles. "Mr. Tighe – Tatty, the potato man."

"Correct," Papa says. "And so near Florence, with its treasures – Ah, Mary." He smiles at her. "This could be the making of you. This could be a whole new *life.*"

Back in her study, Mary sits down and tries to think. On the table before her, her writing-box's lid gleams, unlocked. Did she leave it this way? In the tumult of Miss Boinville's visit with Harriet and then Papa's offer of Italy, she can't recall. All the papers seem to be inside, though – all the notes from Shelley tucked together inside her copy of *Queen Mab,* buried deep under composition exercises and straggling, struggling Greek, with the Mary, Queen of Scots manuscript still on top. Had she stored those pages inside the box, or just abandoned them on the table when she bolted downstairs? That ink bottle, so neatly corked: hadn't she left it open, her pen dripping on the wood?

No matter. Too many other thoughts. Italy is tempting. A room in Lady Mountcashell's house, with that kind woman who'd once been Mama's pupil Margaret King and remembers her so well. Italy: all warm sunshine and white marble limbs and Tasso and Dante and scandalous

Boccaccio and the Borgias and creamy blue sky. No more Skinner Street, no more dust or laundry or jingle of the bookshop door. No more gray Januaries or empty fireplaces. No more marrowbones and teabags boiled past their use.

And no more Shelley.

But, of course, that is the point.

She rummages *Queen Mab* from the box and opens it to Shelley's inscription. *For my Mary. PB Shelley,* its dedication to Harriet stricken through.

Oh, Shelley.

She lifts her pen.

This book is sacred to me, she writes, *and as no other creature shall ever look into it I may write in it what I please.* She pauses. *Yet what shall I write.* Oh, Shelley. *That I love the author beyond all powers of expression.* Italy, Lady Mountcashell. A whole new start. But – *That I love the author and that I am parted from him.*[10]

Shelley's deep blue eyes with their chips of black. His insistent mouth. The smell of him rises to her nose and her tongue.

Her pen gathers speed. *Dearest & only love by that love we have promised to each other although I may not be yours* – the words tangle, tripping over one another – *I can never be another's – But I am thine exclusively thine – by the kiss of love by – By –*

Oh, how to write of it? The moment when he lifted her and bore her away under the trees–

Words are coming, fit and ceremonial and sad, but they are someone else's, whose? That maroon book with the corner she dogeared, again defying Godwin's rules of book-handling – Quickly, quickly, she will find it and set those words to the longing inside her right now. Luckily Papa has left his study and so she can scramble through the shelves unobserved. Here it is: Lord Byron, "To Thyrza." What a beautiful name. An Italian girl: part of that country of sun-warmed skin and glorious dim color on the walls of churches, the whole hazy dream world of famous poets and outsized feelings, the world of *elsewhere*. She bears the book back upstairs, props it open, and copies the lines into *Queen Mab*:

Ours too the glance none saw beside;
The smile none else might understand;
The whisper'd thought of hearts allied,
The pressure of the thrilling hand...

I have pledged myself to thee, she writes, *& sacred is the gift...* She trails away. Shelley's presence presses around her like Jupiter visiting Io in a cloud – his hands, his tumbling curls, his lean excitable body.

And, oh! I feel in that was given
A blessing never meant for me;
Thou wert too like a dream of Heaven,
For earthly Love to merit thee.[11]

Too like a dream. And if she goes to Italy, that's exactly what Shelley will become. She will leave him behind, become an author like her mother, writing learned books that – as Papa said of Mama – will make strange men fall in love with her on every page. But Shelley is the one she loves. And he loves her. The ugly pain of never again touching him, never being touched again by him, twists her against her chair. The pleading faces of Harriet and Miss Boinville float before her. Ianthe and the second baby are small squalling red presences whom she cannot bring clear. So are the infants in the arms of the women waiting outside Coram's to draw the red ball or the green. Two truths duel in her brain: *I love him. He has done this sort of thing before.*

"What say we all get back to work, hmmm?" Mrs. Vile at breakfast is smug, skewering a last curl into place. "Your father has gone to see some... associates today and won't be back until the afternoon. With so much commotion lately" – she flashes a look at Mary – "we must rededicate ourselves to our various employments. I know I need to get back to the translation of Monsieur Lapin for the Children's Library, Claire, you can help me, and Fanny, your new dress is coming along nicely, perhaps you can finish the bodice..." Mary drifts away. She won't write to Shelley; she's given Papa her word. She'll return to Mary Queen of Scots in her lonely castle. Perhaps her novel can become a real paper book in Papa's shop and earn some money to shrink that stack of tradesman's bills on Papa's desk. Maybe Papa has gone to speak to Shelley. Maybe.

An hour later, high up in her schoolroom, Mary has written to the bottom of one page and reached for a fresh one when she hears the front door burst open. Rapid footsteps bound upstairs louder and louder, two at a time, past Mrs. Vile's shrieks, until Shelley bursts in, brandishing a small glass bottle in his fist. His eyes are feverish, his hair wild, his shirt untucked and stained and rippling from his narrow body like a sail. "Mary!" he shouts. "We shall be united. Now!" He uncorks the little bottle and shoves it toward Mary. *Tincture of Laudanum.* A third of the liquid is gone. "By its embrace you shall escape from tyranny. And this shall reunite me to you." From his breeches pocket he draws a small pistol, cocks it, and presses the barrel to the sharp corner of his jaw. Claire and Fanny shriek. "Get back!" Mrs. Vile shouts, shoving them behind her. "The fool will kill us all!"

"Shelley," Mary breathes. The little bottle trembles in her hand. Very slowly she sets it on the table and reaches for him. "Give me the cork." The pistol wobbles against his neck as he gasps. From deep inside his blue eyes, something watches her, laughing at them both. It is a demon, it is a ghost, it is a spectre, it is the laudanum and something the laudanum has only heightened, not created. *You'll never stop me,* it taunts. *I live here inside him. And I always will.* She will not let it see her fear. She will not let it take Shelley from her, and from the world. That demon will not douse his bright eyes, will not blow his red brains across her schoolroom windows on this ordinary Thursday afternoon as the world goes about its business far below, all cart-wheel clatter and Smithfield-market criers and strangers careless of them both.

"Shelley," she repeats. She takes a step toward him. Eyes fixed on her, he sets the cork into her palm. She pushes it into the bottle's neck and nudges the laudanum away. "You know this will not do," she says. The pistol wobbles. In his eyes the demon rattles its cage-bars and rages, sinking to the floor of its cell. "Please."

Shelley gives one tearing sob and lowers the pistol from his throat. In one motion he ejects the bullet from the chamber, whirls, and throws it at the window. The central pane shatters and Mrs. Vile screams. Shelley hurls himself at Mary and seizes her. "Please," he sobs, his face against her neck, "please, please, please."

"I will," Mary says. "I promise you." His tears are cold on her skin. His breath is warm.

"Get out before I call the Watch!" Mrs. Vile shouts, seizing Shelley by the arm. He shakes her away and looks at Mary. "I promise," she says. "I do. I will."

Shelley rakes both hands through his hair, then sets both palms flat on the table and leans on it, panting. Sweat drips from his forehead and spots the wood. "Sorry," he mutters, uselessly. He tugs the empty pistol from his pocket and hands it to Mrs. Vile. "Sell this and you can pay the glazier. Keep the rest for your trouble." He blinks, taking in the broken glass on the floor, Fanny and Claire's tearful faces, Mary's white shocked silence. "Forgive me." He turns and leaves the room. Down the stairs, his footsteps fade.

At midnight comes a pounding on the door. "Mr. Godwin, sir," pants the red-faced man on the threshold, "I'm here from the Saracen's Head. Mr. Shelley has taken laudanum and is like to die. We've got him up and walking, but he sent for you—"

Mary collapses – the first time she's ever fainted – and wakes on the parlor sofa with the morning light seeping steely-blue through the window. "It's an awful time, the morning," Claire observes, "when you think somebody might die."

At breakfast they learn that Papa followed the man back to the inn and walked Shelley up and down the floor all night. Papa's face is gray, his eyes red-rimmed. "Shelley will live," he tells Mary. "But how much longer this can continue I would not care to say."

My dear Mary,

How can I ever atone for the events of yesterday, in your eyes even more than in my own.

I am sincerely sorry for the grief and damage I have caused. Only believe that I was overwhelmed by love for you, without whom I cannot and do not want to live.

Please let me see you. Please come to me. Anything. Please.

My dearest Mary,

I lie in my room here in this wretched inn and think of you and long to have you near –

Do you remember when at your mother's grave we pledged ourselves one to the other and we swore to love – oh Mary I have not forgotten it –

We must leave London. We must fly. A life apart from you is insupportable.

Mary,

You swore to me you do, you will – as do I – then why do you not come to me – although your note brought by Claire has given me fresh life, my darling –

I now make bold to tell you some intelligence of Harriet: the child she now bears may not be my own. Friends say she is intangled with a man called Ryan, an army officer. Oh! – where love has gone there is no true marriage, there cannot be – only between souls allied like our own – Fly with me, run away, run away – to the Continent, to Switzerland, to Italy and love –

Mary please

Mary please

Mary please

Oh my dearest best Mary you have made me the happiest man in existence—

Then it is set then – corner of Hatton Garden and Holborn, July 28, four o'clock in the morning – the dawn will rise on a new birth of freedom and liberty and love that we shall share as no two beings ever have – your S

The little third-floor room with its trapdoor to the attic is forlorn in the light of the last sundown Mary will ever witness in her father's house. The Queen Sophonsiba dress and stolen lanterns still lie in the dark over her head, where she and Fanny and Claire left them. She needn't take any of those things with her, having retrieved her mother's carpetbag from its hiding place. But she will leave something behind. From the bottom of her writing box she draws the single page of her first attempt at a story: *Once there were two sisters and a papa and a mama's ghost.* She folds it into a rectangle, then slips it into the gap between the baseboard and the plaster under the single window.

Just one more thing to write at this table. *Dear Papa, I am travelling with Mr. Shelley to the Continent. We love & are pledged to one another. He will die without me. Your loving daughter. Mary.* She folds the letter, ready to leave on Papa's desk before dawn. Then she sets the carpetbag on the table and tucks the writing box – with her Mary Queen of Scots manuscript and Shelley's *Queen Mab* safely inside – into the bottom. With the bag in her hand, she steps through the door and closes it. Down the stairs, she orders herself. Don't look back.

From the kitchen come the sounds of Fanny and Mrs. Vile preparing dinner. Swiftly, Mary packs the rest of her things. Her tartan dresses, her plain muslin, her petticoat, her second pair of shoes and stockings, Mama's pewter brush and comb; the stays are Fanny's by right. The little stack of coins assembled from her Wollstonecraft aunts' infrequent gifts and one shilling from Papa for working the shop till. A little stack of coins. The Channel, ahead of her, so wide. What she knows of life on one side. And on the other – the unknown, thrilling country of *elsewhere.*

True, this is not her only chance of Italy. At Pisa is Mrs. Mason – Lady Mountcashell, Mama's pupil Margaret King, to whom Papa might send her. But woven with that is a fate like Mama's friend Miss Hays, determinedly self-improving spinster, ambling among the ruins with a guidebook in hand. Alone.

Life without Shelley: insupportable.

When the hall clock strikes three, Mary slips out of bed – poor tired Fanny sleeps like an ox – and draws from underneath it her carpetbag, her shoes, and her sturdy black worsted dress, which she's folded on top. She'll finish dressing downstairs in the shop, will smooth and pin up her long braid before Shelley sees her sleepy dishevelment. But the most important thing is to get out of the room before –

"I know where you're going." From the doorway, Claire's whisper startles her. "And I'm coming too."

Damnation. Claire has sworn she won't read the notes she carries back and forth from Shelley, but – Then Mary remembers her writing box lid neatly shut, the stacks of paper suspiciously tidy after Cornelia Boinville and Harriet's visit. Claire has spied. But it's useless to put her off here or she'll raise the whole house. Furiously Mary motions her into the hall. "I'm coming too," Claire hisses. "I can speak French, better than you." Her round black eyes fill with tears. "I can't stay in this house."

"We've made our arrangements," Mary protests, "we can't –"

"I'll tell Mama," Claire murmurs. She takes a step toward Mrs. Vile's door. "Mary. Take me with you. Please."

"I have to ask Shelley," Mary flounders. Damnation. Any minute now Mrs. Vile will be stirring. And all will be lost. She sighs. "Get your things. And be quick."

"I have them," Claire whispers. She slips back through the bedroom door and draws a small bag from under the trailing blankets of her cot. When she emerges from the bedroom, she too carries her travelling dress and shoes in her hand. Her eyes shine. "I'm ready. I've been–"

"For God's sake, hush," Mary hisses. "Wait for me in the shop." She gathers her bag and her dress and tiptoes down one flight of stairs to Papa's study. As usual he's left his desk ready for the next day's work, with a clear space right in the center. She sets her letter there. *I have not deceived you,* she pleads. *And anyway, a falsehood can be defensible if it is used to save a life. Without me Shelley will die. And I without him.*

She turns and meets her mother's eyes in the portrait above the fireplace, that painted smile tender and ironic, forever fixed in place.

Mama. You would love him too.

She stretches up, touches her fingers to her mother's painted cheek, and turns away.

Downstairs in the shop Claire, fully dressed, gnaws on a dry roll left over from dinner. "Here," she whispers, tossing one to Mary. "Breakfast."

Mary catches the roll and looks at it: food is the one thing she's forgotten. "Well," she says, uselessly, "time grows short." She stuffs the roll into her bag next to her nightgown, then tugs her traveling dress over her head and laces up her shoes. There on the shelf is the green leather-bound copy of her mother's letters from Norway in which Shelley tucked his first note to beckon her out of this house. Surely it isn't stealing to take her own mother's words of instruction, the record of a model adventure. *Gain experience! Ah, gain it* – She snatches the book and shoves it into the carpetbag and closes the latch.

Once out of the shop door – careful not to jingle the bell – and into the street, Mary runs, heedless of Claire, Mama's carpetbag bumping against her legs, her skirts flying. Surely it's not yet four, not too late! Down the street and left at the corner, then right again, and there's a carriage, horse's nose steaming in the cool morning air, driver slumped drowsily on top, Shelley's trunk strapped to the roof. And there's Shelley himself, pacing back and forth. At the sight of her his whole face brightens and he runs to her, snatching her out of the air. "Mary!" he breathes. And then Claire draws up to them, out of breath. His eyebrows lifts, and he smiles.

"I'm coming with you," Claire pants, "to help speak French."

Shelley's smile widens. "Well," he said. "Another sister. Get in." Mary tumbles with her bag into the dim interior, Shelley after her, Claire last of all. He leans over and shuts the door, then collapses next to Mary on the seat, grinning, as the carriage lurches forward and gathers speed. "What a lark! We'll soon be in France. And I promise you, you won't regret this choice you've made." He gathers Mary against him and kisses her, then beams at Claire in the opposite seat. "That all of us have made."

Part Two

Germany

SUMMER 1814

The Creature huddles in the ruins of the Castle Frankenstein and peers down at Mary and Shelley splashing in the river below. For once in their summer's ragged scramble across the Continent, dodging the soldiers trudging home from Napoleon's war, they've had a good dinner: beer and sausages and sour cabbage, served by the innkeeper's daughter, who blushed at Shelley's German ("danke, meine Schatzi," he'd said, smiling; perhaps he's what humans call *handsome?*) The evening is warm, and Shelley has a whim for swimming, and he's teased Mary into the water too. Mary goes wherever Shelley wants, because she loves him. And now she's hugging a secret to herself, a gift she's bearing inside her body. The Creature understands this, somehow. Does Shelley understand Mary's offering, her love? He hopes so, for her sake.

Within his own bruised flesh the knowledge tugs: he hopes, he desires, he wants the same bright thing that's flickering in the dusk between the two people down there.

The guide who haunts this inn has rattled off his spiel so many times the Creature himself could recite it: *ah meester and mizziz, English, welcome! Allow me to prezent you* (the guide leans heavily into his *s's*, like a saw into a tree) *ze Castle Frankenstein, ruin of the alchemist Konrad Dippel. An evil man, a very devil! Believed he could summon ze life into ze dead veins of a corpse, dug up in ze night from ze churchyard. Ze villagers, zey burn him.* "Like the Smithfield martyrs," Shelley joked sourly – four weeks of threadbare traipsing across France and Switzerland and now Germany have jaded him, but even from a distance the Creature could see the story captured him. Mary, too, although Mary is always hard to read.

The guide's words landed in her like dandelion seeds, settling and grounding themselves to reach for the light in some time to come. She turned her eyes toward the pile of rock on the hill where the Creature hid and for a moment he froze, terrified he'd been seen. But Mary doesn't know he's here. Not yet.

She stands now in the shallows on this warm evening, her shift's hem darkening to beige in the water of the Rhine where it flows past like a song on its way to a silver sliver of ocean that soon Mary and Shelley and Claire will cross to go back home. Shelley is hip-deep in the current, grinning, beckoning, but Mary is shy, laughing. He extends his hand and she balances at the edge of it like a butterfly, from rock to rock and then she's waist-high in the current too and Shelley is drawing her close. But not before she bends her neck to bend her gaze, and Shelley's, to the place where her belly is swelling in a new curve, where the current eddies and touches, soft.

And Shelley sees what Mary intends he should. He drops to his knees, heedless, in the river and kisses Mary where the child is growing now. *The child?* Yes, for suddenly the Creature knows there is a child there. His heart twists. Shelley's arms have gone around Mary's waist now and her hands are in his wet curly hair and they are both murmuring to one another words the Creature cannot hear. He blinks. His eyes are hot. Konrad Dippel made a man come to life, but this is the generation of life by other means. His blue Milton book hums with it: two creatures named Adam and Eve, formed for one another, happy. And looking on is God, who says he loves them both. Where, in this story, should the Creature place himself?

Where in this story, indeed. What *is* this story? The Creature does not yet know. Each day of his existence in this healing, hardening flesh is a sensation of prodding at the world, gingerly, like a finger to a bruise. And the world prods back in stern unthinking injunctions of pain: *no. Not this. Not for you.* But when will the world say *yes?* When will he learn why he has been summoned out of his father's rooms with their vats and knives and wires to follow this girl?

When the girl herself learns to see him. When the girl herself learns what she is following, and why.

And in the meantime, he must trudge through this bewildering world, drawn onward by the ghost up ahead – always ahead – of his father, the one who laid out the knives and warmed the vats and sutured with such care the container of flesh into which the world pours with such reckless ease. He must continue to slip up to the ragged soon-to-be-ex-soldiers' camps and snatch their bread and butchered rabbits from their fires without being caught and hear them curse Napoleon in English and Flemish and French: *goddamned little bastard*. He must remain distracted by these glimpses of Mary that tug at him, catch at his throat with a feeling like tears, like the thorn bushes in this forest that snag his skin. Distracted? Maybe there is purpose, though, even here. Maybe the thorns, too, speak a language he can read. Here is the sun, they insist, that brings even creatures like us to life. Here is the path along which we throng and reach for the light. Here, deep in our angry hearts, is our fruit. Partake. You have a long journey yet. You cannot stop.

Mary bends over Shelley's bowed head, over their child unfurling in its warm unknowing dark. They could stand here for days, heedless of anything but one another as the thick green leaves over their heads blaze red and then gold, as the ruined stones settle deeper against the rock and brace for winter, as the river runs on and on into the sea. This, then, must be love.

The Creature turns roughly and scrambles back into the ruins. A pebble bounces downhill in his wake and lands *plonk* in the water but no one heeds it. Mary and Shelley sway like reeds in the current, their arms around one another. And in the window of the inn a woman's figure, candlelit, watches them as the summer night swells and darkens: Claire, in her single room, alone.

London

SEPTEMBER 1814

Alone at a rickety table in a rented flat on Marchmont Street, Mary gathers herself, touches her belly – the child is larger this week than last – and begins. *My dear papa: I scarce know how to tell you of my sensations at this moment.* The images swirl in her: musty inn beds, the rough Calais crossing, the Swiss chateau chopped into apartments, Shelley bargaining for a mule, the scent of war hovering over roads and fields like smoke from a fire that's supposedly been doused. Their six weeks of adventure are all run out now, along with their money. *Chief among them is my hope that I may be received, together with Mr Shelley, back under the roof where we have long found such shelter now that we have returned from* – ahem – *our delightful adventure on the Continent.* A roof, she thinks wryly, that's upheld by Shelley's money. Better not to mention that. *My mother's example ever before me, I have sought to live as a free and rational being, following the dictates of pure love such as that which Mr Shelley and I have found in one another, and you found with my mother herself.* Please, Papa. *As I now find myself in condition to become a mother* – she swallows hard, flattens her left hand on her belly – *I hope that you will welcome me home.*

Godwin's reply comes by return post:

My daughter: I scarce know how to reply to such impudence and boldness as you have demonstrated in your rash elopement with Shelley and in your return to London except to say that I must forbid you both my house as long as you remain attached to him. Consider the position of your sister Frances, whose reputation and whose future possible courses of action – already limited enough, poor girl, by her birth and scant native attain-

ments – must be stained by your infamy, which continued contact with you can only turn to a deeper dye. Therefore, I have asked her not to undermine my position with regard to you and your partners in folly. Mrs. Harriet Shelley, presenting a most pitiable spectacle, has appealed to us for assistance we are wretchedly unable to give. Your stepmother and I have suffered much from our supposed friends in the wake of your absence. She asks that you convey to her daughter that she may return home if she will separate herself from you and from the man who has cast you both into a deeper shade of opprobrium than you can yet perceive. I ask that you do not speak to me of your mother again.

William Godwin.

Mary turns the page over, but nothing more is written there. Numb grief spreads like fire in her chest, leaving only black scorched earth behind. She crumples the letter in both hands and bursts into tears. A stricken sorrow stretches her mouth square in a bellowing howl closer to that of a menagerie beast than a girl. And then her grief gives way to rage. How dare her father cast her out for doing only what he and her mother had done. How dare he reject Shelley as the man who will surely – due to his *honor as a gentleman,* due to his *promise to support a man of liberty –* continue bankrupting himself to give Godwin and Mrs. Vile money even as he and Mary will continue to scrape a hand-to-mouth life in dingy London lodgings, one room for herself and Shelley and one room for Claire (she's so tired of Claire trailing after them, smiling gamely, wistfulness crossing her face when she looks at Shelley) and a sitting-room in which they all must rub together, dodging the bailiffs who will come for Shelley if he can't pay his debts. *You liar,* she flings at Godwin in her mind. *You God-damned hypocrite, taking Shelley's money while forbidding us the house. I will think of my mother and speak of her to whomever I please. It is you who are not worthy to speak of her to me. You coward. I will make my way without you and God-damned Mrs. Vile.* Tyrant. He'll never be Papa to her again. She closes her eyes and presses both hands to where her child and Shelley's floats in its dark silence. A traitorous thread of grief seeps from under the firm wall of her anger, like rainwater through old ceiling-plaster. She fights it back and crumples Godwin's letter, then rips it into pieces for good measure and drops them in the slop-bucket. Sweeping her draggling hair back from her face with both hands, she decides to take it down and brush and repin it. But this alone will not do; she will go fetch water for a proper wash, and take the slop-bucket and her father's words out of these rooms for good.

Mary edges down the back stairs with the water-pitcher in one hand

and the slop bucket in the other. This is the routine of life on the road with Shelley: finding the nearest pump and the nearest discreet gutter. Pushing open the back door, Mary enters a small green yard with a patch of kitchen herbs, a clothesline, and a gnarled old mulberry tree shading a pair of wooden chairs and a wooden table underneath. Even in London, there's always a tree. Red geraniums in pots bloom on both sides of the back gate. As soon as she's gathered her water and washed her face, she'll bring her writing box out here and set to work. She's seventeen, soon to be a mother. She'll make some money by the productions of her own mind. By God, she is the daughter of Godwin and Wollstonecraft.

Nearly three months ago, straggling east across France, she and Claire and Shelley came upon the village of Nogent, burned by Cossacks. People scratched hopelessly at the nubs of green vegetables in a landscape of black char and ash. Against a tree sat a girl Mary's own age, staring at nothing. Hesitantly Claire – whose French was best, Mary had to admit – learned what happened. *Cossacks*, the girl said. *They walked into town and did not leave until the army of the Emperor cast them out. They stole, they burned, they— They took the mayor with a rope around his neck and walked him through the town cracking a whip over his head and laughing, as if he were a horse. They herded us out of our houses and they saw old mother Gélin with her diamond ring, her little diamond ring, on her finger and they cut it off to take it from her. She bled to death. They took the horses and the cattle. And – us. They took the girls.* The danger of the war floats over Mary again now, brushing her with its great dark wing. She and Claire and Shelley had been fortunate in their impromptu scramble (*foolhardy*, Mrs. Vile would rage) not to encounter such a fate themselves. She sees that now.

On the deck of the Rhine barge back to England, Mary had tried to scratch the beginnings of a story, without success. Now she's sitting at a real table with her writing box open before her in the greatest city of writers in the world, sheltered by the Channel and the broad shoulders of the Duke of Wellington, and she has no excuse. A daughter of Wollstonecraft cannot fail to make of this horror a tale to rouse the pity of the world. She dips her pen and addresses herself to the task. *Injustice: A Story by Mary Wollstonecraft Godwin.* A girl named – Mary taps her quill – Clementine has been raped by Cossacks and is now in condition to become a mother but has been cast out of her village by her prideful father, who attempted for years before the raid to arrange a marriage between Clementine and the local nobleman in order to secure his own fortunes but now finds her – Mary's mouth twists – *spoiled.* Fathers only care about money, after all. Well. The dark wings of the war beat and lift away in the clear light of a certainty that, for now, Mary will not examine too closely. Godwin will read her story and see the error of his ways. So will everyone. That's what stories do. Isn't it?

By the time Shelley and Claire return in late afternoon, Mary has finished a draft of the story and stacked the pages neatly on the table, next to a sprig of the red geranium floating in a teacup. Humming to herself, she sets forth what's left of the bread and cheese. "Oh, hello," she says as Shelley and Claire trudge in, talking disconsolately, something about Lord Byron (Claire has some wild scheme to approach him, but Mary puts more trust in Shelley's bankers.) From their faces she can see they've obviously had no success. "I finished my story today."

The flash of jealousy across Claire's face is swamped by the delight in Shelley's eyes as he seizes her and hugs her. "Mary," he says, "how wonderful. May I read?"

"I'd rather you not," Mary blurts. "I – I'll fair-copy it and take it to Godwin's" – she swallows – "publisher tomorrow."

"Magnificent!" Shelley enthuses. "Let me go with you."

"No," Mary says. "I want to go alone. I have a feeling – Please." She kisses Shelley, ignoring Claire's surly face. "I want to do this by myself." Her mother went to Mr. Johnson's offices with her own manuscript in hand, running on nothing but a mustered-up conviction of the world's need to hear exactly what she had to say. Mary can do no less. Mr. Johnson knows Godwin, as well; he actually introduced Mama to him, then published *Political Justice* and the novels after that. Into her memory drifts a dim picture of a short man with a wide forehead and a quiet, hesitant voice, turning toward her at some long-ago Skinner Street dinner: *Why, Miss Mary. Don't you look like your dear mother. Rest her soul.* And he brought those crates of books to the Skinner Street shop when her father surely could not pay him. *You've been a good investment, Godwin,* he smiled. *We'll settle up in some future time.*

The following morning Mary brushes her hair and pins it neatly and puts on the least faded of the tartan dresses. The seams under her arms are starting to rip and rot from wear, but it will have to do. Soon, she'll sell her story and earn money to repair it. And the other tartan. And her petticoats. And her poor black traveling dress, ragged from mule-backs and carriage seats and boat decks from London to Paris to Lucerne to the Castle Frankenstein and home again.

"Here," mumbles Claire, emerging from her room with a deep-green, black-satin-fringed shawl. "Bought this off a stall. It'll cover the worst.

And set off the green in the tartan, too." Awkwardly, she loops an arm around Mary's shoulder, and squeezes. "Good luck."

Mary emerges from the door of the house, ties her bonnet strings snugly, and starts walking east, in the direction of St. Paul's Churchyard. Briefly, she wishes for Shelley. She needs the reckless-edged excitement he casts around him like some minor sun. No one in his vicinity can help absorbing his effortless conviction that the world means him only good. But she's on a mission to secure their future in London, as her mother did, arriving with her face also set against a tyrannical father and a bundle of pages in her hand and – at least part of her time here – a child under her heart. Mary, too, will do this alone, and share the news with Shelley after the sale is accomplished. He'll be so proud. So will Mama. Wherever she is.

Claire's borrowed shawl provides a welcome bit of warmth in the mid-September morning chill as Mary continues south and east, toward the river. Carriages and carts rumble past and Mary keeps carefully close to the buildings, veering around shop-boys rolling up awnings. She lingers at the great tempting tables of flowers and fruit, presided over by stern-faced women whose faces close when they see Mary's shabby dress, her swollen stomach, the worn shoes through which paving rasps like a pulse with every step.

An increase in bail-bondsmen's offices and moneylenders' bureaus tells Mary she must be approaching Newgate Prison. There it is, its stone bulk emitting a near-visible odor of human filth and human despair, as the slave ships approaching the Jamaican shore are said to do. It's dreadful in prison, everyone says. Even if you're a gentleman imprisoned for debt. No one will listen to your cries for mercy. You'll be thrown into a cell and left to rot until your debts are paid. Even if you have two girls in rented lodgings and an unborn child and a hypocritical old philosopher dependent on you. Even if you have a woman back in her parents' house who's still technically your wife. Even if you're Percy Bysshe Shelley, son of Sir Timothy Shelley, Field Place, Sussex.

Mary turns eastward again onto Fleet Street. The dome of St. Paul's now floats in her path, its pale outline nipped by the jagged edges of roofs, chimney-pots, and the envious spires of lesser churches. Here the carriages are light and dashy, the crowds on the walking-path quick. Most are young men, clothes spotted with ink, gazes keen and impudent. Shops display broadsides and books and prints. *Various Beasts of Different Parts of the World*, reads one amid a scene of fantastical animals: a great ox with long sharp horns and a ridge of fur along its spine, two long-tailed cats with shaggy coats, a family of monkeys. There's the notorious Lord Byron turning his famous profile to the light: ah, Thyrza, those romantic lines she scribbled in *Queen Mab* which now, in the steely light of *afterwards*, make her flinch. Surely she must have misheard Claire's silly scheme, for how could such a man ever hearken to a random threadbare girl? Another print depicts Napoleon seated backward on a donkey. *The journey of a modern hero to the island of Elba,* the caption reads. Furiously kicking spurs into the donkey's flanks, brandishing a broken sword, he's also lifting its tail to release a string of words like a fart: *The greatest events in human life is turned to a puff.* A shopboy standing in the door grins at her. "Mr Gillray's latest," he says. "You should see the ones ain't fit for young ladies. Like Miz Fitz'erbert and the Prince. Just shows their two pairs o' feet. But that's enough to tell they're getting' up to" – his grin deepens – "some'at nasty."

"Insolent scoundrel," Mary snaps in Shelley's voice, turning away and marching up Ludgate Hill. The massive, melancholy sprawl of St. Paul's Cathedral looms over the commotion of people and carriages in the yards around it, its dome smoke-tinged against the blue morning sky. Already there are tiny figures on the dome's external gallery, pointing toward the river or leaning on the rail, sheltering against its great flank like chicks against a mother hen. Tourists. No real Londoner would ever pay the fivepence to make such a climb and view the same shit-clogged river and the same crowded streets they can see for free every day, willingly or not.

Mary dredges in her brain for the memory of the time she came here with Godwin to deliver a manuscript. They'd come up the little hill to St. Paul's Churchyard and turned... left, where the brilliant morning sun glows now against the pale steps on the cathedral's northern side. Most of the publishers' offices stretch to the right, in a row of buildings huddled with their backs to the river. There is the alcove known as Pissing Alley, and there are the men slipping in and out of its shadows, hands on their breeches-buttons: "a suitable location," Godwin had muttered, smiling to himself, "for the center of London's publishing world." Were there so many publishers and booksellers here before? With a prickle of apprehension and longing, Mary surveys the tables of books set out in the sun, the people browsing among them, the clusters of men walking by twos and threes, heads together, voices intent. Thankfully, she recognizes the name *Johnson* on a shop window: *Johnson & Hunter.* Perhaps Mr. Johnson has taken a partner. But surely he'll not refuse to see the daughter of Godwin and Wollstonecraft.

The door of Johnson & Hunter is sticky, finger-smeared but yielding to a shove. Its front room is lined with bookshelves, with some of the paperbound titles on stands face-out. Mary skims them quickly, but her parents' books aren't there. From a half-open door at the back, men's voices murmur: "well," one says regretfully, "given the Crown's paranoia, we must be vigilant."

"Can I help you?" A young man with boils on his chin and a stiff, comb-tracked pompadour looks up from behind his desk. "I'm afraid Mr. Hunter is busy."

"I'm here to see Mr. Johnson," says Mary, striving for gracious ease. "I'm the daughter of William Godwin and Mary Wollstonecraft. And I have a story to sell."

"Oh." The young man's voice goes flat, his face smug. "Oh, dear. Mr. Johnson has been dead for some years. Mr. Hunter is his partner. And a story by the daughter of Godwin and Wollstonecraft" – he pauses – "would not seem to be commercially viable at this point." He peers at her. "Wait. Are you the girl who ran off with that radical?"

"I don't know what you mean," Mary stammers. "I want to see Mr. Hunter."

"Mr. Hunter is busy, as I said," declares the young man, smiling. "But he has empowered me to act on his behalf." He extends his hand across the desk. "May I?"

Mary hesitates. She could storm past this boy into Mr. Hunter's office, but doing so would brand her a girl at the mercy of her fancies. And such a girl could never write a story worth a publisher's time. Reluctantly, she holds out her hand and lets the boy take the bundle of pages covered in her best handwriting. A stillness settles over him and his eyes flick back and forth. He sets the first page down, then the second, before finally looking up at Mary again. "Good title," he observes, sweeping the pages back into a pile and thrusting them across the desk at Mary. "But, I'm afraid, an implausible plot."

"You didn't even finish reading it!" Mary protests.

"When you have read as many wild tales by young ladies as we here at Johnson and Hunter," says the boy, "you don't need to complete a manuscript to make a sound assessment."

"As *we?*" Mary snaps. "Have you really been here that long?" The boy's eyes widen and his neck turns red. Mary fights for control. "Ask Mr. Hunter about my parents," she pleads. "Their books built this whole enterprise."

The back office door creaks open and a stout white-haired man hurries out, glancing at Mary. Then a tall slender man, his dark hair frosted with gray and his cravat rumpled loose around his neck, enters the front room, rubbing his eyes. "What's the difficulty, Cecil?" he asks. Then he spots the pile of pages in Mary's hand. A dismal, professional smile leaps to his face. "Thank you for your interest in our firm," he recites, "but I am afraid we are not able to—"

"I'm the daughter of Godwin and Wollstonecraft," Mary blurts, "and I've written a story." And she holds out her pages to him.

"Oh," Mr. Hunter says. He studies her as several thoughts shift on his face. "Why don't you come back to my office," he finally says, "and we'll discuss it?"

Mary settles into a wooden chair in front of Mr. Hunter's desk. Behind her, he shuts the door, then edges around her to a tea-tray teetering on his paper-piled credenza. "Luckily," he says, "Cecil just made some tea for my... associate and myself. May I offer you a cup?"

"Yes, please," Mary replies. She's never seen such a disorderly room: stacks of paper everywhere, open books lying face-down, pots of ink with pens sticking out and corks leaving their little black hoofprints on the paper underneath. Near the window dangles an etching set crooked in its frame: a surgical theatre with a man splayed on a table and fat-faced men in wigs standing around to peer at him. A string of guts spool down from his cut-open stomach. Underneath the table crouches a dog, gnawing furtively on the end.

"Ah, Hogarth." A smile brightens Mr. Hunter's tired face as he turns, a cup of tea in each hand. "The greatest artist England has ever produced. That's the last of the Four Stages of Cruelty." He grins, looking around distractedly before handing Mary her tea and seating himself behind his desk. "The other three stages are in this office, somewhere. Now, to our business."

"I have written a story," Mary falters, "and I wonder if you would like to publish it." She sets her pages – suddenly, they look so small – on Mr. Hunter's desk. "I am happy to wait while you read."

"Then I certainly shall," declares Mr. Hunter, taking a sip of tea and leaning back in his chair. "Huh. Good title."

"That's what Cecil said." Mary hopes this will help.

"He's still learning the trade," Mr. Hunter admits, "but he does show some promise." He fixes his eyes on the pages and falls silent. "Hmm." He sets down the first page, then the second, then the third, his forehead creasing. "Hmm." Finally he flicks the last page over the others and gathers them slowly back into a pile. "Miss Godwin," he finally says. "With your parentage and the obvious promise these pages show, you cannot help but be a woman of sense. So I will be frank." He sighs. "We are in a political moment where any subject remotely controversial can be very dangerous."

"I don't understand," Mary blurts. Dangerous? What has that word to do with her story? Or the money she and Shelley need if they are going to survive in this city?

"Unwed motherhood," Mr. Hunter says. "I know, I know, *unwed* is grossly inadequate as a term, especially for a such a character as yours." He steals a glance at her stomach and looks away, blushing. "I mean, the girl in your story, of course. But in the wake of the wars –" He falters. "Your parents and Mr. Johnson," he finally says, "fought one version of our government's fear of a revolution such as the one in France. I, alas, am fighting another. And dare I say, one even more insidious." He looks down at Mary's manuscript, then up again. "Any material that is seen as undermining the sanctity of the *family* –" the word spins bitterly in his mouth – "is seen as potentially seditious and therefore subject to...legal action. These are, to put it mildly, conservative times, despite the licentiousness of those in power. Such as our fat Prince Regent with his string of mistresses and his Brighton banquet-house." His lips thin in an angry line. "We are watched, Miss Godwin. Especially a house with a history like that of Johnson and Hunter."

"Which published my parents," Mary says slowly. "Which published Godwin and Wollstonecraft." *Scandalous,* tease the half-remembered words of the reviews Godwin tried to keep from her. *Radical, revolutionary. Virago and her consort. National disgrace.*

"Precisely," Mr. Hunter murmurs. He peers at her. "I didn't want to put it to you in those terms, Miss Godwin. But you must have noticed your father's...difficulties."

"I have," says Mary. So this is among the reasons for the cold fireplaces, the shabby clothes, the reboiled teabags and marrowbones of Skinner Street. "And my own name is linked to this – difficulty." Godwin's neat agitated handwriting floats before her eyes: *Your step-mother and I have suffered much from our supposed friends in the wake of your absence.* The story must be in every bookseller's and publisher's house in town. *You're the girl who ran away with that radical.* And here she is walking among them, with the curve of her belly to confirm it.

"I'm afraid so," Mr. Hunter sighs. "Understand me. We could publish it pseudonymously, but the subject matter might still bring – difficulty. Even in a gazette tossed away after dinner." He hands the pages slowly back to Mary. "That is not to say, however, that further stories from your pen might not be useful to us. Please do favor me with a look at anything else you might write."

"I will," Mary promises, mustering a smile. "Goodbye, Mr. Hunter. Thank you for your kindness." He starts to rise from his chair but she shakes her head. "Don't worry, I'll see myself out."

"Goodbye, Miss Godwin," he says. His smile is sad. "May I say, you are very like your mother. She visited Johnson when I was junior clerk to him, no older than Cecil there. I remember them laughing behind this door. Great friends, they were. That was in the time of the *Vindications*, three glorious years in the history of thought. A memorable lady, and a noble one." He extends his hand to Mary and she shakes it. "She would be proud of you."

Mary resettles Claire's shawl around her shoulders and pulls Mr. Hunter's door gently closed behind her. Cecil looks up. His officious smile widens. "Goodbye, Miss Godwin," he chirps. "Do try us again with something more suitable. Perhaps a nice children's tale."

Mary thrusts her pages into her reticule and strides up Ludgate Hill away from St. Paul's Churchyard and its whole infernal cackle of publishers and books. Damn them all. Why not try another office? But if Johnson and Hunter are not willing to take on the notorious daughter of notorious parents, then why would anyone else? And if none of these men of letters will risk a story of a girl made the victim of prejudice against her will – a girl made the victim of a war thrust into her village and her body by men – what sort of men are they, after all? Cowards. *These are difficult times, politically*, Mr. Hunter said, yet she pushes the image of his weary face from her mind. Cowards. When she and Shelley risk everything for principle – like Socrates on trial, Dante in exile, Galileo hoisting his telescope to look the Church in the eye – why cannot the rest of the world?

In the shop window's reflection stands a small spindly girl with an angry face and fist of round belly under faded tartan skirt. Mary is shocked to recognize herself. Ashamedly, she remembers trading giggles with Shelley as they trudged toward Switzerland, mocking the big London tavern-men eating their plates of liver-and-lights. *Liver-and-light-eater*, Shelley had scribbled jokingly in their journal; they'd been trying to learn the names for the money and thought the pun would help them remember *livre*. Learning money, to buy food and a bed. What a little fool she'd been to scorn anything like meat. She'd happily pull up a chair and tuck into a plate of pig guts right now. Unwillingly, shame creeps through her brain: about what other certainties has she been so serenely wrong?

On the corner of Fleet Street stands a man cooking pork chops on a blackened iron brazier. The rich scent of roast meat floods her mouth. In her pocket she has three pence. She shoves one of them at the man and – looking at her belly, then away – he pries the biggest chop from the grill with a pair of tongs and extends it to her. "Thank you," she mutters. Seizing the chop by the bone, heedless of the sizzling ribbons of fat and the pedestrians shoving past, she gnaws it until the last morsel is gone, then snaps the bone, sucks its marrow, and tosses it into the gutter. Shelley will be disappointed in her. But their child can't live on tea and bread and air.

In an alley to her right, a sign dangles above the entrance to a lead-windowed pub: *Ye Olde Cheshire Cheese.* Mary ducks into the alley and reaches for the door. She'll storm up to the counter and order a pint, then sit in one of the high-backed nooks and brood. If *Injustice* will not sell, what will? Yet a seventeen-year-old girl entering a pub by herself will draw down more trouble on her head than a pint of ale is worth. The insolent printers' boys are only the beginning. The door is narrow, the interior very dark. Any man could be drinking in there in the middle of the day. And any unaccompanied girl at a tavern counter will be his prey. She'd written it herself, and so had Mama. This would be Claire, if she succeeded in attracting Byron and he tired of her. Flung out, determinedly smiling, haunting counters like this: the fate of women in a world of men. The world. God rot it all in hell. Every last stinking dreg.

Mary turns away from the pub and peers up the crooked alley. Pinched by the buildings on each side, it's dim even in the middle of the day. From around the corner come shouts and thuds, the clink and stamp of horse and harness. Suddenly a rangy red fox, white-tipped brush held aloft, uncurls itself and trots up the alley on narrow black paws. Here in the heart of the city, with rat-terrier-men and carts and cruel boys with stones, it's made a den, although she can see no opening in the brick. Pausing, it turns to look at her. Something flinty and factual flickers in its eyes. *Well, girl. Here you are. What are you going to do about it?* And, flourishing its tail, the fox disappears.

The walk back to the flat in the sinking sunlight is a drudgery, worse, even, than the summer's trek across the Continent. By the time Mary rounds the corner of Marchmont Street, she's viciously tired. The old man who lives in the downstairs flat snarls out of his window at her, like a badger from his hole. Maybe once Claire can be foisted off on Byron or anyone else, maybe once Shelley settles his suit with his father and establishes his income, maybe then they can have a home of their own that's not this dingy little flat with its whitewash-slopped floor, where no amount of rearranging can make the rump-sprung armchairs and the teacup-ring-scalded tables attractive. For a moment she lets the full, shameful, petted-princess complaint of it billow up in her head. *Shelley, I didn't run away with you for this.* Hand to mouth. Snatching a chop on Fleet Street and sucking the bone. Papering the inside of her shoes. Hungering, just as if she'd never left Godwin's chilly house.

On the corner of Marchmont Street, thirty yards from the door that Mary still can't open on her first try, a man and woman emerge from the shadows, then stop to kiss. Automatically, Mary averts her gaze. But then she looks again. The bodies tighten and turn together, drawn slowly into the shop window's light. One is Shelley. The other is Claire.

Mary's brain goes white. If Shelley and Claire can reach for one another on the street so heedlessly, what might they have done when out of sight? In the very rooms through which they have all shuttled since leaving Skinner Street? On the long afternoons when the two of them go out and Mary – laden with the baby growing under her heart – stays behind? Harriet's face floats before Mary's eyes. *He left me for you.* Cornelia's face follows, sympathetic, factual. *He has done this sort of thing before.* A jagged blur of memory tumbles through Mary's blood like a rock in a stream: Shelley's skin on hers. His hands in her hair. The warm deliberate weight of him turning to her in bed. Each edge of each image cuts, and bleeds. His mouth on her breast where their child will be – oh, soon, their own child – draws a painful bright strand from the deep meeting-place of her body and brain out up into the world to fly loose and forlorn. Betrayal of this bright thing flings Mary staggering against the door. If he can bring Claire to himself that way, then she has left Skinner Street and traipsed across the Continent for nothing. She is carrying this baby that cast her out of her father's house and the known prim hypocritical world for nothing. She has trusted a rogue and a scoundrel, as her mother trusted Mr. Imlay. She's been a fool. And worst of all, she's consented to her own ruin. Like any other girl seduced into a corner of a dark street, she'll now be left to wander, along with all the other castoffs of so-called gentlemen. Like any other girl whose singing blood has, fatally, drowned her brain.

Mary wrenches the street door open. Shelley and Claire turn to her. Before they can speak, she yanks the door shut behind her, runs up the stairs, and locks herself in the flat. By God, she will not let them in. She snatches one of the old chairs and jams its top rail under the knob as Shelley begins fumbling with his key. "Mary," he calls. She runs to the old dresser in the corner and, with her fingers hooked in the drawer-slots, yanks it across the floor – carving raw tracks in the boards – and shoves it against the door too. The baby inside her quivers, then subsides. Shelley and then Claire knock and plead, but Mary will not open the door. There is no way to handle this whole sorry mess but to make herself entirely clear. "Don't come back," she growls, "until you've sent her somewhere else, for good." Mama wrote scornfully of the downtrodden woman cowering like a pet dog, *smiling under the lash because it dare not snarl.*[1] But look at how in her letters Mama pleaded with Mr. Imlay. And it did her no good. Mary must learn of Mama's error, for error it was. A man she must whimper like a spaniel to keep is a man who does not love her and never will.

"Mary, please." In Shelley's voice rings a thrilling note of fear. "Let us in."

Mary puts her forehead against the door. "Go away," she snaps. She stomps into the bedroom and slams the door – the old man downstairs will raise hell, but who cares – and tiptoes back to judge the effect. First a blur of whispers. Then reluctant footsteps on the stairs to the street, going down. But not before she hears Shelley's voice through the door, dangerously soft. "All right, then. I will."

CHAPTER 3

St. Pancras Cemetery

LONDON 8 MARCH 1815

Under the willows that border the melancholy little River Fleet, where it runs away to the Thames, the Creature huddles and waits to witness what has summoned him here. His brain prickles and stirs – setting, firming like a pudding in a Somers Town bakery window – with what someone (Father?) would name a *deduction* or *knowledge:* he finds himself in a new place when there is something there that must be seen by Mary or someone who cares for her, when there's something that must not be forgotten. Right now, Mary herself – watched over by Fanny – is back in the shabby flat on Marchmont Street, unable to rise from her bed. Her body and mind are torn open and bleeding around an aching, bewildered hole. She should have a baby to hold and nurse, that baby that bloomed inside her as she and Shelley stood ankle-deep in the River Rhine. But she does not.

The squat square tower of St. Pancras Church rears against the sky, scraping the moon where it floats almost low enough for the Creature to touch. Against the soles of his great blackened feet, the riverbank hums: the Fleet is a straggly thing, urban and dispirited, but, like any river, it can speak. This patch of ground has also been witness, to a summoning of something out of the air – a force that made a child, a kind of energy of which the river approves. Mary and Shelley made a child on this spot. And now that child will be –

The iron gate of the churchyard creaks and the Creature ducks into shadow. Two figures steal up over the little hill and weave through the gravestones toward him. Shelley, tall and hatless, carrying a small white cloth-wrapped bundle in his arms. And behind him, Claire, with black curls springing from under the hood of her cloak, bearing an unlit lantern and a spade. They make straight for a tall square stone near the willows, and Shelley kneels and deposits his small burden at its foot. Claire tosses back her cloak's hood and rummages in her pocket for a fire-flint and strikes a spark and lights the lantern. She looks down at Shelley's bowed head with an expression that the Creature cannot read. And then she begins to dig.

Shelley remains kneeling, head bowed. "What has the dead clay to do with the vital spark." He's reciting words, trying to convince himself. "What is the body to do with the living self, the..." He sets one hand on the small wrapped bundle where it's rounded at one end. His hand curves gently, like it did when he stood in the shallows of the River Rhine with Mary, cupping her face. This is, the Creature deduces, what humans do when they *love;* Shelley loves this small bundled thing. Experimentally, he extends his own giant knuckly hand, curves it into a shape in the air: one-half of an incomplete parenthesis, a yearning outstretched in the dark. But this dark is busy with centuries' worth of yearnings, careless of him. Ghosts of priests and warriors wisp past his ears, barely pausing to look at the humans with their lantern and their corpse, at the Creature frozen in the dark. *Mourn,* the willows murmur in their strange language. *Mourn. For what you see now. And for what you will see, before this story ends.*

"She is your child." Claire's voice is taut with a brisk factuality stretched over some other feeling. "We promised Mary." She digs, pauses, digs, testing with the spade's tip, widening and lengthening the hole. Shelley remains silent, head bowed. And then Claire's spade strikes something in the dirt with a hollow *thunk*. It is a wooden sound, like a knocking on a door. Like a window, flung back into its frame, when it is opened.

"Stop." Shelley's voice is thick. He gathers the little bundle in his arms. Quickly Claire kneels, too, and reaches into the hole with both hands – she is touching that wooden thing, the Creature surmises – and then Shelley leans forward and lowers the small white bundle into the ground. Abruptly he shoves dirt into the hole on top of it as fast as he can. Claire leans back, startled, then sets her fingertips against the upright letters carved into the stone. Her face is yearning, dissatisfied. Reaching for the wooden thing underground, reaching for the name on the stone the Creature can't read: what is Claire seeking? "Buried with Mother." Her voice is tentative, testing a sentiment that makes the Creature wince.

"Mary Wollstonecraft is not your mother." Shelley's voice is cutting.

He sets both hands flat on the fresh mound of dirt and pushes down. "It is time to be factual, Claire."

"Says the man who –" Claire is choking, stuttering on her sudden anger, leaning close to Shelley. The Creature cannot see her face. "Says the man who –"

"I know who I am," says Shelley, his head still bowed. "And what I've done. Believe it."

"I don't believe it," Claire blurts. She's raging now, the words unstopped. "Strung me along and ran off from a wife and – Mary, and the *baby*, just two *days* ago, Shelley, she's – And even then you strung me along, you made me believe you — "

"Stop." Shelley's voice hardens. "Don't humiliate yourself."

"You don't know what you've done," Claire spits. "Not a God-damned bit. You—"

Shelley lifts his face, strained white and blank. "So take it back." His voice is defiant, weary. "So take it all back and stay in Godwin's house with your fat insufferable ma*maa*" – the mocking spin in his voice is Mrs. Vile's false-fronted French – "as if nothing had ever changed. As if I'd never come along. As if you'd just stay on Skinner Street forever, selling a book per week, if that, and waiting on a man to walk through that door."

"Do you think I need *you*?" Claire's voice tumbles, propelled by fury, toward a precipice. The Creature's heart twists. She is sixteen. She is so small in the vast dark night, with none of Mary's self-possession, with none of Fanny's humble practicality. She is a girl with no one. Just a fat insufferable ma*maa*.

"You do need me." Shelley's smile is small and terrible. "Don't you?"

"I'm going to write to Lord Byron, like I said," Claire flounders, gasps. "I mean it, I'm going to write to him and suggest a meeting and he'll be too astounded to resist, he'll be –"

"He'll be curious." Shelley's eyebrows lift. "That *is* an item in your favor. So they say." He looks at Claire, carefully. And then he smiles, wider, keeping his eyes on hers. "And once he sees you, surely he'll want to reward your curiosity. And his own." A slow wind rises, swaying the willow fronds against the Creature's face. Something passes between Shelley and Claire that spins the Creature in place, just as it did between Byron and Robert Rushton in crumbling Newstead Abbey. Even at a distance, it emits a heat. *I don't say no. I can't.* In spite of her anger, in spite of the small dead baby at her feet. In spite of Mary. In spite of everything, Claire can refuse Shelley nothing. The Creature swallows hard. He wants this thing crackling between the humans it's been his lot to encounter. But – does he want *this*? This need and shame and anger that still can't stop the need? Is this desire inevitable? No matter what ruin it brings?

"Mary is waiting for us." Shelley rises and dusts his hands on his trouser knees. "And Fanny. We need to go and help...." He hefts the spade and slings it over his shoulder. For a long moment he stands, staring at the dark spot of oblong broken ground. Then he turns and strides away, lifting his sleeve to his face to scrub away tears. Claire snatches up the lantern and follows. "I'll write to Byron," she calls uselessly. "I'll write to him. I *will*."

CHAPTER 4

Geneva

SWITZERLAND MAY 1816

Swish of oars, slap of plank on waves, creak of wind-filled canvas, cry of inland gull and piratical, harbor-lurking swan: with Shelley at the tiller, Mary sails, at last, toward all he's promised her. The morning is dazzling, with a green, intoxicating smell of wind in spruce and pine. Behind them, on the northern shore of Lake Geneva, squats the Hotel d'Angleterre, where Claire has stayed behind to mind baby William and await Lord Byron. Just visible ahead, on the southern shore, is the village of Cologny, a cluster of houses where she and Shelley will meet the estate agent whose card waits brightly on the hotel desk for the pleasure of English travelers such as themselves. With a home, and with William, their second child – their *child*, she corrects herself – she and Shelley will be travelers no more.

At her back, the rudder creaks, turned by Shelley's hand. He's carrying her into the life they've been chasing since the dark threadbare days in London, when dodging bailiffs from the debtors' court meant she and Shelley could only meet on Sundays in the shadow of St. Paul's, just up Ludgate Hill from the publishers' offices and the ghosts of all the books they'd strangled at birth (*try us in the future, Miss Godwin, perhaps with a nice children's tale),* when she waited in vain for a letter from her father – *Godwin,* that was all he'd be to her now – and reboiled tea and stewed the limp vegetables from the back of a Covent Garden market-stall (*'alf price,* said the girl, averting her gaze from Mary's swelling belly and un-ringed finger) and told herself that once the baby came everything would be different.

And here, on the lake, on the Continent, maybe it is. Although as ever there's the clinging matter of Claire, unresolved, still trailing them from room to rented room. She claims to be no more welcome on Skinner Street than they are, claims to be pursuing plans for singing lessons and governessing work. But so far her only visible plan is Lord Byron. Amazingly, she did write to him, out of the blue, although God only knew what those letters contained; at Mary's inquiring look, Claire had only blushed and smirked. "We are now," she said grandly, "*involved.*" Then Shelley's own arrangements for the Continent, his own man-to-man letters to Byron (no one thought it strange when the son of a minor nobleman wrote to a famous poet out of the blue), got tangled with Claire's obvious hopes that Byron would open the trapdoor from her spinster poverty to a real-life Queen Sophonsiba dream. Claire, they all decided, would follow Mary and Shelley to Geneva and meet Byron there. Because, after all, he is separated from his wife. He is, in theory, available.

Separated from his wife: even Mary, who spurns gossip (*what damage*, Mama would sigh, *is wrought by idle tongues*), knows the gist. Famous for his profile and his Oriental epics (Mazeppa, Lara, the Corsair, and now the continuously unrolling, coyly autobiographical scroll of *Childe Harold's Pilgrimage*, in canto-by-canto installments) and his rakish lifestyle (gambling, debt, boxing with Gentleman Jackson at the Fives Court despite a lame leg), Byron married a wealthy girl named Annabella and quickly became a father – to a daughter, if Mary remembers rightly. But this January, Annabella took her baby and fled Byron's house in the middle of the night. Unlike Godwin and Mrs. Vile, her parents took her in. And in March (when Claire had all the gazettes, and Shelley more letters to his bankers, spread over the table each morning), Byron and Annabella had signed a decree of separation. *He is insane. He stays out all hours with actresses. With boys. He has – formed a connection. With his half-sister. Mrs. Leigh. And he once asked his wife to do – Oh, such things!*

Claire has persevered in attaching herself to Byron and apparently won. Yet even the possibility of a Claire-less household can't dispel Mary's unease. Each morning, at the Hotel d'Angleterre, Claire badgers the desk clerk for news of Byron's arrival, glares at the giggling girls in the lobby clutching their copies of *Childe Harold's Pilgrimage* (ah, such a tormented hero – perhaps like the poet himself?) and instructs the clerk – despite his obvious disbelief – to inform any such supplicants that Lord Byron's affections are already engaged. "What do you think of it?" Mary has asked Shelley, alone in their room. "This plan of hers?" By now, she knows when he's smiling only to resist the downward tug of his own thoughts: lips tucked together, the corners of his mouth quirked backward, his eyes dark. "Well," he says, "we *did* make the choice to be – free. All of us."

Two years, now, it's been since Mary slipped out the door of the Skinner Street shop and out of her furious, solitary life. Into this moment, here. Where their real life can begin. Where they'll be free. Against the sun, Shelley is a solid bright shape, hatless, coatless, his shirt billowing with the sail. His hand on the tiller, he turns to look at her and smiles. The wind parts his auburn curls down to the root, splashing them across his cheeks, his eyes. She feels, as if in her own body, how the breeze touches his very blood through the layers of bone and flesh, lighting him with an electrical current like those he sought to isolate at Oxford, where he labored in his room as she did in hers over the pages that would never come right, over her Mary Queen of Scots who would never quite rise and speak. But Shelley is always quickened by the world, kin to the elements it contains. For this is the nature of the man she loves. Water. Wind. Flame.

On the dock ahead of them stands a small figure in a blue velvet coat and black trousers, clutching his hat against the wind: the estate agent. He meets Mary's eyes and lifts his hat, as experience has surely trained him to do: *the gentleman pays, but the lady decides.* Mary smiles back as Shelley maneuvers the sailboat's nose against the post and springs out, the coil of mooring-rope in his left hand and his right already extended. "Shelley," he says – only the single name, always – and the little man beams. "Beauvoir," he says, clutching Shelley's hand in both his own. "*C'est mon plaisir* to show you to your new home."

Two years in Shelley's wake have taught Mary to keep her real-estate expectations in check – there are the houses she dreams of, and, inevitably, the shabby rented rooms Shelley's patchworked finances will afford – but as she follows Monsieur Beauvoir up the path from the dock and along the lane, she allows herself to hope. And as Monsieur Beauvoir stops at the gate of a small white house in a cluster of birch trees, then ushers her through the gate and up the front walk, the hope grows to excitement. "La Maison Chapuis," Monsieur Beauvoir declares, beaming. "Three rooms up and the large rooms here as you see, and the view of Lac Leman, *charmant.* You have children?"

"Yes," Mary falters, "one, a boy," but Shelley has already brushed past them and is striding into the large front room, where an old but sturdy sopha stretches under the uncurtained window and two armchairs face the fireplace. Dust swirls gently in the light, but not much: the place is clean. Solid floors, no water stains, no buckled plaster. Through the archway hulks a giant battered table with five chairs clustered around, a massive black stove, and a back door to what promises to be something like a garden. Shelley halts, turning slowly, his face bright with what's kindling in Mary too: the familiar new-lodgings hope of *possibility*. Monsieur Beauvoir smiles. "The upstairs," he exults, "it is also furnished!" Indeed, Mary finds, it is. One big room to the left. Two smaller rooms to the right, each with a bare bedstead: the ropes sag but could be tightened, fresh linen mattress-sacks bought and stuffed. And on the wide landing where Mary stands is a sun-faded, splintered wooden desk, with a sloping top and a small brass lock.

Of course, Mary must take due diligence; she's a mother now, not a naïve girl. So she returns to the kitchen area and opens the back door, standing in what is indeed a small back garden with a narrow stone terrace and a rain-bleached, rickety table and chairs. Next to the cistern, a shrub is striving to burst into flower; an orange-and-brown butterfly clings to a leaf, flattening its wings to hold on as a breeze suddenly lifts. Behind Mary, Monsieur Beauvoir draws breath to speak, but Shelley interrupts. "What," he asks, pointing, "is *that*?"

On the hill above them rears a four-story mansion, surrounded by overgrown vineyards and cattle paths winding through tall grass. Its pale stuccoed walls are peeling; its windows stare over the lake with imperious blind eyes. Rust clings to the wrought-iron rails of the second-floor balcony, and one shutter dangles loose. The roof, pierced with small dormer windows, has a faint but definite sag. All the window-glass is still intact, but only because the steep hill deters casual mischief. You'd have to be bent on mayhem to make this climb. And you'd have to be brave. Something about the house looks not just forlorn but haunted, remote and ruined as the Castle Frankenstein. *They say he went mad. They say he killed—*

"Ah," says Monsieur Beauvoir, "the Villa Diodati. Allow me to present it to you." *No*, Mary signals to Shelley, *I like this one!* But Shelley is already brushing past her, nearly treading on the shorter man's heels in his excitement. The tall mad boy from Eton; how he loves a ghost story. Mary sighs and starts to climb the hill after him. Have they not had enough draughty windows and chilly rooms, enough of rearranging meager furniture on blank expanses of floor? But she must not leap to conclusions. Must be realistic. At least in such a house, Claire could have her own room. Her own floor, come to that.

The path winds back and forth against the steep upward face of the hill. Rocks and tree roots buckle its surface. A pale brown cow wearing a bell on a leather collar lifts her head and blinks; Mary dodges a heap of dung, then a hoof-printed mud patch at a hillside spring. "You can see the old vineyards," Monsieur Beauvoir huffs, "the traces of the days this was a grand estate. Diodati family – *famille très ancienne*, first to translate the Bible into Italian during the Lutheran time." He stops, wheezing. "And as you can see, the *view*!"

Mary and Shelley turn together and gasp with delight. Beyond the scattered roofs of houses and chimneys poking through the trees, Lake Geneva sweeps, deep and dazzling blue. Clouds soar over mountains covered in their summer green. To the west, where the Rhone River empties into the lake, the city tumbles, brown and gray. There's the tiny dot of the Hotel d'Angleterre, with tinier dots of people strolling on the quay – maybe Claire is one of them, pushing William in his pram, scanning the arriving guests for a sight of Lord Byron – but to the east there is nothing but water, scuffed into tiny whitecaps by the wind. Mary stands in a trance of pleasure, looking. *Italy,* she realizes, *is that way. France, over there. I can see it all.* A brisk wind flows through her clothes, against her skin. She has never been confronted by such limitlessness. What would it be to walk out of one's bedroom onto a balcony and see this every day? What could she not imagine – and write – with such a prospect ahead?

They step into the house's long shadow – there are the traces of garden-beds, a wisteria arbor, a conservatory with a roof of mildewed glass, a well with a rusty iron lid – and climb through the straggling grass to the front door. "Luckily," puffs Monsieur Beauvoir, "I have the key." He draws forth a jingling ring from his pocket and pries the biggest, oldest-looking key from the bunch. With a stiff squeak and a click, the lock yields.

The doors swing open onto a long hall that runs straight through the house to wide windowed doors and a terrace at the opposite end. Dim archways to the left and right indicate other rooms. Benches cushioned with cracked leather huddle against the walls, and dusty chandeliers loom over Mary's head. Here and there, underneath the dark brocade wall-cloth, the plaster has cracked and bowed outward from its moorings in the wall. For such an outwardly imposing house, the Villa Diodati feels small inside, dark and cramped rather than expansive, forlorn rather than grand. And lonely. Mary swallows hard. Something whispers to her, *go.* Something else whispers, *stay. I need you here.*

"When was this house built?" Shelley asks. "It seems quite old."

"Two hundred years ago, I believe," Monsieur Beauvoir replies. "The family has been here ever since. But" – he pauses – "they have experienced some difficulty."

"Ah," Shelley says. "The old story. House-rich, cash-poor." He smiles wryly. "We English ought to know."

"If you will just step this way –" Monsieur Beauvoir begins. From behind the nearest door comes a faint scuffle. Then the door opens, with a rusty click. A small bent figure emerges. It's a woman, ancient and stooped, with strings of white hair scraped back along her skull and knotted at the top. Her dark dress is shapeless, its dusty hem frayed to gray rags. Slowly, she lifts her face to them and raises one hand. "Dove è la mia cameriera?" Her voice is raspy and faint, her eyes huge and watery, their brown irises purple-edged with age. "Dov'è?"[1]

This is Italian, Mary knows, but the few scraps she's learned back in England blow away when she tries to reply. Shelley is frozen, wide-eyed. Monsieur Beauvoir clears his throat and pitches his voice louder. "Pourquoi êtes-vous ici?" he asks. "N'avez-vous pas trouvé une nouvelle maison? On vous a dit que cette maison est à louer et que vous devez la quitter."

Mary's French rouses itself and stumbles after him. *Why are you here? Have you not found a new home? You have been told this house is for lease and you must leave it.* Imperious disgust stirs in the old woman's eyes. "Je suis née dans cette maison," she says. "Elle est a moi." *I was born in this house. It is mine.*

What is this woman's name? Where has her family gone? "Comment-vous appelez vous?" Mary stutters. "Où est votre famille?"

The old woman does not answer. She peers sharply at them and straightens her bent back a fraction of an inch. "Je ne vous ai pas invités," she declares. "Vous voudrez bien partir." *I did not invite you here. You will kindly depart.* She turns and retreats into the room again, calling the same unanswerable question with which she greeted them: "Dove è la mia cameriera? Dov'è?" The door shuts. With a rattle, its lock clicks into place.

"Damn," Monsieur Beauvoir mutters. "I was told she'd been –" He shoots a glance at Mary and Shelley. "I apologize, *monsieur, madame.* I was told she'd been – relocated. To a home more suitable for a lady of her –" He falters. "Condition. My correspondent in this matter has been the great-nephew of this lady, a young Monsieur Diodati who is resident in this city –"

"So that is Madame Diodati?" Shelley interrupts.

"*Oui*," Monsieur Beauvoir admits. "The youngest daughter of the family. Her grandfather built this house after the family came to Geneva from Florence. *Laisse-moi réfléchir...*" With relief, he gathers himself, summoning the shards of rumor and memory that help agents sell houses. "Cultivated people, merchants of fine wine, scholars, linguists. A Charles Diodati was a friend of the poet Milton!" He flourishes one hand. "You can see that even in its... present condition, it was built by people of taste."

"True," Shelley says. Abruptly he turns and hurries out the front door. "Let's talk about this in the light." As the three of them stand on the stone courtyard, Monsieur Beauvoir smiles, but Shelley's face is noncommittal. "We like Maison Chapuis very much," he says finally. "About Villa Diodati we are less certain. But we will be in contact very soon." He bows. And then he turns and starts down the hill. Mary follows him. Impulsively she turns to look behind her but can see no face or form behind the windows, only a glaze of sunlight that turns the house's gaze skyward, imperious, lost.

They reach the bottom of the hill and pause at Maison Chapuis. The butterfly rises from its back-garden shrub and resettles on a different branch. All the windows are sound, the roofline straight. And here is the dock where their sailboat still bobs, only a few steps away. From here, Mary could walk to the market or the town, whenever she likes. She could stake out the desk on the upstairs landing to make a start on something more successful than Mary Queen of Scots or *Injustice: A Story by Mary Wollstonecraft Godwin*. And Shelley could sail, all the way to Italy.

Shelley holds out a hand to help Mary into the boat, then unties the rope and shoves off to point them back toward the Hotel d'Angleterre. On the hill above, the Villa Diodati is nearly hidden by trees. Together, she and Shelley stare at it in silence as their boat skims away. "I don't want it," Mary finally admits.

"I don't either," Shelley replies. "Isn't that odd? A wild and ruined place otherwise appeals. But – that poor woman." A shudder twitches his shoulders. "And anyway," he continues, his tone brightening as he bends to steer, "we must be sensible. Decide on a routine. Work, walk."

"I agree," Mary says. Relief floods her; this time, there is not to be a mustering-up to the bright side, cudgeling herself to follow Shelley no matter what. They can have the little Maison Chapuis with its yet-to-bloom shrub and tenacious butterfly and its desk with a view. "Do you think that old lady's uncle was really a friend of Milton?"

"Well, he might have been," Shelley muses. "Milton did go to

Florence, and he wrote about it, where is it, somewhere in the *Defensio Secunda*?" He twitches the tiller to the right, contemplates and decides against lowering the sail. "I must say," he finally says, "I don't want to end the summer with nothing more to show for it than I have right now." He's thinking of that unfinished poem that makes him so shy of meeting the prolific Byron, its title still in question marks: *Alastor?* "And I can't press harder on money with my father, for a while, at least. Maison Chapuis, we can afford. And we can heat it, too." He shivers. "At least until this chill breaks. What a late spring this seems to be."

Yet in the following week, as they sign a lease on Maison Chapuis and browse the shops for mattress-sacks and a kettle and a fresh supply of paper and pack the trunks to be hauled on a wagon around the end of the lake to Cologny, and as Claire's standoff with the clerk reaches a new phase – "*Non, pas encore,*" he now declares, without looking up, as soon as she enters the lobby – Shelley's thrift doesn't preclude an unexpected suggestion: hiring a nurse for William. "We said *both* of us would write, remember?" Shelley asks. "I don't want you to be ground down by the old man here." He gives William his finger to clutch and the baby squeals and grins. Accordingly, Elise Duvillard – a woman of about thirty, with brown hair and observant hazel eyes – is found and engaged to come to Maison Chapuis every morning except Sundays. "*Ma mère, elle est vielle,*" she explains, "and I must sleep at her cottage with her. Every night. She won't have it otherwise." A bitter smile flickers over her face, so quickly Mary thinks she's imagined it, replaced by a bright glance from Shelley to Mary and back again. "I will be able to be here with you, Madame, and with Monsieur and with Guillaume –" she pats William's cheek – "all day. Whenever you like."

And as she and Shelley and Claire unpack their trunks and settle William and his new cradle in his upstairs nursery, Mary realizes she is now the mistress of a real, grown-up house. *Fine lady*, Godwin's voice mocks in Mary's mind, *what a little madam you are!* Elise's presence, however, quickly becomes indispensable. Because a real, grown-up house, with a six-month-old baby, is demanding. It's terrifyingly easy to become overwhelmed with William grizzling and the bed unmade and Shelley's shirts slumped like battlefield casualties all over the floor, no matter how sternly Mary tries to get herself in hand: *remember, domestic chores will be the end of art, if you let them. Just ignore them.* But pursuing her Greek, as she has promised Shelley, is difficult when the washing-up or the weedy front walk tug at her attention like mendicants, pleading, cunning: *give me what you have, give me all of it.* How had Fanny managed all this, back on Skinner Street? Why does there never seem to be time for Mary to write to her and ask? Elise, however, is calm. She wipes the mysterious, inevitable baby-stickiness from table and chair and boils the diaper-cloths in buckets of water hauled from the lake and hangs them to dry. She tames the stove's balky flue and lights fires in its terrifying belly. She musters Shelley's abandoned teacups from all over the house. Even more magically, she can straighten his papers without reading them, and without provoking the irritation with which he snaps at Mary: *can't you see I left this here for a* reason? (*Left this here* is indeed the phrase: Shelley, unlike Mary herself, does not prefer a desk.) Elise combs and gathers the raveling ends of the morning as neatly as straggling hair, tidying it, readying the day into a unit of time that will not go to waste. "She's a treasure, as my mother would say," Shelley declares happily. "More time for the boat!"

Shelley's sailboat – with *Ariel* painted in black letters in Shelley's hand on its bow – is always moored now at the Cologny dock, only a few steps from Maison Chapuis' front door. *Ariel* is now, Mary can't help thinking, Shelley's favorite room in the house. He's as delighted with it as a small boy; on their walks around London he made a paper canoe out of whatever was in his pocket, setting it adrift on puddle or running stream. Now he clamors to take her and William out on the lake. And, caught up in his enthusiasm – nothing is more contagious – Mary has gathered their baby son in her arms and stepped onto the dock before the gray doubt wisps across her brain: *what if.* What if the boat tips, too far from shore to set her feet on the muddy bottom and hoist her son above the waves? What if Shelley tumbles overboard and strikes his head on the rudder? An ugly vision sparks in her brain: the *Ariel*, round hull up, bobbing like a bloated fish, with William and Shelley and herself sunk below the waves for good. How long before their bodies drift back up into the sun? Yet another vision replaces it: Cornelia Boinville's rueful gray gaze, leveled at her in the Skinner Street parlor: *he's done this kind of thing before.* Deserted the wife who'd become a drudge, a drag, an encumbrance, the corpse yoked to his in loathsome and horrible communion, for the girl who meant *freedom* and *liberty* and *fun.* The girl who is *spontaneous.* The girl who will not tell him *no.* The girl who does not ask *what if.* The girl who's followed him to this lake, this house, this sun-warmed deck, right here.

In her arms William stirs and yawns, his hand wavering over his face. So odd a baby's hand is, fat at palm and wrist with such delicate fingers. So starlike and small, the tiny nails at the tiny fingertips. She has seen such tiny fingers before, still, lying quiet against her chest. Before the tiny body was lifted up and away from her, for good.

"I don't think –" She forces a smile onto her face. "Let me call Elise."

"Ah, Mary." Shelley's voice is warm, indulgent. "See what a calm day. We'll go out and right back again. Delightful task! To teach the young idea how to shoot, to breathe the enlivening spirit, and to fix the generous purpose in the glowing heart –" Mary's mind reels and catches itself and recognizes: James Thomson, *The Seasons*. Shelley, of course, is quoting someone else's poem. To support what in theory she also wants: to bear their boy lovingly and proudly into the world, to let experience fill and lift him like a sail. *Experience!* Here are Mama's words, again. *Ah, gain it –* But if the boat tips, William will drown.

This won't happen, though. Because this sailboat's tiller is fitted so well to Shelley's hand. Because Mary herself won't let it. She can turn herself on her back with William in her arms and float and kick, some-how, until they reach the shore. She can save her boy, no matter what. *Any creature* – it is not quite Godwin's voice, but close enough – *has the instinct to save itself, in any element.* And its child. The red and humble body with its networks of muscle and nerve can be counted on. Surely.

Not until they've skirted east toward the River Rhone's inlet to the lake, hugging the shore (Shelley can see her nervousness without being told, he will care for her and William, why can't she just *trust* him?) and returned to the dock (half an hour, maybe less?) that she asks it directly: "Shelley, can you swim?"

His back is turned, his shirt clinging to the blades of muscle along his spine as he secures the ropes. Relief at their safety bolts suddenly through Mary and releases itself as desire: she'll touch him there, when they're alone, run her hands all along him, moor him to her and to this world. How can she doubt that he is hers and their boy's, and that he will keep them safe? "As much as any sailor needs." His voice is brisk, laughing. "Enough to keep upright till the first mate throws down the rope." He takes William from her arms and hoists her onto the dock and pulls her close, one arm around her waist. "Now. Let's have our dinner. Yes?"

Behind an oak's veiny trunk the Creature hides, pausing in his southward-and-eastward journey, watching the beloved ones. All in pairs. Going somewhere with a friend. A husband. A wife. He lingers on their tender bodies inside the capes and jerkins that are as ragged as his own shirt and trousers, snatched from a washerwoman's line. They're carbuncled and dirty and fat and rude but yet they are beloved. Because they are not alone among their kind. Alone, as he now knows himself to be. Unlike Byron and Robert, twined together in the dark. Unlike Mary and Shelley in the river below the Castle Frankenstein, drawn together in the cold, sweet current. Unlike Mary and Shelley, who are settled now with little William in a house not so far from here. He is bound to find them. Now, he doesn't have so far to go.

A black-jawed man with a round red belly peeking under his shirt-hem comes trundling up the road in a green-painted cart. His horses are plump and shiny gray, like the barrels of the musket at his feet. He lifts a lidded tankard to his mouth, takes a sip, then suddenly snaps it shut and bolts upright. The Creature has hoped he can't be heard above the wheels, but maybe he's wrong. Freezing, he huddles close to the tree. Its blessed indifferent blood runs up and back into the earth, kinder than his own heartbeat in his ears. Oh, to be a tree. To be a simple homely thing that grows and lives its whole life in one spot, exactly where it belongs.

"Who's there?" The horses' ears flick and swivel. Their thick skin shudders. They smell the Creature, of course. "Who's there?"

The Creature closes his eyes. *Please*, he prays, *don't let me be seen*. To whom? He can detect no larger hand guiding this tale in which he finds himself, this thing he reckons as his life. He's been wandering so long. He's been beaten and kicked, chased away from cabin and vegetable garden where a few cold-roughened turnips shoulder up forgotten through the dirt. The soil is cold on his fingers, but the bitter rush of food is good. His shoulder is rubbed by the sack in which his grimy blue *Paradise Lost* rides, dusted now with dirt and ash. His feet are cut to pieces by stones and frozen mud. The smell of smoke from the DeLaceys' burning cabin will never leave his nose as long as he remains alive. But *alive* is what he's realized he wants to be. Sharp on the tongue, on the flesh, is the world to this body – this mortal and terrifying thing that is nevertheless so precious.

Safie the Turkish girl was so lovely that no one cared she couldn't speak. When Felix DeLacey saw her – there in the cabin's yard, out of the blue – his whole face went still and his eyes grew huge, shocked and softened out of his usual bitter rigidity. Her father had cheated them in the time before he and his sister Agatha and their old blind father had been exiled to this hut in the woods where the Creature had found them and watched them for so many weeks and dreamed his foolish dreams of belonging to their family. But Felix obviously cared for Safie. Perhaps he had once kissed her, like Shelley kissed Mary. Perhaps he only wished he had. But like Adam in *Paradise Lost* he awoke and found his dream come true: suddenly there was Safie on her mule, trailed by her loyal servant, blinking wearily and smiling at him. "Merhaba," she had murmured shyly. "Burayı bulacağımı hiç düşünmemiştim."[2] And Felix's sister Agatha had rushed forth and then their father had come hobbling out and in the general rejoicing the Creature was able to slip out of his usual hiding place (that little storage shed against the hut's north wall, warmed by the borrowed heat of fire through the cracks) and into the woods. They might need to rummage in the shed for spare bedding or a larger cooking pot, so he'd absent himself, just in case. At least they'd have plenty of fuel: he'd split and stacked two cords of wood next to the door, gratified by Agatha's surprise. "A good spirit!" she'd exclaimed. This was better than some other names that had been flung at him.

Learning to speak, Safie had been quick, but not as quick as the Creature himself. *I am happy to see you. How are you today? You are my friend.* Safie mouthed the words for Felix and Agatha and their father to hear. Behind his log wall, in silence, the Creature did the same. In the dirt he scratched the same words Safie scratched on her slate, marveling as meaning took shape like tongues of candle-flame. *Good. Dearest. Happy.* He hoped it was not what the father called *the sin of pride* to admit that his skill in reading and writing was greater than Safie's. But unlike Safie he could appeal to no friends. At least, not yet.

For weeks, hidden in his stolen shelter, the Creature had planned to approach the old father. He'd tried to be realistic. He knew the risks. He knew he must practice what Felix called *hard work* and *self-reliance* – although without Felix's bitter smile when he looked at the withered winter garden and the dwindling stock of potatoes. The Creature would need speech for what he had in mind. He knew that. He knew many things, by then, that had helped him formulate a plan. And – even now, he clings to this – the plan had been good. The father had been his friend. He'd not been wrong in that. He hadn't misinterpreted the kind gaze that skated over his own face, the hand outstretched, inquiring, in the air: *ah. He's blind. No wonder I don't frighten him.* He'd been quick to disappear when Safie and Agatha and Felix returned to the hut from their expeditions, smiling indulgently at the father's account of *the friend who came to visit me today.* But the Creature had sat with the old man and read aloud Volney's *Ruins of Empire* and his own *Paradise Lost,* which at last he can understand. Oh, yes. He is that quick. And, newly self-confident about reading people, he knew he was interpreting accurately the flicker of the thing among Felix and Safie and Agatha and the father, just as among Byron and Robert and Old Joe and Fletcher – shared worry, and, thus, companionship. Because he felt that feeling himself. He still does. He can hear and feel. He can respond. Even if he never did answer the father's final question: "Great God. Who are you?"[3]

Of course, officious Felix was bound to spoil everything. He burst in and beat the Creature and chased him away and by the time the Creature returned to the hut from where he had been hiding in the woods, sobbing, all four of his beloved ones had gone. Then there was no language for his rage except to burn the hut to the ground. Sometimes he wishes the four of them had been inside. Maybe it was good that they had fled. *Know thyself.* Someone from the father's books had advised that. Someone with two smooth pink arms and two smooth pink legs and a loving mate and family. Someone safe and warm. Someone quite naïve.

Of what a strange nature is knowledge! It clings to the mind, when it has once seized on it, like a lichen on the rock.[4] Whose voice is this unfurling in the Creature's head right now? It's not Milton's, not Felix DeLacey's or Safie's or the old blind man's. Gently it suggests: what you feel is pain. Gently it suggests: there is no language on this earth in which pain does not exist. Except the vast blank darkness from which the Creature flinches even as its presence shadows him: death. Death is real, to be feared, to be fled. No words need attend it. No more need be said of it. Except a fact: death can be brought upon others, or upon oneself.

The Creature extends his own long hand – broken-nailed, sunburned, black-veined, immensely strong – into the air before him. Not pink. Not small. It is an ugly thing. A humble one. And humbly it serves him. Loyal red heart. Blood unknowable and bright, busy at its rounds. Bones and muscles bending to their task companionably as peasants in the fields. So ordinary. Yet: a wonder. Entirely his. At the thought of destroying it, the Creature snatches his hand back and wraps his arms around himself, involuntary, shaking. Only much later will he fit language to the fact that this embrace is the only one he'll ever know.

So. Let him discipline his mind by completing his tale in memory. His rage built and spent itself and then there was nothing left. The heat of the burning cabin defrosted the ground around it and so the Creature could scratch the last abandoned turnips from the dirt and thrust them into his pockets before he took to the road. He is meant to be somewhere. But not, apparently, with the family he'd mistaken for his own.

Now, huddled against the tree, squeezing his eyes shut against the carter's voice – he'll give up, soon, and cluck to the horses and move on, *must have patience*, the old man had said – the Creature renews his vow. Somewhere up ahead is Victor Frankenstein, who can explain to him what started in the room near the river with its vats and wires and knives. And he will find that man. Father. No matter what it takes.

Each day, Claire walks to the Hotel d'Angleterre, six whole miles around the tip of the lake to its opposite shore and back again; "he won't like it if I've run to fat," she declares, brushing off Mary's concern. And one day, she returns with the news that Lord Byron has arrived. "There's his name, right in the hotel register," Claire burbles. "I made the clerk show me. Age listed as one hundred. How witty!" Her laugh rattles, overwrought. "Poor man. He must be exhausted. Coming all the way through Belgium. Oh, imagine the wreck of that battlefield." For the rest of the day she's tense and distracted, picking things up and putting them down. She's left a letter for Byron at the hotel, along with a short note from Shelley: *Welcome to Geneva. We shall call on you on the morrow.*

Mary takes extra time with her hair the following morning, pinning it carefully and tying a lacy scarf over it to keep off the wind in the boat. Surely Shelley will laugh at her. Yet once Mary and Claire are side by side on one of *Ariel's* bench seats, with Shelley at the tiller, and Mary can get a good look at him – there's been such a rush to get William breakfasted and settled with Elise and his colored blocks – she sees that he too has dressed carefully, wearing a cravat for the first time in weeks. He grins and ran a finger theatrically around his neck. "The gentlemen's garrote," he quips. Mary laughs and looks to Claire, wearing an unfamiliar blue-green silk dress, the color of the eye in a peacock's tail, rigidly upright on the bench. Mary squeezes her hand. "You look lovely," she whispers. "Don't worry."

"Mama would tell me to remember Cleopatra." Claire's laugh is nearly a bark. "She made men wait on *her*."

"A wise woman indeed," Mary murmurs. "But look! You too are being carried in a barge." She's relieved to hear Claire's laugh soften.

By now they're drawing near the hotel's dock. Swans drift along the quay, leaving dirty tufts of down in their wake and eyeing the *Ariel* like pirates. Men and women stroll; carts rumble past. Yet around the door of the Hotel d'Angleterre is a thick crowd, mostly women, craning for a glimpse through the windows. "Look," Shelley says, pointing. "Is that—"

The door springs open and Byron bursts through the crowd. As fast as his limp allows (so the rumors are true – he *is* lame), he strides for the dock, twisting to snatch himself free of clinging hands. "Achète-toi une vie!" he snaps into the crowd, and they falter back. In spite of his haste, his waistcoat is faultlessly buttoned, his coat flowing behind him, his cravat worn with an ease Shelley's can't match. "Just in time," he calls. "Get me *out* of here."

Shelley's mouth falls open, with surprise Mary knows must be reflected on her own face – Lord Byron, here in their boat? Lord Byron, to whom Shelley hasn't even been introduced in person? – but he recovers himself and draws *Ariel* up to the pier, clasping the post in one hand. Byron drops onto the bench in front of Mary and Claire, seizes an oar, and fits it into the lock. Shelley snatches up the other oar, and he and Byron propel the boat backwards just as two young women come thumping onto the boards. They're plump and vaguely poxy-looking, with bleached hair showing dark at the roots. Catching Byron's eye, they snatch their skirts and waggle them above the knee, grinning. Their dimpled knees are strapped with lacy garters that have cameo frames set into bows, Byron's picture in each frame. "Childe Harowld!" they screech in French-accented English. "Come back! *Nous t'aimons!*"

"I'll do nothing of the bloody kind," Byron mutters, bending to the oars to help point *Ariel* back across the lake. He and Shelley pull so hard the boat leaps, nose-up, like a dolphin. "Shelley, you have rescued me. Saw you coming from the window upstairs. Timed it perfectly."

Mary twists to look behind her at the dock. In front of the girls now stands a young dark-haired man in a gray coat, waving one arm frantically over his head. "Lord Byron!" His voice reaches them in snatches, broken up by wind and splashing waves. "Wait for me!" The girls shove him and he shoves back, staggering near the edge of the dock. Byron hunches lower, glowering, and shakes his head.

"Who's that?" Shelley asks. "Do you know him?"

"To my lasting misfortune, I do," Byron sighs. "That would be John Polidori, who calls himself my personal physician. Hired by Murray to spy on me." At Mary's questioning look, Byron nods. "My publisher. John Murray. He's concerned for my health." He rolls his eyes and tries to smile. "I can't *imagine* why."

"Should we go back to pick him up?" asks Mary.

"And let those French bitches in heat swamp the boat?" Byron snaps. "Hell, no. You have the makings of some tea across the lake, correct?"

"And you are welcome," Shelley says. He grins. "Even though I haven't actually introduced myself. I could be anyone. A pirate kidnapper of famous poets."

"Better than that mob at the hotel." Byron turns to Claire and his face goes steely blank. "And who are *you*?"

Mary freezes. But Claire is quick, rising to a cue she already knows. She draws herself up and gives Byron a haughty glare. "Not one," she snaps in a Piccadilly-drawing-room drawl, "to suffer your insolence." Thrusting her chin forward, she lowers her eyelids and stares at him, with Queen Sophonsiba's old imperiousness. "As you soon will learn." She stretches one foot forward and twists it, crushingly, into the boards. Byron's blank face breaks into a smile. He and Claire hold one another's gaze. Shelley's ears turn red. "Well," he blurts, his voice suddenly Eton-schoolboy-shy, and he leans to the oars again. "We'll soon be on shore, eh?"

Mary tries to calm the blushes rising up her own throat. Byron is at least ten years older than Claire, yet this difference seems exciting. A fresh and herbal smell breathes from him, perhaps the pomade that makes his dark curls shine, perhaps cologne dotted carefully on his collar. But there's a heaviness on him, too, darkening his blue-green eyes like a cloud above the lake. A premonition of rain. *Childe Harold's Pilgrimage* is a brilliant poem. But Mary knows the rumors. *Two actresses, one on each side of him, all naked.* Ha, ha, ha.

Mary turns her back to the Hotel d'Angleterre and the crowd on its dock, still watching them like terriers at a badger hole. Maybe they'll get spyglasses to sharpen their view, or even trek to the Maison Chapuis itself, now that they can see where Byron's gone. Well, that can't be helped. She can serve tea in the garden, leaving William's morning nap undisturbed. With Elise to assist, she needn't be ashamed of their modest house. An escaping lord can't be choosy as to where he lands.

Shelley ties *Ariel* up at the dock below Maison Chapuis and helps them all out. Byron comes last, staggering a little on his lame leg. "Aah," he sighs, rolling his head from side to side. "Just got to Geneva but it's already time to move. I'll be damned if I linger at that hotel to be gawped at like Bruin. Pet bear in my rooms at Cambridge... I'll tell you later. What about *that*?" He nods up the hill to the Villa Diodati. "Is that available?"

Shelley stiffens. "Mary and I investigated, with our agent," he begins, "but there's –" He shifts his gaze, still rattled. "An old lady living there. Last of the family, apparently a distinguished one. Diodati, the first to translate the Bible into Italian during Luther's time. And they came here seeking haven, I surmise."

"Leaving behind a fairly acceptable villa," Byron says. "Might you oblige me with your agent's name?"

Not *leaving behind*, Mary thinks. The old lady is still there, wandering through the dim rooms, calling out her unanswerable questions. What will Byron do with her? But the worry dissolves as she hurries toward her own front door. She starts to call for Elise but thinks better of it. If William is wakened, he'll fuss and whinge and discomfit Byron, who's their guest even though, technically, he's invited himself across the lake. Byron himself has a baby, back in England. But he doesn't seem like a man to tolerate a grumpy child. Well, with the child and her mother fled from him, that won't be a concern.

"We serve tea in the garden, madame," Elise murmurs, meeting Mary at the door, "since Guillaume, he's still asleep." The teakettle's subtle chatter rises from the kitchen. Mary shoots her a grateful look and hurries through the house and out the back door to check the garden. Claire bolts up the stairs, doubtless to primp and smooth her hair. All is in order on the patio, with the two chairs pulled up neatly to the little table, except for William's cloth diapers spread over the shrub to dry. Damnation. Mary snatches them up and turns toward the kitchen. Maybe they can be strung on a line above the stove to finish drying. No good cramming them in a basket to wait till Byron's gone, she can't afford to lose the drying time today, William is almost out of clean diapers and when he wakes, he'll need –

"What's *this*?" Byron stands in the door, glancing at the wad of cloth in her hand. His eyes roam the little yard and land on one diaper she's missed, fluttering from a twig. "Ah." He grins. "The white flag of childhood. Before which all else must surrender." Shelley, just behind him, snickers. "Particularly art."

Anger bursts in Mary's brain, fighting with the restraints of proper hospitality, of *letting it go,* of *respecting the famous poet. How dare you. Invite yourself to our house and then insult* – The image of William asleep upstairs in his bed joins it: William, the tender spot through which the whole alarming world can enter her now. *How could you understand what he requires of me, you who've abandoned the duties of a father?* The anger rocks her like a vase tilted and wobbling on a shelf. A chill voice within extends a cool hand and holds her upright. *Do you think he truly understands what he has said to you?* Of course he doesn't. He speaks out of the same wealth of careless assumption that secures him everywhere. Art is total. A gentleman needn't devote himself to any other requirement in life if he doesn't choose. And women will take care of everything else. He wouldn't have said this to her if he were seriously considering that women make art of their own. Or that they even could.

So. The cool voice continues its inquiries. *Is this what it will be to be a woman among the poets, to continually tamp down, justify, tolerate, and smile? To be the only one to consider the old lost creature roaming her family's home on the hill above – the old lady, abandoned by her family, who's now only an inconvenience to a visiting lord?*

Byron and Shelley settle themselves on the wrought-iron chairs. Claire emerges from the house wearing her most dazzling smile. Shelley leaps up to fetch two more kitchen chairs. Mary waits to speak until she has set the tea-tray down in front of Byron. "The white flag of childhood," she says brightly. "That's a good phrase." She lifts the pot and pours him a cup. "And as the example of my mother shows, art and motherhood need not be incompatible."

"It's true," Shelley says loyally. "*Letters from Norway* is a wonderfully spirited book."

Byron looks at Mary. She sees him registering what he's said, and what she's made of what he's said, and why. Incredulity, then acquiescence, flicker in his face. Beyond them, the diaper still dangles from the bush, twitching in a breeze. Byron lifts his teacup and smiles. "Incompatible for the common run of women, perhaps," he says. "But, apparently, not for you."

Claire, smoothing her dress and obviously meditating on the most attractive way to hold her teacup – she does have good hands, good wrists – looks at Mary with a mixture of resentment and respect. Claire can't afford Byron frightened away. Perhaps Mary should have been a gracious hostess and let this little rudeness pass. But no woman who even claims to have some sense can let such remarks go unchallenged. Byron's obviously a man who'll affect to disdain any intelligence in a woman while secretly admiring it. Yet whether that admiration will extend to Claire, as well as Mary herself, is uncertain.

Elise appears in the door. "Madame," she murmurs, "there is a man here seeking Lord Byron –"

"I am his personal physician." A plaintive voice drifts into the garden. "I was hired by John Murray *himself.*"

"Oh, for Christ's sake," Byron sighs. "Polidori has found me."

"Pollydolly?" Shelley asks, confused.

"One of his names, like Legion," Byron says. "He'll answer to anything." He grimaces. "Well, now that you've found us," he calls, "you'd better come through."

Polidori edges through the door into the garden, talking in one nervous, out-of-breath stream. "I saw you get in that boat and cross the lake and so I got a carriage at the hotel and rode all the way around the end of the lake to where I saw you land on this opposite side because Mr. Murray *did* instruct me to tend to your health at all times –" Barely older than Mary herself, Polidori is slight and stooped, with dense dark curls and large, slightly bulbous eyes. He's the youngest physician Mary has ever seen. Such a boy must be forgiven: he's only tending to his duty, and that must be a difficult task. Especially when that duty involves pleasing a lord who, despite his complaints, would complain equally if he felt neglected.

The scowl line on Byron's forehead deepens, and he fixes his eyes on Polidori until the young doctor winds down, blushing. "Behold, my publisher's thrift," he snaps. "Declares he'll hire a physician for his prize author, then saddles me with a boy just out of medical school."

"I passed all my exams," Polidori protests, "with honor."

"Have some tea, Dr. Polidori?" Mary asks. The young man's hands tremble as he takes the cup from her and settles on the low stone wall that surrounds the back garden, crossing his legs awkwardly. "We were just talking of –"

"Art," Byron says smoothly, "and its relation to life."

The Creature is under a house-roof at last with a new beloved one: an old woman who is no longer beloved by anyone but him. No one comes but an occasional emissary from the village, sent by her guilty nephew to drop a basket of bread and cheese against the massive wooden door. *The Villa Diodati,* he hears the villagers whispering as they pass the rusty iron gates, slowing their steps in the lane. *Haunted. No, it is! Anyone can see that.*

At first these words – delivered to him by his mercilessly clear hearing, which can count the mouse-pups in their nests behind the plaster – frighten the Creature. But if people really believed this house was haunted, they'd have to act. They'd come to wave crucifixes amid the solemn babble of a priest, and then they'd burn it down. No. They're only teasing themselves with tiny thrilling fears built out of words. How strange, the pleasures people take.

The days are long in this house, but there's much to learn. He pries apart the damp books on the library shelves – there is a Shakespeare he'll keep – and puzzles through them while the old lady naps. He reads aloud to her as she sits upright in a chair. He follows as she paces from window to window to heavy front door. Sometimes he hums to her a lullaby of his own making, hoping it will tincture her dreams with memories of some other time. From the dark wells of her eyes, blue-rimmed with age, she watches him. Sometimes, in her sleep, she smiles.

While she sleeps, he prowls. In the cellar, he tries on a pair of mildewed old boots but rejects them as too small. He uncorks cobwebby bottles here and there, tasting and comparing: apparently it makes a difference when a wine is born, although he knows better, now, than to mistake that pleasant warmth of wine in the brain for *happiness*. He can bide his time. Because there's something in this house he needs, and that needs him. He burned the DeLaceys' cottage in a fit of rage. He won't make that mistake again. *Cut off your nose to spite your face and you'll only bleed to death.* As ever, humans speak the truth most in their jests.

Madame Diodati ignores the estate agent's letters pushed under the door, but the Creature opens and reads them. The nephew is impatient for an income from this place, which means the agent is impatient on his behalf. But apparently they're limited in precisely how they can act, although they are warning of *measures we must take*. And meanwhile, Madame Diodati abides. Sometimes she cracks open the great front door and breaks off a piece of cheese and mouths it into mush; the Creature finishes it (this *Gruyere* is justly praised) and drops the basket neatly at the gate to be refilled. Sometimes he snares a rabbit in the tangle of old vines on the hillside and roasts it in the fireplace. He wanders into and out of the rooms, including the old lady's own; she is so often asleep, so small and curled and lost in the vast dingy four-poster bed. The floor is dusty, but he manages not to sneeze. He can't stay away from the treasure that he's found, right there on her mantelpiece: a music box.

When he opens the lid and the string of notes swirl upward, circling back on themselves and then rising higher, like the curls of smoke after a candle flame goes out, the Creature's eyes prickle and he feels a vague angry shame at being so overtaken, every time, but he would not have this feeling depart from him for anything. Tiny black letters are painted on the underside of the lid: *Gluck / Orfeo ed Euridice.* He can see how the mechanism works – the tiny gold teeth strummed by the sequence of more teeth on a turning cylinder, it's all just automation, just logic – but this knowledge never stops the tears. And he's glad. He stands holding the enamel lid open in his huge black-nailed hand and forgets the old lady asleep in her bed and the drowsing mouse-pups in the walls and his own huge bare pilgrim's feet on the dusty floor: everything but the rapt blood singing in his veins. Shakespeare obliges him with words: *Now, divine air! Now is his soul ravished. Is it not strange that sheep's guts should hale the soul out of men's bodies?*

People and their pleasures. At least they've left him this.

Once he musters the courage to approach his own reflection in the mirror above the parlor's fireplace. His own eyes flash; their darkness, pupil and iris blended imperceptibly, is always a surprise. Shakespeare has words for this too: *This thing of darkness I acknowledge mine.* He cannot look upon his bony face, his naked flesh that blends corpse-gray and bruise purple-yellow and windburned red, his obvious unfitness for the world of neat pink-cheeked humans cloaked in normalcy and cheer. Madame Diodati avoids the mirror, too, so he hoists the heavy thing and hauls it to the cellar and leans it against the wine-vault wall, where rows of dusty bottles in their wooden slings stretch deep into the dark.

At night, lights come on in the little white house down the hill. Through the windows he can see small figures on chairs, raising and lowering teacups and forks to their mouths. Mary is there, with Shelley and their little William and the nursemaid, setting a palm against her neatly swept-back hair and frowning, looking suddenly out the window and up the hill. He always stands back from the window when this happens although he knows she cannot see him. Not yet, anyway. He will stay in the Villa Diodati. And at this little distance from Mary, although no farther. There is something with her, in her, that he needs.

Having signed a lease on the Villa Diodati, Byron sends a note from the Hotel d'Angleterre: *Prepare ye the way of the Lord – B.* Then, two black horses pulling the largest, gaudiest carriage Mary has ever seen come heaving up the steep hill. The window rattles down and Byron's long white hand, framed by a cuff of blue velvet, waves to Mary and Shelley where they stand behind Maison Chapuis. In front of the carriage bounds a big brindled mastiff, and behind it trundles another wagon, laden with crates of books and a Chesterfield sofa Mary remembers spotting in a shop near the cathedral. "How in heaven's name has he accumulated so much plunder?" Mary asks. "He's only been in Geneva for two weeks."

"Well, some of it must have come in that carriage," Shelley says. "It *is* fairly large. Says he modeled it on Napoleon's." Even on this overcast day, the gilt trim of the carriage sparkles, surrounding great panels of bright red and bright blue the color of Byron's velvet cuff. In the center of each wheel-hub, a giant B revolves. On each door a coat of arms and motto are drawn in gold: *Crede Byron*. Trust Byron. What a motto for a man of such bewildering changes and such mystery, who bolts from the crowds at the hotel yet emblazons his name on his carriage for all to see. Who claims to seek privacy yet has rented the largest villa on this side of the lake. Whose cameoed face is warmed on the gartered pink knees of the girls from whom he flees. Oh, well. What is man, Godwin would say, if not a mass of contradictions? Doubtless Byron has also explored the warren of shops at the top of the hill in the old city, around the cathedral and Calvin's chapel and what is rumored to be the house of Rousseau, leaving their thrilled owners to broadcast his presence in the city even more widely. Across the lake, Mary can just see the sparkle of spyglasses in the crowd outside the Hotel d'Angleterre, watching them all.

Of course there can be no question of orderly morning work now. Mary and Claire gather a loaf of bread, a wedge of cheese, and a bottle of wine into a basket – food is dear, but they have to show some hospitality – and follow Shelley up the hill. Byron meets them all in the stone court-yard in front of the gate, with Monsieur Beauvoir, the estate agent, smiling behind him, jingling his keys in his hand. Beyond them, all is chaos. The big dog rushes barking at the wheels of carriage and wagon, which jockey for position as the drivers back them toward the door, cursing at one another in some Genevan dialect Mary guesses she's better off not knowing. The red and blue carriage draws aside, under a great tree that spreads its branches over the courtyard. From somewhere inside it comes a distinct animal scream. Just climbing out, a wooden box clutched against his chest, is Polidori, who catches Mary's eye and shyly waves. Mary waves back. A tall man with one ear squashed like a boxer's directs two young men as they struggle with a crate of books. "Set it down there," he barks in a thick Nottinghamshire accent, pointing a thick finger to a spot near the wall. "Got to get them bookshelves off first." The young men's faces are blank. "Bookshelves!" he says louder. "*Book*shelves!"

In the center of the chaos, Byron is serene, even jovial. "Thank heaven," he says, taking the basket. "Seems the only thing in all Geneva I haven't bought is food. Why don't you come see my new home?" Expansively, he loops one arm around Claire's waist and leads them all toward the front door.

The rattle of keys must have brought old Madame Diodati out of her hiding place, or maybe it's the commotion of carts and voices in the stone courtyard outside. When the heavy front door swings open, she stands before them, under the dusty chandelier, silhouetted against the square of light from the French doors at the end of the hall. They yawn open, admitting a cool wind that licks at her skirts and lifts the straggling white wisps of her hair. "Je ne vous ai pas invités!" Her voice is louder this time, harsh and definite. "Vous voudrez bien partir!"

"What the bloody hell?" Byron whirls on Monsieur Beauvoir, who stands openmouthed. "You told me the house was empty!"

"Young M'sieur Diodati assured me," Monsieur Beauvoir stammers, "he had made the arrangements, he –"

Behind them, someone coughs. When they turn around, a burly man in a dirty smock is standing there, with a middle-aged woman in a gray dress and starched white apron just behind him. "We were delayed," he says in oddly accented French. "My apologies." A smile ripples the blank professionalism of his face as he scans the group of them: Byron and Claire, Mary and Shelley, the flustered Monsieur Beauvoir, Madame Diodati now edging backward down the hall. "Which one is our patient?"

Monsieur Beauvoir points at the old lady and the woman in the starched apron steps forward. "Now, madame," the man's voice booms, "you will please come with us. Your great-nephew has engaged us to –"

The woman shoots the burly man a look of intense dislike and lifts her hand to silence him. "Madame," she begins softly, taking a step toward the old lady, "I am Mademoiselle Legarde, and I am here to assist you. Would you like some tea? Perhaps a little refreshment?" This will pique poor Madame Diodati's interest, Mary thinks. Surely there's been no food here for some time.

"Dove è la mia cameriera?" The old lady's voice is a querulous keen. "Dove sono mia madre e mio padre?"

With a quick rustle of footsteps, Polidori is in the hall. "Sua madre e suo padre l'aspettano in città," he says, extending both hands to Madame Diodati and smiling. "Sono il dottor Polidori e mi hanno chiesto di portarla a loro."

Italian. Of course. The old lady peers at Polidori, touching his arm. "Avrò bisogno di una camicia da notte?"

Polidori hesitates, glancing at the beefy man in the dirty smock. "Forse," he finally says. "Questa signora l'aiutera a confezionare un paio di cose per un pernottamento. Le altre cose saranno inviate se ne avrà bisogno." The old lady nods and turns toward the room at the end of the hall. The nurse in the starched white apron glances gratefully at Polidori, who takes her by the elbow. "Help her pack a few overnight things, her nightgown and such," he whispers. "Keep her calm. I believe she is ready to accompany you. She's asking where her maid is, where her mother and father are. I have told her they are waiting for her in the city and they have sent me, sent you, to bring her to them. She is prepared for an overnight stay. But for heaven's sake, keep her calm. Perhaps we should all go outside –"

Byron nods and turns, but the burly man steps forward. "It does no good to postpone these things." His voice is flat, loud, disastrously confident. "We have been commissioned by this lady's relative to make the house ready for –" He glances at Byron and adjusts his tone. "To ensure her care." Brushing past them, he strides down the hall to where Madame Diodati is emerging from the farthest room with the nurse behind her, bearing a shabby carpetbag. He catches her arm and pulls. "Come with me," he declares, "or it will be necessary to compel you."

"No!" Polidori shouts, rushing forward. "This is not the way!" But the big man has fastened to the old woman's arm, and, with it, to a notion of her that locks over him like an airless cage: she will be the mad patient, in need of firm treatment. Madame Diodati's eyes widen and she twists back and forth in his grasp, letting up a thin horrible wail. Byron and Shelley and Claire stand frozen. "This isn't right," Mary blurts. But no one hears her as the big man drags the old lady down the hall, the nurse and Polidori tugging at him. Madame Diodati's arm juts upward at an awkward angle, but he does not release her. "Figlio de puttana!" she spits, glaring. "Figlio del diavolo!" Her bodice-seam splits with a long ripping pop and reveals a pale slice of wobbly flesh, the grayish curve of a rib.

"I say," Byron begins uselessly, "this hardly seems" – But as the old woman approaches the door where he and Claire and Shelley and Mary stand in one useless gaping group, she wrenches herself out of the big man's grasp and turns to fix Byron with a stare that has suddenly turned deadly flat. "I curse you." The rasping voice is English now. Has she known it all along? Her huge eyes sweep the group, glaring at each in turn. "I curse you for what you do. You take my home, you throw me aside." She pauses. "I am not alone in this house. I have a friend. He will avenge my dishonor."

Polidori, standing behind the old woman, gasps and lifts his fingers to his forehead, flinging them aside with a strange forked gesture Mary has never seen. The old woman does not turn to look at him. Disdaining the hands of the nurse and the burly man, she lifts her carpetbag and steps through the door, blinking in the light.

"Wait. I'll come with you. Just a moment." Polidori puts his hand on the nurse's arm, and she nods. Then she turns to follow Madame Diodati to the carriage. The old lady peers at the sky, looking all around at the clutter of moving-in and the rustling of the great tree and the tangled grapevines along the walls. The sunlight reveals the frailty of her small body, the blue veins under her skin, the dusty gray of what has once been black silk.

Polidori turns to Byron with an uncharacteristic flash of anger. "Admit it," he snaps. "To what have you delivered her?"

"It wasn't me!" Byron protests. "It was the family, this agent! They must have made this – arrangement weeks ago. Tell them!"

"It's true." Monsieur Beauvoir jingles the bundle of keys in his hands. "I have been in contact with the young Monsieur Diodati for some weeks. These – doctors –"

"They can't be doctors," Polidori growls, "not by my lights."

"These – specialists," Monsieur Beauvoir stammers, "have been paid to take Madame to a private home where, ah, she can have –" Under the strain, his English flees. "Un peu de repos pour l'esprit."

The big dog presses close to Byron's leg and he plunges his hand into the fur around its ears. The gesture seems to calm him too. "Here," he says, rooting in his pocket and drawing forth a handful of francs. "Take this and give it to that big fellow, see that she's looked after."

"Not to him," Mary interrupts. "To her." She points at the nurse in the starched apron, now helping Madame Diodati into the carriage. The old lady wobbles and nearly falls, but the woman braces her with a hand on her side, touching, gently, the place where the ribs show through the ripped dress. Madame Diodati's face is turned away, so she can't see what Mary can; the nurse is on the verge of tears.

"Quite right." Byron nods and shoves the money at Polidori, avoiding his eyes. "Go with them and see to it, there's a good fellow."

Polidori folds the money into his coat and looks around. Luckily, the big man in the dirty smock is turned away, testing the latches on the carriage door. So there's a chance, Mary tells herself, that the old lady's care can be secured, that Polidori can pay the nurse to take special notice. The nurse is honest, obviously. With Polidori there to see Madame

Diodati settled in whatever sort of place this is, a place of *rest for the mind, repos pour l'esprit,* surely she can be cared for, surely –

By now the old lady is out of sight, shut in the carriage behind a window covered with narrow iron bars. Polidori shakes his head and looks at Mary sorrowfully. "Così una signora normale diventa una strega," he murmurs. "This is how an ordinary woman becomes a witch." Again he makes that strange gesture, raising two forked fingers to his head and flinging them to the ground, before climbing into the carriage and shutting the door behind himself. And the carriage rolls out of the courtyard and down the road toward Geneva. In silence, all of them – even the big Englishman with the squashed ear, even the two Swiss boys moving furniture off the wagon – stand and stare after it.

Finally Claire touches Byron's elbow. "We should eat," she says gently. "There's still the bread and cheese, and some wine. Let's go sit on the terrace, enjoy the view of the lake."

Byron swallows hard and nods. "Quite right," he says. "Poor host, I am, today." He gives a short trembly laugh and follows Claire down the hall. As he passes the old lady's room – last on the right, its door still open – he averts his gaze, as do Claire and Shelley. They emerge onto the terrace with relief and begin the comforting bustle of lunch, dragging forth some chairs, setting out the bread and cheese, wrestling the cork from the bottle of wine.

Mary lingers in the door of Madame Diodati's room. It's nearly bare except for a massive four-poster bed, canopied and quilted with age-yellowed white silk, carved with fierce clawed feet like a lion's. Small elfin faces laugh from tangled vines and flowers all up and down the posts. Against one wall a wardrobe looms, its door dangling open where the nurse must have rummaged to fill what's no longer just an overnight bag. It's empty except for a pale muslin gown, trimmed with lace, in the style of seventy years ago. Underneath it huddle a pair of dancing slippers that have once been pink. Here's a dressing table with a dusty skirt, and more dust on its top outlines a missing brush and comb. And on the mantelpiece, under a pale square of plaster where something large once hung – a portrait? A mirror? – sits a small enamel box.

Mary goes to the mantel and lifts the box down. Pandora, she is, whose curiosity will kill them all. She will double the curse Madame Diodati has laid on them, which surely can't be lifted even by Polidori's counter-charm, the forked fingers, the hurling-away of evil invisible things. She has no right to peer into the last precious object left behind by a woman forced out of her home. Yet here it is, asking, like any box, to be opened.

The tinkle of music from under the lid startles Mary so much that she nearly drops the small glossy thing in the fireplace. Tightening her grip, she opens the lid further and listens. It's a sweet tune, with a lingering melancholy that tightens her throat. She's heard it before, back in London, at what Godwin had called an *evening of culture,* beaming as he brushed the shoulders of his coat and gathered herself and Mrs. Vile and Claire and Fanny to walk to the theatre. It had been a chilly night, early in the autumn, when London's winter damp was hovering in the smell of wet leaves pasted to the cobblestones, horses blanketed, smoke lifting toward the sky. Mary had settled next to Fanny on the cheap-seats bench in the balcony, peering down at the rows of heads: the lines of hair-partings, the bald spots, the tousled hat-lines. Yet when a young man in black walked onto the stage and sat down at the piano and begun to play, she forgot everything. His pale face was rapt, lost. This same melody had tumbled forth, the same yearning climb of notes over the strumming, sad left hand. *Dance of the Blessed Spirits,* said the blurry printed program, *from Gluck, "Orfeo et Euridice."* She knew this story: the lute player who descended into the underworld after his lost love, then killed her all over again because he could not stand not to look. He had to turn and see. And even though Euridice loved him she had paid for it with her life. He had lived thereafter with the knowledge of what he had done. A rich, strange throb of pain gripped Mary in that moment and bowed her head toward her lap. Mama was also there in the underworld, consigned to the land of the shades, because of her. But here in the halo of the music, the thought of her brought something more than pain. Fanny's hand clutched Mary's, and when she turned to look, she saw that Fanny was crying too.

That same song is here, now, in the music box. This is the only sound Madame Diodati must have heard for days, other than the scuttle of mice in the walls, the breath of wind from the lake, and, when the silence must have been too great, her own voice. There was no need to have seized and shaken and compelled her. *This is how an ordinary woman becomes a witch:* the bumbling false certainties of men who persist, all evidence to the contrary, in thinking they know more than they do. That airless cage of righteousness that drops over them when faced with something beyond their ken. That frightened creature made malevolent, where moments before had stood only a fellow being hungering for kindness. A creature, born instantly, of fear.

Mary sets the music box back on the mantel. Tears sear the backs of her eyes, and she hurries from the room. Out on the balcony, Byron is perched next to Claire, sipping from the bottle of wine, one hand twined in hers, the mastiff slumped at his feet. Shelley, leaning against the railing, looks at Mary worriedly and hands her a hunk of bread and cheese. "I'm all right," she murmurs, taking the food. "I'll be all right." Nestling under his arm, she follows his gaze. Along the lakeshore road, far below, the carriage bearing Madame Diodati and Polidori and the *specialist* and his nurse trundles toward the city. So gleaming white, it is, so innocent, with its bars over the windows that can't be seen unless you're standing close. Or unless you're trapped inside, watching what was once your home get smaller and smaller until it disappears.

Near Madame Diodati's bedroom window, in a square of moonlight on the floor, the print of a large bare foot lies quiet in the dust, unseen.

Lightning flashes over Geneva and Father is pursuing the Creature but it isn't yet time to be seen and so he must flee. The words he'll say to Father haven't sorted themselves into any shape that can match his giant hungers and so with his blessed inconvenient strength he's scrambling up the steep hill into the old city, through the warren of cobblestoned alleys in the shadow of the great cathedral, past the chocolate shops and the stationer's and the banker's (*M. Hentsch,* reads the name on the gold-lettered plaque, even in his panic he can pick out the words in the dark), past one clockmaker and another and a Lutheran chapel and a shuttered café, under a web of paper lanterns strung over the street in some festival that does not include him, all their candles gone out. A sign in a window in fake-Gothic lettering reads *English Antiques / Antiquities Anglaises.* It's dark here, three a.m., according to the deep chime of the cathedral bells overhead. He gallops through the courtyard and in front of John Calvin's chapel he crosses a spot of cold – of firm not-quite benevolent will, of malign intent calling itself *good* – that freezes him in place. But Father's scrambling up the steps into the plaza behind him and so he dodges down the next street, past a house where someone has splashed *ROUSSEAU* in bright red letters on the plaster wall, down the opposite side of the hill and onto Plainpalais, the market field. Rough sleepers huddle in the shelter of the stalls and the Creature trips and goes flying and scrambles up. Lightning flashes. Father is closing in but the sleepers stir and rise like the dry-boned dead from their graves and snatch at the tails of his good

black frock coat, at his watch-chain swinging across his panting chest –
ah, sir, have ye no coin for a poor beggar, so hungry in such a deep night –
and Father curses and shoves but is delayed long enough for the Creature
to scramble away. Then there is only one place left to flee: straight up
Mont Saleve, a jagged face of rock, directly in his path.[5]

Lightning crackles and fat raindrops slap the Creature's rag-clad skin.
If he's going to climb, he'd better do it now, before the rain intensifies and
makes the rock too slick to grip. He hurls himself at the stone, hooks his
fingers on a crag above his head, and hauls himself up. Father is a dark
shape in the greater dark, drawing closer, cursing, shouting, heedless of
who might hear. But the Creature is heedless too of all but escape. He
thrusts himself upwards, toes in crevices. The rain is slashing at him now,
the lightning flying around him like a flock of white birds. Father can see
him climbing, but he cannot stop. He reaches for a higher rock and slips
– *fall, ah,* blood-shocked clench of loyal red heart – and catches himself
and scrambles up. Up. Finally there's a ledge for his huge broken-nailed
feet. Finally, there's a cave. He flings himself panting onto his belly – the
cold wet stone presses up against him with each breath – and coils himself
around again until he's gripping the lip of the rock and peering down at
Father. A single sodden man, a tiny white dot of face turned up, almost
invisible in the slashing rain. *Poor fork'd creature. Poor houseless wretch.*
Ha. Shakespeare has scaled the cliff with him, then. Poor pursued creature. Poor inconvenient strength. Dear blessed knowledge. Dear clinging
words. Dear stubborn life. Dear rage.

The Creature wakes sodden and sweating, shaking to the dreams that
have flung him deep into the cave. An uncertain glow brightens the
ceiling of the rock. He drags his giant palms down his face. Heaving
himself to his knees – wincing at the new constellations of pain – he
stands, bracing himself against the stone, then shudders and stretches and
wanders toward the light. Stamped in tears and blood is the red print of
his giant right hand, pointing north.

Gradually, the sky goes dark. The first days in Geneva had been bright, if
a trifle brisk: put it down to the mountain wind, Mary had thought, to
the cool waters of the lake. But now, when Shelley pushes the *Ariel* out
from the dock – having left a nest of scratched-out papers in a heap on
the sopha – even he wears a coat. The lake is strangely still. Against her
will, Mary remembers when Mr. Coleridge came to Skinner Street for

dinner and recited his *Rime of the Ancient Mariner* to Godwin and Mrs. Vile as she hid under the settee, disobeying her bedtime for the thrill of those screaming ghosts, those glittering eyes. *Quiet as a painted ship upon a painted ocean*, the lines ring in Mary's head as she watches Shelley through the parlor window, with William oaring along the carpet on his stomach, with Elise building up the fire in the kitchen stove, again. In the garden, birds' voices are subdued. The air is cold. And then comes the rain.

At first, there seems no reason for more than mild annoyance. "It will pass," Shelley speculates, "and then the summer will be here." But at the market with Elise, Mary isn't so sure. The tables under the canvas tents are arrayed, like Covent Garden or Smithfield, with haunches of mutton and sheaves of shining fish on bins of ice stored in sawdust from the winter, with eggs and curious hens in a cage, with baskets of dark brown loaves. Yet there's almost nothing green, except sad string-bound bundles of dandelion leaves. The faces of the other women are pinched, their voices sharp. "For such a price," snaps one, turning away from the mutton-seller's table, "I would expect the lamb of God!" Only one seller stands behind a box of crisp lettuces, rosy radishes, and – miraculously – a pyramid of jewel-like oranges: a young blond woman with a fixed, professional smile and, behind her, a tall man with a pistol in his belt. Mary starts toward them and Elise grabs her arm. "Don't," she whispers. "From the east, Russia, where the weather is not so bad as here. They have ways of packing the food and driving through the night without stopping. And only the rich buy from them, see?" She nods at a trim housekeeper-like woman who's approaching the lettuces, eyes downcast, as the other women glare. Someone shoves her and she stumbles, dropping her coins and flushing as she fishes them from the leaves. Elise raises her eyebrows and turns away. Reluctantly, Mary follows. Raising her parasol against the drizzle, she spots a row of small dark objects on another table: dead songbirds, lying on their backs. And here comes a woman with her hand outstretched, ready to count them into her basket. "Ah, Lorraine," she sighs to the bird-seller, "did you ever think we'd be eating..."

"Damn war," spits the seller, shaking her head. "Damn weather."

In the afternoons, Mary and Shelley climb the hill to see how Byron and Polidori – and Claire, who's always there now – are coming along with their settling-in. She had hoped Byron would refresh the sad Villa Diodati from top to bottom: rip off the dark damp-blotched wallpaper in big strips, whitewash the walls to magnify the light off the lake, open all the shutters and all the doors, and blow the last of the old lady's lonely curses out of the rooms to swirl away over the mountains for good. But for Byron, the darkness of the villa is part of its charm. He's left the old lady's furniture right where he found it: the great four-poster bed with the little faces, the massive armchairs in the parlor, the wide benchlike thing that looks like a Chinaman's opium couch. In the library, dim ranks of books ascend to the ceiling. A handful of light gilt chairs huddle near the fireplace in the otherwise empty ballroom. Even his great Chesterfield sofa, covered in cracked brown leather, looks lost among the big armchairs in the parlor, drawn up around the fireplace big enough for a person to lie in. The rooms seem to grow bigger, and darker, around Mary the longer she's inside them, like rooms through which she dimly remembers having wandered in a dream.

Despite the cold, Byron has pulled back the heavy drapes and opened the doors to draw a breeze into the hall. Fletcher – Byron's valet, the big man with the cauliflower ear – is unpacking his books as Mary arrives, assisted by Claire. They greet Mary with similar harassed looks. "The mold in this place will martyr us," Fletcher says darkly. "I didn't think no place would have damp worse than London."

Mary lifts a thick green book lying open where Byron has left it. An engraving of a shirtless man in knee breeches, widely planted feet, and a stalwart expression – *Tom Cribb, Champion of England* – faces the title page: *Boxiana, or Sketches of Antient and Modern Pugilism*. Ah: a relic of the Fives Court and Gentleman Jackson. Mary turns the pages: pictures of men, names, stories, and then suddenly "FEMALE PUGILISM: To show the *nationality* of BOXING, and that it was not merely confined to *heroes*, we have extracted the following copy of an advertisement, which appeared in a diurnal print, in June, 1722, upwards of *ninety years* since, when even HEROINES panted for the honours of pugilistic glory! CHALLENGE: I, ELIZABETH WILKINSON, of Clerkenwell, having had some words with HANNAH HYFIELD, and requiring satisfaction, do invite her to meet me upon the stage, and box me for three guineas; each woman holding half-a-crown in each hand, and the first woman that drops the money to lose the battle. ANSWER: I, HANNAH HYFIELD, of Newgate Market, hearing of the resoluteness of ELIZABETH WILKINSON, will not fail, *God willing*, to give her more blows than words – desiring home blows, and from her, no favor: she may expect a good thumping!" Mary snickers. Women like this could vault between the ropes at the Fives Court and send even Byron scurrying for his life.

Byron enters the room and crosses to where Claire kneels on the floor. He cups the back of her head in his hand and she leans against him. "We're almost finished!" she exclaims. "All in order, just like you said." Byron smiles and pushes his fingers into her hair, a gesture that reminds Mary uneasily of fondling the mastiff's ears.

"I'd have thought you'd have more of your own books here." Striving for lightness, Mary's voice is merely sharp. "Your poems are wonderful. I remember when Shelley and I first met – when I knew that I – well, I thought of some lines of yours and wrote them down in my own book. The stanzas to Thyrza. Who was she?"

"Ah." Byron keeps his face carefully blank. Finally he permits himself a small, rueful smile. "An early love. Edelston –" He stops. "*Miss. Miss* Edelston. Forerunner of a – Miss Rushton. And then came mad Caro Lamb and Annabella. And then – no more love." He turns to the books, lifting them one by one. After a moment, he looks up and sighs, holding a wooden box. "Thank you," he says to Claire. "Why don't you go find some tea for us?" Claire leaves the room, brandishing a bright smile. *No more love.* Mary tries to think of a way those words could have been unhurtful to her, with no success.

Carrying the box, Byron leads Mary and Shelley down the hall into the old ballroom, their footsteps loud. "Do you think there could ever have been a ball here?" he asks. "Doesn't seem like a setting for much but a funeral." He sets the box on the marble mantelpiece and removes a round pale object Mary takes a moment to recognize as a human skull. Shelley gasps.

"What's the matter, old man?" Byron asks with deliberate offhandedness. "Came with me all the way from Waterloo. Maybe one of Napoleon's, maybe one of ours." He turns the skull ruefully in his hands. "I would declaim *Alas, poor Yorick.* But it would be such a cliché."

"You just picked it up?" Shelley, still wide-eyed, has backed away a step. Even the ghost-story-loving Eton boy cavils at Byron's souvenir. Yet Mary can't stop looking. The shape of a human face is still so clear. Here is the scaffolding of bone, the round sloping ripple of brain-pan, the small flaring roof of the nose, the pleading empty sockets of the eyes. A knob of spine still clings to the nape of the neck, the first brick in the path down which sensation marches into the world and back again.

"Don't worry," Byron says, "Fletcher and I have cleaned it thoroughly." One by one, he lifts more things from the bottom of the box and lines them up on the mantel. A scrap of blue cloth. A scrap of red cloth, blood-stained black. A snapped-off sword-tip. A metal stirrup, splashed with dirt.

"What would this man's family say," Mary flashes, "if they saw how you make sport of him?"

"They turned him over to Napoleon, didn't they?" Byron answers. "To war, the biggest and most foolish sport of all." His eyes darken. "Think of it. How else do we remember *this was real*? How else do human beings get anything through their thick –" A wry, guilty look flashes over his face as he looks into the soldier's empty eyes. "If the living don't remember, the dead have no hope. Touch the world, hold it in our hands, that's the only way to keep it alive. Haven't you ever picked up – well, little mementoes?"

"Seashells on the beach at Calais," Mary replies sardonically. "Maybe an autumn leaf."

Byron sighs. "Perhaps you're right," he admits. "But if you could have seen –"

"Steady on, old man," Shelley says uneasily.

"No," Mary insists, "tell me."

"That battle was a year ago, almost exactly," Byron says. "And yet when Fletcher and Polidori and I went through last month there were still bodies on the field. Skeletons. It's a great flat place, most of godforsaken Belgium is a great flat place, why they ever fought for it is beyond me. Wellington set up his command under a great elm tree near the road. You can see where the damned souvenir-hunters have been at it, chipping away."

"Ah, yes," Mary says, "souvenir-hunters. So *tactless*, aren't they."

Byron blushes. "Anyway," he says. "To see them all still strewn – Some had been gathered, buried, families had come to collect. But others –" He pauses, searching his memory. "Like Dante, it was. *I would not have thought death had undone so many.* All those bodies. Still lying right where they fell." He looks at Shelley, then at Mary again, suddenly pleading. "You can't know how absurd it is to see. Which makes it more horrible. A mass of men decides to pick up weapons and rush at another mass of men with weapons and everyone just starts firing. It's nonsense. That's what's terrifying. Especially for –" he looks away – "the horses." He recovers himself and throws a shoulder of sardonic cheer against the wheel of conversation. "But what a boon to scavengers. Ragpickers came out to pull the coats and shirts off the bodies for rags to make pulp to make paper. And the denture-makers came, with their little tools, to bend over the dead men's mouths and knock out their teeth. They only need the front ones, top and bottom. For verisimilitude."

Mary suddenly longs to be out of this dim room, out from under the sad grinning gaze of the skull. She turns and strides down the long hall into the stone courtyard outside. She'll never bring William into this house. Never, never, never.

"Madame?" A red-faced man with a crumpled paper in his hand stands next to a cart. "I have delivery for Monsieur Gordon Byron?"

"He's inside," Mary begins, but Byron, hearing the rattle of wheels, has emerged from the house. "Your chairs," says the man, "from the Boutique des Antiquitiés Anglaises."

"Ah, yes," says Byron, "almost forgot." He calls for Fletcher, who, with the driver's help, lifts from the cart two Tudor chairs. "Watch that door," he warns, leading them inside. "Now let's take them to this parlor – no, maybe the bedroom—"

Mary stands alone in the courtyard, near the little old cart-horse who's drawn this wagon all the way down one hill and up another. His gray coat is flecked all over with darker gray and brown, and white hairs cluster in the hollows above his eyes. He blinks at her and tips his ears forward, and she rubs the flat hard plane of his head, scrubbing out a skim of dust with her fingers. Oh, the horror of Waterloo: the strewn bodies of horses and men, necks flung back, teeth bared, shattered bones, shattered flesh. Yet they had all lined up for the battle on command. *Good boy, good lad.* Perhaps a cavalryman had leaned down from his saddle to pat the sleek neck he'd groomed so carefully that morning, to flip a tousled hank of mane back into place below the nervous ears. On a summer morning there would have been flies to swat. *Hold still,* he would have muttered, twisting in the saddle to smack a hand down on a rump. All around him, the glitter of buttons and sabers and drums, of that metal edge that holds down the skin of the drum over nothing but empty space. Stomp hoof, fidget, squeal and pin ears at the horse just behind. Raise sticks: drumroll. And he and his horse and all their comrades hover on the brink of some great thing that will tilt and dump them off the edge of the world, like a child's toy soldiers when the playing-board is whisked away. Mary runs her hand down the little cart-horse's neck, into the warm spot under his mane. By what strange will could any man ever take upon himself the right to lift a gun and fire and shatter this flesh, to leave this large brown eye cold and open and staring at the sun? To push another creature across the line between life and death?

Mary walks onto the terrace and leans against the railing, studying the sky. Thick pillowy clouds are piling up in the west, tinged with an eerie platinum light. A subtle chop has begun on the lake. Wind nudges a crisp smell of rain against Mary's face, and the long grass in the cow-field leans backward as if brushed by an invisible hand. Byron and Shelley appear behind her. "There you are," Shelley says. "Time for us to be going. William will be awake any moment."

"Sailors take warning," Byron quips. "Careful going down that hill. See you later?" He shakes hands with Shelley and bows to Mary, then lingers on the terrace, staring out over the lake, as they start down the path to the Maison Chapuis. Just as they reach their own back door, the rain comes. Mary turns to look back up the hill, held temporarily spellbound by what she sees: a silver veil, thickening between them and the Villa Diodati, until its outlines are blurred, its shape nearly lost, the man on the balcony no more than a ghost himself.

The rain continues all night. A stream swells in the downhill path from Villa Diodati, washing a rill of mud against Maison Chapuis's back wall. Shelley picks his way through the slush and discovers a shallow trench along the back terrace, obviously dug for that same reason, then fetches Fletcher, wrapped in a great black oilskin coat, to help him reopen it. Struggling all morning with their spades, they manage to divert most of the water around the garden. But still the patio is flooded. Brown water pools around the pots of Mary's hopeful, shivering geraniums, blurring the outlines of Shelley's long footprints on the stones.

In the night Mary wakes from exhausting dreams that stalk through her and leave her with a tender singed crater inside where something alive has been excised. Shelley claims one can train oneself to remember dreams, but she doesn't want to remember these. Opening her eyes in the dark, she's grateful for the white smudge of his worried face, close to hers. She can't describe to him the feeling of narrow escape from a pursuit by something that's using the dream as an occasion to find her. When it catches her it will crouch on her chest like the beast in Mr. Fuseli's drawing of the Night-mare, pressing down on her like the gray sky that's so leaden over the lake. Some creature is waiting there, drawing the sodden air in ragged breaths. But surely Shelley will not let her sail the sleeping world alone.

The rain goes on and on. Byron will have need of Claire's amusement at Diodati now that no riding or sailing is possible. Maybe, together up there, Claire and Byron can develop something more than the relation of poet to pursuer. Without her in the house, Shelley seems calmer. Dressed in dry clothes, he hurls himself onto the sopha in a litter of books and manuscript pages and lead pencils (Mary keeps him away from inkpots unless he's sitting upright at a table.) In the wet gray window-light, he settles down to sketch lines of poetry, sailboats, flights of steps leading up beyond the margin of the page. But nothing that coheres into a column of lines marching down, from one page to the next. Elise appears without being asked, setting down a steaming cup of tea and bearing his empty cup away.

With an old Skinner Street sternness, Mary takes herself in hand. This is their summer now. William is settled into a pattern of napping and of play with Elise that leaves great chunks of the morning and afternoon for Mary, ostensibly, to dispose of as she wishes. Yet alone at the desk on the upstairs landing, she can only watch the page like a fisherman watching the surface of the lake at the spot where his line disappears under the waves, waiting for a twitch. She opens the lid of her writing box and shuts it again. Nothing moves. Of all the words that swim and flick their tails inside her, none will come close enough to be snared in the gentle net of a sentence, letting her feel that blessed unfolding and welling-up of sense where before there has been none. That had been the feeling as she scratched out her novel about Mary Queen of Scots while dreaming of David Booth. But only someone else's words will come to her now, some mad admonitory thing on strange hand-colored pages that had remained unsold for months in Papa's shop: *There is a Moment in each Day that Satan cannot find, nor can his Watch Fiends find it, but the Industrious find this Moment & it multiply, and it renovates every Moment of the Day if rightly placed.* "Don't despair, Mr. Blake," Papa had told the artist wearily. "This work – *Milton,* is it called? I see – is certainly... unique. A good lesson for us writers." The small dirty man – his eyes wide and luminous, his bald head smudged with ink, his hands splotched brown with printers'-acid burns – had nodded. "To be sure," he'd said, "the world itself is sufficient for the man of art." His gaze flicked to Mary, and he smiled. "Or for the girl."

If she can only find that moment in the day, if she can only be ready with her net when the words come swimming past in their great hidden migration, she can unlock the pattern of her days and of her thoughts and of this unknown thing she is ostensibly taking her summer to write. Seizing that single moment dirty little Mr. Blake wrote about will mean she has seized the whole day, and the pattern of days that will become a life like her mother's: rational, memorable, productive. Yet she feels barren of invention, bashful and furious before the page. *If you can't work at one thing,* Godwin would advise, *work at another.* So she turns again to Greek, to the scrawls of the foreign letters and the squeak of chalk on slate, bending her head into the familiar dusty sweat of brain-labor. Here is her favorite Sappho fragment in the beginner's grammar: τελέϲϲαι, *telessai,* to *happen,* that continuous glowing state of the soul, of annunciation, of being taken-up, that she is seeking. Writing and learning are this state of *telessai,* a perpetual becoming. They make sense, and sensation, out of nothing, just as travel does. The very presence of one idea or word summons forth others, lighting and bathing the otherwise-dull lump of your brain. Yet no feeling like that comes for her as a story now.

So with a furtive mix of anger and relief she turns to what is always there: the work of child and broom and bread-bowl. She helps Elise gather the books and jackets and tiny knitted socks. She casts more socks onto the spiky needles that string the wool between them in a thorny little crown. She smooths the sheets and quilts back over the mattress. She kneels on the floorboards to stack William's colored blocks in a tower for him to demolish, crowing and grinning and clapping his hands. There are chamber pots to empty, diapers to pound and swish in buckets of lye. There is washing to hang on lines strung over the kitchen stove and up in the rafters of the attic, steaming in the heat of copper braziers lit to smolder all day. Mary collects William's diapers: *before which all else must surrender,* come Byron's snide words, *including art.* Elise gathers Shelley's damp shirts, smoothing them gently over one arm – the iron's heat, in the kitchen, will finish them – and raises the attic window to release the smoke. "Ah," she says. "Tant de pluie." On the other side of the shingles it taps and rustles. So much rain.

Polidori brings the invitation, edging down the path in a pair of giant leather boots spotted with mildew and slick with mud. "Found them in the cellar," he gasps, struggling to toe them off and unbuckle his mackintosh at the door. "Sorry for the stocking feet."

Over a cup of tea, he confirms their suspicions: Byron, bored, is ready to throw a party. She and Shelley are to leave William with Elise and gather up all the wine they can lay hands on and bring it up the hill. "Maybe even stay the night," Polidori offers, "if the weather remains so bad. There's ample room up there. To say the least."

The following evening, caped and shawled and stooped over their baskets with wine bottles and a loaf of bread, Mary and Shelley struggle up the hill to the Villa Diodati. The rain has stopped, but a cold wind shakes some last drops from the trees. Mary shivers. Up ahead the villa looms like a sailing ship, candles blazing in each downstairs window. How invitingly warm, how apparently safe.

They find Byron in the library in front of a fire, reading with a bone-handled knife in his hand and his gray boxing gloves abandoned at his feet and his big dog snoring on the rug. The book is obviously brand-new, just a bundle of pages stitched together along the spine and still joined together in their quarto-folds at the top. He's literally tearing through the book, teasing the knife's tip toward the binding and then drawing it backwards along the quarto-fold with a velvety rip to open each new page. "Forgive me for not coming to the door," he says, "but I just got this…" His face is blurred, still half-lost. Reluctantly, he closes the book, the knife handle still protruding from its pages. Mary recognizes that look. *Come on, time to put the book down, your Papa has guests to entertain at dinner and you girls shall be present.* Time to trudge downstairs, eat one's food as fast as is compatible with decency, smile and nod at the other balding men chattering with Papa about the mad King and publishers' advances, and bolt back upstairs, a last piece of bread-and-butter clutched in one's hand, to be alone with the book.

"Where'd you get this?" Shelley drops down on the sofa and reaches for Byron's book. *The Ghost of the Alps,* black print screams, *A Gothic Tale.*

"Down at the newsagent's by the Angleterre," Byron says. "The papers too. Something about a volcano erupting in the Pacific, back in April. Mount Tambora. That's what's still playing hell with the weather, even here."

"I wonder how that can be," Mary says, "when it's so far away." The Pacific is the home of the brown-skinned Otahetians who live happy and free, with flowers on their necks and love in common. *We are the Otaheite philosophers,* Claire had once joked.[6] *A whole tribe,* moving through Europe like gypsies in Shelley's wake, unbound by the dead hand of custom. Yet now even those original Otahetians are overshadowed by gloom, by a disaster Mary can only vaguely imagine: villages drowning in lava and ash, thatched huts ablaze, half-naked people struggling and weeping like those caught by surprise in Noah's flood. Tambora sounds like the name of some bloodthirsty queen. That volcano across a continent from them has caused all this rain? Is the great globe really so small?

"Come on," Byron sighs, slapping Shelley's knee and raising himself off the couch. He picks up the boxing gloves and clasps their cuffs together in one hand. "Dinner should be ready soon. And there's more wine. Fletcher and I got down in the cellars and found a stash of bottles. Someone's been at them. Maybe a servant. The lady didn't look like a tippler." He smiles. "A big old gold mirror was standing down there, leaning up against the wall – caught sight of myself and jumped out of my skin."

"Here we are." Beaming, Claire comes swaying into the room with a decanter and four glasses balanced on a tray. She wears a black silk shawl Mary has never seen. "I've brought it to you here. The roast is not quite done, so we can linger by this fire a little more." She shivers daintily. One by one, she sets forth the wineglasses – gold-rimmed, etched with vines and leaves cut deep and outlined in red – and fills them, handing one to Byron, then to Shelley, last to Mary. "Aren't these lovely? We found them in a cabinet in the kitchen."

"One of many," Byron says. "Obviously the old lady sold most of the family's things. But we keep finding others. This house is vast." He locks eyes with Claire over the rim of the glass and smiles, raising it to his lips. She smiles back, raising her glass as well. Mary's skin prickles. Claire is lovely in her peacock-blue silk dress, dark curls swept high off her neck, flushed with the wine and the warmth of the fire and Byron's gaze. She's happy here, presiding so prettily over the wine decanter and the old lady's rediscovered goblets in a borrowed house she re-borrows now as her own. *I dread to unfold her mind,* Mama wrote, *lest it render her unfit for the world she is to inhabit.* Yet isn't this role – Villa Diodati chatelaine, accepted consort of a lord, woman set like a jewel into the setting of a house and a man's protection, secure at last –what any woman wants, has been trained to want out of the limited, pitifully optimistic range of what's possible for her?

Shelley is watching Claire too, faintly smiling, eyes darkening in the firelight. A thing she recognizes – roving, teasing, wicked, intent – flickers over his face. *He's done this kind of thing before.* What is Harriet doing now, back in London in her parents' house with her two children who have never known their father? Mary draws her shawl tighter around her shoulders. What will she do if Shelley's love drops from beneath her feet, like a trapdoor giving way beneath an actress in mid-line, jerking her into a flailing falling dark? What of William, then, safely in bed in the Maison Chapuis just down the hill? Harriet's face, and Cornelia Boinville's, then Mama's, come to Mary, severe, rueful: *Don't be a fool. To let him see your fear will be to set him on the track you fear the most. Keep calm. Be rational. Just as you are.*

Fletcher appears in the library door, his wide face moist with sweat. "M'lord, it's ready," he announces. "The vegetables, they –"

"Never mind the details, Fletcher," Byron laughs. He leads Shelley and Mary and Claire out of the library, thrusting his boxing gloves into

Fletcher's hands as he passes. "Time for the feast of reason and the flow of soul, eh?" Struck by a sudden thought, Mary lags behind, slipping back to Madame Diodati's old bedroom. The drapes are drawn, the door of the tall wardrobe shut. But the small gold music box is gone. Polidori must have taken it to Madame. What a comfort it will be to the old woman, now surely locked in a room Mary flinches to imagine: bleached white, rough linen sheets on a narrow bed, screams and moans bleeding under the door like the cries of cattle from the Smithfield market. Perhaps the little box will not be stolen from the old lady so suddenly converted from chatelaine to patient.

The dining room is thick with shadows in the evening light. Fire blazes under the big marble mantel and brass candelabras lift their arms on the sideboard. Deep red flocked wallpaper, patterned with vines, is marked with darker squares and ovals where pictures have hung. Against the polished mahogany table, four gold-rimmed white china plates flanked by knives and forks float like moons. "This is rather good," Shelley observes, picking up his plate and turning it over to inspect the maker's mark.

"Found in the house, luckily," Byron replies, "although that 'English antiques' shop up in the city, near the cathedral, had what looked to be some silver from a lesser Marlborough...."

Mary stares at Shelley. Can this really be her republican, her atheist, her mad wicked boy, now standing next to his fellow English nobleman and discussing china and silver plate as coolly as an auctioneer? Ordinarily, to hear him talk of Field Place and the country-gentry world from which he has liberated himself, one would think he'd been bound in chains in a cellar, strait-jacketed into an Eton blazer, strapped to the back of a pony like a man being tarred and feathered. Yet now Mary can see him at his mother's side in the dining room, her voice gentle: *see here, Bysshe, this was your grandmother's china, such things are also good for a man to know.* Shelley flung ecstatically on his back beneath a great elm tree, rapt by the thousand murmuring voices of the leaves. Shelley and his sisters chasing fireflies on the lawn, calling and laughing until the oncoming night has darkened them to pale blurs, flickering like ghosts over the grass. That world can't be so terrible if he can slip back into it so fluently when it is suggested to him. And suggestion is, of course, the key. He's so mutable when Byron is around, so willing to be turned like a jewel to let the light glance off a hitherto unknown facet of himself. *An English lord.* And it's Byron's hand that does the turning.

Mary shakes herself awake and smiles at Byron, who's guiding her to the seat immediately to his right. On her other side, Shelley draws back his chair and fits his knees under the table, banging something that makes the glasses rattle. "Ouch!" he yelps.

"Sorry, old man," Byron says, settling into his own seat at the head of the table, back to the fire, draping his napkin over his lap. "I find this table's just a hair too low." *It fits me perfectly,* Mary starts to say. But then, she's the shortest of the four of them, Shelley the tallest, fitting Claire and Byron together between them like a pair of bookends. And Claire and Byron are together even now, shooting oblique glances, sharing smiles as Byron pours everyone more wine. Claire's body shifts in her chair. She must be reaching her foot toward Byron under the table, teasing his leg with her stockinged toes. And – although his face remains politely fixed on Shelley – his shoulder tips toward Claire.

Fletcher, in a rusty black butler's coat, enters with a slab of beef on a platter, already sliced and breathing warmth across the table. Mary's mouth waters, and she takes a big slice when he brings the plate to her. Shelley stares at the beef, wavers, then shakes his head. "Oh, that's right," Byron says. "Your principles. Well, there'll be vegetables next."

"Vegetable love," Claire quotes, smirking, into her wineglass. "Vaster than empires, and more slow."

"Marvell-ous." Byron's smile is pleased. "Ha. Ha."

The vegetables are startlingly delicious: a salad with vinegar and oil, spears of asparagus with special little tongs to serve them out, and baby carrots, glistening with sweet butter. Crusty white bread with more butter follows them. "Mmmm," Shelley murmurs. "Elise says there are shortages at the market, in this weather – the farmers are in difficulty. Poor devils." His face turns sad. "How'd you come by all of this?"

"I have empowered Fletcher to make certain excursions," Byron says vaguely. "And we have a friend from the East now. Yuri, thug of all the Russias. But that's not for you to worry about. Just enjoy." His smile softens, his gaze flickering over Shelley's lanky frame.

But Shelley, lost now in guilty thoughts of the farmers, only stares at his plate. Mary nudges him. "Eat," she whispers. "Not to do so ill respects their labor." Not to mention the invitation from Lord Byron. And Shelley must keep up his strength. Even on food that must have come from the blond woman with her determined smile in the market, and the big man with his hand on the butt of his gun.

"True," Shelley murmurs, lifting his fork.

"The house is much improved since moving day," Mary says, turning to Byron. She slices off a chunk of beef and takes a bite. "Where's Dr. Polidori?"

Byron's face twitches. "Visiting Madame Diodati," he says. "He stays so late and they so often feed him at her...home that I didn't expect him here." So to this party, Polidori has not been invited.

"He visits?" Mary asks. "So she can talk?"

"In a manner of speaking," Byron says. "Talk. Speaking. Ha. Ha." He shoots a sideways glance at Claire, who smiles lazily, her foot – yes, it has to be – still teasing him under the table. Desire rises like smoke between them, obscuring the forlorn figure of the old woman in her rotten dress, calling for her mama and her maid. Mary doesn't try to conceal the disapproval on her face. Of course Byron can now dismiss Madame Diodati. He has had the poor old creature carted away to a madhouse so he can occupy her home with its cavernous rooms, its cellars still filled with her wine. *Just like any man,* rises a caustic voice in Mary. *Women are either an aid or an obstacle, to be encouraged or cleared away accordingly.* Has Mama written this somewhere? Or is this – maybe – a voice of her own?

"His concern is laudable," Mary says. "Yours is... obvious."

Byron looks at her, but before he can answer Polidori walks into the room and heads straight for the fire, rubbing his reddened hands together. "It's blustery as November out there," he complains. His smile is tired. "Are we sure it's still only June?"

"How was your visit to Madame?" Mary asks.

"Well enough," Polidori sighs, ambling to the table and dropping into a chair next to Mary. "She's being treated kindly there. Having some trouble eating. But then..." He pauses. "In one so advanced in years, that symptom is not unusual."

"Where is the home she lives in now?" Mary asks.

"Up in the oldest part of the city, on the top of the hill," Polidori answers. "By the cathedral." Mary remembers the first time she and Shelley and William climbed that cobblestoned hill and emerged into the plaza in front of the cathedral and Calvin's chapel at the old city's peak, the rows of windows watching them. Had there been lost old ladies behind those windows even then, women like Madame Diodati watching as she and Shelley pushed William in his pram? In London there had been so many rumors of child-stealers, creatures between criminal and witch: *they'll take your baby, sell him to some rich woman who can't have none.* Mary shivers. What presences wait beyond any bright day to snatch up her boy and press him close no matter how much he struggles, no matter how he cries for her? What dark things gallop through the air as lighting flashes around the hill, as Calvin's severe ghost tries unsuccessfully to banish them? She shakes off the sudden dark stain of fear, angered by it. *The first thing a woman must control*, Mama would declare, *is her own mind.* "So that is near the cathedral," she says instead, "and Calvin's chapel where the refugees came. Back in Bloody Queen Mary's reign." She remembers the names still on display in the chapel's register, preserved under glass: 1556. *Sir William Stafford. William Kethe. Catherine Willoughby, Duchess of Suffolk. With Richard her husband and with infant.*[7] Refugees. Like her.

"When England was burning Protestants, Geneva was making 'em a church," Byron remarks. "How little has changed."

"O tempora, o mores," Polidori jokes. "And all that sort of thing."

"For the end of the meal," Byron announces, "a treat." Fletcher comes forth with oranges neatly segmented on a platter, their bright skin coiled around them. More food from the Russians. With a cry of delight, Shelley leaps on the fruit, dispatching one piece in two quick bites. Across the table, Claire has barely touched any of her food, although she's been steadily sipping her wine, a blush climbing her throat underneath a blue chiffon scarf wrapped around her neck. Unusual choice for a decoration, Mary thinks, but there is a chill in the air. "Time to go into the drawing room," Byron drawls, "such as it is."

"Wait," Claire says, shooting her a significant glance, "Mary and I will just stay here for a little while longer. The fire is so nice." Byron shrugs and nods to Shelley and Polidori, who push back their chairs and follow him out of the room. As soon as they're out of sight, Claire leaps on the cooling beef and vegetables and devours them, neatly and voraciously. "Albe doesn't like to see a woman eat," she mumbles between mouthfuls.

Albe? "Well, that's too bad for him," Mary says. "He can't starve you."

"Yes, well," Claire says. She loosens her gauzy blue scarf, tucking it back to avoid meat-juice stains. A red scuffmark, bruise or bite, streaks down her neck below her ear. When she sees Mary looking, she smiles. "He is very...." Her grin turns wicked. "Ardent."

What would Mama say? *A dependent creature, smiling under the lash because it dare not snarl.* How could Claire let him make such a thing of her? Yet, watching Claire fork up her borrowed food out of Byron's sight, the words scatter and blow into the air like ashes from a fire. Like the rough fires in all those inns and fields all across France and Germany in the days of wandering with Shelley. So long they've traveled to get here. So many times she's hoped for Claire to find a poet of her own. Maybe this is just how it is with Byron, or any man. Sit serenely at his table, and feed yourself in secret. When you dare.

In the library, Byron, Shelley, and Polidori crouch on the sofa, their heads bent together over some shredded dark substance in a blue china bowl. A single candle burns before them. Each of them balances a small silver pipe in his fingers: Shelley awkward, Polidori apprehensive, Byron matter-of-fact. With a tiny silver spoon, he ladles the crumbly black stuff into the bowl of the pipe. "Like that," he murmurs to Shelley. "Not like Polly. He always takes too much."

"What's *always?*" Polidori complains. "I hardly ever..." But he trails off, shaking his head, and taps a tiny heap of the black stuff into his own pipe bowl. "Careful," he says, handing the small spoon to Shelley. "Don't spill."

"What is this?" Mary blurts. "What are you –" Claire elbows her. Byron raises his head. "A little diversion," he says. "A little something to lighten the mood. To lighten –"

"The pain," Shelley mumbles, "my stomach's giving trouble. Like the times I took the drops, Mary, remember? This is the same medicine, only in a different form." He swallows. "Byron recommends it, he's done it often, he's—"

"Under the supervision of a doctor," Byron intones, with a light, lethal smile, tipping his head toward Polidori, "just as one should."

The same thing as the drops. The same thing that set the laughing demon curling its fingers around the bars of its cage, deep in Shelley's eyes, when he stood in the Skinner Street schoolroom and pointed the pistol at his head. *Mary, Mary, I can't live without you, I will die.* Slowly, Byron unwinds his cravat and wads it up and tosses it over Claire's head into the corner. His blue-green eyes rest on Mary, daring her. *Go ahead. Nag and forbid. Send him back to his wife. Or to your stepsister right here. She never says no.* Mary swallows and glances around the room. Decanter of wine and five glasses ready on a tray. Crooked silver candelabra ablaze with tapers, drooling white wax onto the wood. She should call for Fletcher to come with a rag and blade, or Madame Diodati's sideboard will be ruined. But Fletcher is nowhere to be seen. Fletcher has surely been told not to come near this dark cindery stuff tipped into the silver pipe now held so carefully in Shelley's long fingers.

"I wouldn't do things like this," Byron says conversationally, "except that with all this rain I am bored out of my God-damned mind. And" – he cuts his eyes at Polidori – "my doctor approves."

"Why don't we drink first," Mary offers. She rises and fetches the tray from the sideboard and sets it on the low table. Maybe she can upset that blue bowl and scatter the black stuff all over the floor. But no, Byron is shifting the bowl out of reach, glancing at her coolly from underneath his dark brows. "Certainly," he says. "Pull up a chair. And pour out."

Claire drags two chairs up to the little table as Mary unstoppers the decanter and tips the wine into each glass. The rich red smell mingles with the acrid black breath from the bowl. Shelley sets his pipe down on the table and reaches for the heavy glass. Polidori follows suit. Byron shifts his silver pipe to his left hand and reaches for the goblet with his right. "My pistol hand," he observes. "Need a strong grip." He sips, then sips again. "So. Miss Godwin. What shall we talk about?"

Firelight leans lower against the table and catches the rims of the glasses, the silver, the gilt edge of the earring dangling against Claire's throat. In Mary's glass the wine is black and flat. Smoke breathes from the logs. Flames shriek in tiny shrieks. She takes a sip of wine. How long can she sit here? How long can she keep the little silver pipe out of Shelley's hand? Down the hill, William sleeps in his bed, watched over by Elise. So serene. So far away.

"Maybe," she says, meeting Byron's gaze, "we could talk of poetry. Of how it moves and breathes. How it gets its life."

"A proper Godwinian gambit," Byron declares in mock approval. "I'll play." He sips his wine and turns his silver pipe in his fingers. "Polidori, obviously, knows nothing of this topic. Shelley, what say you?"

"Well," Shelley begins. His eyes light with a familiar thoughtfulness that, thank heaven, has nothing to do with the demon in its cage. "It moves in us, the writer and the reader alike. It moves over us. Like the wind. It stirs into new life the mind that without it would fade as a coal fades, burning itself out, smothered in its own ash." He shifts his gaze to the candle flame on the table. "But for it to have that effect it must bear some relation to experience."

"Yes," Byron agrees, "experience. That thing too many calling themselves *poets* affect to disdain." He snorts. "So much tepid and cerebral so-called poetry out there, all fake Arcadia and shepherdess simpers. Leave the nerves untouched and just diddle the mind. What bullshit. What a dry-bob of a thing. Much like my marriage. Ha." He grins sourly. "But of course the ones who write such trash don't know enough in books or any *other* area" – he glances at Claire, and smirks – "to tell the difference."

Mary takes another sip of wine. Is this, then, to be the Byron of the evening, the bawdy one, the sexual adventurer, the lord. How tiresome. "Men know so little, in my experience. Especially of what can make up books. Of what can make up people's ordinary lives." Until Byron and Shelley and Polidori stare and Claire's face hinges open in fear, Mary doesn't realize she's said the words aloud. She flushes. Shelley will be angry, he'll – but no, he's watching her, eyebrows cocked, his blue eyes dark. She is, after all, the daughter of Godwin and Wollstonecraft. The trained bear like Byron's Cambridge Bruin, the trained thinking woman, who has been trained for this.

Byron's face is still, determinedly polite. "Say more." His voice brightens. "I can't wait to hear what men don't know. Bad drawing and worse French? Housemaid's knee?" With elaborate care, he sets both pipe and wineglass down and folds both hands primly on his lap. "Or maybe how to spread out diapers in the sun to dry."

Damn him. "Certainly," she says. "If the writer is to speak of experience, then experience it should be. All of it. Is not the birth of children of great moment in any life, man's or woman's?" It looms ahead of her, the thing she mustn't say, but she's hurtling toward it anyway. "Even if a man may leave his children when a woman can't. And journey, say, to Switzerland." Too late it strikes her: this is true of not just Byron but of Shelley. Now he hauls himself upright and gapes at her, hurt darkening his eyes.

"In which endeavor" – Byron's voice is poisonously soft – "young misses may accompany him."

"I say," Claire blurts, "why don't we –"

"Case in point," Byron continues, "both of Godwin's daughters, trailing after the same –"

"Enough." Shelley lifts his glass and tosses down his wine. He doesn't look at Mary. "Too much, old man."

"Right, bad form," Byron mocks. "Bandying a lady's name." He leans forward. "All right. What if we all think of a story, and –"

"A ghost story!" Claire breathes, rolling her eyes teasingly. Yet with the shadows in the ceiling corners and the thick drapes pulled against the night – shutting them in with the strange heaviness in the air, with the image of Madame Diodati struggling against her madhouse-keepers, with that laughing thing pacing back and forth behind Shelley's eyes, with the weight of all the unseen attic rooms and black spaces pressing down above them, with the whole house creaking like the Ancient Mariner's mad reeling ship – Mary can imagine nothing more suitable. "Why don't we *all* think of a ghost story?"

"What counts as a ghost?" Polidori asks pedantically. "Need it be the spirit of someone actually dead, or –"

"I am thinking of a murdered baron," Shelley breathes, "poisoned, stalking his palazzo in Venice –"

"Here's a tale I heard," Byron interrupts. "A creature, half-dead, half-alive, who was once a man but has passed over the border between life and death." His tone grows somber, his eyes widening. "He sleeps by day and wanders the world by night. He's three hundred years old, maybe more. To remain alive he must kill. He must drink the blood of living people, young people. Because that keeps him young as well. He comes from the black forests on the border between East and West, where the mountains are sharp as teeth and wolves and men walk beside one another on solstice-night, when one year becomes the next, although at other times they are bitter enemies. Because they both fear this ghastly being hungry for their blood. His name is –"

"Vampire," Polidori breathes. "I heard her tell you. It was Waterloo, that hag on the battlefield who was picking over –"

"Just a story," Byron snaps, "but it has promise." He looks at Mary. "Miss Godwin. What will be your tale?"

"I?" Mary asks. "A ghost story? Ah –" White panic floods her brain. They are all looking at her now, Byron's expression studiously polite. She sips her wine and waits. No words ribbon up inside her but bitter ones, laden with unsayable things. How about a Sussex gent who flees his wife and child to gallop away across Europe with a supposedly rational girl, racing away from reproachful English shadows? How about an old philosopher who sucks the money from his pocket while prating about *principles?* How about a limping semi-Scottish laird who traps people in his rented villa to smoke some ominous black stuff that can release a demon? Or an old lady thrown into the kingdom of the mad like Lear onto the heath?

Byron's eyes are steady on Mary's, his mouth curling into a smile. "I can think of no story at the moment," she murmurs. "Perhaps with a bit more time, I could –"

"Ah," Byron says. "What any would-be author needs. More time." With elaborate courtesy, he lifts the little silver pipe. "Here," he says, "an inducement to the muse. Since you have yet to follow your father and your mother and Shelley" – *and myself*, he doesn't need to say – "into print, this may assist you in your labors."

Damn him. Some ugliness is loose in this room and he's delighting in it. But he hasn't seen Shelley's demon rise and twist against its cage-bars. He doesn't know what will happen once Shelley puts that little silver pipe to his lips and stumbles into some thorny forest and becomes lost to

William, to Mary, to himself. But Mary mustn't shout or plead. She must be rational. Or else Shelley, watching her, will begin what poor abandoned Harriet surely saw – a deadly polite withdrawal, so very English and so impossible to stop.

"If I can't achieve an invention unaided, how can I be sure it's mine? I can't." The voice from her mouth is Godwin's, surprising, firm. "And I want my invention to be my own."

Byron shrugs, then sets the stem of the silver pipe between his lips and lifts the candle-flame to the bowl. The black powdery scraps inside begin to bubble, then to smoke. A sweetish steam rises from them and Byron inhales deeply through the pipe stem, then lowers the candle and settles back against the sofa cushions. "Ah." He pinches the pipe between his fingers and holds it immobile in the air.

Mary stares at Shelley. *Look at me,* she pleads silently. But he does not. Clamping the pipe stem in his teeth, he lifts the candle and heats the bowl, his eyes intent on the bubbling black stuff, then draws a single ragged breath. Maybe he'll miss taking in as much of the vapor as Byron has. Maybe his amount is insufficient to rouse the demon. Maybe Polidori will recognize some sort of physicianly responsibility and forbear to light his own pipe so he can be present to his senses if – Mary fights to clear her own head from a sudden darkening at the edges of her sight. But Polidori, too, is setting the silver stem between his lips and lifting the candle. Claire slumps backward in her chair, held in Byron's gaze like a bird before a snake. *Snakes.* With horror Mary feels a panicked conviction rise: a scaly band of amber and black, just like the pythons in Mr. Pidcock's Exhibition of Wild Beasts back in London, is wrapping itself around her heart. Lazily the long muscle tightens around the frantic pink scrap that jumps and pleads in her chest *you're killing me, what of William* – and does not stop, not even when the serpent lifts its spade-shaped head to stare at her and from deep inside its yellow eyes Shelley's demon dances in triumph, waving a knife. *See*, it shouts, *I can go anywhere, and I have found you here.*

I'm thinking of a story, whispers some voice deep in her brain, *in which a dead child comes to life.*

Mary gasps and lurches to her feet. Cold sweat springs from her armpits and soaks her good dark-green dress, which she had made back in England when she and Shelley conceived their William, brother to a tiny baby sister he will never know –

(*That baby of whom she cannot, will not, think –*)

(that trailed-off line still bitten into the page of her abandoned diary, FIND MY BABY DEAD – A MISERABLE DAY---)[8]

(oh, nameless girl – oh, William –)

(Don't think of him or the demon will have him too!)

– before they came here to this city of ancient churches and castles tumbling down a hill into the lake and this house where old mad Madame Diodati wandered, lost, in her rotten black gown that ripped down the seams to flutter from her ribs like the Ancient Mariner's ship of death with its shredded trailing sails, *the nightmare life in death is she –*

A dead child come to life.

Mary stumbles out of the room. Reeling against a table in the hall, she clutches its edge. If this – or worse – is stalking the inside of Shelley's head, he'll go mad. She should drag him out right now, no matter how he fights her, no matter how Byron smirks. But she cannot go back into that room. If she breathes the black air of that room again, she will die. And without her to protect him, William will die too.

William. She will go home to him now. But not until the last shreds of horror clinging to her brain have gone. She will give them a moment to dissipate, like leaves caught and swirled by a sudden wind up to the air and then out to the river that will bear them away.

River. And she is there. The great Thames in its stinking curves, taverns and church spires and the dingy moon of St. Paul's drifting above it. Homely, beloved, infuriating, safe, London unfolds itself in her mind. The Thames rustles in its black glittering bed. And entwined with its rushing, Mary hears a voice. *Come on, my girl, get up.* She knows this voice. Coming from the river itself. Calling her. *Come on, my girl.*

Down the slippery stone steps at low tide she edges, ignoring the bump and scrape of someone's tethered boat, the shimmer of torch and window-light from all the crowded rooms above, the stink of shit and river mud, the dark span of the bridge tramped by hooves and feet and wheels like armies passing on into the night toward a battle that will never end. She steps onto the shingle foot by foot: it's low tide, pebbles crunching, the river lapping and mumbling to itself. She is alone here. Not alone. A woman stands here, skirts drenched, hair half gathered up, half loose and streeling down her back. Some lady mudlark out for pickings. A knife-slashed purse, discarded. A child's china doll, slipped from a sticky hand over the bridge-rail. A sailor's clay pipe flipped into the waves from deck, intact enough to smoke.

But then the woman turns and Mary sees her mother's face. Smudged with dirt and water-straggled hair but glowing underneath with life, pink as the painted cheeks on Mr. Opie's canvas. Her skirts are sodden, ringed with mud the rough cloth has absorbed. Her eyes meet Mary's, her lips upturned in a smile. Mary fights to clear her head. Damned smoke. Damned – But it isn't only smoke that brings her mother to her now. It is the voice inside her own head that taught her to climb onto the chair in Papa's study all those years ago, that said *Hold still. Hold still and use your mental eye.* When the painted brushstrokes broke and swam before her and reassembled themselves into the warm living picture of Mary herself as the small red-faced baby held in her mother's arms – the long chestnut hair tumbling across her mother's breast as it does now, here in the dim river-light – that was no drug. It is no dream. It is the truest place inside herself. It is where words assemble to march forth in search of right things, lonely and brave. It is the place her mother had gone every day, no matter what grief or loss or abandoning man stranded her on another shore. It is where all good things live, memory and honesty and love. Mama is waiting here, for her. *Come on, my girl.*

Mama. Mary's mouth stretches open in a wondering smile, her cheeks cold with tears. She takes one step forward, then another, and enfolds Mama's sturdy figure in her arms. Wiry muscles, small square hands, thick hair coarse and singing as piano wire, a beating heart under the river-cold cloth of stays and shawl and camisole. This is her mother, this warmth, this breath, the smell of Thames and linen in her nose, the firmness and the mercy in those hands. This is her mother, embracing her at last.

Mama releases her slowly, setting one hand on each of Mary's shoulders and standing back. Around her eyes the skin is creased; her rosy lips are chapped with cold. She smiles and turns and takes one step along the waterline, and then another. Mary follows. Pebbles and crockery and oyster shells crunch beneath their feet. *It can't be a dream, can't be the smoke,* argues some corner of Mary's waking mind, *I hear it!* But Mama is turned away from her now, stooping to comb the shingle with her fingers. She flicks some small thing into the river, lifts another and slips it into her skirt pocket. And then she rises with a third thing in her hand and rubs it on her skirt to clear the mud and lifts Mary's palm and presses the thing against it. A cold, round, small thing, gleaming in the river-light. A Roman coin.

Mary brings it close to her eyes. Just bigger than an ordinary shilling, hammered into a ragged round shape like a pie crust more than a thousand years ago. On one side, twiglike clusters that must be words. On the other side, one of the Caesars in profile, cheek blotched by river-rot. This coin fell from some consul's purse back when this place was the muddy pit Londinium, when maps were drawn with sea monsters and blue-faced Celtic Britons haunting the edges of the world, where sea dripped off into empty space. That general had been sent here to subdue their queen, Boudicca of the Iceni. She and her people, like anyone, had been heedless of other existences but their own until war broke their lives open from the inside. Praying to the force that moved the clear blood through the hearts of trees. Sleeping and birthing and making love on heaps of skins in mud huts, around their smoking fires. Tearing out the livers of their enemies and hoisting them on sticks. This was what the Romans found when they invaded, and when they killed Boudicca's husband, the pagan king. They had captured Boudicca as well, and her daughters, beaten her, raped the girls – the oldest no more than thirteen – before her eyes. *Subdue her. Show her who we are.* And she had risen from her bed and brushed her hair until it hung down past her waist and climbed into her chariot and gathered all her husband's men yet living and rode southward into battle and died there, laying about her with a sword to slaughter every Roman she could reach.

This coin had been in someone's pocket then. At a thrust of sword, a stagger backwards, it had been jostled loose to fall and be trodden deep into the muck of the field of battle with its great trees gazing from the hill and all the gods trapped, helpless, in their hearts. And over hundreds of years of winter thaw and frost-heave and rain it had worked itself loose and tumbled into a stream and been washed down into the pull of tides until it came upon the shingle and into her mother's hand.

Boudicca had loved her daughters, had struggled against the laughing soldiers' grip at what they'd forced her to look upon. There could be no greater suffering than this. Your child torn and bleeding. Your child of seven months' birth lying dead in her cradle on an ordinary morning, her lips blue, her tiny starfish fingers open on the air.

The coin presses into Mary's palm, its edges warm. Mama's rueful eyes, their color flickering from hazel into green, stay steady, staring into Mary's own. She will not look away. Because she knows it now. This is love, the terrible and fierce and tender place through which the world can enter you. And remaining alive depends on keeping that place open. No matter what comes through on the back of love, what other kinds of knowledge. Such as this: the world goes on regardless of yourself. Small things are made and lost and sifted through the sieve of accident and weather to wash up in a stranger's hands long after people's bones have melted into earth. Calamity of war or flood or volcano or plague breaks over towns and families in a flood more terrible for not being recognized as anything but terror at the time. Only later does it become *history*, that neutered string of slate-scratched names and dates. Only those following the dead and dying in their desire and their rage, flushed with the hope and arrogance of blood in their living veins, can call the flow of time *history* and delude themselves they're safe from it. And only the writer will be left to tell.

On the coin the head of Caesar wavers. Curls sprout and throng toward the edge. The profile sharpens, delicate and fierce. And Caesar becomes Boudicca, queen of the realm that once had been, the realm of what might be. The dull beaten silver becomes gold, with a deep luster like living skin. Against Mary's palm the coin grows warm, and pulses. One. Two. Three. Time is moving forward here and always in this place of dream and hope and remembering, where armies stumble and rage, where queens vow vengeance, where tree-gods summon water from the earth and transform it into air, where only the river will always be the same. This is the place that makes art, that makes words and memory, that makes the truest things.

Mama lifts Mary's hand and presses her fingers against Queen Boudicca's chiseled face. Her smile is loving, rueful. She puts her arms around Mary and holds her. The breeze lifts strands of her long hair and pastes them to Mary's cheek. And then she turns away and walks into the river. *Wait,* Mary stutters, *don't leave me* – But Mama does not turn back. The river touches her skirt-hem, wicks itself into the cloth and climbs. It reaches her knees, and then her hips. Each step a deeper splashing noise, a pause of seeking footing further in. Her shawl-fringe touches the current and trails toward the east. *Stay with me,* Mary pleads from the shore. *Mama. Please stay here.* But Mama is out in the current now, her long hair eddying around her. Into the dark water, glittering with all its shore-flung light, Mama's square shoulders, then the round shape of her uplifted head, disappear. Mary strains to pin her gaze to the spot but cannot identify the moment when her mother goes away from her for good.

She raises her head and stares into the gold-framed mirror above the hall table. The features of the person staring back – white round forehead, hair straggling from its pins, eye-pupils round and black – cannot be assembled into any picture she recognizes. Around her the Villa Diodati rustles and hums, each room and each forgotten drawer a separate chamber of some half-indifferent brain: the wine cellar where rat tails trace patterns on dusty bottle-flanks, the bedrooms with their ceiling-canopies of gathered silk into which woman after woman once looked without looking, clasping a man's heaving weight against her hips, the attic trunks where lacy christening gowns and tiny knitted socks lie yellowing to dust. From the door beyond her, Byron's voice burbles, low and confidential, and laughter bursts behind it: Claire's anxious giggle and Polidori's chortle and a high gurgle that must be Shelley, close to some edge over which she should not let him tumble now. But she can't go back into that room. All down her ribs her dress clings to her, sticky and cold. Tightening her shawl around herself, she strides to the heavy front door and opens it enough to set herself free.

The space between morning and night is moist and loud with frog-song and a single bird. Where the sky touches the dark line of the mountains, a faint pale line glows. Far out on the lake, a lantern bobs: some fisherman at work. The world is still here, beyond the villa with its black-smoke dreams. Mary breathes deeply, flooded with gratitude. That little boat will draw up at Geneva city docks in an hour or two and the fisherman will haul his basket over to the ranks of tables waiting under their canvas tents, sluice yesterday's dried scales and blood away with a bucket of water, and temptingly arrange the fat shining fish, their red gills gaped wide to trap the fatal air. And this morning, she will go buy a fish for William's dinner.

Down the muddy path she edges, toward the house in which her child sleeps. A flickering animal shape crosses her path, then stops to peer at her: a fox, its eyes curious, its tail held high. She steps forward and with a rustle the fox vanishes into the high grass. Has she seen it? Has any of this been real? She remembers the cobblestones of Fleet Street underneath her ragged boot-soles, the shrewd eyes of the flame-red London fox trotting toward its hidden den. *What are you going to do about it, girl?* She closes her hand and opens it. Against her palm still burns the coin of some lost emperor who believed that he would never die, an emperor who, in her mother's dream, has been transformed into a queen.

Mary wakes from the dream with her whole body clutched into a single sharp point. Her mouth strains open on no sound. The moon hangs full and gray in the window, starkening the room with its light. Three o'clock, maybe four. Gripped by the dream, Mary gasps. Is she awake right now? She can't be sure.

In the dream, a tall man leaned over her, plucking her insides apart with a knife. She was the body on that table and she was the dream-vision watching the doctor at work, his straining back under a stained smock upturned to her from where she hovered near the ceiling, looking down. He had stolen her, stolen it, stolen the body from its grave. Huddled with Shelley on the steps of St. Sepulchre's she had seen the resurrectionists, edging across the square with the tall man in their wagon. That single giant hand dangling from under the canvas, fingers curling up.

Mary's waking shock has tipped Shelley toward the waking edge of his own dream, in which he now begins to seek her, eyes flickering behind their veined luminous lids. With thigh and hip and the sharp sudden warmth where his nightshirt is rucked up around his waist, he comes to her like Jupiter to Io in a cloud, surrounding her as the dream has done. Melted-into, she enfolds him. At the familiar joining-place there is no urgency, only a pulse, floating her deeper into a place that is neither waking nor dream and holding her there until she knows that she will die if she does not rip out of herself the gasping growling shout that is roiling up but that she cannot loose because to do so will be to wake them both and lose the dream. She will not open her eyes. She knits both hands deep into Shelley's hair and closes her fingers to clasp in place the last scraps of the dream fluttering, vanishing, melting from them both. The delicious explosion, the wrench and fall, Shelley panting, his lips travelling her face, finding her eyes still closed. And into sleep she drops again as heavy as a stone, her body heating and curling itself around something that was not there before: a glaze of moonlight on a patch of moistened skin. A wrinkled palm, unfolding. A single eye opening on a darkness, its pupil and iris all one shade of deep, bewildered black.

She doesn't write of it at first. First there is William to lift murmuring from his cradle and nuzzle and change and dress. Shelley kisses them both as if nothing at all happened in the Villa Diodati last night. Did he actually smoke the little silver pipe with its curling black shards in the bowl? This morning, the deep-blue light of his eyes is clear and sane, a little preoccupied. His shirt is fresh, his curls, as usual, sluiced with water then tumbled into place with a thrust and shake of his fingers at the roots. "Lets the thoughts rise," he laughs, "straight up from my head." Now he smooths William's blonde hair and follows Mary as she bears their son downstairs. So there will be no talk of Diodati. All right, then.

The stove is lit, and Elise is out on the patio with the washtub. She catches Mary's eye through the window, but Mary waves her away: *I'll get the breakfast.* And there are the eggs and milk, waiting on the table: ordinary, marvelous things, haloed in the last light of the dream. Mary sets the iron skillet on the stove to warm. She sets six eggs gently into a bowl of water, watching, with satisfaction, as they sink – this means freshness, with the yolk still plump and floating in its place inside the shell. Then she cracks them one by one into another bowl and whisks them with a fork. She carves off a curl of butter from the butter-jar with a knife and flicks it into the skillet, where it bubbles and grows pale. Just before it browns, she pours the golden soup of egg into the pan. Ropes of yolk swirl and settle and thicken. In a jolt, the image of the dream stirs and quickens between her belly and her brain, behind her heart. It's a live thing, stirring and murmuring, and it wants words. It will magnetize those words to itself with its own weight, like the top of the great sleeping earth draws a compass-needle. *Here. Here's where you go. Lift your pen and I will tell you what I want to be.*

She mustn't burn the eggs, mustn't startle whatever this thing is inside. Carefully, carefully, nudge the edge of a turning-fork under the opaque white and yellow mass to keep it from crusting along the rim, lift the pan to ease the pressure of the heat, slide the fork back and forth through the eggs that will in a moment be food for husband and child and self, let self be lost in the strange tug of the story inside that is implanting, latching on, settling, working itself deeper in, thickening like the long strings of egg cracked and spilled out into the world from which until that moment they have been hidden in secret –

Just as the egg is stiffening toward the overcooked state Shelley will grumble about and possibly refuse to eat, Mary tips the skillet and slides the eggs into a bowl, dolloping another curl of butter onto them, then fluffing them with a fork. "Mmmm," Shelley says, tugging William upright in his basket. "Eggs, old man!" William crows and waves his hands. Grinning, Shelley clinks his spoon on his plate. "Food!" he roars like a Viking. "We are hungry!"

"Silly," Mary smiles. She scoops out two heaps of eggs onto plates and sets one in front of Shelley, then carries the second plate to her own seat, next to William's basket. He's just taking solid food now, which Elise says is normal for a six-months' child. "Look!" she encourages, spooning up a fragment of egg and popping it into her own mouth. "Good!" William's eyes follow the spoon back to the plate, and he squirms with excitement, opening his lips like a bird. "And!" Mary slips the egg-laden spoon into his mouth and draws it away clean. "Egg!"

Elise reenters the kitchen. Just before she closes the door, she casts a look backwards at the gray morning sky and frowns. Another gloomy day.

"The eggs are good, Elise," Mary says. "Thank you."

A smile flickers under Elise's frown. "I had to pay more for them than last week," she says. "The man with the hens, he tells me he burns lanterns in the hen-house in the daytime to keep the light so the hens will lay their eggs. These are darker days than he has seen before. No one knows what else to do. For the lanterns, then, he has to buy more oil and he has to pay a boy to watch them so the henhouse doesn't burn. So the price of eggs goes up."

"Exploitation," Shelley declares. "The rich always take advantage of the poor, they –"

"Shelley," Mary says, "a chicken farmer's not exactly rich." Can't he see that? She looks at him again. There is his wet hair drying in its usual tousled shapes, nothing in his eyes of last night or of the silver pipes, nothing but indignation he considers righteous. He didn't see her fear as Byron taunted her with the candle and the scraps of that black stuff in the bowl. He's outside this space she's entering right now. Almost too soft to hear, the voice inside her speaks: *don't speak of me, let me grow in private. All right,* she whispers back. *I'll be with you soon.*

After breakfast, birdsong-racket fills the trees and robins hop after worms through the grass. Maybe the sun will come out this morning after all. A rosy light filters through the gray layers of cloud, accompanied by pale platinum streaks of what might become sun. Shelley gathers up his papers and lead pencil, moving toward the door to the small back garden patio. "The lines are here this morning," he declares, "I feel them, they –"

Just as he reaches the door, a handful of fat raindrops splash against the window and the would-be sunlight fades as if someone has yanked down a curtain. "Damnation," Shelley mutters. He swings his gaze wildly around the kitchen. "I'm tired of being shut indoors. Maybe if I call its bluff, the rain will…" He grins at Mary, squares his shoulders, and sallies forth through the door onto the patio. Settling himself in a chair, he twists his long thin legs around one another, hooks his right foot behind his left calf, and props paper and pencil on his right knee. "Now."

"Shelley," Mary protests, "you'll –" But the birdsong is loud all over the hillside: a lilt and flutter of notes that tilt upward like a question, an insistent repeated squawk, the murmur of little birds all underneath. A summery ghost of damp grass – this is June, after all – reaches her nose. Perhaps he'll be just fine. And anyway –

"I'm going upstairs to work," she tells Elise, "you have him?" Sliding the egg-streaked plates over one another in the dishpan, Elise nods. On a blanket on the floor, William wobbles happily on his stomach, lifting one hand in front of his face and staring at it with wonder. "Yes," she says. "*Bon courage.*"

On the landing, at the desk, Mary sits and opens her writing box. She must be quick. Following the dream, the words are massing as they haven't for days. Knowledge shimmers around the image of the single open eye; only writing the words, one by one, will unfold it. She mustn't be frightened by her own desire for perfection. She mustn't hesitate. Get words onto the page as the nails and splinters of something to be later rebuilt. Hasn't Godwin said it a hundred times? "Perfectionism is for the amateur, who can afford to fondle every single word. The author who would make a living, who would actually accomplish something, must –"

She brushes her father's voice out of her head and begins to write.

It was on a dreary night of November that I beheld my man completed; and with an anxiety that almost amounted to agony, I collected instruments of life around me, and endeavored to infuse a spark of being into the lifeless thing that lay at my feet. It was already one in the morning, the rain pattered dismally against the window frames and my candle was nearly burnt out when by the glimmer of the half-extinguished light I saw the dull yellow eye of the creature open – It breathed hard and a convulsive motion agitated its limbs.[9]

It has hold of her now, the image gifted by the dream and all the clouds of meaning trailing it (Wordsworth? Brush that other voice away, too, it doesn't matter), the bewildered open eye, the strange knowledge that has seized her: that eye belongs to a made creature, and the voice she hears is its maker.

But how can I describe my emotion at this catastrophe, or how delineate the wretch whom with such infinite pains and care I had endeavored to form. The limbs were in proportion and I had selected his features as handsome. Handsome, Great God! His yellow skin scarcely covered the work of muscles and arteries beneath, his hair was flowing and his teeth of a pearly whiteness but their luxuriousness only formed a more horrid contrast with his watery eyes that seemed almost of the same color as the dun white sockets in which they were set –[10]

A slash of rain on the window-glass jolts her up from the page. Through the streaming blur of it she peers into the garden below. Shelley still sits there on the little iron chair, head bent over the page, resolute. Through his stringy draggling hair, his scalp shows white; his shirt plasters itself to his back. Useless to write when the ink is washed away by the rain, when the paper itself will melt under his hand. What is he thinking?

She reaches for the windowsill and stops. The rain will come in on the floor and she'll have to either go fetch a rag or mop it with the hem of her own dress and then endure the damp slap against her ankles for the rest of the day in the chilly house where even the burning braziers in the attic take hours to heat the trousers and petticoats and diapers hanging from their strung lines under the eaves, barely separated by a layer of shingle from the constant rain, gradually growing the faint dismal smell of mildew. Either way she will have been teased away from the page by her own restless mind. By that nervous never-not-present warning: *the dishes! the unmade bed! the dirty floor!* By that part of her always leaning toward Shelley like a woman listening to a child's voice from a distant room. *Dependence,* Mama would surely say, bred into a woman's habits like the hollow where the collar rests on a cart-horse's neck. A woman can come to depend for her purpose even on the distractions she claims to spurn. Being a writer is retraining yourself for a different purpose. Remaining in your seat and meeting your daily quotient of words. *The mind is its own place, and itself can make a hell of heaven...* Like Odysseus sailing past the Sirens, she must lash herself to the mast, stop her ears. And Shelley must look to himself.

Here is her beloved writing box, companioning her all the way from Skinner Street to the Continent, twice over. Here are the sentences before her on the page. Here is the unknown voice at her elbow, polite and insistent. *Ahem.* She will not betray them. Again, she lifts her pen.

But how can I describe my emotion at this catastrophe, or how delineate the wretch whom with such infinite pains and care I had endeavored to form. The limbs were in proportion and I had selected his features as handsome. Handsome, Great God![11]

A thump and squelch of footsteps up the stairs and Shelley is behind her. She turns to look up at him just as a chill raindrop slides down one curl and splashes onto her face. "Alas," he says cheerfully, "the elements prevail." He peers at her page. "Hmm. Catastrophe?"

"No!" she protests, laying her forearm over the page. "Don't read. You're all wet!"

Shelley grins and kisses the top of her head, then squelches away, humming. The footsteps stop and she hears him clutch the banister, brace himself, then give a mighty sneeze. Lovely. Now he'll be laid up on the sopha with a cold –

But he chose, says the factual voice inside her, *to go sit in the rain like a madman.*

She removes her arm from the page and looks at the words. Thankfully, the ink has been just dry enough not to smear onto her sleeve. *Close your eyes,* Mary badgers herself. *Concentrate. Can you see?*

The pale student of unhallowed arts. The words arrive and Mary scribbles them. Pale man with long knobby shaking hands and a shirt stained with scorchmarks and blood as Shelley's shirts are stained with ink. Pale man drawing a needle and thread carefully through flesh. A heap of flesh under a sheet like that thrown over meat in the Smithfield market to keep off flies. And from under that sheet dangles a hand, large as the hand of the stolen body Mary and Shelley had spotted that night in St. Sepulchre's churchyard.

He is building – He is building a –

Under that sheet, where a face would be, breathing stirs. Rising and falling. Denting the cloth with moist breath like Shelley's when in the bed in the inn that first night of freedom at Calais – just escaped from Skinner Street, never again to be cold, never again to be lonely – she had covered him, then inched the sun-smelling linen downward, kissing from hairline to nose to mouth.

A shroud. The cloth had been pulled over the nameless baby's soft round forehead, then her eyes, and Mary had turned away so nothing could be printed on her brain that would be called *the last sight of her child.*

Claire's avid face in the attic candlelight at Skinner Street scanned the paper – *the body of the murderer, attempting to revive...*

What has made her think of this? What sort of woman would imagine –

He is building a –

The heap of flesh beneath his hand is very large. It wants only life.

Peel back the sheet and look.

Apply the vital fluid and see if it –

"For heaven's sake, Mary," Godwin snaps, "get on with it."

He is building a man. A man come back to life but larger than any other born thing.

Her nameless first baby came forth as a figure in wax, a bundle of stick limbs with a head attached, screaming, coated and slick and yellowish (*vernix caseosa,* that's the name for it). Kneaded out of shape by its brutal ordinary twist through Mary's body and its gate of bone. Blood pushed against the surface of the face, the ceiling of the fragile skull, the puffy red swelling of the genitals, *can this thing be a girl?*

(Mary remembers it now, all of it) –

— this terrifying thing that yet aroused such fierce grieving desire, such yearning –

Pale student of unhallowed arts snatches back the sheet and as the rain lashes at the window high above – *dark, it's surely dark, I see the candle lit* – the being on the table shudders the world into its lungs in one great gasp and opens its eyes.

No, not eyes. Just one. Its face not working properly, the being blinks and droops and hitches and drools. But that one eye – its iris bruised and purple-brown, ringed black – is open on the world for good.

Poor creature. How will life fall into that brain, write on that soul? If soul it has?

Same as life does for everyone. Stretch one large hand toward the fire, toward the door, toward the blurred face, toward the voice. And see what answers you. What voice. What sensation. What pain.

Poor creature. The making of him began with good intentions. She is sure of that.

I had selected his features as – Carefully Mary scratches through the word *handsome* and replaces it with *beautiful*.

Now the rain has let up. She wraps herself in her shawl and slips out the back door, walking along the spine of the hill above Lake Geneva, under the sullen sky. With each step, knowledge gathers, and the story takes shape.

All of London knows how the anatomists work. John Hunter in his two great houses linked by the passage between parlor and laboratory is only the most famous of them, in the city where flesh is for sale. They haunt the sideshows and the burying grounds for monsters and marvels: the Irish Giant, the Sicilian Dwarf, the young wife wrapped in the same soft winding-sheet with her baby, its small face tucked against her neck. They know what to do. Slip coins into dirty hands and steal the corpse and back the wagon to your cellar door and slide your goods into the dark. Cut it up as careful as a chicken – careful not to crack the joints, those masterworks of weight and counterweight you'll study like Leonardo in his Florence attic. Slip what is left of the naked flayed thing into the pickling fluid and put it in a cabinet and lock the door. And then sluice your hands in a basin and towel them dry and go off to open a living woman's womb and draw forth a baby like a heart drawn from its chest. Hold it to the light. Look, see the chambers here. See how it breathes and moves and screams. See how fiercely it clings to life –

Here on this threshing-floor that makes us all so fierce. Dante had it: the wide threshing-floor that is the world itself.

Monster is only a medical term. Before leaving for the Continent, when she was newly pregnant with William, Shelley took her to visit his doctor, William Lawrence, who was famous for the contents of his laboratory and the contours of his daring. He'd dissected the spine of a hanged man, opening the bundle of silver cables on which the vertebrae were strung (*the spinal cord is fibrous,* Shelley says, *like the strings of a violin bow – a single string, made of many.*) And now all the images come crowding in. The living human tooth grafted into the living comb of a rooster, perfused with blood. The dead Ethiopian's leg grafted onto the white man's cancerous, amputated stump. That feat was performed by Cosmas and Damian, patron surgeon-saints of Ingolstadt. Where – she knows it now – her own pale student of unhallowed arts will learn his trade. *Anachronistic,* Godwin would nag. *You're confusing dates.* But Mary brushes her father away. Why not surrender voluptuously to her story, let it magnetize all the images and sounds and bloody bits it wants into a shape that suits its own intelligent will? Why not make all of it her own?

(*I am making a book, Father, such as you never could.*)

(*Father, did you sleep on Mama's grave? To protect her from the resurrection men? I'll never know, will I?*)

Lawrence met them at his front door that day, drying his hands on a towel. Short and capable, with a wide mouth and thick, messy salt-and-pepper hair, he nodded at Shelley and smiled at Mary. "If you will be so kind as to wait, for just an instant," he said.

Accordingly, Mary wandered into the back garden, where a barefoot boy, no more than eight or nine, dressed in a pale linen shirt and brown knee breeches, sat under a mulberry tree with a book in his lap. A marmalade cat curled against his thigh, flicking its tail. "Hello," Mary offered, approaching, "what's that book you have there?"

The boy raised his face to her, and Mary bit the inside of her cheek to hold back a gasp. The boy's entire head was misshapen in a way Mary had not known a head could be. His large, light brown eyes were set far back behind his nose, and his brow slanted steeply away from her under a thin fluff of hair. The collar of his white shirt brushed his chin. Otherwise he looked like any other boy, knuckly dirty hands with bitten nails, coarse breeches, bare feet with long toes. He thrust the book at Mary and blinked. He wanted her to sit down, she realized, and read to him.

And so, in the afternoon sun, Mary had lowered herself and her pregnant-with-William belly into the grass and opened the book: a little story about a family of birds. The boy sat next to her, his gaze averted, his hand sunk deep in the orange cat's fur. "The robin family lived at the very top of the tree...." Mary's voice wobbled, steadied. "And then one day, the smallest robin decided to seek his fortune..." Suddenly the back door banged open and Shelley ran straight across the lawn to them. "Monster!" he had shouted, "Mary, don't let him touch you!" Lawrence, right behind Shelley, had calmed him with a stern glance and, of course, an explanation. And now, as Mary paces the ridge of the high hill above Lake Geneva, Lawrence's voice unspools in her head, winding itself like a bright thread around a spindle as her story gathers it into its own hands, loop by satisfied loop.

Oh, "monster" is only the medical term. In the field of anatomy and physiology – I have just begun to write of this – a monster is simply a creature in whom the body in general, or some large and conspicuous part of it, deviates remarkably from the accustomed formation.[12] *It might be called the term for a child of nature in her, shall we say, sportive moods. However cruel those moods may seem to us, as cruel as Tom Tabby over there.* (Lawrence had pointed at the orange cat huddling behind the bee-skep, watching a sparrow peck the gravel path). *But ours is merely one point of view. Christopher has another, although he cannot tell us it. His fondness for Tom Tabby is perhaps ironic. For note how the eyes, when viewed in connection with the retreating surface of the head, give to the whole a striking resemblance to the head of a cat, so that the fetuses have been called in Germany* katzen-kopfe, *cat's heads. Much of the brain is simply absent, the rest deficient. No one has charted the full possible length of such a life. And yet, Christopher has been with me some time. Eight years, in fact.*

Poor creature, Mary had blurted. But Lawrence had looked puzzled. *Poor? Only from one point of view, perhaps. He likes his friend Tom Tabby, and Mrs. Trimmer's robins, and a kindly voice. He seeks the interchange of human sympathies. As do we all. It is an old wives' tale that such productions of nature as Christopher may be called have anything to do with what the mother sees or doesn't see, fears or doesn't fear. They don't. Think about it. With most such children, the hour of their birth is also the hour of their death. Yet should any such child live, the mother is eager to find some reason, eager to attribute any cause, to what has befallen her. What human being can live in such unknowing guilt, and, thus, in such fear?* Maternal impression, *the fallacy is called. A hare jumped from under a hedge as I walked. I was frightened by a rabid dog. And thus my child came forth in animal shape. Who wouldn't seek to know a cause?*

And therefore, Mary thinks as she walks, a woman takes that cause upon herself. *Maternal impression.* Something I touched, ate, saw, drank, distilled unwittingly through my own body into my child's. Something I let pass the portals of my sight. *Control the gaze* is the injunction to nuns and women, or what happens to you will be your fault. What your child becomes: that is your fault too. *Maternal impression*: birth a child and watch your body dissolve to a circle of wax, yielding and tender with the terrible vulnerability of love, stamped by the thousands of chances and accidents entirely beyond your control.

It's interesting. Lawrence had paused, peering at Mary. *For reasons unknown, most of the children with Christopher's condition are female.* He paused again, taken by a thought. *Monsters; that's the term we're taught to use. But I like your own term better. Creature.* He smiled. And as Mary followed him inside, Christopher had slipped through the door behind them and disappeared down the hall, the green-backed book still clutched in his hand.

That boy was not a creature with no portal to the world. Perhaps no creature ever is. Perhaps each creature feels, yearns, loves.

Does the pale student ever feel pity for them, his cut creatures, the flayed beasts on the table? As he separates the nerves of the arm to thread them back together around a stronger hand, as he teases the tip of the probe between the long bands of muscle – pinkish-blue with death and cold, but veins intact – touching the bone, scraping it, does he flinch? Does he pause?

For Mary knows he does not stop.

The flayed face on the table looks up at him with its one whole eye. Through the hole in the cheek its teeth are bared.

Have a care, Frankenstein! (Here is that name, just when she needs it, her brain handing to her the moment in the ruins above the Rhine.) *Life is dear to me and I will defend it.*[13]

From deep in her brain, the chill voice speaks: *You thought, Father, that I was just a girl.*

Pale student of unhallowed arts Victor Frankenstein cuts a human body open and stitches it back together in a different shape and shocks it into life to see how it will work. To study it. And then it becomes a creature that can study him.

The creature is walking out there now. Surely it is watching Mary too, catching her sidelong in the roving bewildered gleam of its dark bruised eye, in its searching gaze, which is sharpening now toward intelligence. Consciousness. Cunning. And grief. All the aspects of itself it has been waiting for her to see, so that she can write them down.

Come up to dine at Diodati, Byron's note says, casually. So they do. As the big dog rushes forward to greet them, Mary's face stiffens at the animal fug rising from the carpets and the wide floorboards, which are scored now with the long scrabbles of claws. Byron smiles. "I let him out at night," he observes. "Keeps the French bitches away." Polidori is bent over a lap desk, writing. Claire's face is feverish, bright, her hands clenched against her peacock-blue dress which – Mary can't stop a flashing glance up and down – fits differently, bosom overflowing just a bit more, waist not quite so— In a distant room, some other animal rattles its cage.

"You've been rearranging, old man," says Shelley cheerfully, surveying the great hall: now the leather Chesterfield sopha hulks before the veranda windows, its back to the front door, so that anyone sitting in it can contemplate the lake and the endless rain.

"Yes," Claire volunteers, "we love to sit and watch the fishermen, don't we, B?"

Byron turns, stares at her, and takes a step away. "What's my name?" His voice is ominously soft. "What's my name, again?"

"What are you writing, Dr. Polidori?" Mary cuts in to avert her sudden, dismal vision of an evening lowered over by Byron's storm-cloud pique. There's no point in letting herself be angry at him, since that anger can have no outlet around Polidori, his forehead by now crimped in a perpetual anxious frown, or Claire, smiling forcibly, or Shelley, grinning at Byron and his sopha as if nothing at all is amiss.

Polidori looks up, startled by his own delight at being noticed. "That idea of the vampire that we talked about," he blurts. "I thought I'd try a sto–"

"He's writing his usual report to my publisher." Byron keeps his eyes fixed on Mary. His breath is red with wine although no wineglass is in sight. "Murray pays him like a goddamn Venetian state spy. Like a goddamn tool of the Doges. Like a goddamn Medici assassin."

"Italy has been much on our minds lately," Polidori chirps. "We have been thinking of removing there."

"No *we* about it," Byron snaps. "Just one English milord bored out of his mind."

"Pandaemonium," Claire blurts. "Which way I fly is hell, myself am hell."

Amazingly, Byron turns to her. "And quiet," he agrees, "to quick bosoms, is a hell."

"Putting yourself next to Milton," Shelley jokes. "Well done."

"That's where he belongs," declares Claire. "*Childe Harold* is a very great poem."

"Flatterer," says Byron, but nevertheless he smiles and leads Shelley away. Mary starts to follow them, but Claire catches her arm. "I saw you looking," she hisses. Her cheeks are red. "Yes, I am with child. And he knows."

"What?" Mary stammers, but Claire has already dropped her arm and marched away, smiling at the two men who are seating themselves in the deep sopha, murmuring about something Mary can't hear. "You wouldn't credit," she calls, "how cozy that couch is when it rains." With playful effort, she inserts herself onto Byron's lap. Byron looks at her, and at Mary, then at Shelley, whose ears have turned red with embarrassment he's straining to hide. "Beautiful Turkish boy," he says conversationally. "Had a cock like a fucking Clydesdale. A seventh wonder of the world."

"Oh!" Clare squeals, pretending to slap him.

Byron's face darkens and he pushes Claire off his lap. "I never asked you here, you know," he says. Snatching an empty wineglass from the floor next to the couch, he strides to the decanter without looking back. Mary stands, pinned by the knowledge that there's nothing she can say. *Did God exist*, her father's voice echoes in her, wryly, *you'd be prudent to thank Him for sparing you the nature of an ordinary girl.*

As soon as Mary nudges open the wooden door of the watchmaker's shop, she is caught and cosseted by the velvety chorus of clocks. Each set of hands points to twenty-nine minutes after ten, one hand up and one down like two halves of a crooked mustache. Here and there, a blue and gold constellation-map turns beneath the hands, tracking the worlds beyond this ordinary day. Grandfather clocks – one almost touching the ceiling – stand ranged along the back wall and along a corridor leading to a hidden room. Someone is sitting at a table back there, drinking tea; she can hear the rattle of chair legs on uneven floorboards, then the bright *ting* of cup-edge back into its dish. On the counter is a small square wooden mantel-clock with a silvery face, just large enough that she needs both hands to lift it. Such a clock would be useful for her, helping to mark the point in the morning when she can launch away from the shore of *chores* and into the deep water of words.

"Ah, oui," a voice calls from the back room. "Moment." Uneven steps rise and tilt along the corridor. The guts of the big clocks rumble and chime as the floor quivers and an old man comes forth into the front room, jerking his chin upwards to see Mary plain. White hair drifts from his pink scalp. One eyelid droops over a shrunken, cloudy sliver of gray; the other eye, a large, brilliant blue, fixes on Mary. He straightens the cuffs of his rusty black coat and folds his long hands neatly in front of him. "Vous voudrez de l'aide, Madame?"

Mary stumbles toward the French for *I'm only looking,* but at that moment, every clock in the room reaches the half-hour at once. A massive foresty slithering and rustling of springs rises, and then one single note rings from a hundred clocks: a choir of strikes and chimes, bass to treble, brass to tin. Mary's ears buzz. "All at once," she blurts, smiling, once the shimmer of the strikes has faded from the air. "How do you stand it?"

The old man nods and tucks his chin toward his chest. She's spoken English, Mary realizes too late, floundering – *arrogant foreigners, come here and don't even know our language.* But the man is smiling. "It is not so much noise," he offers, "when you are in the shop every day. And better when all the clocks are together. More –" he lifts his long hands and shapes some invisible container in the air – "beautiful."

Every working man is a philosopher, Godwin would say, *with a metaphysics of his trade. Ask and you will learn of it.* What invisible wheels and gears can this one-eyed watchmaker detect, turning behind the curtain of ordinary sight? Behind him hangs a glass-fronted box full of watches, arranged in concentric rings. Large gentlemen's pocket-watches circle smaller ones, which circle the smallest watch of all: a gold and ivory face dangling upside-down from a clip shaped like a ribbon bow, meant to be pinned to a woman's dress.

Fanny. Her birthday has passed this spring – May 14, almost two months back – and Mary has completely forgotten it. Fanny is trapped back on Skinner Street with Godwin and Mrs. Vile because Mary has floated away to the Continent with Shelley on their raft of Sir Timothy's post-obit loans, just as if she were the only rational Wollstonecraft daughter dreaming of love. Fanny didn't get to go to the Continent or to Dundee or even to the horrid school at Ramsgate. *She didn't seize experi-*

ence, argues Mary to herself, *I did.* Yet if Fanny had awakened on that morning two years ago and pleaded, like Claire, to come with her, would Mary have said yes? Probably not. She flinches, then rallies, as guilt descends. *Can't take charge of everyone's happiness. Just my own. I was sixteen, I was just –*

What ever faults I may have I am not sordid or vulgar, Fanny has written, in one of the letters Mary has not answered. *I love you for your selves alone. I endeavour to be as frank to you as possible that you may understand my real character. I understand from Mamma that I am your laughing stock – and the constant beacon of your satire.*[14]

Grief tears Mary at the thought of her sister, a grief on the obverse of which glows terrible need (*but I could not let Shelley pass from me, could not be without him.*) Like a woman on a tightrope she wobbles, grasping the firmness of anger to pull herself upright against the weary, guilty headwind of *home*. Of course Mrs. Vile (so Fanny calls her *Mamma* now?) is spreading rumor and dissension, dropping, like Hamlet's uncle Claudius, poison in the ear of one who cannot move away. Fanny too is the daughter of Mary Wollstonecraft. Fanny too is a rational woman, clinging even in her letters to Mama's words: *I have determined never to live to be a disgrace to such a mother. I have found that if I will endeavour to overcome my faults I shall find being's to love and esteem me.*[15]

Superfluous apostrophe, whispers Mary's brain. And that's the pattern of things, isn't it? Fanny writing, reaching, pleading, Mary vaguely bored and irritated, twisting away from her clutching hands. *The dreadful state of mind I generally labour under & which I in vain endeavour to get rid of...*[16] Well, Fanny, don't we all feel so sometimes. I've lost a child. I'm trying to rear another. I'm writing a book. I'm making a home. Look to yourself.

But this is not the honest way of things, is it? Fanny is sad because she has been left behind by Mary, the sister she loves, and who claims to love her.

"Permit me," murmurs the watchmaker. He unlatches the glass door and swings it open and removes the watch to place in Mary's hands. The edges of the bow-shaped pin are tarnished with touching. So is the rounded case, where the hands, suspended upside-down, now read, faithfully, twenty-five minutes till eleven. The old man sighs. "It is well made," he volunteers. "Here in Geneva, we know the craft. Even in such times..." Mary can see that, like the little wooden mantel-clock, this watch has been brought here to exchange for money long spent, money that must have gone for food in this cold-blasted spring. And this man surely needs money now.

"I will buy this," Mary hears herself saying, "to send to my sister for a gift. Back in England. And" – she yields to the impulse – "this little wooden one, too." It will fit so well over the fireplace, and she does want a clear marker of time, more than Shelley's *later* or Byron's *sometime this evening.* These clocks won't cost much. Shelley's been apprehensive, but now relieved: *the annuity will be deposited. Father is amenable, for now.*

The old man smiles, turning his single-eyed blue gaze firmly on Mary. "I believe she will be pleased," he says. "This belonged to a lady of quality. And it is something good, to give a loved one a gift of time." He wraps the gold-bow watch in cloth and places it in a small velvet box. "Time will move," he muses. "The matter is, we will move with it? Yes, no? Not let it run away, like horse and carriage, with each of us trapped inside. Will we sit inside or on the coachman box? Will we be the driver or the passenger?"

In Mary's palm the round gold weight remains, even after the small velvet box has been packed for sending across the Channel, even after she has wandered back along the lakeside road to Montalegre and up the hill to her own house and set the little wooden clock – now hers – on the parlor mantelpiece above the fire. "He is sailing," Elise volunteers, "with Lord Byron." Mary nods and drops onto the couch and closes her eyes and loses herself in a fervid blurred dream where the hands of a clock on the wall of a room – a room where something terrible has happened, a room where shining instruments lie arrayed, a room where a girl has just departed – is permanently stopped at ten minutes till seven o'clock.

At dusk, Mary climbs the hill to Diodati. Since Shelley and Byron have been sailing all day, she girds herself for the faint Byron-ness – the sharper edge to his charm – that seems to seep into Shelley whenever he's spent any time in Byron's company. Like a child with a disreputable playmate. But to forbid him that playmate's company is to make him want it more. Mustn't pester. Mustn't drive her man away.

Byron and Polidori are out on the balcony, dancing. No, fighting. This must be pugilism, the gentleman's delight, which Byron reads about in his big green *Boxiana* book. Each wears thick gray gloves, with which they swipe at each other like bears: Polidori flailing, Byron leaning back and in, jabbing with his left arm and then his right. Deliberately, he clips

Polidori over the ear. "Move!" he barks. "You're meant to be following me, goddammit! Pick up your feet!" Balanced on the railing, two of Madame Diodati's thick wineglasses glint in the cloudy light. Shelley must be down in the cellar, fetching another bottle. She waves at them and smiled. Byron yanks Polidori against his chest, glares, then thrusts him away. Polidori reels back and lifts one arm gallantly into the air. "Permit me to escort thee," he calls, in a voice loosened on its hinges with drink and Byron's clip on the ear. Before she can stop him, he hoists himself over the balcony railing and jumps. He hits the ground badly and hard. His ankle folds beneath him and she hears the faint tear, like the husk being ripped from corn.

"Oh, hell." Byron's voice is cross, dismayed. He limps hurriedly around the corner of the balcony, calling for Shelley and Fletcher. Mary rushes forward. "Stop," Polidori gasps. He leans sideways and vomits neatly into the grass, his face white in the gloom.

By the time Fletcher has bandaged Polidori's ankle and settled him in bed with a supper tray and a drop of laudanum under his tongue – "that ankle," he sighs, "it'll be talking to him in a few hours" – and Shelley and Byron and Claire and Mary have picked over the cold chicken and bread that they've rustled from the kitchen, it's completely dark. Together, they settle onto the big Chesterfield in front of the window. The cloud-shrouded lake and the long spine of mountain behind it are lost, with only a scattering of lights on the opposite shore. Even though Shelley's shoulder is pressed cozily to Byron's, he reaches out to take Mary's hand and nestle it against his thigh; he is hers again, darting and sweet. "We've decided," he says, "that we should go see Mont Blanc. The road to Chamonix will be clear in summer. Even such a summer as this."

"What about an inn?" Mary asks. "Shouldn't we write ahead to see?" Chamonix is fifty miles away, too far to travel and return in one day, particularly in Byron's ponderous monogrammed carriage. And if Byron is along, they can't take William. One night in an inn enroute both ways, at least two nights in the inn in Chamonix: how much will that cost?

Of course Byron, sunk in the center of the giant sofa, doesn't deign to answer her. He can angle his sarcastic disapproval like a man using a candle-shield to adjust the light. *Tiresome little housewife.* Just like her sister back in Skinner Street, sentenced to life as a drudge. And Polidori, laid up in bed with the laudanum bottle, isn't there to deflect him. "But truly"—she pushes the thought of Fanny away— "don't we need to ensure a place, don't we –"

"Surely it won't be hard," Byron muses, "to find a room for two gentlemen, alone."

Mary's breath clicks in her throat. Alone? Byron would leave her and Claire here with Polidori and William and Elise like a passel of children, abandoning her like one of the *ephemeron triflers* her mother had scorned in book after book, who have no greater concern than the grain of the ribbon to pull through a cutwork sleeve. She's come here to the Continent to escape just as he has, not just from a family but into a life that will expand, someday, into books like her mother's, and his. Fury thickens in her. "Well," she says, striving for a tone just shy of his pointed indolence, "I have begun a book of travel-writing, and surely an account of the Alps would be the high point for any publisher." She keeps her eyes on the dark falcon-curve of his head and shoulders. "Paris, the plains of France after the war, Geneva, the Rhine, now the Alps. The sum of" – her mother's word rises in her, the welcome knife ready to hand – "experience, gained by traveling with my dear Shelley." She pauses. "Wherever he goes."

Surely this last shot is too much. Byron will store it as return ammunition. But, more importantly, will Shelley be shamed? Before this man of the world, his new friend, to have a woman, not even a wife, attaching herself so publicly, harridaning him? But Shelley is nodding. "Mary is hard at work," he confirms, "on a manuscript."

"Have you seen it?" Byron's face is still averted. "This magnum opus?"

Shelley's face darkens. Silently, Mary exults: he's not so under Byron's sway that he's blind to Byron's scorn of her. "I have," he says. "She goes to her desk and labors away, adding to the pages, much more than you or me. Admit it, we don't exactly *labor*." He permits himself a wry smile. "It's bred in her bones. Daughter of Godwin and Wollstonecraft, remember?"

"I doubt" – Byron's voice stings – "that any of us will be allowed to forget."

"What about me?" Claire's voice bursts from her perch on the end of the big sofa, too near Shelley and too far away from Byron. "Don't I get to see the Alps?" Her dress strains against her belly, revealing a new, hard curve. She fluffs and resettles the fabric without looking down. "Just imagine how cozy it would be, all of us in –"

"Our own little Inferno." Byron heaves himself out of the chair and stumbles. Mary can't see his eyes. "Stay here with Polidori. He'll take you to the asylum. Visit the mad former mistress of this house. And learn of her." He pivots around the end of the chair and ignores Shelley's outstretched hand. Mary and Claire, fixing their eyes on the tossing trees outside, listen as he limps down the hall – thud, *slish*, thud, *slish* – and slams a door behind him.

"He always has that stiffness in his leg," Claire murmurs eventually, "when he's been sitting for a while."

The morning of the trip to Chamonix dawns cold but bright, with a white sun half-shrouded by pearly shreds of cloud. Elise sends them off at the coaching-stop. "What you might find there in the mountains," she says, her face somber, "no one can tell. They say it is the haunt of demons, that it is inhabited by a race of..." She turns away and hoists William higher, raising his chubby arm and waving it with her own hand. A breeze tickles the blonde hair around the edges of his blue knit cap. "Bonne chance!" she calls. "Goodbye!"

Waving back from the coach window, Mary notices with a pang that William isn't crying for her. He has Elise, who feeds him, who changes him, who helps gather his wooden blocks and sets them back in a tower to knock over again. But he's a big boy now of nearly seven months old. Her story has no name yet, no shape beyond the flickering light over that creature on its table. The pages ride in her bag: she can't be parted from them. Right now, they need her more than William does.

Mary settles into the corner of her carriage seat and fixes her eyes straight ahead (this sometimes keeps her from queasiness), then closes them. That morning, she'd hurried up to borrow food for their trip from Fletcher's apparently bottomless larder. Byron was folded into the corner of the big Chesterfield, scribbling on a paper propped on his green *Boxiana* book. "I had a dream," he read to himself, testing his own words, "that was not all a dream. The bright sun was extinguished, and the stars did wander darkling in the –"[17] Then he turned his head and saw Mary. "Well." His voice was unreadable. "Off to Chamonix on something like a honeymoon? Enjoy yourselves." A smile twisted over his face. "Of course, something *like* a honeymoon would be the precision of language most suited to the daughter of Godwin and Wollstonecraft." He paused. "Mary. Marry. A pair of words that seem to match more closely than they actually do. You don't think he's *really* going to marry you?" His tone was factual, interested. "The son of Sir Timothy Shelley, Baronet, of Field Place, Sussex? Who's got one wife already although he doesn't seem to remember it? *Please.*" He grinned. "Perchance to dream. As the Bard might say."

Mary felt Fletcher hovering at her elbow, powerless. "So says the lord" – she *would* talk back, by God – "who left his own wife, and his daughter, to play at being his own imaginary self. Childe Harold? *Please.*" Of course, it *was* a brilliant poem. But she'd die before she'd admit that to Byron. "Stumbling around in some Oriental fantasy. Your daughter will never want to set eyes on you again in all her life. I wouldn't. Thank you, Fletcher." She grabbed the basket and strode down Diodati's wide central hall and slammed the big front door behind her.

Now, she cracks her eyes open to rest on Shelley in his seat opposite. Twining one strand of hair around his finger, he's riding backwards and reading, both of which would nauseate her within seconds. *He'll never marry you.* What if Byron is right? What if there will always be another woman, somewhere else?

The coach stops for the night at an inn on the flat plain below the mountains. An old man sits at the door. Next to him, on a chipped wooden chair, is propped a cage of sticks bound at the corners with twine. He catches Shelley's eye and grins. A single tooth shines through his lips. "Écureuils!" he calls. "À vendre!"

Shelley, Mary, and Claire step close to the cage. Inside, flashes of gray and brown fur seethe into terrified life. "Un écureuil!" The man opens a door in the top of the cage, plunges his hand inside, and withdraws a struggling animal in his fist: squirrel, or chipmunk? English squirrels are long-bodied, fluffy-tailed. But this is a little gray-brown creature with a long slender tail and beady black eyes and tiny paws. In the man's hand, it wrings its body, then goes limp. Best to accept the inevitable when you're small, borne skyward in someone else's claws. In England, it would be sold for a child's pet. But here, in this cold summer, it must be food.

"Quel est le prix?" Claire asks. Shelley stares, horrified. Before the man can answer, he snatches a handful of coins from his pocket, flings them at the man's rag-bound feet, and overturns the chair. The cage shatters and squirrels pour onto the dirt, bolting for the grass with their tails up. A red-armed woman in a kerchief, rounding the corner with a dishpan, screams and hurls the pan in the air, plastering her skirts against her legs with both hands. Luckily, the pan is empty.

"Merde!" the old man shouts. "Êtes-vous fou?"

"No," Shelley says coolly, "just a person of feeling." With a familiar mix of love and irritation, Mary sees he's decided on lordliness: he'll assert his humanitarian principles, no matter what. The old man, his face resentful, is nevertheless bending down to pick up the coins. He'll lace his cage back together and buy food elsewhere. But what food is there, here, to buy? The plain is all brown grass and shaggy fencerows sweeping up towards the mountains, with a few disconsolate cows huddling under a leaden sky. To the inn's eaves, someone has pegged a string of squirrel skins like tiny gray jackets, their tails pointing down. Mary swallows. Thank God for their basket with the carefully wrapped loaves of bread and Fletcher's savory Gruyere cheese and the salted shoulder of known and customary meat.

Inside the inn, Shelley stoops over the counter and scribbles a tangle of shapes into the ledger. *Mr Percy Bysshe Shelley, Madame son Epouse, Theossteique la soeur* εκαστοι αθεοι.[18] *Atheoi.* He's announcing them as atheists, in Greek, to be recognized by his fellow gentlemen on this path to the famously sublime Alps: Claire as his sister, Mary as his wife, flying them all under the banner of his notorious name. Maybe he's also remembering those first days of flight across France, pursued by the angry ghosts of fathers and proprieties. Two years ago. How has the time gone so fast? She squeezes against his elbow, looks up at him, and smiles. The old defiance rises in her. *Mary W Shelley*, she writes. Destination? *L'enfer.*[19] Let other English travelers gasp and shake their heads. They can go to l'enfer, too.

Up in their room, Shelley hurls his satchel of books and shirts on the bed with a happy sigh. Mary sets the basket on a table in front of the window and begins unpacking it: bread, meat, wine, cheese. Something soft that might be cake. A knife and fork. Another knife and fork. Two small plates. Suddenly Shelley's arms come around her, his lean chest firm against her shoulder blades, his lips on her neck. She leans backwards into him, then turns to meet his mouth. Her fingers dig into his long curls and she loses herself. Here is the old delicious drowning, right on the edge of danger. He smells of salt, like the sea. Drawing back, he grins. "Remember," he asks, "what happened the last time we were alone in an inn in France?"

"With no child," Mary agrees, giggling. All the republican arrogance and Byronish wickedness has leached out of him, and he's just her lanky irresistible boy: her Shelley, so susceptible, taking his color and heat, like the chameleon, from whatever rock on which he comes to rest. And here, now, he is entirely hers.

She remembers their first night in Calais, freshly fled across the Channel from Godwin and Mrs. Vile. The maid had brought a bottle of wine and a giant roast chicken they'd attacked with all their fingers, and then they had looked at one another, suddenly shy: they'd never been alone in a room with an actual bed. Yet she had smiled at Shelley – the smallest possible smile, a teasing smile from somewhere new inside herself – and he had drawn her lazily with him onto the bed with its quilt made of scraps of rainbow-colored silk. Tipsy and giggling, then rapt, she had sunk her fingers into the narrow channel of his spine, drawn him down to her as she had done under the willows in St. Pancras Churchyard. No matter what, no matter how many children and books and journeys arrive to shape their days, she will never be able to take this for granted. She will never be weary of him.

Outside in the hall, footsteps approach and hesitate. Then comes a knock on the door. "Oh, for –" Shelley sighs, strides to the door, and yanks it open. "What the hell –"

Claire stands on the threshold, eyes downcast, her traveling bag dangling from her fist. "The innkeeper says," she recites, "that he has no room for a woman alone, that he must give the room next to yours, which was to be mine, to another family. So I must stay, now, with you."

Shelley stares at her. Mary steps around him and glares, trying to pry Claire's gaze loose from the floor. "Are you telling us the truth?" she demands. "Is that really what he said?"

"Mary," Shelley protests, "surely she wouldn't..." He lets the words trail away. A cluster of cheery French voices mounts the stairs, in a thump and rustle of bags. "You might as well come in," he sighs, turning away. Mary follows him, seething. This is their room, by God, with their own picnic supper waiting on the table. Two plates, not three. And – in a flare of glad spite – she sees that Shelley's disappointed. She, not Claire, is the one he wants right now.

Claire slips in, closes the door behind her, and waits there – probably smiling, ingratiating herself – but Mary won't turn to see. She slices the ham and sets one piece on Shelley's plate; chewing a mouthful of bread, he waves it away. "You need strength," she insists, "for mountain climb-ing." She cuts off a bite-sized chunk of her own ham and pops it in her mouth with exaggerated delight, as she does when feeding William. "See!" she mumbles in the high-pitched voice William likes. "It's good!" Shelley snickers. The key is to make it seem obvious, natural. And not to remind him of the squirrels. He must be so hungry, traveling on bread and tea and nerves.

By the time they've prepared for bed – Shelley absenting himself politely from the room so Mary and Claire can use the necessary pot and put their nightgowns on, like little girls – Claire has helped herself to the food in the basket, venturing *thank you*, but Mary has been able to summon only a tight smile. Like Shelley, she's propped herself behind a book: *Paradise Lost,* with Shelley's father's name on the title page (what *is* Sir Timothy like? Will she ever meet him?) Shelley is reading Greek, bending himself into shape to match it: thighs crossed, ankles hooked, twining one curl around his index finger.

Two years ago, they would have plunged into the same bed, Mary in the middle, fellow Continental vagabonds in a companionable heap. Now, without discussion, Shelley bunches up under his greatcoat on the chaise-longue and Mary and Claire take the bed, Byron's baby weighting the mattress between them. Mary falls asleep with the dismal familiar presence of what had once been a sister opposite her. Grieving knowledge leaks from Claire like cold air through a window-frame: *I have made such a mistake.* Deep in the night, Claire begins to cry. On the other side of the wall, there is only silence.

In the morning, the driver changes the horses for two stout, shaggy beasts with hooves as large as dinner plates, ears and eyes almost hidden in masses of tumbling black mane. Hissing and mumbling to them in dialect, he unbuckles the harness and lets out the collars and hames as far as they will go, then buckles them again. He checks the boxes and bags on the coach roof – mail and supplies for the village of Chamonix, Claire's and Mary's and Shelley's own portmanteaux – and climbs to the driver's seat and lifts the reins in one hand. With the other, he makes the sign of the cross.

The road winds upward away from the plain. Mountains rear on either side – massive, jagged points of black and gray rock, laced with snow and ice where they meet the sky. The foaming River Arve runs far below, fed by streams that tumble from cliffs into thin air. This land is like the ocean, so foreign an element it is difficult to remember that it, too, is still part of the ordinary earth where people wash shirts and write letters and feed their children breakfast. What are William and Elise doing now? Mary slides down the window in its squeaky wooden frame and cranes her neck to try to see the tops of the mountains, but she can't see past the near-vertical rock on one side of the road, or the fog that thickens over the mountaintops as they climb.

"Mary," Shelley whispers, "are you ill?" She shakes her head without turning around. In Geneva, these cold summer days have suffused the whole city with a palpable, pleading hunger. The women in the market and the shopkeepers along the quay let the scornful question rise on their faces as she picks over the wilted weeds or the precious hothouse eggs: *Anglais, so rich, where do you get your money?* No way to explain to them the acrobat-nets of post-obit loans and promises on which she and Shelley and William – and, of course, Claire – are traveling, or her own fears about what will happen if old Sir Timothy snips those threads. But here in the mountains, something lives that doesn't need food, or money, or fathers' approval. *They say there are demons up there,* Elise had worried. "Power dwells apart," Shelley is muttering, "remote, unreachable... No, *inaccessible...*" He digs in his pocket for his pencil, and, finding no paper, scribbles the word on his shirt-sleeve. *Inaccessible.* From this, Mary knows, the whole poem will depend in his mind, like a dewdrop from a spider-web, until he returns to the Maison Chapuis and writes it all down.[20]

At midday the coach stops in the lee of a cliff. On a sunny day, this would be a comfortably warm spot, but today it is just a chilly lapse in the fog. Next to the road, a stream trickles into a basin of rock. The driver leaps down and opens the carriage door. "Let's get some water," Claire says, "before he turns the horses loose at it." Climbing out, all three of them stretch their arms and amble stiffly to the stream. The driver, too, takes a drink before he leads

the horses, steaming gently through their shaggy coats, to the pool. He watches them carefully, allowing only a bit at a time. Hot horses shouldn't be let drink too much, Mary remembers. Where has she learned that?

"Now," Shelley suggests, "a little lunch." But there is nowhere to sit. The rock rises steeply from the surface of the road itself, which is wide enough at this spot for two coaches to pass each other. Yet theirs is the only coach in sight on the road, which loops around the flanks of mountains, climbing higher above the gorge through which the River Arve tumbles far below. Claire props the basket in the open door of the carriage and fills her hands with hunks of bread and meat. (*Eating for two:* no one needs Mary to make that joke.) The driver pulls a chicken leg, wrapped in a dirty rag, from his pocket and leans against the front wheel. Shelley rips the heel off a loaf of bread and wanders toward the cliff, chewing. After finishing the bread and dusting the crumbs from his hands, he glances left and right, then fumbles at his trousers and aims himself over the cliff. Mary snickers – pissing into the void! – then saws off a slice of ham, lays it between two slices of bread, and takes a bite.

Chewing, she walks toward the water-spring where it emerges from the rock –

A scrabble and slither in the brush and a creature leaps out. A bony ragged thing, fluttering with rags, staining the air with feral stink. Wild hair stiff with dirt, clawlike hands bleeding. Its eyes in its skull-like face are very dark. Mary freezes, her bread and meat outstretched. The creature snatches the food from her hand and thrusts it into its ragged clothes and whirls to scramble back up again. It staggers, slips, hurls itself at the rock. A pebble flies and grazes Mary's cheek. "Fils de pute!" Behind Mary the driver curses, lunging at the reins to hold the terrified horses. Shelley bounds towards her, shouting, "Pistol! *Un pistolet!*" Far away, Claire screams.

The creature scrabbles upward, fleeing them. Bigger than a normal man but climbing in the shape of one. Dirt and bruise and blood and scars. Hair bristling in matted locks. Bony bare feet and hands with nails broken on the rock. Strong. Hungry and strong enough to steal. Without looking back, it lunges up and reaches a ledge and scrambles into the brush and out of sight.

Where can it possibly have gone? Heedless of Shelley, panting at her side – "Mary! Mary! Are you hurt?" – Mary scans the cliff, all rock and scrub and cloud, melting into forest above the road. Across the valley a similar wall of jagged gray and black looks back. No other living thing moves, anywhere. That creature must have a cave, some hideout in this dizzying wilderness of stone. It must be risking its life to come up and down that rock to the water and the road. But when you're hungry, Mary thinks, you don't care if you fall.

Even after they climb back into the carriage and trundle forward again – the driver muttering to himself about demons, demons in these Godforsaken mountains, why hadn't he listened when they told him he should hire out his horses for the plow like any sensible man – and even after Shelley has calmed himself and Claire with rational sympathy ("these are hungry times with the weather so strange and food so dear, who knows what would drive a poor soul into the mountains, so far from anywhere?") and even after he has wetted his handkerchief to sting the blood away from the pebble-cut on her cheek, Mary keeps straining backwards, her face against the glass, to see if something moves. So nimble, the dark ragged body scrambling away up the rocks. Gone so completely, now, as if it never existed at all. She touches her fingers to her cheek. No. It is real. That creature has been here.

✳

The village of Chamonix is a huddle of steep-roofed, small-windowed wooden houses, muddy paths, and pens: brown cattle, black and white sheep, brindled hens pecking disconsolately at the dirt. Up the low flank of a mountain, a child with a stick leads sheep to look for grazing. If food is dear in Geneva, and in Europe as a whole, as Byron's newspapers have it, then with all their animals these people might be an exception. Where you have cattle and sheep and hens you have cheese and meat, you have milk and wool and eggs. Yet the sky is gray and low here as in Geneva – lower, actually, given the fog that clings around the mountains. You can't grow vegetables, or corn for animals, in a sunless world such as this seems to have become. Across the valley a thick, grayish braid of ice reaches over the mountain and down nearly to the houses: a glacier, trapping thousands of years in its icy heart. She shivers and pulls her cloak tighter around her shoulders. Is this really July?

In the inn that night there is no trouble about rooms, because there are no other guests. The landlady – delighted by the three of them and speaking slowly enough for even Mary to understand her French – says the cold summer has kept most of the usual visitors out of Chamonix, even the mountain-climbers. "But that means," she intones, "more food for you!" She sets a small burner and tripod on the table, then lights its flame with a long straw. With a flourish, she places a blackened, fat-bellied pot over the flame; something pale and sweet-smelling already bubbles inside. "Our specialty. Fondue! Our good cheese, from this valley, here. You take the bread, so –" She spears a bit of bread on a long fork and swirls it in the pot – "and, la!" She extends the fork to Shelley, who pops the steaming chunk into his mouth and chews. His eyes close in bliss. "I believe," he pronounces at last, "this may be the perfect food. Made from the milk of cattle, given willingly."

"And wine," the landlady adds, setting a bottle before them. "Bon appetit!" Freed from Byron's disapproving stare, Mary and Claire lift their forks and attack the food. Soon, the bottom of the pot comes into view, coated with a lacy, crispy brown layer of cheese. "La religieuse!" the landlady exclaims, pointing over Claire's shoulder. "We call that *la religieuse*, it is, how to say in English, a nun?" She smiles. "Called this because the monks, they took the soft cheese and left this on the bottom for the nuns to eat. What they do not know: it is the best! So do not waste it!" She wraps a rag around the pot's short handle and sweeps it off the flame, then scrapes around the bottom of the pot with a bent knife until she's dislodged a brittle gold circle that falls into the center of the table and breaks into three neat pieces. "Three!" she exults. "Very good luck!"

"A good-luck nun," Shelley laughs. The wine bottle in front of him is empty, but, for once, his stomach is full. "Three crispy pieces of the Trinity!" Ceremonially, he hands one shard to Mary and one to Claire, then holds the third piece aloft. "For the *atheoi*." He crunches the golden cheese between his teeth and grins. "For the nourishment of the body and the poetic imagination. Let's see what there is in these mountains to find."

In her *Letters from Norway*, Mama had complained about the beds in the country inns of Germany and Scandinavia and mountains like these, with their *stupid* inhabitants and their *none-too-clean linens* and their beds, she wrote, *with high wooden sides like coffins; I expected to be suffocated by morning.* She might have heard what Mary hears as she tumbles carefully into the high-sided bed with Shelley, giggling: the distant bells of the cattle, swaying in a line along their path to the barn, milked to keep this village alive. Surely for Mama the window glass rattled like this in its loose mullioning as the wind kicks up and dies again, like the sigh of a mountain-demon turning over in its sleep. But even she, eventually, must have slept.

Tucked up in the wooden bed, Mary and Shelley lie face to face. The faint sweetness of early spring grass still breathes from the linen, spread to dry in the sun before a volcano in the Otahetian Islands blotted out the sky. The cold summer has upturned the normal world but made this moment right here, with the two of them, alone.

So much has brought them to this place. The carriage waiting in the Holborn street before sunrise, Shelley's trunk strapped to the top. That first summer of scrambling across France and Germany, lucky not to be torn by the dark beast of war that swiped at girls and soldiers with its careless paw. The death of the baby – *No.* The birth of William. Byron magnetizing them into Switzerland and up the hill to the villa with its mad Madame. *Diodati* means *given by God, chosen by God to speak.* That might be said of Shelley, too. *He is a god, slightly damaged. He is an angel, dented around the edges. He is a demon of some merciful variety. He is a married man. A man you cannot trust. Great brilliance, undirected. You will never enter this house again unless you give him up.*

She has refused to give him up. And look at all that he has given her.

They have not lain like this, so quiet, in so long. High wooden bed-walls around them, sweet grass-smelling linens underneath, soft wool mattress padded with the willing gifts of the mountain-grazing sheep. No Claire tonight, knocking on the door; "place her far away from us," Shelley had told the landlady, smiling, "she snores." No William in his cot, flushed in his deep sleep that can nonetheless break in an instant, swiftly as a swimmer darting for the surface when some underwater beast nibbles his foot. Geneva with its peering English eyes is two days' ride behind them. Beyond that lies England itself, across all of war-scarred France and the Channel that tossed them in their little hired boat. They have fought all this way and come to the mountains at the edge of the known world. And now they are entirely alone.

Alone now she can look her fill of Shelley. All blood and nerve. All hers. Her gaze rests on the fine pale purple-shaded skin between his cheekbone and his lower lid, where long dark lashes shadow the bright eyes through which the world flows into him. His wide mouth twitches into a smile, his warm breath brushing her lips. Her hand rises and her fingers slide into his hair, clutching the warm curve of his skull. *Shelley*, she thinks, *you're so alive in there*. He turns his face and sets his lips against her arm's underside, stroking his cheek downward against it like a cat. He curls into her and gathers her against him and she wraps her topmost leg around him and tightens her grip and they are joined, like that, still looking. She holds his head in both her arms and buries her face in his hair, its reassuring ocean smell of salt and wind. At one point she feels her body hitching, gasping, her face wet with her own tears. It is a place she has not yet touched with him: ecstasy, grief.

Much later they fall asleep. She knows it, then. A door in her has opened to him and it will never close. Forever it will hang a little on its hinge, knocked sideways by his passage through. From behind that door shines now some light by which another creature is navigating up into the world. Step by step but always moving closer. And it will not stop.

The morning dawns gray but clear, the fog blown away by a teasing west wind that flutters Mary's skirts, then, emboldened, returns a moment later to shove. "Don't go up there," the landlady frets. "On a windy day, it's dangerous, you might fall –"

"Well, we came to see the Mer de Glace," declares Shelley, "and that's what we'll do. You said you have some ponies?" This is his milord-makes-problems-disappear voice, brushing away objections with a perfect friend-liness that, like ice, can slow and halt the progress of any opposing current. Accordingly, the ponies are produced, Shelley hands over more coins, the girths and stirrups are adjusted (two shabby sidesaddles for Mary and Claire and something little more than a blanket with straps for himself) and they start up the muddy track between thick straight fir trees growing out of furrowed rock. The valley, glimpsed between the trees, drops further away. A pebble tumbles from above, skittering toward them, and Mary flinches. "Just one of those little squirrels, like we saw at the inn," Shelley calls back without turning. "I can see him from here. You'd think he'd be grateful to us for letting his family loose." He snick-ers. Mary lets herself be calmed. It won't do to jump at every little thing for the rest of the trip. Surely the creature who snatched her bread is only a madman, a sad but singular outcast. Surely this village with its cattle and its crispy *religieuse* broken from the bottom of the pot doesn't harbor more than one Lucifer descending from the rocks. *Whichever way I fly am hell, myself am hell...*

The track ends and the ponies emerge from the trees into sky and cloud. Hundreds of yards below their feet, a river of ice – the glacier – winds around the gray base of a mountain, its surface jagged with sharp, frozen waves. For millions of years this ice has been flowing in this rough channel between the mountains. Ice, flowing: an inherent contradiction but a natural one here at this thin upper edge of the world, so close to heaven itself.

Mary slides off her pony and ties him to the hitching post next to a warming-hut, then walks to the edge of the ravine and looks down. She stares, now, directly into the heart of one of the glacial caves, a purer, deeper blue even than the heart of the imperial diamonds in the Tower of London treasury. Godwin had walked her and Fanny past them once, muttering about aristocracy and waste. Yet Mary stared into the diamond's heart, even when Fanny shrieked for her to come see the raven tearing the sinews from its dinner ("leg of old beef," the Yeoman Warder had explained matter-of-factly, "your raven's too intelligent for just a slab of mutton, nothing there to exercise his mind.") In the heart of that diamond, and down in that cavern of ice below them now, is a tunnel to another world. This place is the sharp edge of the world they know, just like the mapmakers' *terra incognita*, where the ocean drips off into a void. That edge is surely located around the farthest curve in this river of ice, just beyond her sight. A river of ice, surrounded by rock, with a ceiling of infinite sky.

Shelley takes her elbow and stands next to her. The wind whips their clothing like sails. "I have never seen such a place," he declares. His voice is flat, stunned. "Never even imagined it."

Slowly, the cloud shifts. A square of sunlight strikes the mountainside opposite. Only this bit of it is visible among the clouds – but that bit only makes the mountain vaster, and more unknowable. Far above, across the glacier, a fierce wind whirls a spume of snow from the top of a peak. No human foot has ever touched that expanse of white, that slate-gray point of rock that she is looking at. Mary blinks. This must be the *sublime,* that bookish word she reaches for even as she tugs it away like a too-heavy bonnet blocking her sight. What can a word like *sublime* do to name the feeling this place has lit in her bones? Shelley is struggling too. "Power dwells..." he's muttering, "remote, serene..."[21] But *serene* is not the word, for this is no quiet place. It is a space to stand and shout and declare yourself while accepting the chance that you will summon up out of that white silence something that you do not want to answer you.

The clouds shift again. Over the glacier, the sky brightens to silvery blue. The muscles behind Mary's eyes clench. Far away, at the bend in the great frozen river, a ragged black shadow flutters, upright and vaguely human-shaped. It's coming toward her, at a more-than-human speed. It grows taller, stretching itself higher, as it approaches. The blue crevasses under its feet don't hinder it. It's coming. It's the road-bandit ghost, the food-stealing creature drawn into her human orbit by some more-than-human need. It has climbed up here into the highest of the mountains, and it has found her. Her throat thickens in sudden terror and she gathers her breath to scream. But when she blinks again, the black traveling shape is gone.

"Snowblind," says Claire. She peers into Mary's face. "Stare too long and you'll hurt your eyes." Gratefully Mary lets herself be led into the little warming hut, past the three ponies, who stand at the hitching-rail with their heads tucked and their tails turned toward the wind.

Inside, the hut is cool and dim and relatively quiet. The ringing roar in Mary's ears gradually dies, and the dazzled white rims around her vision burn away. Claire hands her the little water-jug from her saddle and she takes a long drink, then crosses the little room and stands before the bank of windows facing the glacier. Etched initials fill the corners of each glass pane like drifted snow: *EB + RS. Willi. Te amo M.* And Shelley's school, left by some Grand Touring old boy borrowing his wife's ring: *Eton '96.* You have to have a diamond to cut your name on glass. Have there been so many travelers here, with such wealth as to not only wear a diamond but risk it on this mountain? Up here it might be stolen by another creature leaping from the rocks. Or it might simply be lost, the tiny gold teeth of its setting loosening to drop the stone over the cliff's edge, into the clear blue heart of the ice. Diamond returning to diamond. Heart returning to heart.

From his hole in the rock the Creature watches the man sitting on the glacier just below. Victor. Father. Master. Traitor. He isn't dressed for this altitude: faded black long-tailed coat, ragged scarf, thin-soled Geneva shoes that scrabble on the ice. Ah, the Creature thinks. His mouth twists. Victor Frankenstein. Always so well-prepared. Always so adept at reasoning all the steps before he embarks on a mountain expedition. On a course of study. On a grand design to track the origin of life to its lair and make it move and speak to his will.

You don't know me, Victor Frankenstein. But I know you.

Arid wind scours down the great valley of the glacier, whirling snow up from the jagged frozen sea and from the surrounding walls of rock. Clouds tousle in the sky. Patches of sun strike the mountain's flanks and vanish. Deep in their hearts, the ice caves glow blue. The Creature's eyes water. It is vast here, so cold. Good thing he has Mary's stolen bread and ham, burning like a coal in his belly. He hugs his cloak tighter. He wears only the homespun cape and ragged trousers and shirt he stole before he stumbled onto the DeLaceys, before the terrified son tore him from the blind old man, before the ridiculous flowering of hope into flame that burned their cottage to the ground. Huddled on his rock far below, Victor, underclad as he is, is nevertheless dressed in ways becoming a man. Parts and pieces of cloth are fitted to the parts and pieces of his body. Each with its own garment. Each with its name. Unlike this shambling tower of flesh in which the Creature must accustom himself to be. *This thing of darkness I acknowledge mine.* (In his sack, Madame Diodati's Shakespeare nestles with his stolen *Paradise Lost*, its grimy but still-blue cover cheering to his eyes.) *Poor houseless wretch.* Shall this stolen cloak defend you from this world? Obviously not. He can bear with some equanimity the cold that is obviously shriveling Victor on his rock. At least the cloak and trousers cover the purple wrinkled pointed thing that dangles from where the Creature's legs join the rest of him, that thing whose clenching and rising – never predictable, darkly obliterative, and always, afterward, the root of a terrible grief – fills the Creature with a mixture of rage and shame. The cloak can hide this flesh of his. It's good for that.

And he must keep this flesh, and the scouring winds of feeling in his heart, hidden from Victor's sight when he makes his request.

From the side where I now stood Montanvert was exactly opposite, at the distance of a league; and above it rose Mont Blanc, in awful majesty. I remained in a recess of the rock, gazing on this wonderful and stupendous scene. The sea, or rather the vast river of ice, wound among its dependent mountains, whose aerial summits hung over its recesses. Their icy and glittering peaks shone in the sunlight over the clouds. My heart, which was before sorrowful, now swelled with something like joy; I exclaimed – "Wandering spirits, if indeed ye wander, and do not rest in your narrow beds, allow me this faint happiness, or take me, as your companion, away from the joys of life."

As I said this, I suddenly beheld the figure of a man, at some distance, advancing towards me with superhuman speed. He bounded over the crevices in the ice, among which I had walked with caution; his stature, also, as he approached, seemed to exceed that of man. I was troubled; a mist came over my eyes, and I felt a faintness seize me; but I was quickly restored by the cold gale of the mountains. I perceived, as the shape came nearer (sight tremendous and abhorred!) that it was the wretch whom I had created. I trembled with rage and horror, resolving to wait his approach, and then close with him in mortal combat. He approached; his countenance bespoke bitter anguish, combined with disdain and malignity, while its unearthly ugliness rendered it almost too horrible for human eyes.[22]

"Mary," Shelley calls from downstairs, "Byron and I are going sailing, I'll be back..." A crow of delight rises from William, and laughter from Elise, as Shelley (she can tell) picks William up and tosses him. There's a farting noise and a squeal of joy: Shelley blowing a raspberry on William's plump tummy. This is their happiness, father and son.

"Enjoy yourselves," she calls. She does not lift her head. The front door closes. Her pen scratches and re-dips. Her handwriting stretches into a fluid, racing line. The story can't be left alone right now.

❄

So. The Creature settles back against the wall of blue sheltering ice. Outside the mouth of the cave, the wind scours down the mountain toward Chamonix. That's my story. What do you think?

If he weren't so exhausted by his tale – wrung out like Agatha DeLacey's scrub-cloth – the Creature would almost enjoy the expression on Victor's face, equal parts confusion and wonder. *It worked!* the Creature can see him thinking. *My homunculus, my flesh automaton, can reason and speak! He's been reading – let's see – Milton, and Volney, and Locke. All that language of obligation and right, it must be Locke, with perhaps some Rousseau. This is Geneva, after all. And he actually spoke to peasants. I must say, I'm impressed.*

But will he truly hear? The Creature's heart quivers. Will he heed?

It is remarkable— Victor finally manages.

(He won't say *I'm proud of you,* the Creature warns himself, don't expect it. But he is a scientist. Trust his curiosity to lead him on.)

—To have made your way so far alone, to have learned to read and write with such facility – Victor stares, his lips parted, rapt. Yet a cooler layer of that gaze assesses the Creature's bony face, his hands, his hair matted into icicle shapes with the weeks of dirt and sweat and snow. Then his face flushes and twists. You fiend. You killed – A child who never did you harm. My own little brother – Victor's eyes film with tears – an innocent ...

Yes, the Creature sighs. I was wondering when we'd come to that.

You – you demon! Victor lunges at the Creature. The Creature springs to his feet and twists aside as Victor's momentum staggers him toward a crack in the back corner of the cave, a deep blue seam of endless fall. Should the Creature let him fall? No. He shoots out one giant hand – *in color and apparent texture like that of a mummy,* whose words are these, scribbling themselves suddenly across his brain? – and grabs Victor's arm. His fingers completely circle his father's flesh and bone. Sit down, he growls. The rage on Victor's face is rinsed through now with fear, and he's glad. I'm not finished. I need you to be alive. Because you're going to make another one like me.

Victor blinks, reels backwards, straightens his spine and firms his mouth. I will do no such thing.

Oh, yes, you will. The Creature smiles. Fresh fear stains Victor's face. And let me tell you why.[23]

❄

It feels good to sit at Byron's table in the evening, emptied of story and, therefore, able to be polite. It feels good to take a sip of wine and smile as Shelley chatters about their swift wind-driven voyage up the lake to the castle of Chillon ("You should see it, Mary, so picturesque and wild") with the dungeon in which Byron, of course, has scratched his initials ("Increasing its value for the punters to come see – the keepers will be glad of it.") Something else flickers below the conversation's surface – something about the sale of Byron's home, Newstead Abbey, back in England, silenced with a meaningful look between him and Shelley. "Ninety-five thousand guineas," Byron mutters, "there's an old Harrow classmate, planter in Jamaica now, perhaps he'd ...." Mary lets her mind drift. Tomorrow's words stir inside her, stretching themselves with the lazy pleasure of cats. What will the creature say, exactly? How will Victor Frankenstein respond? The large ruined face, all black and yellow and purple, rises in her mind, its eyes sad. The one large hand reaches out, again and again. *It is impossible to suppose a giant the object of love,* wrote Mama's old adversary Edmund Burke. Yet no one has ever read about a giant like hers. *Love* is not unlike what she's come to feel for him.

"You must let me teach you to swim, old man." Byron's voice is cool. "The rest of you would never believe what I saw of Shelley here out on the lake. When one of those little storms came up, he put down the oars and crossed his arms and waited to be swamped. Shelley, old man, I said, can't you swim? No, he said, no more than any sailor." Byron flicks a glance at Mary. "So I said, let me teach you. You have a – you have Mary and the child, after all. But he laughed." Byron's smile at Mary is victorious, rueful. "Even this *atheos* trusts Providence. And me."

Mary trembles, suddenly, but must not let it show. "Indeed." She lifts her glass and takes a sip. "As must we all. All of us here in our mortal bodies with our little –" She lets her eyes drop to the place under the table where Byron's lame leg is. "Infirmities."

Outside, the wind rises and rain lashes the tall windows. "God damn this place to hell." Byron stands and screeches his chair backward on the floor. "It's not even August and I'm selling my birthright for *this?*" He flings his arm at the darkness beyond the glass, at Mary's and Claire's and Polidori's startled faces. "Polly, when do we go to Venice, again?"

"End of the summer, milord." Polidori's voice is determinedly cheerful. "We've got to see out the lease here, and I've written to Duchess di Robilant about Palazzo Mocenigo, but –"

"She'll take whatever money she can get," Byron spits. "Just like the rest of the Venetians. All pox and gambling tables, they are, sinking into the sea. An empire gone to ruin."

"But you're eager to get there, nonetheless." Shelley's smile is shrewd. Every so often, the old Scotch puritan in Byron heaves itself above the waters of his dissipation like a whale's back in an ocean, and Mary isn't the only one who notices. This is how to be a friend, she reckons: make note of someone's contradictions and crotchets while still enjoying their company for sailing or dinner with wine from the Diodati cellars. But more than that, it's how to be Byron's friend: take what he presents to you at any given time and sail on regardless, looking sharp to keep your own boat upright.

"So would be any man of sense." Byron's voice is sullen. "Maybe it's time we all moved on from old Geneva. What are your plans?

"Well," Shelley says, "we haven't determined on anything quite yet." Byron flashes a glance at him – *no plans, with your woman and child and nursemaid in tow?* – but Shelley won't be drawn, sitting as pleasant and imperturbable as one of the Chinese statues back in the British Museum. Mary stifles a rueful grin. *Shelley's never made plans in his life,* she thinks. *That's what has brought us here.* When she looks up, Byron's eyes are fixed on her, his face turning white with anger. He thinks she's laughing at him. Suddenly, she's weary. Let him think what he likes. Managing Byron and Shelley together is like managing a whole second child, equivalent to William – a sulky invisible homunculus of English lordship, bellying about and battening-on like the vampire in Byron's tale. Let him make his plans for Venice alone.

A letter from Shelley's father catches up with them the next day. *Sir Timothy Shelley, Field Place, Sussex.* Shelley lifts it between his fingers and carries it into the back garden, where he paces back and forth on the little stone patio, grinding his hand into his hair, clenching his jaw. He storms back into the house and throws the letter down. "Read it."

My son: Having been made aware of your chain of post-obits stretching from London to the Continent, and seeing no prospect in sight of your adopting sufficient reasonableness to cease this course of action on your own, I am driven to take the action of removing you from my will pending your return to the country of your birth. ~~Beware the strain of madness in our~~ *My son I am aware you have a son now of your own and I cannot allow you to deplete his legacy in addition to your own in fruitless wanderings about the world. Return to England or I must remove you from my will. Son, I must tell you that I wish we could be more congenial and --*

Shelley snatches the letter from Mary's hand. "Look how he signs himself." His voice is bitter. "Your obedient servant, Sir Timothy Shelley, Baronet. Behold the emptiness of convention. He obeys no one but his own tyrannical self."

"He sounds like Papa," she stammers. Cold fear sticks in her throat. This is the man whose continued tolerance, if not actual support, has floated them across the Channel and into Geneva. What if he stops Shelley from drawing any more post-obits? They'll have no more money, then. Shelley has earned nothing from writing but the scorn of his Oxford dons. Neither has Mary herself. Perhaps the story of *Frankenstein* will... But remembering Cecil's casual contempt in Johnson and Hunter's office stops her. She can't count on money from it until a contract has been accepted and signed. Perhaps not even then. Who'd believe that she, a girl, has made such a book?

Ah, fathers: the old fury swells in her again, and she lets it. How they try to call you back to them from along the path you're forging for yourself, dangling money or love over your head. Something in them loves the sight of your bowed white neck, like a French aristocrat's before the guillotine. Yet she can't deny Sir Tim has a point. With all of his post-obits – advances on his inheritance, at ruinous rates of interest – Shelley is gambling against his father's own death. And if he does come into that money, it will be drawn right down by taxes and interest payments, like blood from a fever patient's vein, before it ever lands with them in any form they can spend, let alone hand over to Godwin, as he'll surely continue asking them to do. What will Mary do if she ever finds herself caught between the fathers and Shelley himself, with Shelley's son at stake? Shelley's sisters are unmarried. Where, then, does that leave William? Shelley would frown if he could see these calculations. So *grasping*, he'd call them, so typical of the world from which they'd fled. So unlike the daughter of revolutionaries. *So like,* she thinks back at him, *a woman who must care for her son in the world as it is.*

Today is the first day of August. In three days, Shelley will be twenty-four. In twenty-nine days, Mary will be nineteen. William is eight months old, crawling along the parlor floor to the blocks Mary and Elise nudge just out of his reach to stretch him, expanding his capacities and curiosity. Perhaps they should plan a celebration. For, now, they are all grown up.

Byron huddles on her back patio with Shelley, engaged in some intent conversation that Shelley breaks off as soon as she opens the door. He won't meet her eyes. But Byron does. His smile has something alarming in its depths, like the outline of a pistol in a coat pocket.

"Byron has asked," Shelley flounders, "that I accompany him and Claire up to the villa so that we can... so that we can make arrangements for...."

Claire's baby. Of course. That curve of the stomach that no one has even mentioned aloud. Claire must be upstairs now, gathering her shawl. She'll hold it around herself as they settle down at the table, tighten it around her elbows, look up and fix her smile in place. Holding her fear in place, too. "Should I come?" Mary asks. "Maybe she'll need me to..."

Byron shoots a look at Shelley from under his dark brows, and Shelley flushes. "No, ah, actually," he stammers, "just the three of us, that'll be sufficient, that'll.... Why don't you stay here and work on your manuscript?"

"To hasten the day," Byron adds, "when we will all savor the productions of your particular genius."

Damn him. Mary forces a smile onto her face. "A consummation," she intones, "devoutly to be wished." She brightens her smile and lets the Shakespeare set him on his heels, then turns to go back indoors. Why doesn't Byron want her there while they talk about Claire's baby? At least they are making plans for Claire, and Shelley's there to help.

So: the dark, chilly summer is mutating, changing, drawing to an end. "As all good things must!" Mrs. Vile would chirp. *Has* this summer been good? In her rented parlor, with her baby son squirming across the floor, Mary ponders this sequence of days. On that night of visions, her mother appeared to her. She surrendered her bread to a creature scrambling down from the mountainside to snatch it away. She curled with Shelley into the box of the inn-bed in Chamonix. She set her hooks, like an Alpine mountaineer, into the great hidden mass of her story – her creature? Her story? Her creature's story? – and began to climb. Right now those pages lie in her writing-box upstairs, breathing sweetly in their sleep. She couldn't have written them in the contracted world of Skinner Street. Travel, Shelley, William, even Byron – all these have widened her life, made space for her and her work to become something she is surely meant to be, even if she can't tell exactly what it is. *Telessai. Happening*. But with the summer ending, and with Shelley's father drawing in on him, surely they will not stay here.

Shelley bursts through the door, his breeches and shoes muddy from skidding down the hill in the dark. "Come up to Diodati," he pants. "I've got an idea." An uncertain smile flickers on his mouth. "Byron wants us to. All of us. It's all right. I just need to get…" He darts through to the kitchen and emerges with the metal fire striker and flint-stone in his hand, then bounds upstairs. A rasp of a trunk across the floor, then a rummaging, before Shelley gallops down the stairs again with one of his limp white shirts and a sheaf of papers wadded in his hand. With an apologetic look at William, and a nod from Elise, Mary follows him out the door and climbs uphill against the setting sun.

The atmosphere in the Diodati dining room is tense, overlit: Claire upright and rigid, battling tears, Byron sunk deep in his chair, glaring at his empty wineglass. Candelabras smoke against the mirrors. Plates with smears and crusts of food – ham rind, blackened bread-bottom – have been shoved into the center of the table. Claire's hands grip the chair-arms, her belly rising between them. Neither of them looks at Mary or Shelley as they enter. A decision has been made. And it's not a happy one.

"So now it's settled" – Shelley's voice is bright – "let's go launch the fire balloons. To celebrate. I've got everything right here."

"Do you really think," Byron mutters, "this is the time –"

"What a good idea." Claire's voice is brittle. "A little festivity. Now that such an obvious problem has been solved." Surely now Byron will snarl and say something cutting. But he only gestures submissively at the French doors onto the balcony – *after you* – and Claire rises and stalks after Shelley into the night.

Mary peers at Byron but he still won't meet her eyes. All of them are hiding from her now: Shelley in his frenetic activity, Byron his silence, Claire in the stiffness Mary recognizes as terrible anger, an anger Byron is letting her express. Why? Because he is ashamed? Or because this, too, is a power the lord retains? Let her display her sensibility, for his delight. Let him ponder his own incapacity to feel. What a novel sensation.

Claire and Shelley are bent over Shelley's spare shirt and the heap of paper. For a moment Mary panics – *he'll burn my story, he's taken it!* – but no, this is Shelley's own writing, spiky and black and covered with sketches of ruined temples and laughing little demons. He folds the largest sheet of paper into a rounded upright sphere like a hot-air balloon, pinching its corners together along the seams. "Now I just need the wick," he mutters, "and the spirit…. Byron, fetch me the whiskey?"

Byron sighs but turns and limps away. "Bring a candle, too!" Shelley calls after him. Soon Byron is back, setting a burning candle upright in its holder on the railing and thrusting the bottle into Shelley's hand. "Not sure why I'm letting you burn up my good liquor," he says. "What on earth are you –" Shelley rips off a bit of his shirttail – too quick for Mary to protest – and soaks it in the whiskey-bottle's mouth and whips a piece of string from his pocket (Shelley always has a piece of string, and a pencil) and nets it crosswise over the top of the paper orb and ties the wet cloth on tight. Without a word, Claire passes him the candle and he holds it to the cloth. The wet rag catches and sputters and burns blue, then gold. "Fire!" Shelley exults. Cupping the paper orb in his hands, he carries it to the balcony's edge and, tossing it gently upwards like a released bird, he lets it go.

Amazingly, the balloon takes flight, wobbling on a light wind up and away from them. Mary leans against the rail to watch. What if it lands on someone's roof? Then it will set the house on fire and the burgher will come up after the Anglais at the villa, demanding money – But then Shelley presses his little telescope into Mary's hand. And there are Shelley's words, backlit by fire, rising through the night. So sharp is the view through the lens that Mary can read them, briefly: *scatter the sparks of thought... mankind, the world...*[24] "Typical of his methods," Godwin had said scornfully. Yes, this is typical of her beloved mad Shelley and his desires: writing words and setting them on fire to send them out and light a fire somewhere he will never see. The brass ring of the viewing-piece is warm against her skin, warmed by Shelley's skin too. This must be the world as Shelley sees it: one great event, always on the verge of flame, disastrous and thrilling in indeterminate proportions. The little balloon wavers down the hill, sinking lower, until it settles in the grass and winks out.

"We made balloons of silk, back in Wales," Shelley mutters, "perhaps this old..." He lifts the shirt in his hands and ties the sleeves in knots, closing the cuffs. Then he gathers the long tails together and ties them too, making a balloon-shell of the whole upside-down body. Yet it still gapes open at the neck, with no way to close it further or suspend from it a wick that will lift the whole contraption into the air. Shelley leans out over the balcony and dangles the shirt upside down, puzzling. "Come now," Mary suggests, "that still has plenty of wear, let's go back home and –"

Suddenly Claire steps forward with the candle and touches it to the collar's edge and the whole shirt catches fire in Shelley's hands. Shelley yelps and flings the shirt away from him. For an instant it floats upside down, arms outstretched, in the air. Lifting on its own heat, the chest catches fire, and then the right sleeve, and the left. It rises and drifts, then settles back and, with a sullen *whump*, hits the damp grass. The flames dim and the shirt smolders until there is nothing left but charred black cloth and smoke. Claire's back is resolutely turned. Far out on the lake, a fisherman's lantern bobs: out earlier than Mary's ever seen, before any hour that can reasonably be called the dawn.

Behind them, Byron sighs. "Well," he declares, "looks like the party's done." Deliberately he turns away and walks – thump-*slish*, thump-*slish* – back into the dining room and shuts the French doors. Through the glass Mary watches him blow out the candles one by one. The great Diodati dining room flickers into black.

Back in their own house, Mary learns the truth of it. Byron offered to have Claire's baby raised by Augusta Leigh, his half-sister, back in England. Claire protested. Eventually they decided that the baby could remain with Claire – "he said," Shelley relates, "that she could pretend to be its maiden aunt" – until such time as Byron decides to absorb it into his own world. But Claire has sensed accurately what lies beneath: Byron will not love her, will not keep her. He'll move on to Venice with Polidori and his other pets. Which means that either Mary and Shelley and William and, yes, once again, Claire will follow him, or they'll return to England. For now, at least, the summer is over. And there is nowhere else to go.

The Creature comes upon a girl. She lies asleep in the straw of a rough farm shed like the one in which he spent months spying on the DeLaceys, peeking through the cracks of his loneliness at the life so normal for everyone but him. He stands at a distance, struck. Tall grass washes against his legs with a sound as soft as water. Overhead, in a giant poplar tree, one bird sings, pauses, sings. The Creature breathes shallowly and lightens his step so as to remain unobserved. He moves closer. From humans, he's learned this much of stealth. And desire.

How would humans classify this girl? Her hair is brown, drawn back in two bands over her ears. She wears a rough brown homespun dress and a stained apron with a tarnished gold watch pinned to its strap. Her nose is long, her forehead pinched with worry even in her dreams. She is an afterthought in the cold dusty house where she lives, a spinster sister, perpetually smiling and hoping to be smiled at in return and asked, *Well, Fanny, how is it with you? (Fanny?* How has that name come into the Creature's head? He'd thought she was *Justine.*) She is a girl who watches her sisters chosen by men and carried away, who marshals, each day, what's left of her will and her self-control: *Mama would be proud of me. Oh, I remember, so dim but I remember her, standing on the deck of the ship* – She does not think herself, or her memories, of great account. Yet to the Creature, she is lovely. Her hands curl gently against her pillow of straw, each finger capped with its own luminous pink nail. A loose straw in front of her face waves back and forth with her breath. And suddenly the words in the Creature's mind are not the girl's but Shakespeare's. *What a piece of work is man. How noble in reason, how infinite in faculty. In form and moving how express and admirable. In action how like an Angel. In apprehension how like a god. The beauty of the world. The paragon of animals. And yet to me, what is this quintessence of dust?*

The Creature looks at his own hands – twice as large as this girl's, knotted with purple veins and broken black nails – and lets the words twist his mouth into a bitter smile. *What a piece of work. And what is it to me.* What indeed. I am loved only by the blind and the mad. My body is misshapen and horrible to look upon. But my memory is excellent. So are my endurance and my strength. I may well be able to go on as I am forever.

Thank you, Victor Frankenstein. What a gift is this life of mine you've made.

The Creature puts his hand into the pocket of his stolen trousers and leans over the girl. (Fanny? Justine?) She stirs but doesn't wake. Her gold watch ticks, just loud enough to hear. In his hand he holds the small oval picture of a woman: painted in delicate pinks and whites and browns, her auburn hair gathered up under a dark green cap, a smile on her face that is not quite happy and not quite sad, her arms encircling the round form of a second sleeping child under her white gown. From the gold frame trails a narrow black ribbon, snapped by a single tug.

The little boy in the woods had been wearing this picture on its ribbon around his neck when the Creature approached and snatched him up. Perhaps this thing called *human life*, called *companionship*, was only a matter of training. A child wouldn't spurn him. A child, like old blind DeLacey, wouldn't send him away. A child might even grow to be like – the knot of desire in the Creature's stomach tightened – a son of his very own.

But the child had thrashed and struggled and shouted in his imperious little voice that his papa was Monsieur Frankenstein of Geneva and the Creature had better put him down or he'd be sorry, ugly old monster, he'd be sorry.

A tightening of the fingers and the little voice stopped for good.

Monster is only the medical term. Some doctor had written this, intending its neutrality as comfort.

Logical. The Creature must be logical. He had snapped the ribbon from around the small neck and put the woman's picture in his pocket. This object would later reveal some use.

And here, with the sleeping girl at his feet, he's found it.

Power swells in the Creature's heart. He can do what he likes with her. A flurry of tearing and screaming beats in the Creature's head, confused as an animal thrashing in a thorn bush. He will not – touch her, no. But he will –

(What is the sadness that radiates from her even in her sleep, tugging at his heart? Someone loves her but not enough to show her that. Why?)

The Creature sighs. Of all the human characteristics that cannot be known, here is one that can: Objects framed in gold are valuable. This picture is framed in gold. It had been worn by the Frankenstein child. So it is a valuable thing belonging to the Frankenstein family. This girl in her rough dress is obviously not a person who can buy such valuable things. Ergo, to put this valuable thing in her pocket will be to imply that she has stolen it. Sleeping alone on her straw, with only the ticking of her watch for company, she will not be missed. At least, not for very long. Everyone around her is so busy, after all, with love-filled lives of their own.

Theft brings suffering to its victims, and to thieves. The Creature learned this when he took the DeLaceys' food and firewood from their cottage in the early days of watching them, before his own cursed compassion drove him to gather and stack more wood than he'd ever stolen, before that compassion flickered slowly into hope that he had no way of knowing, then, could never live. He stole Mary's food on the mountain road (*I'm sorry*, he whispers, hoping she can hear.) This girl will be accused of stealing the picture of this lovely woman who whispers to the Creature of all the things he can never know: *Wife. Friend. Mother.*

And then Victor Frankenstein will punish this girl as Victor has punished him.

Unjustly. But then, suffering does not always land on those who merit its sting.

The Creature rallies himself against the voices of doubt and shame gathering in him like clouds. The child died because he lifted it from the ground with his fingers around its neck. The child died because of him. But the child was prejudiced against him like all the other people in this miserable fascinating world who have the power to look upon his face. So

– the Creature sets his mind to it, hard, as if he's leaning into a contrary wind – he eradicated that prejudice where it stood. He nipped that prejudice in its swelling bud, before it bloomed. Really, he had no choice.

Of course, Frankenstein will be furious with him. But fury is better than indifference. Fury will drive Frankenstein to seek him out, to speak with him face to face. To look him in the eye. The Creature can know, then, that Frankenstein has seen him plain. And once Frankenstein gets within range of his speech, he will make his request. Again. More clearly this time.

You gave me language, Father. A quick wit. A retentive mind. Cast me out and I must use them how I can.

No matter what it costs the girl left behind him on her bed of straw, sleeping with the stolen picture of a mother she remembers only in shadow, standing on the deck of a sailing ship, laughing as the sea carries her into another world and out of sight.[25]

CHAPTER 5

Bread Street

LONDON DECEMBER 30, 1816

St. Mildred's Church is dark and poky, with a leaf-litter of missionary pamphlets in the vestibule and broken-backed hymnals on the pews. A smell of the Thames rises through the open door amid the rumble of wagons and the bells of St. Paul's to the east. No one seems concerned with this small church two days before 1816 becomes 1817, when London is preoccupied with the next new year. But it doesn't matter, because any church will do for the ceremony that will now be undergone: Mary's marriage to Shelley, and his marriage to her.

Two weeks ago, Harriet drowned herself in the Serpentine. Found by a dog-walker in Hyde Park, her body is identified, her death confirmed. Now Mary can be Mrs. Shelley. She can travel with him and sign registers and brush off the skeptical look in innkeepers' eyes: *just two runaways, mad man and ruined girl.* She can banish the tense crouch of uncertainty: *he could leave you at any time, he's done this sort of thing before.* Harriet's family can see that Shelley is making the effort toward respectability, and perhaps allow him custody of his children Ianthe and Charles; three and two years old they are now, and Mary has never set eyes on them. Perhaps they will come to live with her and Shelley and William. *Our William will lose his pre-eminence and be helped third at table – as his aunt Claire is continually reminding him.*[1] This is the attempt at a joke she's written to Shelley, desperate to animate these days with something like happiness. But she wants Ianthe and Charles. She wants to be a married woman. She wants Sir Timothy to welcome her, eventually. She wants their family. Of course she does. Because the alternative is unthinkable.

Harriet is drowned and Fanny is dead. Two months ago, Fanny's body was found in an inn in Wales, identified by her stays – the stays from the top drawer on Skinner Street, stitched MW in red thread – and the gold watch Mary sent from Geneva and a suicide letter from which Godwin, scrambling after Fanny from London, had torn off the signature, to avoid scandal. He hadn't told Mary what the letter said. One gold watch. Thirty pieces of silver. Guilty, self-justifying gift of a penitent Mary, too late. *Well, Fanny must look to her own happiness.* Well, Fanny had drunk laudanum and sent herself to sleep alone in an inn miles from home because she knew herself to be a bother and a burden. Because Mary had left her on Skinner Street while she went to *gain experience* as if her sister were not Mary Wollstonecraft's daughter too.

Gain experience. Let the dead bury the dead. Get married. It is practical. It is for the best. And Godwin thinks so too. Once, he wrote that *marriage is the most odious of all monopolies.* Now he writes, *My daughter, I confess that despite my previous views on the matter I am glad to hear that you and Mr. Shelley will be solemnizing your union in London. This will indeed aid your stepmother and me in attending, and we thank you. We will meet you on 30th December at the church.*

But Godwin and Mrs. Vile aren't here. Shelley paces before the altar, jerking at his cravat, which he's insisted on tying all the way up to his chin. "Just loosen it," Mary says, reaching for him, "if it pains you." But with a martyred expression, Shelley twists away. "Never fear," he jokes sourly. "I've done this before."

The vicar approaches with a harried expression, rolling down his water-splashed sleeves: he's been making tea, or washing up. "So you are gathered to be married," he begins, brushing his thinning brown hair off his forehead. "Splendid, splendid. Where's the ring?"

Mary blinks: in all the confusion, she's forgotten this part. "The ring will be arriving with the bride's parents," Shelley answers, in his your-lordship voice. "We await them now."

"Does the bride have an attendant?" The vicar smiles at Mary. She shakes her head. *No.* The words ring in her as clearly as if she's spoken them. *I have a stepsister who's hiding her pregnant belly from her mother. And a half-sister dead by her own hand because she believed herself unloved and I did nothing to convince her otherwise.* Helplessly she imagines them, Claire on the left and Fanny on the right, brushing tears and grave-dirt from their faces, clutching hothouse violets in their hands, the gold watch she'd sent Fanny from Geneva ticking *reproach* with every second. Were it not for her, they'd both be here right now. Harriet – of Harriet she dares not think. Bad luck for a bride on her wedding day. But perhaps bad luck is no more than she deserves. *If ye know of any impediments why ye may not be joined –* What would happen if Mary answered that question *A wife and a sister who killed themselves from loneliness?* The church roof would crack and crumble, the vicar and the stained-glass reflections on the walls would puff away in colored dust, and only Shelley would be left – his eyebrows raised, his lips firmed in anger – before he vanished too. Without him and William, Mary has nothing now, except her Creature's black eye blinking bewildered in the dark, an unfinished manuscript that has no home, not yet. She cannot lose Shelley. She must become his wife. In spite of everything.

The heavy door at the end of the aisle creaks open and a small elderly man edges inside, peering around at the ceiling and the baroque altar-piece. *Wren church,* he's surely thinking, *earlier period, sadly neglected, but still quite –* Then he catches sight of them and his face brightens and Mary realizes the old man is her father. He has now almost no hair left – the high round dome of his forehead bulges, vulnerably – and his whole face has bunched itself in lines around his spectacles, which, obviously, he seldom removes. The brown coat with the inkstain on the sleeve is the same one he'd been wearing on the day she last set eyes on him, when her secret plot to run away with Shelley was swelling inside her. Tears prickle her eyes, press upward on a rush of unnamable feeling. Papa. Godwin. In her head, he looms so large. Here, he is so small.

Mrs. Vile, of course, is right behind him, fussing with the strap of her reticule as if it contains anything worth stealing. *If they're so short of money,* Mary wonders sharply, *how come she's still so fat?* But a sneaking undertow of pity tugs her as she assesses Mrs. Vile's navy-blue dress, pressed along the seams to smooth where they've been turned, and her short-sighted blink: she needs spectacles as much as Godwin, but *between the two of them* – there's that unkind Jack Sprat and Mrs. Sprat rhyme, again – there's only enough money for one pair. Here's a woman clinging to what she deems *respectable.* But it costs money to put up that partic-ular shop-front. Especially when your daughter and stepdaughter run off with a radical. When the sweet sad spinster who scrubs your floors and fetches your eggs is dead by her own hand and you must parry prying neighbors with a lie: *oh, she's gone to her aunts in Wales.* Thank God no one has told Godwin and Mrs. Vile about Claire's pregnancy. Thank God Claire has stayed behind in the rented rooms in Bath. *She's taking the waters for her health,* Mary braces herself to explain, *the jolting of the trip would have been too much for her.* Technically, this is not a lie.

"Mary." Godwin stands in front of her, blinking, smiling. He reaches out both hands and clasps Mary's, more than a handshake but not an embrace. "We – we are here."

"And happy for you on your wedding day." Mrs. Vile steps around Godwin and seizes Mary. Against her own cheek Mary feels the muscles of Mrs. Vile's jaw clench in a smile. Well, she, also, will smile. And as she stands next to Shelley at the altar, that's what she does.

How is it that having once dreamed of a moment, you can remember nothing of it once it actually arrives? There must have been familiar words: *love, honor, obey. As long as you both shall live.* There must have been an exchanging of rings, because there it is on her finger now: a simple gold band, slightly worn. "Mary," Godwin murmured as he withdrew it from his pocket and handed it to Shelley, "this ring was your mother's." Then Mary remembers only a spider high in the corner of the church ceiling, spinning lazily as a Chamonix mountaineer on its rope down and down through the light, serenely confident in the shimmer of its slender thread that any hand at any time could snap.

"The ceremony," Shelley mutters sarcastically as they turn away from the altar, "so magical in its effects." But he kisses Mary, and he shakes Godwin's hand, and Mrs. Vile's. Out in the street paper blows against the storefronts and whirls up to the sky. Intermittent cold rain dashes their faces like drops flung from a housemaid's mop. Men lean over a scrap of fire to light their pipes. She is a married woman. Now it is done. There is her mother's ring on her own finger, placed there by Shelley. *Gain experience. Ah. Gain it.* He's her husband now.

It isn't until the next day that she finds the letter to Claire, fallen out of Shelley's pocket onto the floor: *The ceremony, so magical in its effects, was undergone this morning at St. Mildred's Church in the City. Mrs. G. and G. were both present, and appeared to feel no little satisfaction. Indeed Godwin throughout has shown the most polished and cautious attentions to me and Mary. He seems to think no kindness too great in compensation for what has past. I confess I am not entirely deceived by this, though I cannot make my vanity wholly insensible to certain attentions paid in a manner studiously flattering. Mrs G presents herself to me in her real attributes of affectation, prejudice, and heartless pride.*[2]

The black slanting letters have an intimacy that strikes Mary to the heart. That quick, racing hand, relaxed – You do not write to a woman this way unless you can unbind yourself with her. You do not nearly leave yourself anonymous, knowing you are known, by just one careless scribble in the corner of the page: *your S.*

He's done this kind of thing before.

The Creature huddles with little William while their parents are arguing in the other room. Sharp words, voices surging and then suppressed. Names are hurled: *Fanny. Harriet. Claire. Admit it, you never really wanted to* – Objects are suspended in the air, shaken: the tiny bottle from which Shelley takes the drink that makes his eyes wild, that sends him to his stacks of papers or out to the streets to walk in the rain or to his own settee in the parlor, moaning. The stacks of papers on which Mary is writing her story. She must finish it. The Creature is sure of this. Shelley's poetry is less certain. Some good lines. But little that is yet completed, ready to send to Shelley's friend Leigh Hunt. *He'll help us, Mary,* Shelley pleads, *I know it.* But no one helps a writer who doesn't write. Even the Creature knows that. No matter how eagerly the Creature himself haunts the edges of the human world, waiting to be born. As only Mary's writing can help him to be.

On the mantelpiece ticks Mary's wooden clock from Geneva. At the Creature's feet, William flounders on his stomach, pulls himself upright, and stares frankly into the Creature's eyes. His blonde hair is thick as milkweed fluff packed in its pod. There's always something sticky on his hands and face despite the best efforts of Elise, who's followed Mary and Shelley to England. Mary is so tired. There will be another baby very soon. Perhaps a little girl just like the one who died, the firstborn who slept in a drawer in threadbare rented rooms. The baby who never had a name. The baby of whom Mary never lets herself think.

Wuh, William declares. Pop! Pleased with the sound, he makes more. Mum mum mum.

Bub bub, the Creature volunteers. Good boy.

William's face cracks open in delight so total and unfeigned the Creature's heart dissolves: a lady-novelist's cliché, but useless to deny. He flattens himself on the carpet, then props himself up on his elbows to bring his face closer to William's. Mon mon mon, he says gravely. It means, in French, *mine.* But we need not concern ourselves with that. He crosses his eyes and grins idiotically and sticks out his tongue and William squeals with joy. It seems this is a thing to do with babies. Talk to them. Laugh with them. Toss a rope of words over to where they swim in their own worlds, the colorful puddles of lives as yet without language to explain any of the sensations built anew inside them every day. Take them seriously. And before you realize it, they'll be on the shore of what is called this ordinary world with you, perhaps having forgotten the language they once spoke and so desperately wanted others to understand. *Our birth is but a sleep and a forgetting.* Mr. Wordsworth wrote that, once. The Creature has learned to speak this way, with what effects – he smiles grimly – the world will someday know. If Mary only finishes her book.

William looks up at the Creature and sets his hand flat down on the carpet. The Creature puts his own hand over it. How tiny William's hand is, fluttering against his own. How sturdy and alive. Hand, he says. This is your hand. Your hand in mine.

Mon! William declares. Han! Man!

Man. The Creature hesitates. He raises his voice a bit to mask the voices through the wall. Man is what your Aunt Fanny – may she rest in peace – used to call your grandfather Godwin when she was a little girl. He brought her a little china mug with F for Fanny on it as a present, when he came to see her and your grandmother – he pauses – your grandmother, Mary Wollstonecraft. This was before he was your grandfather, of course. I understand there was some controversy about the marriage. But oh – From some astonishing unknown place his eyes prickle with tears. They were very happy. And thus was born your own Mamma. And thus you.

And where was I? God only knows. Best not to shade that darkness into the air this blue-eyed child breathes. Just one year old. With all his life ahead.

CHAPTER 6

Hampstead

LONDON FEBRUARY 1817

Raindrop circles thicken in the gutter and overlap in the slant of candlelight from the window at which Mary stands. *Thicken.* Is this the word for circles made drop by drop in the Hunts' clogged gutter, the right tailoring of word to world? This questioning is always in her now that her stack of story-pages has grown so thick, now that she is – dare she say it, in this house so full of them? – a writer. A modern Prometheus. *Be careful to whom you compare yourself,* Godwin would joke, now that, theoretically, they are on speaking terms again. *No writer should invoke the punishment of the gods.*

Over a chair by the tiny room's fireplace, her damp cloak steams. That afternoon she's been walking out on the Heath in the rain. Inside her a dissatisfied searching beast sidles from corner to sill, rubbing its withers on the doorjamb, raising itself with its paws on a window-ledge to peer through her eyes at the huddle of houses in the rain. *What would be a name for this before my eyes right now? The name for circle upon circle of raindrops on this roof? The mysterious thing that even a village becomes in the night?*

Is it wrong to wish she were still out there on the Heath? Probably. Tonight, the Hunts will be entertaining a young man Mary's never met, and she and Shelley should help. The Hunts are generous friends, sheltering them until their rented house at Marlow will be ready. A home in England will help Shelley with his lawsuit for custody of Ianthe and Charles, the children Mary has still never seen. Curt letters from Harriet's father's lawyer bristle from his pockets. *Sir: My client stands amazed that after all you have done, you nevertheless ask for – Sir: My client refuses to consider – Sir: It is the belief of my client and, we must confess, of this firm that it would be unsuitable in the extreme for two children of such tender years, after their sweet mother's death, to be subjected to –* Perhaps they've been too quick to settle on Marlow, come to think of it. Hampstead is so quiet and green and clean with its bright-windowed shops and coffee-houses. So unlike Holborn, which has only grown grimmer and darker in Mary's years on the Continent. So blessedly free of Mrs. Vile, of whose last blast of fury Mary prefers not to think: *you traipse off with your – with him to Switzerland and you think you can just come back here and live on our charity?* But now she won't have to. In Marlow, there will be space for herself and Shelley and William and Elise. And Claire. And her baby girl, Byron's daughter.

Claire gave birth in a rented room in Bath on a cold day just above a month ago, when the windows of the Pump Room steamed over and the fine ladies tucked their faces deep into their fur-collared cloaks and hurried, shivering, from shop to shop. When Mary wrapped the small red creature and placed her on Claire's chest, Claire embraced the child and began to weep. For hours, she stared into the small face, smiling, breathing words Mary couldn't hear. She opened her dress to feed the child and drowsed off, upright in her chair, as the baby's small mouth slackened into sleep. On a piece of paper, she scratched names for the baby – *Albe, Alba, Allegra* – over lines for letters she would not send to Byron: *If you could see how lovely she is. If you were only here.* It fell to Mary – signing herself *Mary W. Shelley* and snickering at the impotent spite this would draw from Byron – to write him in care of his banker, Monsieur Hentsch in Geneva, that he had a second child, named Allegra after all.[1] Perhaps he's still at Diodati, perhaps in Venice already. No way to know.

Back in England, the tumble of life with Shelley caught up Mary and Claire and their babies like dice in a cup: first more temporary lodgings in London, then out to the village of Hampstead, where Shelley paid for a room for Claire and Allegra but accepted an invitation for Mary and William and himself to lodge a little while in the crowded house of his new friend, the journalist and editor Leigh Hunt, with Hunt's wife Marianne and their seven (soon to be eight) children and Marianne's unmarried sister Bess and a housemaid Mary only ever seems to spot out of the corner of her eye, scurrying away. The Hunts' house is like a cottage in a fairy tale, stretching or contracting according to the number of people it wishes to hold inside. Always through its walls are the sounds of liquid trickling or one child slapping another or a stifled cry of pleasure or papers rustling or floorboards creaking or the sharp brown tang of bread left in the oven a minute too long or a snuffed-out candle's impatient ghost. But Hunt drifts upon it all, magnificent and calm. "When you have been imprisoned by His Illegitimate Majesty," he declares, shoving back his shock of black hair, retying the knot of his maroon satin dressing-gown, "for two years in the Surrey County Gaol for daring to write the truth of what he is, in his corrupt and corpulent body and in his rotten soul – 'a fat Adonis of fifty, a violator of his word, a libertine over head and ears in disgrace, a despiser of domestic ties, the companion of demireps, a man who has just closed half a century without a single claim on the gratitude of his country or the respect of posterity' – well, then this happy overcrowding holds no terrors for you." He grins at Marianne, then at Shelley. "'Fat Adonis of fifty.' That *is* a better phrase than the original."[2] *And of course he knows his own words by heart,* Mary thinks sardonically. But Hunt is charming, and potentially the London-literary introduction they need. In his paper *The Examiner,* a year ago, he gave Shelley's book of poetry its first and so far only review. "I declare you one of the three new voices of our age," he'd told Shelley at breakfast today. "The second is John Hamilton Reynolds – you don't know him? Good poet, good writer on boxing, too. And the third – you'll meet him tonight. He's walking out from the city, where he works as a – Well. Just wait." Shelley had smiled politely. His own name has obviously crowded out the other two poets from his mind. But a new friend – Mary and her new husband can always use one of those.

Downstairs the front door slams and voices rise: Hunt and Shelley back from walking, Marianne calling to them. Mary smooths her hair and descends the stairs. Hunt, slinging his greatcoat onto the wall hooks, beams; Shelley, underclad as usual in his old brown jacket, reaches for Mary and gives her a kiss. Marianne emerges from the passage to the kitchen with woolen oven-mitts masking her hands and a single curl of hair straggling from its knot; no doubt the effect had been enchanting two hours before. "He's here," she says to Hunt, accepting his hand in the small of her back and turning up her narrow face. "In there."

Hunt nods and leads Mary and Shelley through the archway to the parlor. It's decorated in green, with a white bust of Shakespeare and a piano and overflowing bookshelves and, on the ceiling, a blurry pattern of daisies painted enthusiastically by hand, as they'd been painted on the ceiling of Hunt's prison cell, where he spent two legendary years at the pleasure of His Illegitimate Majesty. The chairs are still shoved into groups from last night's activities: Marianne cutting silhouettes from candlelight on the wall, Bess and Hunt playing cards, Shelley and the Hunt boys folding paper into boats to reenact the Battle of Trafalgar. Thankfully, there's a fire already to warm the little room; the ground around the Hunts' house is apt to be damp. "The Vale of Health," Hunt laughs, "talk about a wishful name for a plain old swamp."

On the settee in the corner, a young man stirs and rises from sleep. He throws off the dark green coat he's tugged over himself and gently disarranges Falstaff, the Hunts' orange cat, who's curled against his shins. Quickly, he stands and shoves his bare feet into his unlaced, battered brogues. He isn't much taller than Mary, with curls the color of dark honey and huge, liquid eyes. His nose and mouth are large, his lips fine-cut and firm. Some restlessness wakes in his expression as he smiles and comes forward, extending his hand. "John Keats," he says. The Thames twists through his vowels, first to the south, then the east. "Sorry. I overslept."

"Mr. Keats is a physician," Hunt explains, "and he walks the seven miles from Guy's Hospital to Hampstead each Saturday when his work is done."

"Not *done*." Keats' smile is wry. He shakes hands with Shelley and with Mary. His hand is large, big-knuckled, rough, and warm. "Having reached a temporary pause. Let's call it that."

Marianne appears with the teapot and cups rattling on a tray. "Have you seen the children?" she asks Hunt. "It isn't like them to miss their teatime. Even when the gypsy life awaits." At Mary's questioning look, her smile grows ironic. "Ah, yes. We've sent them to the Heath to play at gypsies. Thornton is quite capable." Keats clears a litter of books from the low table before the settee and Marianne sets the tray down and begins to pour. "He wants to test his skills at fire, both the making-of and then the putting-out. He vows he will overcome the rain. His brothers and sisters are helping him. We try to let them govern themselves."

"No other way to learn, is there." Keats' voice is factual. "What do the other gypsies think?" Everyone laughs, Mary notices, except him.

"Mr. Keats wrote a charming tale for Thornton," Hunt explains as they draw their chairs into a circle and sit down: Shelley near the door, Hunt next to him, Keats at the window. "'Old Meg, she was a gypsy...'"

"Do you have children, Mr. Keats?" Mary sips her tea.

"No." Keats' smile is rueful. "Two brothers and a sister. Somewhere else."

"'On Looking Into Chapman's Homer!'" Shelley interrupts. "I remember now. Stout Cortez!" He turns to Hunt, his face darkening under a smile. "A damn good sonnet. Which Hunt apparently did not mislay. As he mislaid my own." No wonder, Mary thinks: Hunt's tiny study is as chaotic as Mr. Hunter's, back in the shadow of St. Paul's, with its snowdrifts of paper and the ghosts of Johnson and Wollstonecraft, laughing, plotting their next *Vindication*. Here in Hampstead, Hunt is plotting, too, something for Shelley and Reynolds and Keats, his trio of champion poets. Maybe he'll make room in his plot for her. If she ever finishes her book.

"I confessed to that in print." Hunt's good cheer doesn't break. "The only cure for one's faults is to confess them. As Mrs. Shelley's father once remarked." Shelley opens his mouth to speak but Hunt overrules him, smiling. "Keats. What've you seen at Guy's this week?"

"Another childbirth." Keats hesitates. "A coal-heaver with a crushed leg. A baker with the flux. But, really, I don't want to –" His large mouth stretches closed, lips thin. He snaps his fingers and Falstaff the cat leaps from under Mary's chair. Balancing on Keats' thigh, he shoves his round skull into Keats' fingers. Keats rubs the thin skin of his ears and the cat leans closer, eyes shut. His raspy purring crackles, like the fire.

"Have you done surgery?" Until the words are out, Mary doesn't recognize the voice as hers. Like a child, her story has turned in her and bumped its head against the ceiling of what's real. *Let me learn of the world, let me through.* She's nearing the end of her manuscript, but there's a fog at its heart she can't dispel. Victor Frankenstein: how has he actually done his work? How has he actually joined limb to torso, muscle to nerve? In order to write it she's patchworked a mental picture out of memories: Shelley in his bath, her own hands and Fanny's on the pattern of a dress. On the page the slippery limbs join somehow with the obedient parting of cloth and the suturing of two rent things into one neat seam. But here is someone who has actually opened a body with a knife. *Ask him.* The creature inside her takes her hand gently in its teeth. *Learn just one more thing to make me real.*

"My last operation was the opening of a man's temporal artery." Keats doesn't look at her, or anyone. "I – I did it with the utmost nicety. But." The words rise through his unwilling throat. "It was an arterial wound to the head. As my father had suffered when he –" He pauses. "Reflecting what passed through my mind at the time, my dexterity seemed a miracle." He looks at Mary. "I will not take up the lancet again."[3]

Mary's face grows hot. Shelley and Hunt and Marianne all stare at her. "I'm sorry," she finally managed. "I didn't mean –"

"I know." Keats' smile is fleeting. "It's simply that..." His face brightens. "I went to see a boxing match one time. Jack Randall –"

"The Nonpareil!" Hunt exclaims.

"Fighting some poor chap out at Moulsey Hurst," Keats agrees. "And some writer was asking him how he did it, you know, what was passing through his mind when he was in that ring, and he could only say, 'I don't know, I don't speak of it. I just *do.*' And if you could have seen him..." With his left hand still sunk in Falstaff's orange fur, he pivots to the right and taps his fingers on the window-glass.[4] "The blows so rapid. Every one straight home."

"Like your sonnets." Hunt's voice is sincere. "And soon you'll have a book of them." He sweeps a glance around the group. "Mr. Keats, you see, is no half-painter, who has only distinct ideas occasionally, and fills up the rest with commonplaces. He feels all as he goes."[5]

"Surgery's like that," Keats says. "The best surgeons seldom talk of it. Like boxers. Except – if I can turn to poetry instead, I won't be a surgeon anymore." He grins. "But maybe I could still be a boxer, what say you, Hunt? I used to fight at school. All the time." His eyes widen in delight. "Maybe it's not too late to turn to another kind of – science."

Hunt snickers and lifted his glass – "well-punned!" – and Shelley looks between them, baffled. "I wrote a poem about a cat once, when I was a boy," he says. "A little thing to amuse my sisters." He leans awkwardly to tickle Falstaff. "'A cat in distress, no more or no less...'" The cat stirs in irritation, leaps down from Keats' lap, and stalks away. Mary sighs. Sometimes Shelley is a chameleon, wanting to blend in: sometimes a bright serpent, determined to stretch himself in the sunlight of everyone's gaze. Always a slightly odd member of any coterie.

"He must've heard about your electric experiments, Shelley." Hunt's black eyes sparkle. "Shelley, here, as a boy, tied a kite string to a cat's tail to be like Mr. Franklin –"

"No!" Shelley protests. "I never should've told you that." Everyone laughs. Keats stretches his mouth obediently into a smile; his eyes, watching Shelley, are cold.

"So, Chapman's Homer. Why Chapman? A translation?" Shelley's voice is apparently sincere, but a warning prickles Mary's neck. Godwin had complained about his rich pupils, swotting up on holiday from Eton: *They consider Greek the domain of gentlemen, and therefore shameful not to know. Yet watch the vacant eye of the rich boy rolling about – as your mother would say – endeavouring to avoid his lessons and you'd never guess what a value they place on Homer. What a privilege they squander. Like so many others.*

"Well." Keats looks at Shelley for a moment. Between them, tension flares and subsides. "Latin is the chief language of my school. I got no Greek. And when I found Chapman I found" – he pauses – "the same energy of voice as in Shakespeare, the same phrases that leap to the tongue, and the brain. I'll never forget it. 'Sea-shouldering whales.'" He closes his eyes and smiles. "And when Odysseus staggers up onto the shore of the Phaecians—"

"—Just before he sees the girl," Marianne breathes, dropping her hands, busy with a small torn stocking, into her lap. "I love that section—"

"—Chapman renders the moment with a magnitude," Keats says. His eyes are still closed, his smile rapt. "'The sea had soaked his heart through.'"

"Consider what a gift the translator gives," Mary adds, "how particular is his art. Or hers. My mother, in her first years in the city, earned her bread as a translator. Mr. Johnson gave her work from the German."

"And women may work at translation" – Marianne's voice is soft – "when they may not work at anything else."

Hunt sets his hand on his wife's forearm, stroking the pale skin of her wrist. "Indeed," he says. "Mrs. Wollstonecraft, as always, is a welcome reminder not to confuse the social machinery of this world with what is real. Or good." He gazes at Shelley, his black eyes direct. "And as Plato instructs – in or out of translation – we must always consider the good, what is best and most worth striving for on this temporary earth. As I am fortunate to do. Right here in the Vale of Health. Such friends around me." He smiles. "Two poets of such gifts, here in my own parlor. And a dear wife I adore." Mary lets the tension of the moment relax away from her. Hunt can be so willfully, maddeningly oblivious. But sometimes, he says the right thing.

The front door opens and children's voices babel into the house. "We found Aunt Bess!" Thornton Hunt, the oldest of the pack, age ten, appears in the parlor door, followed by his brothers and sisters. A stoutish young woman with an incongruously pointy face – Marianne's on a body a bit too large for it – stands among them. "I'm back," she says, unwinding her shawl. The cold has roughened her voice, tugged her hair loose from its knot in a million waving strands. She cuts her eyes at Hunt, then Marianne. "They found me after all."

Shelley laughs obediently, as if Bess is joking. Maybe she is. Her level tone and unblinking gaze make it impossible to tell. "I escaped from the house onto the Heath and a band of gypsies building a fire – unsuccessfully, I might add –"

"We had it going!" Thornton protests. "It just went out 'cause the wood was wet, from where we got it, down by those trees, and the rain –"

"—Surrounded me and have now returned me to captivity," Bess says. Hunt smiles gamely, as if to will Bess's words toward a joke. Marianne watches him, her forehead creased. *Captivity?* But Bess has no prospects that Mary can see beyond fair-copying Hunt's manuscripts and proofreading the new *Examiner* numbers and helping her sister make beds and mend the children's clothes. Doubtless it does feel like captivity, sleeping each night in her attic above the bed where her sister sleeps with the man Bess looks to on entering any room. Keats's eyes rest thoughtfully on Bess, now, too. Who knows what Hunt is thinking? Who ever does?

"Come sit with us," Mary offers. Guilt stabs her. This is what she should have said to Fanny. But Fanny had been left back on Skinner Street to slave for Godwin and Mrs. Vile in the poverty and cold. Claire, that other sister loitering on the edge of the circle, had been left to look to herself. Well, that was what the Byron dalliance, as Mrs. Vile would call it, had gotten her. A beautiful illegitimate baby girl and a handful of nights with an elusive poet who has galloped away to Venice on the fat white horse of his own will, its tail streaming behind him impudently as the long veil of the Staubbach Falls. "The falls," Byron had told Shelley in Geneva, "are magnificent for so slender a thread – they remind me of the tail of the pale horse that Death rides on. You know. In the apocalypse." Typically, and flippantly, Byron spoke as if the apocalypse were a long-awaited party for which his own departure had been a little delayed. But Mary had heard him mumbling the poem he scribbled on his knee on the Diodati gazing-couch: *I had a dream, that was not all a dream.* She'd seen his eyes darken when he thought no one was watching him. Claire, like Fanny, like Bess, is an extra sister, longing for a life of *more.* Like any extra sister, she can only reach for the comet's tail of a passing poet, streaking through her ordinary sky. But the white fire of Byron's comet will burn Claire, and baby Allegra too, as it streaks on, heedless, into the dark. Toward whatever apocalypse awaits. Mary shivers. No way to stop any of it now. No way to know how the story will end.

"Are you cold?" Hunt's voice is solicitous. Mary shakes her head, aware of Bess's and Shelley's eyes on her, with different shades of jealousy blooming in both.

"Thank you for your invitation, Mrs. Shelley," Bess says deliberately, "but my stockings are soaked. I must go change them. And perhaps the children should do the same." She starts toward the stairs. "Come on, gypsies. Let's get cleaned up and dried off." Amazingly – the Hunt children aren't usually so biddable – they tramp after her, trailing cloaks and muddy shoes. Marianne rises and returns to the kitchen; they'll be wanting their dinners when they come down.

In the general commotion, Keats rises and slips out the door, and Mary follows him. The night is chilly, but the rain has stopped. Over the Heath, stars glint through a rip in the clouds. Mary twists her mother's ring on her finger. "Mr. Keats," she blurts, "tell me about the knife."

Keats stops. He doesn't turn around. His voice is quiet. "Why do you want to know?"

"I'm writing a novel," she says. She has never uttered these words to anyone. "About a man who – About a doctor. And when I have the opportunity to ask a real doctor, well..." She smiles, a pleading pressure rising behind it. The book swells in her like one of Shelley's silk balloons, lit by its own fire. *I need this. Feed me. I want to grow.*

"Well." Keats turns to face her. "It was two months ago. Thirty-year-old carter presented with a lesion to the left temple; he was standing up in the wagon and the horses bolted and he fell forward onto the corner of the wagon, just...." One fist smacks the other open palm. "Pow. There was collateral damage, bruising and tearing to the neck, and I was directed to open the artery. Check for occlusion." His tone becomes clinical. "The walls of blood vessels, themselves, are not actually blue. We only see them as that color when we look upon ourselves, when we see our own blood changed by the layers of skin through which it flows. Really, a blood vessel is the same color as any other flesh, depending on how deeply it's perfused –" he sees Mary's questioning look – "suffused with blood in such a way as to join it to the body's other rivers and territories. And." He swallows. "The scalpel is kept so sharp that really you need only touch it to the skin and the skin opens. Yet when I glanced at the carter on the table – unconscious, poor chap, thank God, with the boys there to hold him just in case – something about the angle of his head, something about that bruise" – he pauses. "I was eight." He looks down at his muddy shoes. "I was eight and my father had been to see me and my brother George at Mr. Clarke's school. On his way home, passing along the City Road and Bunhill where the Methodists have their chapel, do you know it? Well – he fell. Was he drunk? Did some footpad rise up out of the ditch, fed by the Methodists and feeling bold? Did the horse stumble? Who knows? When they brought him home he had a bruise on his head just like that. Laid out in a wagon pulled by two gray horses. A light dapple and a dark, one older, one young. I could only think of how he himself would have marveled. He kept a livery stable, you see. It's hard to find two dapple grays so cunningly matched. He could have hired a pair like that out to every would-be gent in Moorgate." His eyes darken. "Anyway. I was the oldest. Father was dead. Mother was hysterical." His smile holds something terrible in its heart. "Two younger brothers and a younger sister and me. So. I was off to Guy's Hospital to earn a living for us all."

"But Mr. Hunt said, I think," Mary stumbles, "that you aren't intending to practice."

"No," Keats agrees. "Not a decision well-received by – well, some of those who call themselves my family." His lips thin. "But with Mr. Hunt's help I am publishing poems at last. It is in me, the writing. I have to – I can't not try." He pauses. "The apothecary's license – I have finished it. I have qualified. But I feel—" He looks at Mary, then away. "Somehow I feel that time is very short. And I must make my use of it."

As Mary sits on the edge of her bed before sleep, brushing her hair, Shelley's weight denting the mattress underneath her, William fortressed in blankets in the corner, she feels the words settling inside her. Smoothed by the regular strokes of her mother's brush, they're also suffused with the sadness in Keats' eyes: *temporal artery. Perfused. Practicing.* A good doctor hesitates. A good doctor trains, and practices. A good doctor knows his limitations, takes care before he cuts into those delicate river-veins that only look blue from outside. But what if the doctor is not good? What if his *practicing* is in preparation for something not good at all?

"Mary." Shelley's voice – edged with irritation he's striving to disguise – rises from the pillows behind her. "What were you talking to Mr. Keats about?"

What was – What? Mary blinks, recalling herself to the circle of candlelight and the weight of the brush in her hand. A dismal incredulity yields quickly to an irritation of her own. Oh, for God's sake. Shelley is jealous. Although even on their wedding day he wrote to Claire, and has so carefully settled her and Allegra in their little room across town.

"It seems," Shelley continues, "that he was quite charmed." He turns toward her. His body's close warmth presses through her nightgown. He gathers a dangling curl from her shoulder and turns it around his finger. "As who would not be."

"It was a question," Mary enunciates each word, "for my novel." She pauses. "My *novel*. Remember?"

"Of course." Shelley's voice is hurt, subtly victorious. "You know how I cheer the progress of your novel. I've only asked you about it, oh, how many times this winter?" True. As in Geneva, Shelley has lauded the presence of Elise as the thing that will let Mary get on with her writing, even in this crowded place: like Macbeth's castle, the Hunts' ramshackle house is riddled with nooks and outcroppings where writers might cross their straws and sticks to build a temporary nest. And everybody under this roof – even the children – knows to stay away from someone hunched over a writing box with its inkwell snug in its slanting lid.

"Come on." Shelley yawns. His warm hand creeps around Mary's ribs. "Put out the light."

Mary rises from the bed and goes to the bureau, where she sets her mother's brush deliberately down. In the candlelight, she knows Shelley is watching her. She straightens the brush so it's exactly parallel to the comb. She slants to the comb to the left. Then to the right. She turns the brush over so that it rests upright on its thick boar bristles. The tip of the handle sags and taps the bureau-top, flattening the brush's bottom edge. This is why you mustn't store a brush any way but on its back, bristles facing up. This is how her mother's brush has lasted so long. Unlike her mother's stays, which are buried, now, with Fanny. Buried in an unmarked grave in Wales. Wales, where her mother's sisters have eked out their school and their precarious gentility, refusing to take Fanny in and let her mar their fragile selfish peace. Wales. Where Shelley let loose his fire balloons and revolutionary messages in the dim past days of Harriet and her *bitch of a sister* and darkly-hinted-at assassins. Where Mary Wollstonecraft Godwin Shelley, her mother's daughter, hopes never to set foot in all her life.

Dead sister. Dead mother. Dead –

Mary squeezes her eyes shut, then opens them. She will finish her novel, rolling her small boulder forward word by word. The first of May: that will be her deadline. Then she can go to London and get her father to help her approach publishers. Maybe Johnson and Hunter. Maybe Byron's own publisher, Mr. Murray in Albemarle Street, tucked just off roaring Piccadilly with its broughams and bucks and beauties and – because of Mr. Hatchard's palatial shop at Number 187 – its books. Blissfully, she surrenders to the dream of it. Her own words will be transmuted from dauby thumbprinted ink to orderly print, stamped into white rag paper that will release its sweet musty smell of reconstituted cloth when she puts her nose into its pages and breathes, just as she inhales the sweet smell of the top of William's head. Victor Frankenstein's words will be spoken into the world each time someone she will never meet – now or two hundred years hence, oh, thrilling – turns a page. *I am by birth a Genevese.* Her book will come to life. If only she can fill in one last scene. How has Victor come to make his giant man?

Shelley sighs. With a swift rush of sheets he turns over and hunches his shoulders deep into the pillow. Mary flips her mother's brush safely on its back and slips under the blankets and blows out the light. The story waits in her now, opening its single bewildered eye upon the dark.

Victor Frankenstein slips through the surgery theatre door and locks it. In his candle's light, the wall clock reads 1:55 a.m. Now he will be alone with the girl.

He had noted her arrival. They all had. Monsieur Krempe, of course, was not deceived. "Gentlemen," he'd said, his gray eyes sweeping over them, his hand clenched on the lectern to stop the worsening tremor, "remember that gentlemen you are. And do not take –" he paused – "advantage of her."

Of course Victor would never do such a thing. How disgusting. His purpose is a nobler one. As, someday, everyone will see.

But first, a diagnosis. Drowning victim: likely self-inflicted, no sign of struggle, fingernails intact. Lungs sludged with river mud. Lips cyanotic. Eyelids shut now upon eyes of deep carbon-dioxide-saturated bloodshot blue. Height below the medium. Skin gray, beaded with moisture from the ice cave. Frame thin. Hips narrow. Aureolae enlarged but mammary tissue relatively underdeveloped despite advanced state of pregnancy, perhaps one month to term. Hair drying after its hospital bath – as a living girl's would – to auburn, darker in the candle-light.

He will be able, now, to look inside.

Somewhere in the air above his head a voice half-speaks: *Don't do it, don't pursue, must you actually* – Is this conscience? It's more like his father in another room, shouting a warning he is meant to hear. But this is not his father's voice he hears. It's a woman's. Elizabeth's? Justine's? Calling to him across a great distance. Or from within a dream.

No matter. When he finishes this work he will be hailed as the benefactor of men and women everywhere.

This girl is due to be opened tomorrow but he will be the first.

He lifts the scalpel and begins.

The standard Y incision. Left, down. Right, down. Then down. The skin parts with an ease Monsieur Krempe will not feel wielding the knife in lecture tomorrow, after another day of rigor mortis and the invisible progresses the ice cave can't arrest even in so fresh a girl. Inside the layers there's a fading pinkness, a fading yellow of what residual adipose tissue there is. And there's not much flesh to spare. She's been working: note the reddening of hands, the faint gnarling of joints. She's been walking: note the flattening of the ball of the foot, preparatory to metatarsalgia in later life, which for such girls begins at twenty-five. Her body has been giving its child every bite of food. Every spare mineral has been flushed from the bones by wave after wave of the new small being's wordless need: *feed me, build me, make me strong.*

Incision: down. And in. The skin parts on the hillock of her belly and there is the corrugated surface of the womb itself, faintly purple. A muscular veil of flesh. Behind which a child lies curled. A shoulder juts up, hands folded protectively at what Victor knows will be its narrow chest. A head lifts its womb-roof in a gentle curve, pressing up from underneath.

He will open her there. To deliver.

Draw with it, Monsieur Krempe once instructed, before he began to look at Victor with suspicion, before his hands began to shake (it is a degeneration in the nerves, not drink, for Monsieur Krempe for all his severity is an honest man, has raged against the rot of drink in a physician's life, has never been known to touch a drop.) *Hold it with your fingertips. Don't think of it as cutting. Because cutting is too crude a thing. Just draw a line.*

And so Victor does. A careful straight line with the scalpel-blade. The womb's wall is thick and knotty and his small blade bumps and skips but the flesh curls back and there beneath him is the child's head.

For a seven-months' baby it is large, already starting golden fluff around the tiny ears. The round back of the skull is visible, the face turned away. Its skin is pearly blue, still damp. Its knees and elbows bend in tender folds. *Don't look.* There's that pleading voice from somewhere in the air again, or is it somewhere in Victor's own head? *Don't look at me.*

But then such rooms as this are full of phantoms. It's nothing a promising physician such as Victor Frankenstein – until recently top of his class, until recently invited to the tavern each Saturday with his fellow dissecting-room apprentices – should mind. Phantoms are to be expected, really. Given all those cadavers that have been wheeled into the theatre through the left door and out again through the right, freshly opened, fully seen, all those souls in which Victor firmly disbelieves released from the dissecting room into the wailing air of night.

He draws his line down through the uterine wall along the curve of what would be the child's jaw and across its shoulder and down its ribs until, in the protective jumble of folded knees and elbows – for such a journey, Nature packs a child as tender and efficient as a good valet packs clothes – he spots the joining-on of umbilicus to gut, and thus to life. Is this indeed the point of life? Its origin? The blackened cord wrinkles and coils upon itself with blood made livid by the time that has elapsed since this mother's heart last beat. But this point at which cord joins stomach had been the blood-root of that heart – its fondest care, its end and aim.

Perhaps this is the place where life begins.

When Victor builds his man he will replicate this joining-on. What will be the substance that flows through? What vital fluid? That is his puzzle, still to solve.

He cranes and pivots about the gurney and opens, carefully, the womb with one more twist and then another of his knife and moves the candle but in the dimness he cannot see the precise means of the joining-on. What if he were to lift –

From down the hallway to the right, beyond the swinging doors, he hears a distant jingling of keys, then whistling. Damnation. In the instant before he extinguishes his candle, he casts a look around. He's been neat. Nothing to clean up from the floor. He's been foresighted: a roll of catgut suture thread and stout needle are hidden in his coat from earlier that day. He blows out the candle and pockets it and grasps the gurney-edge and rolls it through the left-hand door into the deeper dark. He'll finish his work in the ice-cave. He doesn't mind the cold.

Of Monsieur Krempe's fury when he discovers the stitches in his fresh girl Victor will not think. Of his father's disappointment when he is sent home to Geneva in disgrace he cannot think. Of Elizabeth, the sweet cousin occupying the bride-shaped space his mother carved for him, he does not think.

Have a care, Frankenstein![6] But it is just a phantom's voice. He will not heed it.

For now he sees how he will build and animate a man.

Have a care, Frankenstein! There is the voice again, strong as a living person's. Both inside and outside his head. *Have a care. Stop – Don't cut – Or you may unleash something of which you've never dreamed.*

He lifts his eyes from the girl and scans the ceiling. For the voice is talking not only to him but, somehow, to itself. How does he know this?

On her gurney the girl is coal-ash-gray. The river smell is strong. Her lungs must look like rivers, too, an estuarial map in alveoli and vein, leading from the first sight of that faithless long-gone sailor toward the fatal moment of that leap from a bridge.

Why did you open her? Why did you have to lift that knife and keep on –

Oh, beware of what you let into the world.

But once it's here it is our duty to investigate, and call it by its name.

Too late to turn back now.

Victor trundles swift and quiet through the left-hand door of the theatre, back to whence he came. The jingling keys of the hospital's night watchman approach but no one sees that blinking oblivious man open the door and step into what he vaguely feels is not an uninhabited room although it should be, because the only one who could see him is a young woman behind the window of another place that is and is not another space and time, with light-auburn hair trailing over her shoulders, just-brushed with her mother's brush for sleep next to the husband and the son who have lost themselves in dreams, staring in horror at the pen that's just become a scalpel in her hand.

CHAPTER 7

Finsbury Square

LONDON SEPTEMBER 1817

The great balloon is staked down like Gulliver among the Lilliputians, its blue and green silk dome arching over the chimney-pots. Men scurry around it as it shudders and yearns skyward, scraping its passenger basket against the grass. And, around this wonder, London continues its life. Someone's washing-line flaps between windows in an alley. Three ragged men from the Methodist tent-camp up the road amble past and stop to stare. A woman holds a child by the hand and hunkers down to point at the wicker basket in which Monsieur Blanchard, the famous aeronaut, will stand, equipped with blankets and water and sextants and pens to construct a map of the world from an entirely new angle of sight. Swaying upright between the ordinary houses, the balloon is a creature of unparalleled wonder, longing to leap to the air.

With her manuscript in hand, Mary stops to watch it too. She's overcome with the desire to pat the great flank of silk as she would a horse's shiny haunch. It could only be good luck before she enters the *Temple of the Muses of James Lackington, Bookseller and Publisher* (that's literally what the sign says) on the opposite side of Finsbury Square. Surely Monsieur Blanchard, slight and gray-haired, hurrying about as nervous as a racehorse groom, feels something like what she feels now: throat tight with nervousness and anticipation, waiting for the moment he clutches the basket's edge and bends his knees as one corner, then the other, sways and bucks and lifts from the ground. Inside the balloon, the lantern's flame roars. What might London look like from the air, all the streets and roofs seen top-side first? Mary can form no conception of it. Shelley says the ancient Egyptian hieroglyph for *house* looks like a child's drawing of a house from above, as the gods are thought to see it. Borne over the city in his balloon, this little Frenchman will become a god too.

Lackington's, in the southwest corner of Finsbury Square, isn't Mary's first choice. But John Murray, Byron's publisher, rejected *Frankenstein* after one week: *We regret that we are unable to pursue publication of your most interesting novel...* No, you don't *regret* it, she'd fired back in her head. You just don't *want* it, damn you, and you can't have read enough of it in one week to know how *interesting* it is. Reluctantly, she returned to Johnson and Hunter in St. Paul's Churchyard, where a black ribbon hung on the door and the boy Cecil, two inches taller and self-importantly strangled in a cravat right out of Shelley's nightmares, presided in the office where the Four Stages of Cruelty were now hung neatly in a row. When Cecil saw Mary – in a new gray dress, with her hair neatly pinned and a third baby just showing – he arranged his features to cover an instant, spiteful recognition. Mr. Hunter must have given him a bollocking after the way he'd treated her before. "I'm afraid we are accepting no new authors at this time," he declared. "Upon Mr. Hunter's death, the press of business has grown extreme. But" – he paused, just long enough for magnanimity – "there's always Lackington's."

The sneer in Cecil's voice had been echoed in her father's. "Ah, old Jim Lackington," he sighed. "At the 'Temple of the Muses.'" Scholarly scorn fought with respect on his face. "But no denying, he's successful. That store is large enough to drive a coach-and-four right through. And he loves books. When he and his wife first got to London they spent their last half-crown on a book: 'for had I bought a dinner,' he said, 'we should have eaten it to-morrow, and the pleasure would have been soon over, but should we live fifty years longer, we shall have the *Night Thoughts* to feast upon.'"[1] He laughed. "He loves to tell that story. To be sure, I wouldn't starve for Edward Young. But try Lackington anyway, Mary. He loves to find new authors. And unlike so many publishers who make that claim, he actually *means* it."

The wide green door of the Temple of the Muses opens, then slams, and a stocky man in a plain but good blue cloth coat – obviously Lackington himself – hurries toward the balloon's basket, a piece of paper and a quill clutched in his hands. "Blanchard!" he calls. "Brave fellow! One more thing!" Blanchard lifts the quill and scratches at the page; Lackington shakes his hand and beams, holding the paper up carefully for the ink to dry, then rolls it into a careful cylinder. As he steps away, Mary can just hear the satisfied words he mutters to himself: "first rights!"

"Mr. Lackington?" Mary approaches, fighting a quaver in her voice.

The man's blue eyes, merry and sharp, flicker over her gray dress and the pages in her hand and assess her in an instant: *Author. Aspirant.* But nothing in his gaze says *silly girl.* Nor should it. She is twenty years old. She has fair-copied the whole book again in her best writing, incorporating most of the corrections and changes Shelley scribbled in the margins. Sometimes he went off on some high-flown obsession of his own, inserting into Victor's mouth a speech about ambition or poetry. Those she's left out. But he did help her with spelling. *Igmmatic,* she had written. *Enigmatic o you pretty Pecksie,* he wrote.[2] She'll keep that to herself.

With a cheer from the crew and the gathering crowd, Mr. Blanchard swings one leg, then the other, over the edge of the basket and flourishes one arm in the air. Mr. Lackington jerks his gaze from Mary and watches the balloon. Without speaking, he holds out one hand and Mary gives him the pages, bound tightly with their green ribbon. There. It is done.

Mr. Lackington's eyes swerve between the pages and Blanchard's crew, who are now loosening the ropes one by one. The Frenchman clutches the basket's edge as it bucks and rises. He tugs a cord dangling near his hand and the fire inside the balloon roars. And then the whole basket hovers off the ground, six inches, then eighteen, then a yard and more. The crowd cheers. "Relâchez les cordes!" Blanchard shouts and tugs the fire-rope again. The men open their hands and the ropes whisk through and the great balloon springs into the air like a racehorse from the starting-gate. Cheers rise from the crowd and from the windows of the buildings all around Finsbury Square, where office-boys and housewives and children lean out, waving their arms. Mr. Lackington clamps Mary's manuscript under his arm and applauds thunderously. "Go!" he shouts. "Go, go, go!" And the great silk globe, shimmering green and blue, sways above the house tops. Mr. Blanchard is a tiny shape in the basket, waving with one hand and working the fire-rope with the other. One of the dangling ground-ropes brushes a chimney-pot. And the balloon drifts eastward, towards the Channel, growing smaller as it lifts.

For a long moment, neither Mary nor Mr. Lackington moves. At last, with a sigh, he takes her manuscript from under his arm. He smiles at Mary. "Such a moment!" he exclaims. "As Pliny said, rowing to Vesuvius, chance favors the bold. Now. What's your title?"

"*Frankenstein,*" Mary said, "*or, The Modern Prometheus.*"

Mr. Lackington's eyebrows lift and his smile sharpens. "Prometheus." He scans the sky, but the balloon is a tiny dot now, almost out of sight. "You know your moment, madame." He grins. "Chance favors the bold. Indeed." Swiftly, he tugs the ribbon loose and ruffles the pages. He reads the first page, then the next. He shuffles to the part Mary has recopied and rechecked the most, crinkling the paper: the moment the Creature's eyes open. Finally he lifts his head and crooks his elbow at Mary. "Come into the shop," he says. And Mary sets her hand on his blue coat sleeve and follows him inside.

Two hours later, Mary leaves Lackington's, eager both to linger and to rush away, hugging a bright globe of joy to her chest. He has said *yes*. "I can't remember," he said, "another time I've come so quickly to this judgment. There's just something about this book, and I..." He shook his head, marveling. "You should be proud, Mrs. Shelley. Ten percent of sales. Three author's copies. Reviews: I'll see to it. Date of publication: January 1, 1818. This book is worth a rush. To the new year!" Lackington has launched her book like Mr. Blanchard's balloon. Or perhaps more like a colt or oxen calf, staggering up onto its shaky legs within hours of its arrival in the world. That's good. She needs it to finish being born. She needs it to rise and walk.

The title page won't bear her name. Probably, this is for the best. Like the author of that novel *Sense and Sensibility* and – what are the other ones? – who is certainly a woman too. There will only be a dedication: *To William Godwin, author of* Political Justice *and other writings, this tale is most affectionately inscribed by the Author.*[3] How her father, still laboring at all those other books, stretching out his diminishing trail of sales, will appreciate the reminder to the world that he *has* other books. He has frozen and cudgeled and badgered her but he has taught her to become a writer. She turns her mother's ring left, then right. A strange bashfulness flushes through her, now that she's actually done this thing. *I've made a book. See, Mama. I am here.*

By God. It's real. She has made a creature like no one – even Mama – has ever seen.

By God. It's real.

From the door of Lackington's Temple of the Muses the Creature steps, elaborately casual, and watches Mary's small narrow back, upright in her gray dress, hurrying away toward the City Road. Her joy, as buoyant as that big silk balloon, lifts him too. In fact, her joy has summoned him into this moment: he'd blinked, and suddenly he was browsing Lackington's shelves in sober slate-colored trousers and a long morocco-brown frock coat and suede gloves and boots and a top hat pulled down well over his face as her voice and Lackington's twined excitedly in the office and the store clerk, cheerful and polite, left him to browse (it's an art to be helpful but not obtrusive in a bookshop; Lackington trains his people well.) Mary is so excited, and she's nervous too. Her heart is pounding. Her thoughts are racing: *what will Papa think?*

Don't worry. The Creature hopes she'll hear him. *You don't need Godwin. You've got me.*

To be sure, starting their novel with Robert Walton's voice is risky. Walton's not even the main character, just a sea captain, a poor plodding sod who picks up disastrous Victor Frankenstein on the polar journey that the Creature, and Mary, have designed. (At the top of page three, Lackington had to stifle a question – *where is this going?* – and smile at Mary perched anxiously opposite him, but the epistolary form *does* have its own propulsion.) Then after Robert picks him up, Victor tells Robert his own story, and the Creature's, taking all the credit for himself, as usual. Lackington's impressed with the novel's onion-like layers of narrative: *so complex for a first-time author. And for a girl!* (He tries not to be the sort of man who thinks such things, but he can't always help himself.) But the Creature, of course, is the star. No one can deny that. Lackington was sold on the book as soon as the Creature opened his eyes, on page eighteen. (Of *course* he was!) And now Mr. Lackington's released the Creature out into the world to follow Mary, and Victor Frankenstein, and the book they've all made.

Soon they'll be back on the Continent, following Shelley's restlessness to Italy. Godwin and Mrs. Vile, pinched and old, will wave them off at the docks: Shelley, and Claire with Byron's eleven-month-old baby Allegra in her arms, and Mary and little William, age two, and his new sister Clara, aged three months, and Elise, the grown-up maid from Geneva who tries not to stare too long at Shelley (he is, after all, what humans call *handsome)*, and Milly Shields, the awkward new teenage maid, who leaves behind a life of tending her drunken father's pub in Marlow High Street. The Creature will go with them, three calf-bound copies of their book in Mary's trunk: *Frankenstein, or The Modern Prometheus.*

Byron is in Venice now, having banished poor Polidori back to Soho, scribbling sarcastic letters to his friends: *I was half mad during the time of its composition* – he's talking about his own famous poem, what else – *between metaphysics, mountains, lakes, love unextinguishable, thoughts unutterable, and the nightmare of my own delinquencies. I should, many a good day, have blown my brains out, but for the recollection that it would have given pleasure to my mother-in-law.*[4] Ah, Childe Harold, aiming his famous profile theatrically over his painted backdrop of mountains and lake as the stagehands scurry to lower the lights. *If I could embody and unbosom that which is within me* – What a laugh. The Creature knows what Byron also knows but tries to deny: there *is* no unbosoming, no unbuckling and releasing what you've written once you've done that thing. Authorship isn't so easy as boxing at the Fives Court: you can't just shuck off your mufflers and drop them on the stained canvas floor and take a sip of water and turn your mind to the next round. There is no forgetting a book once you've made it. Any more than there is a forgetting of a child once you've birthed it into the world. Even if you frighten its mother away from your house at midnight, even if its mother drowns herself in the Serpentine, even if you trundle in your ponderous unpaid-for carriage away from it across the Continent, even if it dies and is buried on its grandmother's coffin in St. Pancras Cemetery, it's still out there, connected by a cord invisible to everyone but you. As the Creature is connected, now, to the infuriating, brilliant human world and to the woman who's brought him into it.

The Creature watches Mary until she disappears down City Road. He tugs his top hat very low. Then he turns and strides toward Shoreditch, merging with a crowd of Londoners too concerned with their own business to turn more than a casual eye to a rawboned, unusually tall man in a good coat and trousers, something flickering on his shadowed face that might or might not be a smile.

Part Three

Near the North Pole

First, Robert Walton knows, you train yourself to bear what comes. No matter what that is. Cold. Danger. Loneliness. Because that is the price of *elsewhere* and the dreams that take you there. Since his boyhood back in Derbyshire with his sister Margaret and their grief-distracted father and their visits to their mother's grave after church – Margaret always has a posy for her stone and he a penny for the offering plate – he's dreamed of journeys. Their village is pleasant enough, with its square of cottages around the green and the one-room school where the master soon exclaims in delight *I can teach ye no more, son* and plies Robert with the books he's ordered from London to stoke his own dreams of *elsewhere:* the jungles of South America, the ancient pyramids of Egypt, and the vast wastes of the polar North, where the ocean can bind a ship in ice and where a person of sufficient courage may transform himself from an ordinary Derbyshire boy into a man who has stood atop the globe. This is Robert's dream. To go as far as any human can. To discover the secret of the forces that turn the earth and move the stars. To be forever changed. To have done *more*. Not just to count out his days to the *clink* of Sunday coins in the offering plate and the *swish* of water into the vase at Mother's grave until a new sound wakes in his head: his own regretful voice, whispering *too late*.

To be sure, there are dangers down this road, like the clever boy in the next village, still talked of twenty years later, who went mad. *I will be an anatomist,* he declared, *like the great surgeons in London.* On the night of his thirteenth birthday, he went to dig in the churchyard for a baby's corpse. The boy was discovered. So was his secret room in an abandoned cellar, with the bones of rabbits disarticulated and labeled with pins. Charges were brought. And so the boy's family sent him to Bedlam. Then they sold their house and followed him: all gone, down the road to London after all. Walton will not – out of embarrassing but unshakeable superstition – utter that boy's name, which he well knows from his father's meaningful repetition of the story (*are you listening, Robert? There is always a cost to such folly, for others and oneself*). Because something in him fears that mad focus, respects it, yearns for it. He has never met anyone as ambitious as himself. He has never had a companion. A friend. Who wants *more*, as he does. Who understands. Who will keep journeying forward, no matter what it costs, alongside him.

Even the bankers who've underwritten his polar journey don't comprehend Robert's drive, unless it's put to them in terms of profit: *I will discover a passage across the top of the world from the Orient to the North Sea, and thence to England. Just imagine the movement of trade: from six months to three weeks!* Accordingly a stout ship is found and equipped with sailors and supplies. The men don't seem to trust Robert, despite his cheeriest voice and best smile – he's never understood how to talk to people – but they trust the mission, and the money. Waivers of liability and risk are read out and signed with thumbprints in tar. First installments of salaries are stashed in pockets and left with dockside wives. Margaret hugs Robert and weeps; her husband Mr. Saville shakes his hand. And they sail north, past the godforsaken islands at the tip of Scotland, toward Norway and the farthest ports from which the fierce Vikings took their leave, out of the land-world of white and brown and gray and into a sea-world of dazzling pearly ice and jagged spars and the unearthly glow of polar sky. When the Aurora Borealis dances in green and gold waves like rain blowing across a summer field back in England, all the men join Robert on the deck to watch. And they're united in wonder until Robert ruins it: *now, look here, men, let's get our sleep!* And they turn away, faces dark. Either he says too little or too much. Never the proper words. Good thing he can write his letters to Margaret, which he completes and dates as diligently as his captain's log and holds in readiness to send on the next southward ship they pass. Perhaps his words will reach her. Perhaps.

The compass holds true: they are on course for the North Pole. The ice is thickening and the men grumble but Robert can't afford to heed them: the ship's flanks are thick English oak with iron ribs and they have sufficient supplies (not *ample*, he must honestly admit) for the week's sailing, maybe two, that will bring them to the Pole. But as for passage across the globe's top, he can't honestly recommend this to his investing merchantmen. Not yet. For there is no land here at all. No stations at which to stop and relieve even his unusually hardy sailors. Only a perpetual gloom and a cold so deep he can barely breathe, even through the layers of Margaret-knitted scarf in which he swathes his face. Thank God for the spark of fire in each cabin monitored and fed to bring a modicum of light. For without that light he and his men will not complete their mission. Without that light, he can't scratch out the log and the letters to Margaret that keep his mind in its upright track. Without that light, he and his men will die.

He's awakened by the groan of the ship's timber in his cabin bunk's wall. Ice, tightening its grip. And then, up on deck, the first mate shouts for him. Hurrying up the ladder and following the mate's pointing finger, he sees a blurred shape on the ice near the horizon, moving fast. He blinks. It looks like a man in a dogsled, wrapped in furs. But no man is so large. No man could survive out on this ice in a sled, no matter how well wrapped. There are natives here, Inuit hunters of great courage and craft. But Inuits are short of stature. This is a giant. *Snowblind*, all the old polar voyagers warn. *Ye stare too long across the ice and ye think ye see a ghost. This is how good men go mad.*

"Sir, sir!" Now the cook calls him, beckoning frantically from the opposite railing. Tearing his gaze away, he strides to where all the sailors are scrambling for ropes to lower toward something on the ice down there: a second man, a European, with a straggle of dark hair and iced-over beard, swaddled and shuddering. The floor of his tiny boat rattles with empty canteens and gnawed, frozen rabbit bones. Robert leans over the ship's railing and the man peers at him, blinking through eyelashes silver with ice. "My name is Victor Frankenstein," he says: a cultivated voice, despite his chattering teeth. "Before I come on board your vessel, will you have the kindness to inform me whither you are bound?"[1]

And Robert shivers and hesitates, because the light in those dark eyes is the unquenchable desire of the mad boy from the old Derbyshire village, the boy who stalked Robert's childhood dreams, the ambition that stalks his own brain, here on the ice in front of him, gazing up. Like the wraith from some terrifying poem he read as a boy, the Ancient Mariner, who freezes an innocent churchgoer with a basilisk stare and tells him a story, a nightmare bleeding through the poem into the waking world. *It has found me,* Robert thinks. *The punishment.* In blind unreasonable terror – I'm a *scientist,* he argues with himself, what's *wrong* with me? – Robert admits these words even as he extends his hand and grasps Victor Frankenstein's filthy glove to haul him up. *Here it is. The cost.* On the horizon, the giant shape on its dogsled pauses, observing them, then continues onward, almost out of sight.

CHAPTER 2

Venice

ITALY SEPTEMBER 1818

Shelley, tall and frantic in the haze, is shouting at the gondolier. "For God's sake, man, row faster, this child is –" But Mary's brain will not admit his voice. Only water slapping boat-flank, the creaking of the oar in its upright hooks (*il forcola*, her mad brain helpfully supplies), the incredulous protest of the lithe boy at the helm: "Signo,' we are in center of la*goon*." At her feet is Mama's carpetbag with the random things flung in from the trunks that were supposed to be unpacked methodically and then stored in the attic of the lovely Casa Bertini at Bagni di Lucca, where, in Italy at last, she and Shelley and the children were meant to stay. And stretched across her thighs, straining and convulsed, lies her daughter, Clara, twelve months and twenty four days old. Clara has the fever. Clara is too ill to travel. But Clara was rousted from the lovely house in the cool green woods because Shelley decreed it so. And now Clara must be hurried to a doctor. Because Mary has chased a man – and words – across the Continent, no matter what, her child will be the one to pay.

Mary's little girl is so small in all this light. Her arms are thin as a china doll's. Her mouth stretches square in whimpering that has no sound. Her eyes swell open, huge and black. This silent baby is not large enough to hold the suffering that wracks her in her mother's arms.

Clutching her daughter, bundled in a ragged gray blanket, Mary cannot speak. She cannot stir from the seat of this narrow boat. On her finger, her mother's wedding ring burns. She bends her body over Clara and cranes her face into the white sun, past her husband and the gondolier to where the gray-blue shadow of the city is rising from the sea. Row, row. Slow, slow. Boat through water. On. Again. Breath by ragged breath. Borne like a painted Italian Madonna on a barge, ringed with dead flowers. This is not what is meant to happen here.

First a slim spire, just an arrow-point above the waves. And then another. Then the square fortress of a city wall and then the hilly scape of roofs. With each stroke of the oars, Venice grows above the lagoon's horizon as the Alps grow above the plain between Geneva and Chamonix. But something here is wrong. She travels on water, not land. This is a witches' world, all reversed and upside-down. Solid ground is silt thirty feet down. Deep in that silt – Shelley has talked of it – are sunk the great trees hewn from forests like those of distant cool green Bagni di Lucca from where she and her baby have been hauled, great pines planted in the muck to calcify slowly over centuries, accustoming themselves to holding up the city built on marsh and arrogance and dead men's dreams that no one now remembers, no one but the great trees turned to salt pillars in their grief, eternally upholding this blue-gray silhouette of towers and spires and domes above the waves, their feet held fast in the snapped-shut jaws of the fatal moment centuries ago in which the blood urging itself up and down their veins had said *I'll help you build your life above these waves. Take me.* Before their love turned them all to stone.

Small body on Mary's thighs. Third baby from the bed of her own body. Lips turning blue. Wind twitches pale curls around the old gray blanket folded over small face, turning blue.

Love turns flesh to stone. How can that be true? And yet it is.

Venice surrounds Mary now in walls of crumbling marble and clay rearing from the sea and struck gold by the lowered sun. Balconied houses and warehouses and churches and *palazzi* lean high above her to the left and right, echoing with voices and shouts, curving ahead as ordinary as Piccadilly or the Strand except instead of cobblestones and mud this street is greenish water and the carriages are boats of every size and shape, including sinuous high-prowed gondolas, barges tattered with crates of leaves and fruit and shining fish, little rowboats dashing to tie up at the *palazzo* docks where blue-and-white-striped landing poles rear at the foot of stone steps slippery with brackish weed. Clara shudders and goes still. Mary clutches her child. She'll never get Clara up steps like that once they reach the Ospedale. One more of these convulsions and Mary will tumble with her girl and strike her head and sink to the bottom of the Grand Canal. Daughter and mother, dead together. A crazy brain-babble begins, eerily calm: *Creature and creator. The old moon with the new moon in her arms. And I fear, I fear, my mother dear, that we shall come to harm. These are pearls that were her eyes.*

They must reach the Ospedale or her daughter will die.

If Shelley tries to name the landmarks to her she will push him into the canal herself.

The slim boy shoves the oar deep and the gondola slides forward and hits a passing fruit-barge: *thunk.* High on the barge roof, a wooden crate tips, and three bright oranges tumble over mounds of radicchio and artichokes into the stinking canal water: *splash, splash, splash.* "Vafancu'!" The wiry barge-woman shakes her fist at the boy, but then she sees Mary and the child. Clara is shivering, her cheek hot under Mary's palm. "Al' ospedale." The woman points uselessly at an alley toward which the boy is already steering them. Her right hand sweeps up to her forehead, down to her breast, left shoulder, right. "Con Dio." The horror on a stranger's face chills Mary. The pity there is worse.

Under the Rialto Bridge they float and the day turns underwater-green, ribboned all around with writhing snakes of light and hollow echoes of suddenly-not-human voices. Clara's lips are gray, her eyes now closed. Mary bends close. There it is, the singing rasp of breath drawn through a tiny throat. So small a thread of life.

The gondola shoots down the alley and scrapes the walls, clawing the shaggy muck away in raw stripes. The light glows pink and golden-brown around Mary now, with one slice of blue sky up near the roofs. Five feet of water between one house and the next: thank God no other boat is coming this way. Two plump rats patter along a ledge and a gray cat strains at them from a window, too far away to leap. A man whistles across a footbridge, crossing out of and then back into his own unknowable life. What would he see if he looked at them? A young woman in vomit-stained black travel gown (*seen better days*: the inevitable quick Italian verdict would be true.) That child on her lap, so very still. And balancing in his worn and slippery-footed shoes on the gondola's prow, a skinny white-faced English baronet staring into every window, up into the slice of sky, looking everywhere except at the woman with the dying child on her lap. A man an English court judged *morally unfit* for custody of his first two children. A man with eyes for all the world except for his second wife and his third daughter. Who lies so very still.

Here is the *ospedale* dock and here a red-faced sweating nun rushes forth to take them in, speaking quick Italian that at Shelley's wild gaze breaks into slower words: "Signo,' here.... *Rapidament'*, the child..." The boat tilts and leaps back under Mary's feet and she's on the stone threshold with Clara against her chest, small Clara's body cooler now, the nun calling *Medico, medico,* down the hall where torches smoke and gutter despite the mellow sunlit afternoon outside, then into a bare white room.

A man behind a table holds out his hands. "Lay the child here." The voice is English, the face weary. He stoops over Clara and puts his fingers in the soft crook of her jaw. One heartbeat's worth of time. Then two. His face goes very still. His head bends lower.

If he looks up and Mary sees the knowledge there, it will be true.

Please don't look up.

Shelley hovers, still panting, at Mary's shoulder, but she will not turn to him.

The doctor waits. A stillness settles in his face. Through the neck of his smock, gray-and-ginger beard hairs curl. How strange it is: that unshaven throat pulses with its own heartbeat and a faint unbathed bedside-whiff. This homely alive body is neglected now in its owner's absorption in this tiny body that is not. How strange. He is alive and Clara is –

The doctor's face, turned downward, has at some point in the last twenty seconds become a face with news it fears to break. Two fingers dent the crook of her daughter's jaw, broken-nailed and scarred with scalpel-cuts and acid drops: Clara's life has just passed beneath them like thread slipping through a dropped needle. A silver point, a strand of green, apart and gone. Mary has stood directly over her only living girl and has not seen it. Clara is dead.

Shelley is gathering himself now to speak but Mary will not hearken to him. All is quiet here, inside her and around her now. All is very quiet here.

In her sad ragged blanket the bundle of Clara lies still. The bundle of baby. Bundled-up, bundled-into-carriage, bundled-across-mountains-for-the-benefit-of-interfering-everlasting-never-sister-never-ending-Shelley-longing Claire – for the benefit of *her*. Claire. Baby bundled over Italy as an afterthought. Hefted into weary arms at daylight, letter with instructions crumpled in one hand. *Then it is set then – corner of Hatton Garden and Holborn, July 28, four o'clock in the morning – the dawn will rise on a new birth of freedom and liberty and love that we shall share as no two beings ever have – your S –* That was how Shelley had summoned Mary from Skinner Street. How many years ago now? *Corner of Hatton Garden and Holborn ...*

Imperious excited black pen-strokes, spiky as a mountain range, crumpled in her hand. Carried all that way, so she would not forget.

Oh, she will not forget.

The doctor raises his head. Knowledge has settled there, clear enough to read.

Footsteps in the corridor outside: a flock of nuns hurrying past in wings of white starch and hushed Italian, instruments clinking on a tray. Smell of smoke and brine and blood. The light upon the whitewashed wall turns golden as a peach, browned faintly underneath. That would be the sun, on its way into the stinking sea.

Mary lifts a fold of the old gray blanket and covers Clara's face.

She will have no memory, years later, of the emergence onto the *fondamente* where the sign swings in the wind – *ospedale*, you need no Italian to know that word – and the gondolas bob and nose their mooring posts. Or of the cemetery island, San Michele, rising just beyond, its green points of cypress twitching above its tawny wall. Only the knowledge rising into her, dismal as a flood: *acqua alta*, adulthood, acceptance. There will be the finding of a house, now, to stay in Venice rather than return to the green hills at Bagni because Shelley will want to linger in this city so atmospheric and so *beautiful*, everyone says, so *beautiful*, and commune with Byron. Of course. Byron is here. Isn't that the reason for all this rush, to accommodate everlasting Byron and everlasting Claire and Claire's own baby girl for whom Mary's has been –

Set into a wall niche a foot above Mary's head, three little candles gutter before a bas-relief portrait of the Madonna and her solemn baby son. Three candles glowing in the middle of the day for this mother and child who have been –

Sacrificed. Her daughter has been sacrificed instead of Claire's and Byron's child. And Shelley has arranged it.

"Mary." Shelley is speaking to her now. "Mary. We'll meet the Hoppners, the English consul and his wife, you remember, and Elise and Allegra, and we can find a house to let – Where would you like to..."

Words dart in her brain: Chapman's Homer, the translation that so impressed Mr. Keats. *The sea had soaked his heart through.* That is how she feels. That is how this city surely feels, this intelligent grieving organism in which she's now submerged. The walls of painted plaster, yellowish and pink and golden over brick, lean at an angle, this way, that way, almost unnoticeable. Unsound. Soaked through. Shut out. Shut in. Mighty doors with lion's heads and Moors' heads and Medusas worn shiny with grasping, all firmly shut.

"Mary." Shelley's voice is softer now. No need to rush the hysterical mother, for it will do no good. "Mary – where do you want to go?"

Breath shudders into her lungs. She speaks deliberately: "I do not give a damn."

❄

The publication of *Frankenstein* had been meant to mark the opening into an ordinary authorly life, neat as a book with pages turning forward. Chapter One: the inevitable *bildungsroman,* the scrabbly life of Young Ambition and Young Love, Obstacles Overcome. Chapter Two: where Mary's narrative finds its feet, where like Mama she sees her first book into the world and earns a living as authoress, anchor of a household that now includes husband and boy and girl. But despite Lackington's cheery letters (*the reviews are coming in! Walter Scott, no less, has praised it! That narrative structure, such an innovation!),* the royalties have only dripped into her bank account: one pound, three pounds, two pounds fifty at a time. And despite Shelley's anticipation, Italy, so far, is not furnishing a clear and sunny Chapter Three.

Perhaps things started to go wrong five months ago, on that April night back in Bagni di Lucca, when Mary, Shelley, and Elise hiked down the hill to the Casino to watch Napoleon's sister, beautiful Pauline Bonaparte, playing cards with the men. All the way back uphill to their rented Casa Bertini, Elise had been in raptures. "Did you ever see such a dress?" she asked. "Such magnificent eyes. A woman like that knows how to take a chance. To change her own life. *Mon dieu.* It makes me wonder" – Elise's startled, ugly laugh surprised Mary – "what *I've* been doing all this time."

"You're only thirty," Mary volunteered. "No need to talk like an old woman."

Elise shot a veiled look at Mary. "Thirty? True. That's not so old. But I am –" She paused and put her hands on her hips and drew a deep breath. "Yes, thirty. Not old at all." Shelley watched her. And under his eyes Elise straightened her spine and thrust out her chest, just a bit. She lowered her chin and cut her eyes at him, then at Mary. Then she laughed – loud, false – and lowered her head and continued up the path.

How did some women absorb so naturally that mysterious skill that Mary had apparently missed: the ability to understand another woman? What were you to do when her smile contained nothing you could object to other than a vague, deniable contempt? Elise had followed them from

Geneva to London and now to Italy. And now she had a place under the roof of the Casa Bertini, their rented house high in the cool green hills. She had shy young Milly from Marlow as her second-in-command. She had Paolo Foggi, a handyman to patch the roof and keep the temperamental stove alight, who was obviously taken with Elise, although she mocked the way he swaggered and smoothed his lush mustache. And tomorrow she would accompany Allegra to Venice. Why was she still dissatisfied? Thirty was not so old. Plenty of respectable widowers could still hearken to Elise, with her clear, if sallow, skin and dark brown hair and dark eyes and quick sardonic gaze that softened, when she looked at William and Clara and Allegra, into love. Surely Elise had nothing of which to complain.

Back in the Casa Bertini, Claire had lit a fire in the sitting room to banish the evening chill and was scribbling her letter to send with Allegra and Elise to Venice the next morning. *I am sending you my child because I love her too well to keep her.*[1] Byron, backed by His Lordship in every servant's and banker's salutation, could educate and launch Allegra. Claire had no name other than the one she'd invented, no man other than a notorious poet who'd slipped from her grasp and to whom she must now be polite, pleading, supplicant, not overly demanding, and still-at-least-somewhat-faintly-alluring all at once in letters she must keep short and pleasant to keep him reading about what would happen to their child. Her springy black curls looked dull; purple shadows darkened the skin under her eyes. Mary put her arm around Claire and Claire leaned against Mary. "I don't know what else to say." Her voice was factual, heartbreaking. "I don't know what else to do."

"Let me go fetch you a drink of water," Mary said, squeezing Claire's shoulders, "and we'll sit a while." She crossed the big room with its central dining table, its low-beamed ceiling shadowed in the flickering candlelight, and lifted the pitcher from its place on the buffet and slipped out the back door. If not handled gingerly, the heavy old hinges would squeal and wake the children, who slept three in a row on a bed embanked with pillows: William. Allegra. Clara.

At the back door, Mary paused to listen to the Italian night. Fireflies spangled the dim chambers under the trees, which rang with the throaty hum of frog-song from the springs on the hill. Ahead of Mary in the dusk stood the wellhouse. A woman sat on the well's stone rim. A man leaned over her with lazy intent. Low voices vibrated in the air, too far away for Mary to make out words. Then, from the tall shadow of the man, high laughter crackled, quickly doused. The woman leaned back on the well-cap. The man's shadow merged with hers. And they became one shadow. Moving.

It was Shelley and Elise, as it had been Shelley and Claire back in the threadbare London days. It could not be Shelley and Elise, as Shelley had surely just come out to the necessary and Elise was surely indoors, preparing for her journey to Venice. Mary had just interrupted some mountainside peasant pair at their courting, some opportunistic couple under the shelter of the old Casa Bertini's well-cover in the deep Italian dark. A shadow. Of what else could Mary be certain than that? *He's done this kind of thing before.* But Shelley was her husband now. And surely he would not – Three years ago, on Marchmont Street, Mary had raged and shouted and dragged the bureau in front of the door of the flat to lock him and Claire outside. But now – Her brain leaped into logic, fueled by a fear she couldn't allow to surface. She was the mother of two children under three years of age, in a foreign country with no money of her own. She must be rational. Not jump at shadows and suspicions. Close her hand tightly around Mama's ring, which Shelley had slid onto her finger. Surely, her husband would not –

The space under the well-roof was very dark. The shadows had merged now, swaying gently. It might be only a trick of the light. Only the saw and scrape of frog-song rattled on all around her. Only the light. Only a trick. No need to investigate further.

Mary turned and went back into the house and closed the door quietly behind her. She set the empty pitcher precisely back in its water-stained spot on the buffet. Elise's bedroom door was shut; surely she was asleep. She would need her rest, for Venice was more than a hundred miles away, and Allegra would surely be fretful in the carriage. Luckily Allegra was now asleep, sandwiched between Clara and William, all in a row on their clean white bed. Mary must not overturn the raft on which they floated, the unspeaking security of *breakfast* and *playtime* and *sleep again* to come. Not upset her children's dreams. Shelley was not in her bedroom. Surely he had simply been tempted, alone, by the night into the forest. It was so beautiful here, where they were trying to make a life. The night air through her bedroom window was so cool. So conducive to the sleep into which she fell (with the children, with the walk up and down the hill, she was so tired) without ascertaining exactly when Shelley came to bed.

And in the commotion of the morning that followed, there was little opportunity to ask. Right on time, Byron's Venetian agent, Mr. Meriwether, arrived to take Allegra away. "You needn't be concerned for your daughter's welfare." The words poured anxiously forth before he'd even set his cordwain-leather boot on the carriage-step, before he'd even shaken Claire's hand and smiled at Mary and Shelley standing nervously behind her in the yard. "There is an English colony in Venice as in every Italian city, the English consul Mr. Hoppner and his wife are very generous and active in society and know His Lordship quite well, and they have given me their *personal* assurance they will look after little Alba –"

"—Allegra," Claire said softly, "Albe is *his* nickname."

"—Allegra," continued Mr. Meriwether, "and provide her with everything she may need, as of course His Lordship himself also will." He paused for breath and smiled unconvincingly. "Why, she'll be just like a child back home in Kensington. I saw the most beautiful rocking-horse, dapple-gray, in the window of a shop near Rialto myself just the other day, with a flaxen mane, all of real horsehair, and I spoke of it to His Lordship and he has empowered me to purchase it, little Allegra will love—"

"She's a year and a half old." Claire's voice was still soft. "Not quite a half. A bit young for a rocking-horse." She handed her sealed, folded letter to Mr. Meriwether. "Please give this to your employer."

Elise stepped from the front door in her traveling cloak and sturdy boots, holding her own carpetbag and a new leather portmanteau – made by the cobbler here in Bagni di Lucca to last a little girl indefinitely – in her right hand and clasping Allegra's hand with the left. A teething bracelet circled Allegra's other wrist, just visible among the layers of dresses and stockings in which Claire had swaddled her to ward off any chill. At sixteen months, she was proudly toddling, swatting away arms that tried to lift her, bolder than Mary's own little Clara, staggering behind William across the yard as a spring wind lifted her downy yellow hair. Now, spotting Claire near the carriage, she pulled loose from Elise and toddled faster. "Mamma!" she called. "Mam man bud day." Glee and impatience chased each other across her face: why couldn't all these adults understand what was perfectly plain? "Mam man bud day. Hoss!"

Claire snatched her up before she reached the big carriage-horses, who stretched their noses curiously down in her direction. "Mustn't run under horses," Claire said automatically. "It's dangerous." She clutched Allegra against her. Then she bent her face into the child's hair and burst into tears. Allegra squirmed. "Down," she said. Whatever her mother was frightened of, it was obviously not her concern. "Down. Hoss!"

Elise glanced at Shelley, then Mary, then hurried forward and tucked both bags under the carriage seat. "All the child's things are here," she told

Mr. Meriwether. "And mine. I'm Elise Duvillard. As Miss Clairmont wrote Lord Byron, I'll be coming to look after Allegra. She knows me." Relief slackened Mr. Meriwether's tense face; taking sole charge of a teething toddler on the carriage ride to Venice was a fearsome prospect. Avoiding Mary's and Shelley's eyes, Elise turned to Claire, who stood with Allegra in her arms. "I'll take good care of her," she promised. Claire only blinked, silent, tightening her grip. Shelley looked away. Astonishingly, he seemed close to tears.

Mr. Meriwether helped Elise into the carriage and settled her on its forward-facing seat. Elise beckoned through the open door, and Allegra strained from Claire's arms toward her. And Claire let her go. Mr. Meriwether scrambled in after them and shut the carriage door. The coachman took up the reins and the carriage lurched into motion. Suddenly Allegra set up a wail and Claire lunged forward as Allegra's face appeared at the window. "Mamma!" she cried. "Mamma!" Running beside the carriage, Claire stretched both hands through the window and touched Allegra's fingers. "Mamma!" Then the carriage picked up speed and Claire faltered and stood sobbing in the dust. Allegra's cries faded like a bright ribbon in the air.

In June, Elise's first letter from Venice reached Bagni di Lucca. Safely in the Palazzo Mocenigo, Allegra was delighting her father, wearing little lace-trimmed trousers and sitting on his lap at table and playing with his giant dog. "She cries not so much for Mamma now," Elise wrote. "Milord may let her mamma come to her as the summer goes along." *Delightful child.* Byron's handwriting curled across the bottom of the page. *I thank you, Shelley, for your pains with her. Greet your new wife for me.* Then, in August, the second letter came: Byron had moved Elise and Allegra into the British consulate, the Hoppners' house. *He has a mistress,* Elise wrote. *We seem inconvenient. And I must say only that* – the next words were crossed out – *he jests about his daughter in a most unusual way....*

"Allegra!" Claire screamed, hurling the letter to the floor. "That's it. Shelley, take me to Venice. I'm going to get her back, I'm going to – That devil. I'm going to murder him –" This can't be true, Mary argued, surely the Hoppners would not allow – This is some madness of Elise's, she was so odd at departure – Yet Claire, lit by fear and the warlock-fire of Byron's reputation, would not be moved. And of course Shelley agreed. "It's just a misunderstanding, Mary," he pleaded. "Nothing wrong. You know Byron will listen to me. I'll be back as soon as I can." Obviously Mary could not go: Clara was sick and William was fretful without Allegra and Milly could not be left with them both. *Shelley, will you actually come back to me?* Mary could not speak the words. *Or, on the road with Claire again, will you simply ride away?*

Shelley and Claire had cantered down to Florence and then onto the coaching route to Venice and had reached Byron within a week. Mary knew how carefully Shelley must have planned it, how he would have entered Byron's grand dining room in Palazzo Mocenigo alone, how he would have accepted wine and bread and cheese and Byron's chaffing about his diet ("still no meat?") and admired the flicker of reflected wave-light over the walls and eventually come to the matter. The women and the children are at Padua, Shelley would have said, and, like the Ancient Mariner, I alone am escaped to tell thee.... Laughter. Lordly goodwill. Why, certainly, Byron would have said, bring them to my villa out at Este, it's not so far away but far enough. I'll do that, Shelley would have agreed. And then, once out of Byron's sight, he'd written Mary. *He thinks you're nearby, at Padua, with Claire and the children. We must now make this true. Or he'll be angry, he'll think I'm lying – A good relationship with him is important. For all of us. Please, Mary. Do this for me. And for your sister and her daughter.*

So Mary had thrown the papers and the forks and the sheets into trunks and bundled them over the hills and across the plain to Venice. One hundred and sixty-five English miles in the coach from Florence with William grizzling and small Clara feverish and frail. August was so very hot. At least Byron's house, up in the Eugenaean Hills, once they finally arrived, was cool. But Clara got worse. The doctor couldn't help. "He's no good, you know," Byron told Shelley, "come to Venice, take the child to see Aglietti, my own man..." And so Mary submitted herself to the usual mad Shelley-scramble. Rattled down the hills to Venice. Boarded a gondola across the lagoon. Watched the city rise from the sea as her child died, stretched across her lap.

How will you live, Mary? Surely Papa and Mrs. Vile had wondered it. Now, from her rented rooms in Venice, Mary casts a bitter glance backward at all of them – the threadbare old pair waving goodbye from the London docks, the threadbare young pair departing with their trunks and their maids and their babies and their tagalong never-quite-sister – and knew how she'd answer that question. How she'd always lived, of course. What did she always do? Act rational. Admit the sister who was not a sister to her journey, again. Hoist babies and trunks and smile gamely and pry with her eyes into her husband's distant gaze to flip his longing like a lid up from the warmth that hopefully still smoldered inside. Push down what she must convince herself she did not see under the green-black tree-shadows of Bagni di Lucca and whatever other places her husband went with Byron or Claire and not her. Push off with him into a country not yet known. Push the hours forward like pushing a pen across a page. Read. Write. Make a mark. Be responsible. Get things done. Refuse to admit ennui, boredom, shame, defeat, or grief. Hold close her son; bury her nose against his white-blond scalp and breathe. Travel on and on and on into still-hoped-for sensations through the doorway of the passage booked, the carriage hired, the blank inviting road. Set her face forward and travel on, following her husband into the country of *elsewhere*. The only home he will ever know. Or can ever give her.

Elsewhere had once been a place she desired to travel, too.

Clara is buried on the deserted beach of the Lido, facing the Adriatic Sea, in a radiant haze of pink Venetian sunset and silver chimney smoke. Because San Michele is closed to them – non-Catholics, atheists, refugees – they've wrapped Clara's tiny body in a bedsheet stolen from the inn. To the fishermen sipping their espresso at the window of the hut on the street that crosses the island from west to east, she and Shelley and Milly and William must look like any other bedraggled holiday-makers, trundling toward the Adriatic in the rented donkey-cart painted in incongruous summer reds and yellows. They can't see the small white bundle lying in the back, rocking a little from side to side.

Byron waits for them at the edge of the waves, turning his profile to Greece. From Madame di Robilant's garden shed behind Palazzo Mocenigo, he's brought a spade. Shelley takes it from him and begins to dig. "Ma'am." Milly's soft voice swells with tears. "Come away." Mary can't take her eyes from the white bundle lying in the sand. A curly snail shell – pink and white and glowing golden brown – lies next to her daughter's hidden face. Perhaps as a mother she should pick it up and put it in her pocket for remembrance. But she is not a mother who deserves to keep a precious thing.

Screeching with delight, William staggers toward the waves. Byron stiffens, flashes a glance at Milly – her face now buried in her apron, weeping – and lunges away, limping swiftly after him. "See here, old fellow," Mary hears him exclaim. "Here we are at the edge of the ocean. Has anyone ever told you about a great Englishman named Isaac Newton? Fellow Cambridge man, planted a very famous apple tree, near my old rooms, in fact..."

Shelley kneels awkwardly on the sand. Seashells crunch under his weight. He gathers the small white bundle in his arms and leans forward and lowers it into the hole.

"...And said something quite profound about the sea." Byron's voice rattles on, desperately. "He knew not what other scientists might say of him, but to himself he seemed to have been only a child picking up shells on a shore, much like yourself, while a great ocean of truth lay all undiscovered before him." He pauses. "Now, let's not go *into* the ocean!" William shouts the angry shout he makes when he's been bodily removed, by an adult, against his will from something interesting. Milly lowers her apron, turns, and hurries after Byron.

Now, Shelley and Mary are alone at their daughter's grave. He glances at her and looks down. Wind parts his auburn curls, showing threads of gray. Bending, he shovels up a spadeful of sand from the heap next to the hole. Pink and purple and black and pearl-white bits of seashell sparkle in it. With a careful motion, left to right, he pours the sand onto the small white bundle in the landlady's sheet. The gold laundry pin with which Mary fastened her daughter's shroud disappears from sight.

"Perhaps when you are big you can ride horses here on this beach like your father and I do." Byron is talking on, entertaining William, distracting himself. "If you are unlucky enough to be stranded on this rotting isle when you are come of age." Mary turns to see that Byron, lame foot braced, has hoisted her son to his hip and is lifting his tiny arm, making him point. "We gallop from *there* —" he pivots his torso, and William — "to *there.*" Wildly he swings back again, pointing William's arm to the opposite end of the beach. William laughs and Milly gasps, flustered, "oh, Milord, please be careful..." *Don't worry, Milly.* Mary's cold interior voice bites across her brain like a line of fire into paper. *He's gained some experience. Like me. As my mother once urged. He has a little girl too, now, remember? The one I brought to Venice. At the cost of my own. Experience. Gain it. How much experience is worth a child's life?*

When Mary turns back, Shelley has spread two more bands of brown sand into the hole. Only a single glint of white remains. He offers her the shovel's handle and she shakes her head. She will not be complicit in this thing. If he says anything – anything at all – she will snatch the shovel from his hands and slice it right into his ribs. She strides away up the beach to keep the boiling words behind her lips. Over there is Greece. Over there is Turkey and the hazily imagined Orient. The water is gray and sullen, approaching, receding under the setting sun. Hard to imagine this sky has ever been blue.

"Go mamma!" William is asking, in his own language, to be brought to her. Amazingly, Byron seems to understand, for here he comes, galumphing and puffing, his lame step hidden in the comical humpty-bumptying of pretending to be a horse for her little boy. Borne on his shoulders, both his hands clutching Byron's receding curls, William crows joyfully, then stretches his arms to Mary. His sudden weight nearly collapses her into the sand. Byron catches them both. "Here." His eyes are shrewd, sad. "Put him down."

Over the dune comes a white-haired man with a luxurious mustache and a straw hat, leading two saddled horses – one bay, one gray – right up to them. Professionally, he trains his eyes on Byron and nods. "Cavalli di Milordo," he observes. *Milord's horses.* This man does not mean to interrupt her daughter's burial, although he is. He is just an honest stableman, like Mr. Keats' father back in London (ah, that seems so far away from this beach and her child's grave; is it even possible that she stands now on the same planet?), springing to do the bidding of his best client: *prepare my horses to ride whenever I appear.* Of course it is her husband and Lord Byron, not Milly or herself or William, who enter into his calculations. Mary is a rational woman. She can discern that all these things are true.

"Oh, hell." Byron's voice is dismayed. "Giuseppe...." He flounders, turning to Shelley. The gray horse swivels his ears toward Shelley and Shelley takes the reins and rubs his face. "There's my friend," he murmurs, "there's my good boy." The horse blinks his long lashes and lowers his head to bump his nose against Shelley's hip.

Shelley turns to look at Mary. What he sees on her face – she'll never know, exactly – sends him snatching the reins from Giuseppe and vaulting into the saddle and kicking the gray into a trot, showering sand over all of them. The horse pitches and struggles but Shelley guides him toward the firmer sand where the water meets the land and the horse flattens his ears and leans into a gallop, his gray and white tail whipping a rope of salt water. A churned line of hoofprints points her husband's way north along the beach, dwindling out of sight.

"Go after him," Mary says. "We have to finish here."

Obediently Byron heaves himself aboard the bay horse and picks up a trot, then a canter, down the beach. Mary turns and jerks the shovel free – Madame di Robilant will not want to lose such a rare thing as a shovel surely is in Venice – and turns to Milly and William. "So." Striving for cheer, she sounds merely shrill. "Let's go make a pretty sandcastle for..." she wobbles and catches herself, "your little sister."

Alone on the beach, Mary and William and Milly gather seashells to arrange on top of the mound of sand that after a tide or two, no one will be able to identify as her second daughter's grave. She doesn't know the names, but she lingers over the shapes, the patterns, the colors that blend from pink to brown and blue and white and black. For untold years, these creatures have been going about their tiny lives, careless of her. Now they are beautiful little skeletons that can be picked up and arrayed carefully in the shape of a C, and then an L, A, R, A. Her pale skin stings and she must be burning even in this autumn sunset but she does not care. William totters to her with handfuls of shells, slaps them down, and runs off for more, Milly shadowing him back and forth to the water's edge. There are two sticks of driftwood, a lucky find on this treeless beach. Mary rips a long strip of cloth from her petticoat hem and binds them together, then roots one end of the long stick deep into the sand. Here is a cross to mark the grave of a child whose baptism had been custom, a mere English formality. The daughter and granddaughter of two men calling themselves atheists. But still. You do not bury anyone without a cross to mark the grave.

Shelley and Byron trot toward her in the distance, then slow to a walk. Giuseppe reappears over the crest of the dune, removes his hat, and crosses himself. "Pregherò per lei," he says. *I will pray for you.*

Mary forces a smile onto her face and nods. "Come along, William," she says. He stumbles through the sand to her and whines to be lifted; he's exhausted, with no nap and of course no dinner, yet. She hoists him to her hip. He reaches toward her with something clutched in his fist: a perfect rose-and-beige snail shell, the color of his own delicate ear. "Thank you, my darling," Mary says. She brushes the sand away and slips the shell into her pocket, then trudges across the beach, Milly following her, to where the gondolas wait on the island's opposite side. Surely Shelley sees her walking away from him. Surely Byron will ferry him home in his own gondola, site of so many scandalous evenings, heavy breathings, and parted thighs. She neither knows nor cares. She has marked her daughter's name on the sand, and it will remain there until the wind and the waves take it away for good.

Venice is a blur to Mary for some time after that. Nights of not-sleeping in another spavined bed, hastily signed for by Shelley (no *atheoi* this time, just *Mr and Mrs. Shelley and son, no fixed address*), with William in his little cot at her bed's foot and Claire, Elise, and Milly in the room next door. Days of trailing Shelley through rooms hung with Titian and Tiepolo, pretending to listen to his comments on perspective, the marvelous light on the undersides of clouds. Meals in tiny *traittorias* where she watches the food borne between the other tables: steamed fish glaring upward, ribbons of pasta in what looks like ink ("Venetian specialty!" the waiter exclaims, *"seppie nere!"*) for people to swirl up and devour with black, laughing mouths. She turns away and swallows more wine. When she reaches the bottom of her glass and Shelley finishes tearing miserably at his bread – only William is happy, gobbling the pink shrimps the waiter prepared just for him – they can leave this restaurant and not have to look at other people.

The weather grows cooler. Perhaps there will be snow. Surely Venice isn't cold or dry enough for the hard edge of London snow or the blue-hearted ice of Chamonix. Venice snow will be wet, clumpy, blurring, softening edges of roofs and spires, crowning angels and madonnas. As cozily as stable rugs, it will drape the four horses on top of St. Mark's, freshly returned by Napoleon. It will smell of iron and salt and the sea. It will gather around her and Shelley and root them here as he asks *I'm not yet able to bring Byron to the point about Allegra and Claire – one more week?*

Of course once Shelley comes within Byron's orbit he stays, like one of Mr. Herschel's planets hooked, by a larger one, to its gravitational chain. Then it's time for all the weary stratagems of elsewhere-life in Shelley's wake: find a new house to let, assess furnishings and windows and water-spotted ceilings. Of course, the house they find is a narrow gray one next to Byron's own Palazzo Mocenigo, right on the Grand Canal where it bends to the east. Time, then, to unpack and order the dishes and books and serving-forks slung into trunks back on the weekend of Mary's twenty-first birthday, the point where August became September, when Shelley had written so urgently, on behalf of Claire, that she should pack up William and Clara and anything else she could and trundle over the mountains from Bagni di Lucca so Shelley could present them to Byron as if what he'd said were true: they'd been near the city, waiting, all along. So that Shelley could accept Byron's offer without losing face. Time to unpack her Geneva clock and set it on another mantelpiece and wind the hands to keep life moving forward, regardless. So that things can appear as Shelley hopes they'll be.

When William sleeps, Mary sets Milly to watch him and slips off her mother's wedding ring and leaves it on her bureau and lets Venice draw her out to walk. Sometimes the morning is bright, with the slap of waves and calls of gondoliers clear in the air. Some days fog has come in, so that the sun is felt rather than actually seen, the air lightening from slate to dove-gray. But often the hour after dawn is simply quiet, the pearly light not yet hardened toward day. Then it's as if the city slips a hand under her elbow, teasing her forward: *come*. Quiet is always waiting here, under every sound. She can follow where the city's own preferred directions of travel seem to point – bridge leading to *sottoportego* or sunlight promising a piazza ahead – and find herself in a little church-anchored island of quiet: one spindly tree in a square of dirt, a priest rustling into the dark open door, a tabby cat tucked, eyes shut, on a warm stone ledge. Then, it's as if the whole earth balances there, perfectly. Sometimes the completeness of that instance frightens her: she could be the survivor of a global plague, she and the priest or the housewife sighing along the passage with her water buckets or the pregnant girl pausing to touch the stone Madonna's lips. *And I alone am escaped to tell thee.* With this city so all-encompassing, so apparently infinite, how can she be sure she's not the only person left alive on earth?

Two months ago, back in Bagni di Lucca, she and Shelley rode south down the River Serchio to see the Ponte de Maddalena, the medieval bridge the devil had built. Of course, Shelley knew the story. Saint Julian, the architect, struggled to get the arches right and gave up and asked the devil for help. Certainly, said the devil, but in return I'll require of you the first living soul to cross this bridge. Julian agreed; being a character in a legend, he knew some exit would present itself. The bridge was completed – you could still see it, right there, one arch was much bigger than the other two, giving the bridge an off-center peak like a cake baked in an unevenly heated oven, but charming over the river among those green hills – and the Devil came to collect his fee. Julian whistled for his dog and threw a stick onto the bridge. The dog raced after it – and *voila*. One living soul. One bargain kept. One bridge, still standing even now. Practical, wily Julian became the patron saint of travelers and those who speed them on their way: boatmen, hotel keepers, chambermaids. No wonder Satan in *Paradise Lost* was so vengeful: not only had he been cast down by God but he'd been cheated by a shrewd innkeeper, just like any one of the men in aprons in Calais or Milan who eyed her and Shelley and shrugged and shoved the guest book across the desk.

In Venice, crossing bridge after bridge, Mary can't banish the story of St. Julian from her mind. Shelley had panicked and tossed a lure into the air, a command: *come, Mary, scramble nearly two hundred miles with our children so Byron's child and her everlasting mother can be maneuvered into some polite fiction that will charm the sulky lord into compliance, that will not rouse his temper and spur him to snatch Allegra back and forbid her to her mother for good.* And Mary had obeyed. Whose soul had been thrown across the bridge to tempt the Devil? It had not been hers, now a mutinous huddling presence inside her: *by God, I will not forget.* It had been her own daughter's. Such a short distance, from one end of a bridge to the next. Twelve months and twenty-four days. Clara's small life, blown out like a candle.

October comes, and in Venice, Mary and Shelley linger on. He buys her a pair of blue glass earrings from a Murano shop and she pushes the corners of her mouth into a smile to thank him. They walk. They read. They avoid the determined spinsters and bear-leading Grand Tour schoolmasters pointing up at spires. Everyone has a quire of paper clamped to a board and a charcoal pencil and a Baedeker. Surely Venice will be rubbed bare and dry, shredded like a too-much-erased sheet of foolscap by all this sketching, all this eager gaining of experience. A mother-killing daughter, a wandering creature, killing two daughters of her own: how much more *experience* is she doomed to reap?

But Shelley is content here. He goes out often to ride with Byron on the Lido, boating past the island madhouse of San Servolo, where laughter rackets across the lagoon. Scraps of paper pile up on the table. "Julian and Maddalo," one poem is called, about himself and Byron. (Of course, Shelley has given himself the name of that devil-tricking saint from the Bagni bridge.) *How beautiful is sunset, when the glow / Of Heaven descends upon a land like thee, / Thou Paradise of exiles, Italy!* A letter to their friend Thomas Peacock, back in England, snitching on Byron: *He is not yet an Italian & is heartily & deeply discontented with himself & contemplating in the distorted mirror of his own thoughts, the nature & the destiny of man, what can he behold but objects of contempt & despair? But that he is a great poet, I think the address to Ocean proves. And he has a certain degree of candour while you talk to him but unfortunately it does not outlast your departure.*[2]

Yet Byron keeps his distance from Mary. She sees him from her seat on their balcony in the little gray house next to Palazzo Mocenigo as a foreshortened figure hurrying down the steps into his gondola, a swirl of expensive black cape around a tonsure of balding crown and thinning curls. Sometimes she can hear him laughing semi-ruefully to Shelley about England: "there is some advantage," he said, "in getting the water between oneself and one's embarrassments."[3] Clearly, he's avoiding her. And well he should. He wrestled Allegra from Claire as if she were some treasure – a bargain, an auction find like his English sofa at the Villa Diodati – and thrust her into a corner, away upon the Hoppners, as soon as he'd won. Winning was, after all, the point. By now, he's parked both Claire and Allegra in his villa at Este, so he can live on in Palazzo Mocenigo with his wine and mistresses and swims and horseback rides as if nothing has changed. Because that's the lordly goal. Everything sumptuous and normal. Always, the gliding pretense of ease. Despite the wry-footed limp that anyone can see.

Elise avoids Mary too. Silent and downcast, starting to show a pregnancy, she lives in the downstairs rooms with Paolo – he has followed her from Bagni, hopefully to marry her and take responsibility for what is surely his child – and will not speak to Mary unless spoken to. One afternoon Mary finally summons Elise, who arrives with her hand clutched in Paolo's. Raising herself to firmness, Mary snaps at her: Why did you lead us all to believe Allegra was in danger? What led you to write such a lie? "I did not say such a thing," Elise declares, eyes down. Paolo looks at Mary and grins. "Ah, the lord," he says. "He is so changeable." He flicks a bit of plaster off his mustache and leads Elise away without waiting for Mary to dismiss him. Mary stands alone in the parlor, rigid with rage. Damn Paolo and Elise and Claire. Damn Byron. Damn the whole scheming lot of them. If she were brave, she would know how to handle these infuriating beings: *other people.* Just like La Fornarina.

La Fornarina – whose real name is Margarita Cogni – is a baker's wife who has become Byron's mistress with the baker's apparent consent: "fit to breed gladiators from," Byron tells Shelley, out of what he thinks is Mary's hearing.[4] La Fornarina is tall and plump, with muscular arms and an imperious blank gaze that can shade to outrage in an instant. Once Mary saw a pair of teenage girls giggling and pointing at La Fornarina as she swayed through the *sottoportego* with a basket of fresh loaves for delivery. Serenely, La Fornarina stopped, turned, settled the basket deeper into the crook of her left arm, and dealt each girl a slap across her cheek with her right, then resumed her course, their howls receding in her wake.

"I can't believe her husband doesn't mind," Mary observes as she sits with Shelley on the balcony outside their room. A full gold moon hangs above the roofs and ripples a path across the canal. A small dark object – a swimming rat – cuts through the light. Then a larger dark thing, animal and heaving. "Byron!" Shelley's voice is heedless with surprise.

"Swam all the way from the Lido." Byron's head twists to look up at them. Smoothly his arms churn him up to the stone steps in front of Palazzo Mocenigo. "More than three miles." His voice is tired, victorious. Treading water, he turns his face, a pale white blur, up to them and grins. "Not bad for a dissipated lord."

"Dangerous in the dark—a boat could hit you –" Shelley splutters. But then the giant iron water-gate of Mocenigo swings open and La Fornarina bursts forth. Mary can just see the top of her tousled black head, hair and arms flung outward as she strides across the marble landing pier. She wears a long fur-collared dressing gown – obviously Byron's – and nothing else. Keening, she kneels on the steps to the canal, where Byron struggles to pull himself out of the water. The gown's cloth wicks up the water and darkens to blood-black. "Giorgiano!" Her shriek rattles the window-glass. In the surrounding houses, balcony doors open. One man emerges. Then another man, followed by a woman who quickly turns behind her to restrain a child – "Mamma!" rises a high complaining voice, "voglio ve*d*ere!" Maddened, apparently heedless, La Fornarina does not raise her eyes from Byron. "Giorgiano! How dare you do not tell me where you go?" she shrieks. "I wait so long!" She throws her head backward, flinging her dark curls around her shoulders. Her white bosom gleams under the moon. "You think to hide from me you swim?" Her English is bitten, spat, broken, virtuosic, obviously held in place as a dam against the Italian for which she will soon abandon it, having sufficiently demonstrated to all the Grand Canal her self-control. "Potresti mo*r*ire! You die in the water and I do not know!"

"But *I* would know." Byron's voice cuts the air. He sets both hands on the bottom step and hauls himself out of the water, then stands, streaming. "Because then I wouldn't hear your bloody *voice*." With first his left hand, then his right, he sluices the canal water from his arms and his chest. La Fornarina's eyes follow. Byron steps close to her. His voice drops. He clasps the fur lapels and strokes his hands downward. "Give me back my dressing gown."

La Fornarina steps backward and lifts her chin. "Vieni a prenderlo." She stares at him and smirks. Byron reaches for her and she twists away, moving back through the iron gate of the palazzo. Just as Byron follows her under the arch, he raises his face to Mary and Shelley. And Mary – obeying an impulse – lifts both her hands and applauds. Expressionless, Byron ducks inside and slams the door.

❄

In the parlor, Mary sits darning one of Shelley's stockings. Elise is upstairs, busying herself with William and avoiding Mary, as usual. Paolo has gone out to attach himself to some building crew and earn coins for standing about with a plaster-bucket. Shelley is out riding with Byron out on the Lido again, despite the threat of rain. *I love all waste / And solitary places,* he's written, *where we taste / The pleasure of believing what we see / Is boundless, as we wish our souls to be.*[5] Those afternoons have yielded a very good poem. She will be glad for him. Not irrational. She'll sit right where she is and do her work to keep her family in decent clothes. She will not wander, drawn toward a canal or lagoon in which to dissolve herself. Like Harriet. No, she will not think of Harriet. Nor the shadow under the trees at Bagni di Lucca. Nor will she fear that Shelley is with Claire. Claire, after all, is in Este. Claire will not come to Venice to see Shelley even if she wants to because Byron will not countenance the sight of her.

In Mary's hands the work is threadbare, the silken fabric worn almost past salvation. Cobblestones, gondola-landing steps, the sand of the Lido: no telling where Shelley's walked. Today he's wearing his riding boots. Even in Venice, the horseless city, you can find someone to make you riding boots. On credit, of course.

Mary drops the round wooden darning egg into the stocking-top and shakes its smooth weight into the seam of the toe. Lifting the egg in her left hand, she rests it against her thigh and turns the gathered cloth around until the largest hole is looking up at her. Trailing the needle from right to left and back again, she crosses the space with the first stitch that will make it whole. Now she'll be pinned here, a helpless nest for any thoughts that come to roost, until it's done. But it must be done. The spool jumps a little with every stitch. Back and forth. Money for boots. Money for thread. Money for wine and for mutton Shelley won't eat and for the fresh aubergines and lettuce he promises he will. Money for the laundress and the fish from the Rialto Market. And the rent on this narrow gray house. They'll get to next week, next month, next year, one thread at a time. She cannot leave him. Will not. Money. William. Money. Son. Husband. Not a shadow in the dark at the well. Not him.

Stitch by stitch, the hole closes as clouds darken the sky. Shelley does not come. Perhaps he's at Mocenigo, next door. Both he and Byron would be irritated by her if she sought them, scornful of her need. Back and forth. Back and forth. Yearning after him. As bad as prancing Claire. As bad as pleading Harriet. Left with a child, like Saint-Preux left Julie in

Nouvelle Heloise: free to start fresh game. That's Mama's voice, sardonic, rueful, true.

Unexpectedly, the great door of Palazzo Mocenigo is open. No servant comes forth to greet Mary, but in a Venetian house it isn't hard to find the main room on the *piano nobile,* the room with the best view of the world that's always seeking to look back at you. Three tall windows overlook the Grand Canal; Byron never opens those drapes, avoiding the curious eyes of the marchesas and the English girls. How miserable to be unable to sit on your own balcony on a July evening, waiting for a breeze from the lagoon?

Somewhere on a floor above, a dog barks. But there's no *boom* of a door giving way, no rush and scrabble of claws on parquet. Mary steps further into the dimness. She strikes a spark and lights one half of the candelabra on the sideboard. In the mirror, brightness flares and the hulking shapes resolve themselves into settees, armchairs, card tables with four spindly chairs drawn expectantly close. The pink marble fireplace is wide enough to roast a pig. All is delicate undersea color, glowing in the candlelight: pale green and coral-pink and gold. Long dead Di Robilants look down from their portraits, dark eyes bright, gazes veiled.

Yet the piazza is old. Byron has got it for what he calls *a song.* The silk chair-cushion edges have been frayed by years of sliding thighs. A wet wineglass has left a circle on the side table; the fireplace's mouth is black. Where other palazzi have paintings stretched across the ceilings – a Titian or a second-rate Tiepolo, plump bemused allegories of Prosperity or Love – here there are exposed wooden beams, whitewashed as if someone hoped they'd blend with the plaster. Ceiling paintings are made on canvas. Which means they can be taken down and sold.

In the corner a painted wooden screen conceals something hanging from the beam by a chain. Mary goes to it cautiously: one of Byron's beasts might leap out of hiding and shriek. But it's only a long leather bag, stuffed with something like matted wool. Tossed into the corner are the buff-colored gloves Byron wore on the balcony at Diodati, fists raised, challenging Polidori to fight. *The sport of gentlemen.* And – at least some time in the last century – women. *I, ELIZABETH WILKINSON, of Clerkenwell, having had some words with HANNAH HYFIELD, and requiring satisfaction, do invite her to meet me upon the stage, and box me for three guineas...* Mary sees them in her mind's eye: two sweating red-armed women, glowering. Hannah and Elizabeth. Or herself and Claire? Herself and Elise? Harriet in the corner of the ring, looking on, refusing to speak? La Fornarina could box anyone. Beat them to a bloody pulp.

Then select a man from the crowd – *vieni a prenderlo* – and stride away, not bothering to look back. How would it feel to be strong like that?

The gloves are heavy and strange on Mary's hands, a little damp with what must be Byron's sweat but warming quickly to her own skin. She curls and uncurls her fingers. When she makes a fist, the thick padding comes completely around it. Her ordinary hand is both muffled and heightened now. A blunt instrument. A battering ram. A creaturely paw.

Dormouse, Shelley teased her as she curled drowsily in the bed in the inn in France, on that very first flight across Europe. *Maisie, Pecksie, little mouse.* But this is no mouse's paw. No woman's hand.

(*Have a care, Victor Frankenstein!* Why does she hear her creature's voice now?)

In the candlelight the bag's flanks gleam, darker around the middle. You hit the bag there to strengthen you for the moment when you hit a man.

Upstairs the dog barks on and on, slamming its heavy body against the door.

Byron sent Allegra away from this house so he could live just as he chose. Shelley hurried Mary into a flurry of packing and traveling – on her twenty-first birthday – so Byron wouldn't suspect how close Claire had been to him, all this time. And Mary obeyed. Obedient Dormouse rushed her babies into the coach with their boxes and bottles and stuffed dolls in tow. And her obedience had killed. Her frail little girl – the second girl – had been pushed over the edge of fever by all the ruckus and change, dying on Mary's lap as the boat slid toward the Ospedale. One little life, lost in the commotion, delicate as a china cup slipping off a shelf.

Mary swings her padded fist experimentally against the bag. The shock answers back up her arm: a twinge in the elbow, a jolt deep in the bone. From the fingers, safe in their shell, comes no pain at all. Just a nudge, from the edge of Mama's ring.

The candlelight rises infinitesimally, then subsides.

It isn't as if she has to fear the blows will kill a child in her. That worst thing has already come true, twice. The first daughter. And now the second. Two little bodies from the dark red cavern of her own. Now empty.

Mary angles her fist and punches the canvas straight on. Like a lord with his signet ring, *stamp.* Like the slaveholder stamps the swarthy children of the sun as his possessions: where has she read that? It doesn't matter now. *Stamp.* Punch. *Maternal impression.* The world flows through your eyes and your brain as you follow your husband from England to Italy and it is your second small daughter who pays. *The sins of the mother are visited upon the –*

Sins. Unnatural creature. Mary swings. The bag rocks on its creaking ropes. La Fornarina slapped those girls right across the face. Hannah Hyfield and Elizabeth Wilkinson got in the ring and tore each other to bits. What woman could be so unnatural as to strike out with her fist at another woman, to howl and tear her hair and beat her, enjoying the shatter of teeth, the spurt of blood, the *crunch* of the bone under skin, the shock up her arm of another person's pain? What woman could be so unnatural as to write into life a creature that now stalks some parallel version of the Sea of Ice and the city of Geneva and even London, for all she knows? What woman, having created, could be so unnatural as to want to batter and destroy?

Yet what if the woman herself, in being born, has killed her own mother?

What – or who – is, then, the more unnatural thing?

Mary swings her right fist again, harder. The bag quivers on its ropes. The dog's barking reaches a frenzied pitch. Her left hand hits with a solid *smack*. What's that new sound her body has never made? *Smack:* a ripe flat blow. Why is she smiling? No matter. No one else is here to see. No one will even know she's been here unless they walk in right now. But apart from the dog the house is settled in a silence too deep to be quickly broken by a door-key or an unthinking back-home voice. Shelley isn't quick to come home these days. Surely he complains of her – *Maie's so grievous, still, so cold* – and surely Byron abets him. *One more glass. There's this little place I'd like you to see.*

The shocks land and travel up her arms. She hits with her left arm, and her right. This feels good. This is the release that comes with walking except this brings release so much more quickly than the two, three, four miles over these winding canals and bridges in which despite her best efforts she can never get lost.

The bag swings purring on its chain. Back and forth. She's made this thing.

Soon her arms feel too heavy to lift, and she peels the gloves away and lays them in the corner and replaces the screen around the bag. The candles have burned halfway down but she doubts anyone will notice except the housemaid who'll replace them for Milordo's next at-home evening. Madame di Robilant would be furious if she could see the hole in her beam. But, then, lease your ancestral palazzo to the English milord and you have to let him fight as he wants.

Mary slips out the door and closes it behind her. Through the fog, footsteps are approaching. At first they're just a scuffling laughter-edged echo in the alley: the scrape-and-slap bass note of Byron's lame foot on the cobblestone, descanted by Shelley's quick light steps. Like some compound beast they solidify in the fog: a dark caped shape swinging and tottering, leaning on a slender upright one. "Tired." Byron's voice ripples off the low stone archway of the *sottoportego*. His voice throbs, intimate, for what he thinks is Shelley's ears alone. "Boady is tired. Poor Boady. Drank too much and lost to the God-damned Prince of the Rotting Palazzo of Nowhere and all his God-damned friends."

"Boady?" Shelley's voice is amused.

"Boady. B, O, D, Y." Byron's voice is thick. He tightens his arm around Shelley's neck. "Say it aloud and you'll see. Live in it and you'll see it's a bitch of a bastard beasting thing. It deserves its own name. Every bit of this is Boady's fault." Now she can see the wine spilled down his shirt-front, dark as a stab wound. Anybody will think he's been murdered, that her husband is his killer, drawn by some twist of Venetian myth into carrying his own victim through the city forever. Like the Creature and Victor. Pursuer and pursued. One of them hounding the other out of hell and back again.

"And now Boady has lost Newstead." Astonishingly, Byron halts and claps both hands over his face and begins to cry. "I sold it." The words break through a sob in his throat. "Newstead Abbey. I let the beck go. The little beck where the newts are, where the kingcup flowers always come up first of all. The first watercress. The narrow place where the pony could jump and I wouldn't fall off. And clay for pots to bake in the cooking stove." He is weeping now. "I let it go. And I will never have it back. The little beck where the newts are. Never, never, never." He claps both his hands to his face. "I sold it. And for *this*?" His whole body shudders. "All this frivolous bullshit? Childe God-damned Harold? Why can't I ever write about *home*? Why can't I…" Mary flinches from his obvious pain, the miserable yearning cramping him double. Shelley is frozen. And – she sees with anger – Shelley is embarrassed. A gentleman forced to witness another's weakness. He opens his mouth and closes it again, unable to utter even the humblest words: *Come now, old son. Steady on.* Mary flattens her palms against the stone. She cannot step forth to break this English-manhood silence, the tears of the Harrow schoolboy uncomforted by Eton. Her Shelley. So unconventional. Except when he's not.

I curse you. The voice of Madame Diodati – that fragile lady in her rotten gown, hauled by men's hands out of her own crumbling house – rings suddenly in Mary's throat. Clara's death, Claire's pleading eyes, Mary herself and her children hauled over the sunbaked plain by Shelley's frantic desire to please the lord: all of the anger rears in her at once. Like her Creature raging at Victor Frankenstein, in Adam's words: *Did I request thee, Maker, from my clay to mould Me man? Did I solicit thee from darkness to promote me?* There is Byron, face in his hands; there is Shelley, venturing, now, cautiously to set a hand on Byron's shoulder. She could curse them both. It's a power she's never felt. And something in her is rising to it, eager, cruel, determined, aghast at its own strength. What is that voice? What is it in her that wants to hurt, to torture? To bring down both of these men in front of her?

Shelley is clenching his hand against Byron's shoulder, determined, awkward. "Well," he stumbles, "we all make mistakes."

"Mistakes?" Byron draws himself upright and slashes his fingers across his cheeks. He stares at Shelley and Mary sees clearly the four years between them, which, in this moment, might as well be forty. "I suggest a stronger word. But there it is. If we didn't have things we were ashamed of –" the words burst out of him – "we'd be complete and utter reprobates. That's what pins us to earth. That's what keeps us honest." He draws in a great hitching breath, then exhales the last ragged scraps of his tears to float up into the night. Slowly, he slumps against her husband and leans his forehead into Shelley's neck. Then a shadow of a gondola with two twined shapes ripples past against the corridor wall, to sudden laughter and shouted Italian that holds both fellowship and mockery. "*Vaffanculo!*" Byron jerks away from Shelley. "Fucking fairies!" He snarls and tucks his head lower. "Disgusting."

"You don't deserve to feel this way." Shelley's grip on Byron's shoulder softens. His gaze is wondering, pitying, frightened. Even in all their tavern-roistering and Lido-riding, Byron has never spoken to him like this.

"Yes, I do," Byron declares. "Every bit of it. Don't you see?" He pauses. "*That's* what's terrifying." He opens his mouth and shuts it again. Ducking his head, he twists away from Shelley and hurries into the Palazzo Mocenigo and shuts the door. One by one, the locks slam into place. For a moment, Shelley remains where he is. Thunder rumbles overhead. Then, with a glance at the sky, Shelley unlocks their own door and slips inside.

Mary lifts herself carefully from where she's huddled against the wall.

She should follow her husband indoors. Rain is coming on. Instead she slips out of the little courtyard and under the *sottoportego*, back into the night her husband and Byron have left.

Venice can tip a solitary walker from place to place, through its squares and passages, from one end of itself to another, like a fountain tips water from one basin to the next. You don't have to think deliberately of where you're going. You just follow your own steps, your own thoughts, from one square, one alley, to the one beyond. For in Venice your thoughts are not merely trapped in your own head, circling, rebounding back upon themselves. Touching and twining up the blotched stucco wall of a medieval church, the *swish* of water flung out a door, the window-glimpse of cherub-haunch on a ceiling in some second-floor ballroom high above the street, they draw you forward, onward toward the light of the *something else* that circling thoughts inevitably seek, the *more than me* they must have if they are not to drive you mad. Toward something that changes them, and, in the process, changes you too.

Elise. Elise. The shadow was not her. The shadow was not real. Shelley surely will not leave Mary here in Venice, alone with the one child left to them. *He has done this kind of thing before.* Surely he is no longer that man. Surely she and William can depend on him. They have no other choice. She is an author. There will be other books. She is a woman. There will be other children. She and her husband will love each other again. Into some future, she must walk. No matter what.

Sepia light brightens the long rectangle of a church door against the night. A hum of voices resolves itself into song. Half a dozen nuns stand in a tight circle, singing prayers into the space between. A girl with a wide white band of linen over dark hair, a dark smock, battered shoes – a novice – opens her eyes and turns toward the door at the exact moment Mary passes. The word shimmers between them: *sorella*. For an instant Mary is held in the gaze of Venice itself, merciful with the factual mercy of distance and time. *Well. What are you going to do about it? Pregherò per lei. I will pray for you.*

One raindrop strikes Mary's scalp, then another. With a great outrushing sigh, the rain comes on. And through the rain comes a driving beat, a steady jingle, laughter that resolves itself into song. A corridor of light beckons her into the next street: a shop awning under which a group of dark-haired people in bright rags huddle, three women and a child and an old man. Each wears a giant wooden cross on a necklace-string. One of the women is beating the tambourine, and they are singing, some apparently wordless thing that rises and falls in time with the beat. A sign propped over their alms-bowl reads, in Italian Mary can just unpick, *With the Second Coming will be a New Universe and Joy for All!* Godwin would sniff, *fanatics, watch your pockets, Mary. What kind of fool welcomes the apocalypse?* But in the downpour they're just people, sheltering, eyeing her with interest. She is rapidly becoming soaked, probably some *poor unfortunate* to anyone who sees her travel-worn dress, her shawl-less shoulders, only Shelley's blue glass earrings to show that anyone has ever cared where she goes. Who but a madwoman would be out in this storm? Who but a madwoman who has written a monster and killed a mother and two of her own children? What more can anyone, much less these millenarian beggars, take from her now?

A teenage boy and girl clutched together under an umbrella approach the singers from the opposite corner of the square. Even through the rain, shy yet eager, they shine. Suddenly the boy glances at the girl and bolts from under the umbrella. He jumps up and down awkwardly in the rain, raising his arms, spinning and scattering water from the puddles. Astonishingly, he's dancing. The singers laugh and raise their voices, rattling the tambourine with delight. The boy catches Mary's eye as she approaches. And she finds herself grinning, rushing forward, lifting her skirts to spin in a circle. Astonishingly, she is dancing too. *In a public place, in a foreign city at night, with these thieves – What do you think you're –* And then the reproving words are gone and she's simply dancing alongside the boy as the rain batters them and they flail their arms, grinning, and the singers laugh and cheer *(at the end of the world there will be joy!)* and the shy girl watches from under her umbrella (she is fifteen, surely no more, looking at Mary with a mixture of envy and respect: *such an experienced woman, so bold,* she's obviously wondering, *when will I feel so bold as to walk through the rain and jump up and down and spin in these puddles like this woman, like this shining boy I can't stop looking at as he splashes in the puddles, so full of joy –)*

Nobody tells you when. Mary feels the words rise, from the place within herself that never lies. *You take your joy. Even at the end of the world.*

She finds herself in a small plaza with a canal crossing its farthest end and – that rarest of Venetian sights – a tree rising from the stones. Bowing and laughing as the boy returns to his umbrella and the singers applaud, Mary hurries over to shelter under the tree: a fig tree, with leaves larger than her own hands and a thick trunk and rosy purple fruit the size of a baby's fist clustered on each branch. In the spaces between the branches, all the way up to the sky, there is only a thick inviting dark, a space of night into which she could climb like some latter-day Jack up his beanstalk and disappear. Trees are portals to other worlds: Yggdrasil held the nine worlds of the Viking universe in its roots and branches; the rowan tree guarded the Celts against witches; the great oak at Boscobel sheltered a soon-to-be-restored king. Something might climb down from this tree to meet her. Or she could climb up and wander forever in the nine worlds of this Venetian night. Or tomorrow every householder in this district could come with a basket and ladder and pick the fruit to take home and slice onto plates and press into jars with the mix of spices that Mary had tasted just last week, *mostarda di fico* on cheese, on meat, on bread, the gift of this tree planted here by accident or design too long ago for anyone to remember, the portal to worlds, the matter-of-fact sustainer of life. She twists off a fig and puts it in her mouth and bites down. Its skin is thick, faintly rough with a velvet prickliness soon overwhelmed by the delicate purple taste of its flesh. Mary is soaked. She should be shivering. Instead she is warm all over, glowing, unable to douse the fierce grin that still clings to her mouth. Within her, a beastly shape like Frankenstein's creature blinks its dark eyes, curls its long knuckly hands into fists. By God, she is the daughter of Mary Wollstonecraft. By God, she will have this joy.

The rain stops just as she lets herself into her rented house. Dripping, she pads across her parlor carpet to where Shelley lies asleep on the settee. His long legs are crossed, his long throat tipped back against a cushion, blue-veined eyelids closed over a flickering dream. The familiar scuffed brown *Paradise Lost* with his father's name is open to Book Nine, his favorite. A sheaf of papers spills across his lap; his single candle is still lit. He's been waiting for her. Trusting that she would come back to him.

Crossing the room quietly, Mary slides her fingers into Shelley's tumbled curls. Salty and rough from the wind on the Lido, they spring like grass against her palms. He opens his eyes and she smiles at him. *Like Adam in the garden.* She hears the words as clearly as if he's spoken them. *Waking to find his dream come to life.* She rakes her hand back against his skull and pleasure dazzles his face, pressing his eyes closed like a cat's. Smiling, he touches the blue glass droplets hanging from her ears, one, two. On her finger, Mama's ring burns.

Through the open window the night is cool. Snatches of talk drift down the canal behind the bobbing lanterns of boats. The whole night smells of moon, cool and smoky from the fires of the houses or even the little braziers the gondoliers carry to warm their hands. Boats bear fire across the water like Shelley's own paper creations on the Serpentine. Where poor Harriet had drowned, her body lumpy with another man's child. Ah. Eve's curse. You don't stop needing the thing that kills you. That enters your body and swells it and splits it open as a radiant beast spills out. The creature born of your own hunger to *make*, to *feel*, to *live*. To make something of a moment that was not there before. To write a book. To hold a man. To make him yours. And, by God, Shelley is hers. No matter what she might have seen in the shadows of Bagni di Lucca or Marchmont Street. No matter the sad ghosts of Harriet and Fanny and the two baby girls they have borne and lost. She will have him for herself. And she will never let him go.

Mary runs her hand down the back of Shelley's neck, her thumb testing the bright knobs of his spine and the cool pillar of his throat. He stands up in a spill of papers and reaches for her, but she slips her hand away and retreats before him in the dark. Shelley blows out the candle. His breath catches and hastens. *Maie,* he whispers.

The warmth of him follows her up the stairs and into the room where the bed lies dim white under the moon, next to the window with its view of the roof-planes of curved tile and distant spires and the ragged nests of sparrows. With her back to the door, her face to the moon, she waits, tingling, chin tilted down as she dawdles with the ribbon at the neck of her dress. And there he is, hot mouth on her neck, quick hands untugging the ribbon and then swooping to crush her dress hem in a bundle and tumble the whole sodden heap of cloth up and over her head and hurl it to the floor. She turns in his arms, smiling, into his kiss that becomes smile-shaped too. His hands slow, unlacing her stays hole by hole, drawing the laces, purring, one by one. Sliding both hands under the canvas shell, he opens his arms to gather her closer and splits the shell and drops it to the floor. The whole nervous warm length of him is alive, his ship-stave ribs and the dimples at the base of his spine and the hard ridge of his hip. It is so good to take handfuls of him, to feel him shudder and sigh, flooded from within his own body by what she makes of it. Shirt and breeches and chemise and then only the wide white bed, pale blur under the moon.

She tosses back the covers and slides under them and looks up at him: tall, narrow-hipped, head of flame. How she loves the knowledge of him soon to be next to her, then the slow gathering-against, the deep, deep kiss that seems like to devour her, to bruise her jaw with its force. Cold fire jolts and splits her and she angles her hips to open and lock to him and there it is, again, after so many days, the exquisite straining-against and straining-toward, Shelley whispering to her: *oh, Maie, my love, so long. Need you.* And then the same deep imperious thing gathers and grips them both and they cry out and he spends and spends. She can feel it. The same hope flickers in their minds: *Another child.* Another child. Another city. Another year, and then another. A life together, building itself up as blown leaves settle and melt into rich sweet earth on which, in spite of everything, a woman and a child and a man can stand.

And, then, together, they sleep.

Orkney Islands

SCOTLAND OCTOBER 1818

At last Victor Frankenstein is keeping his promise to make the Creature a wife. *You must create a companion for me, with whom I can live in the interchange of sympathies necessary for my being.*[1] To be honest, the Creature had not entirely trusted Father's assent to this request. His eyes had slid sideways, scanning the jagged Sea of Ice but finding no succor – only what the Creature has come to know is his own unnerving presence, which, in that instance, he exploited without shame. I will be with you, he growled. I'll be watching. Only then had Victor nodded and said *yes*. It was the flare of curiosity in his eyes, that avidity (*the female will present fresh...challenges*) that convinced the Creature: *Father will do this for himself. Not for me.*

Victor books passage on a rickety ferry from John o'Groats, the northernmost point of mainland Scotland, with a hold in which the Creature can stow himself, and they set sail for the largest of the Orkney Islands. The land is jagged cliffs and eruptions of rock from a carpet of brilliant green grass nibbled by sheep and the most magnificent sunsets the Creature has ever seen, a clarity of light that cracks his eyes with a pain that is not only pain but awakening. Surely Adam must have felt thus on awakening from his dream to find it true. *Heav'n's last, best gift, my ever new delight.* The season is changing from the bright constant windswept near-polar day to the dim candlelit windswept near-polar night, but the villagers trundle about at their weaving and cheese-making and beer-brewing, lively and imperturbable. They are stocky, with direct bright blue eyes, ruddy Viking hair and faces, and an impenetrable accent in which they challenge Victor: *whar ye fae?* When he works out the question, of course he lies: *London.* They look skeptical, but don't question him: London is just as far away as Geneva, or the moon. And beyond this island, all strangeness is alike.

Under the guise of tourism Victor makes his way to the town of Kirkwall and its medieval cathedral of St. Magnus: rosy-gold sandstone, melancholy and magnificent. It is from the graveyard's farthest edge that he steals the girl. Like a London resurrectionist he has loitered at the edge of the funeral crowd, pretending to mourn but actually peering over his handkerchief at the dirt-spattered coffin and the name on the stone, prying from the Orkney dialect the cause of death – young wife, first baby – and her name, Margaret Young. *Th'babby's down yon w' her.* Glances dart into the grave, faces sorrowful and avid. Victor makes obsequies, polite murmurs, a small contribution. And that night he returns and the Creature joins him in the dark and in silence they disinter Margaret and her baby and carry their coffin to the remote stone cottage Victor has identified and where he has stored his tools – scalpel, bone saw, Leyden jar – and build up a fire and set to work.

The Creature allows Victor to banish him before the coffin is opened and the job is begun. Surprisingly, he is shy. He does not want to look upon the face of his Eve (*Margaret)* until she comes back to life. And in any form, she will be beautiful. In St. Magnus Cathedral, slipping among shadows in this village at the end of the world, he has discovered an upright stone monument to a Mary Young, dead in 1750 of what, judging from the hourglass and the plump-cheeked skull next to her, might be the plague. She kneels in profile with hands upraised in prayer. Thick curls – notched gently with the sculptor's chisel to suggest living hair – tumble over her shoulders, and the swirling pool of her skirts ends in what looks, in the shadowy church, much like a mermaid's tail. Touching her cold stone face, the Creature is enraptured. *She lived regarded and died regreted,* reads the inscription. His Margaret will never know a moment's regret. She and the baby – for surely Victor will spare a moment's work for it as well – will be a family of three. Wandering and cast out, surely, but eventually coming to rest in a humble place their love can make divine. *We'll go to South America,* he's promised Victor, and a vision of it blooms in him now, soft as a purple-throated flower: all towering trees dropping with fruit and slow meandering rivers and bright-feathered birds and no shouting people to fling stones and fists. A child can thrive there. Definitely Margaret's baby, brought from Orkney. Perhaps a child of his own can join it. For the Creature knows, now, that he is a being capable of love.

At nightfall he steals to Victor's cottage – a huddled stone hut on a pebbly beach, with a thatched roof on which grass tosses in the wind like a madman's hair – and rattles the door and finds it locked. Moving to the single tiny window, he sees that Victor has removed the bodies of Margaret and their baby and laid them naked on a rough-hewn table before the fire. Their winding-sheets are wadded in the coffin, which has been slung into the corner. The Creature has not meant to look. But now he cannot look away. Margaret's hair is long and brown, still holding the shape of the winding-women's careful curls. Her lips are gray. She is smaller than either Victor or himself. Her belly has a puddly softness, striped with the long dark line that until recently marked the baby's place: that baby, there, a seven-months' child with enlarged head and small curled arms and legs, lying on the table's rough boards just out of its mother's reach. With a satisfied sigh, Victor reaches for his scalpel, then his chisel, and opens her chest. Starting the heart: this is how life begins, with a *crack* like a falling rock from a cliff. Or at least a Creature's life. For this is the closest the Creature will ever get to witnessing his own birth. But Margaret will not need to be sutured and pieced-together as he was: Victor has decided simply to begin with an electrical impulse to the heart. There is the Leyden jar with its salt water and curved metal pin sticking from the lid. Victor snatches a woolen cloth and chafes it until it crackles, then passes it close to the jar so that the vital spark can travel into the metal pin. He does this again and again. Then, after a dozen tries, he lifts the jar carefully in gloved hands and bears it to the table. Lowering it to the incision in Margaret's chest, he touches the pin to the flesh of her heart.

Anticipation fades to disappointment on Victor's face. He repeats the process twice more but the heart does not beat. Firelight flickers on the cold gray limbs, the hair now drying from its grave-damp in the heat. The Creature longs to enter the room and chafe Margaret's hands between his own as if she were a drowned girl in the world above – the world not currently being violently overturned by himself and Victor Frankenstein – but the door is bolted and, anyway, he's terrified to interrupt the process or to introduce some fatal variable he can't see.

With a sigh, Victor stretches his back straight and lifts a hatchet from the fireside and goes to the coffin and hacks its lid to pieces and tosses them into the fire. The flames rise and roar. He stares at Margaret's corpse. And then he turns to see the Creature at the window, watching him. For a long moment he only stares. Then he hurls the Leyden jar to the ground. It shatters and a blue spark leaps and vanishes in air. With a single motion, he snatches the baby's corpse and flings it into the fire.

The Creature howls and smashes his fist through the glass and then finds himself pinioned in its teeth, struggling against the rising smell of roasting flesh, as Victor buries the hatchet in Margaret's chest with the businesslike *thud* of a butcher. He has decided to abandon her and to destroy her body in the process. Destroy her to pieces that can never be mended. Victor jerks the hatchet free and stares into the Creature's eyes with a cool, insane determination. *He doesn't want me to be loved,* the Creature thinks in horror. *By anyone.* His giant fingers claw the empty air. Furious words boil in him but nothing will emerge except one howl that rattles the remaining glass and echoes off the cliffs and silences, for a moment, even the swish and boom of the sea.

Heedlessly he jerks his hand free and runs to the heavy door but cannot dislodge the hinges or bolt no matter how he shakes the thick oak. The stone walls are solid, the single shattered window too small to admit the Creature's giant shape. Victor watches him, smiling now. He is enjoying this. He is enjoying the Creature's pain. The Creature's vision blackens with a rage he has not known it is possible to feel. If he could get into the cottage he would drag Victor out and haul him across the pebbled shingle to the sea and hold him under the waves and watch him drown.

But then. But then – he would be alone for good.

It is well. Out of the strings of furious words unfurling in his brain, only these come forth in a growl that, blessedly, wipes Victor's face clean with fear. *I go. But remember. I shall be with you –*

A sudden dim undertow blocks out the light and drags him down into the dark. Before his vision goes he sees only the red glow of fire in the window, and, upright in its frame, a single blood-smeared scythe of broken glass.

Part Four

Naples

ITALY DECEMBER 1818

Elise's baby girl, Elena Adelaide Shelley, is born under the volcano in the city of fire, in the suffocating rooms at 250 Riviera di Chiaia from which Shelley and William and Paolo are banished while Mary and Claire and Milly labor with water and towels and knife. Elise's belly rears high out of the bloody tangle of sheets, quivering, pushing forth its innocent, destructive fruit. With a bitter smile, Claire takes up the midwife position, closest to the bursting cave of Elise's body. "I have had," she declares to no one, "some recent experience of this. Mary, go fetch some more water. And you –" she addresses herself to Elise, patting her stretched flesh briskly – "bear down. Pretend you're driving to Venice. With a little girl named Allegra. About whom you'll write lies to her mother." Her smile is callous and terrible. Elise turns her head into the pillow and squeezes her eyes shut. No one, not even Milly, will meet Mary's gaze.

Paolo is the baby's father: that's what they all, in silence, have agreed to believe. They've brought him from Venice for this purpose despite his obtrusiveness, his arrogance, his ingratiating, infuriating smiles. Angling to get his hands on his brace of Shelley's pistols, he invents excuse after excuse: does Milordo not fear the bandits so numerous in Naples, does Milordo not see the need for the men of the house to protect the women? "So many women," he pleads, baring his white fangs in a grin, "all under Milordo's protection. And children, too. Many children." He clasps Elise's hand and she allows him to hold it, her eyes downcast. "When we are married in our own house back in the village, with Milordo's kind patronage, we will give thanks to him." Shelley smiles thinly. "I certainly hope," he says, "that you will."

Mary longs to be rid of this city with its thick humid warmth – even in December, they can open the windows, which lessens but doesn't dispel the atmosphere of six adults and one child in five low-ceilinged rooms – and the constant lowering presence of Vesuvius in the sky, a tiny plume of smoke always curling from its tip. Even the ground underfoot is not to be trusted: boiled and set by the volcanoes, it's queasily solid as a pudding in a bag. Mary can't disentangle the jumble of villas and slums up and down the hills, the Roman baths, even the dazzling blue glitter of the bay, from Naples's history of corruption and grief. Caligula strung his ships in a continuous bridge across these blue waves so he could ride his horse from deck to deck. In those villas, inbred kings sat in baths of children who swam around them, nibbling their thighs. Here, in the most desperately poor city Mary has ever seen, children are cheap. Like changelings, boys hardly bigger than William – spiteful, rueful, hungry, lost – work in pairs to snatch purses from pockets or pigeons from ledges, lighting fires, dissecting their prey in the shadows of baroque churches whose carvings fascinate the eye down and down into spaces of dizzying black. What would Mama make of Naples? Beauty? Justice? Maybe no city, no mortal, can ever have both.

Mary cudgels her brain to rise and stumble onward after Shelley in his insistence that they continue their writing, that their incessant travel will inspire them, that Mary must compose a novel to follow *Frankenstein*, that he must continue the epics like *Prometheus Unbound* and *Alastor*. After all, this is Italy, the most inspiring country on earth, where genius has walked improbable cities of water and earth and fire to show the fallen world that some not-fallen realm exists. Yet how it might be found again no one can tell, not even Michelangelo or Piero della Francesca or the nameless man who'd mixed the blue and green for the peacock's tail on the peeling frescoes at Pompeii, where bodies burnt to curled twists of ash on the floor of their own homes. Shelley has of course insisted they visit Pompeii, has of course sailed them over the sunken Roman town of Baiae, where mosaics and orderly brick foundations and marble statues of Dionysius and Agrippina Minor are scribbled over by the sea-worm's track, sunk and drifting, all green and algae-furred and covered over with water of a burning turquoise blue. They are meant to be artists, inspired by all this lush, cruel, irresistible beauty.

But Shelley is not well. He complains of stomach pain. His face is pale. He's discovered that if Mary doesn't wind her little wooden clock from Geneva, its hands will pause, quiver, then spin backwards, bouncing faintly as if to a pulse deep in the clock's brass-and-wire heart. So he draws up a chair and sits with his nose to the clock's face, like a cat at a mousehole. "If we could only locate," he murmurs, "some point at which time runs in reverse." He takes a sip of laudanum. "Is it a physical position in space? Like a door?" When Mary approaches, he shoves scribbled papers back in his pocket. "Stanzas Written in Dejection" – what is *that*? But later that evening, when he comes to her with a paper in his hand, smiling, "see here, I think this part's rather good," it's just a letter to his friend Thomas Peacock, back in England. Mary scrawls a greeting under Shelley's slanting script. She doesn't dare to write *who is my husband now? What's happening to us?*

When Elise can rise from her bed, Shelley and Mary and Milly, with William in tow, accompany her and Paolo and the baby to the Naples registry office, where three thick ledgers are splayed open on a table: *Partos. Matrimonios. Decessos.* Reluctantly, Milly accepts the baby to hold while Elise and Paolo stand at the bored clerk's desk and Mary, Shelley, and Claire bear witness. From a street vendor, Paolo has bought Elise a bunch of yellow roses with thick green stems, which Mary holds as Elise says her simple vows and signs her name. Like prisoners of the Bourbon kings, the yellow roses' heads wobble oddly on their necks; they're broken blooms from some florist's tip, wired on to green-painted sticks.[1] This is Naples in a nutshell, Mary thinks sourly: such inventiveness, devoted to deceit.

"You must all sign the registry," Paolo declares, baring his fangs, "Italian custom." The clerk leans against the records cabinet and shrugs, allowing Paolo to stage the scene he's determined to play. Paolo snatches a thick book and turns it ostentatiously to Mary. "Your signature, first, Signora," he declares, "as witness."

Mary hands the broken roses back to Elise and steps up to the table. But the word at the top of the page is *Partos* – births – not *Matrimonios.* And there in the clerk's round careful handwriting is Elise's baby's name and her date of birth, two days prior. But the baby's name is written as *Elena Adelaide Shelley.* And there is the familiar spiky tangle of Shelley's own signature, right next to it.

Mary looks up and meets Paolo's satisfied gaze. "É colpa mia!" he declares. "So sorry, I make a mistake." He whisks the *Births* registry away, slams it shut, and pokes the *Marriages* registry under Mary's nose. "Mettilo lì," he orders, and Mary scribbles her signature next to his black-nailed finger, having seen what he intended she should. What is Shelley's name doing there? Maybe an English lord's name is protection for poor spinster Elise and her girl. But with Paolo here as husband, his own signature so floridly tangling with Elise's in the *Matrimonio* ledger, why not just call this little girl *Elena Foggi*, as she so certainly is?

Paolo stops Shelley as they all leave the office and grips his hand. "I will tell the world," he says, in malicious, impeccable English, "that this child is mine. Out of my pride, of course, which is so great. You are a father too. You understand."

"Of course," Shelley says, tight-lipped.

Paolo beams at Shelley and opens his mouth to say something else but at that moment William's grizzling breaks out into a full-scale sniffling cry – this sad little wedding has interrupted his nap – and the baby twitches and sniffles too and Mary and Milly gather the children to hustle them down the stairs and back into the sun. Through the commotion, Mary detects the clink of coins, arising from the corner where Shelley and Paolo now stand, their heads together, their backs turned. Elise watches them, the bruised roses drooping from her hand.

Paolo, Elise, and the baby depart the next morning for Bagni di Lucca, where Paolo has declared his intention to return to the casino as a croupier, maybe open a little shop – "I thank Milordo for his patronage!" he calls, grinning and waving from the coach, Elise's face set firmly ahead, Elena Adelaide (*Shelley?*) clutched in her arms. Shelley watches their wagon trundle away. "Thank God they're gone," he mutters. "Now. It's a beautiful day. And Mary, I think you wanted to see the Sibyl's Cave?" It's his Milord-makes-problems-disappear voice, used to rent ponies at the Sea of Ice and chivvy bankers from London to Venice. It leaves Mary no opening for questions, for inquiring looks, for anger. *Shelley, if that wasn't you in the dark at Bagni, if I am your wife, if we're ever to be happy in Italy, why did you give that baby your name?*

Luckily, in Italy, there are guides to any place of classical myth. One has only to loiter on the docks at Bagnoli, obviously English and expectant, with bread and salami and cheese and Shelley's *Aeneid* in a knapsack. The fishermen ignore them, but within five minutes a young man strides up to them, smiling. "Io sono Marco," he says in Italian – thankfully, not the Neapolitan dialect – "vi porterò alle grotte."

Mary has read of it in Shelley's copy of the *Aeneid*, with the Latin on the left-hand page and Mr. Dryden's stately English couplets on the right. The Sibyl is part prophet, part novelist. "Leaves" blow into the mouth of her cave (they could be leaves from a tree or actual papers; the ambiguity is in the original Latin, Shelley says), and she reads their pattern where they fall, like so many pages blown off a desk near an open window. But the Sibyl won't rearrange those pages, or clarify their meaning. The Sibyl doesn't give a damn. She scorches wandering Aeneas with her words: *O goddess-born of great Anchises' line, / The gates of hell are open night and day; / Smooth the descent, and easy is the way: / But to return, and view the cheerful skies,/ In this the task and mighty labor lies.* Apollo courts her; she refuses him, asking for *as many birthdays as the grains in this handful of sand* she's snatched up from the mouth of her cave. Snickering (he already knows the ending, being the star of a classical fable with a sting in its tail), Apollo grants her wish. Only after her skin begins to droop and her hair to turn white and her whole body to shrink does the Sibyl realize her colossal mistake: she's forgotten the most important codicil, eternal *youth*. By the time Aeneas seeks her, she's seven hundred years old and still a virgin. And she'd been such a beautiful girl, once, accounted so wise.

Mary follows Marco and Shelley past Nero's thermal baths and the Lake of Avernus and then up the hill. At the top of the path, they emerge into a ruined rectangle of stone ringed with olive trees and waving grasses and wild herbs. The bay and the sky open before them in a thousand distinct shades of blue, with the islands of Procida and Ischia to the south. Wind lifts Mary's drifting hair. "Monte di Cuma!" Marco exclaims. Shelley stands rapt, muttering to himself his own lines from Venice: "where we taste the pleasure of believing what we see... is boundless, as we wish our souls to be..." Of course. Shelley's doing a little writing: revision of "Julian and Maddalo" from Venice, letters to Peacock, his signature in the Naples registry of births. Italy is so inspiring, for fantasies of all kinds. *That was not my husband in the dark.*

The path leads down the opposite side of the hill and under a flank of blond stone, sculpted into ripples by water and wind, riddled with holes. The lowest one is a cavern wider than the double doors of a church, several feet higher than Shelley's head. Someone has candle-smoked a pair of names on the wall, like the graffiti in the Doge's Palace cells: *Elena + Attillo.* A wine bottle's been slung into the corner. Of course: lovers. If you don't know the Sibyl's story – or maybe even if you do – this is just another place to come with a girl you want. With a man who secretly has his eye on someone else.

Marco draws a flint and a rag-wrapped torch from his pocket, strikes a light, and leads them down the passage. The darkness wraps them thickly, something thirsty in the air soaking up the light. "Where does that lead?" Shelley points to a passage opening to the right.

Marco shrugs and points his torch through the arch. Water gleams underfoot, stretching away into the dark. "È peccato," he says. "Conduce alla grotta della sibilla." *It's a pity,* Mary realizes: *it leads to the Sibyl's Cave.*

Without a word, Shelley steps forward, snatches the torch, and ducks into the passageway. "Che cazzo!" Marco exclaims. He bursts into a torrent of Neapolitan, mixed with only a few Italian words Mary recognizes, *ghosts* and *death* and *danger,* but with his torch inching out of sight in Shelley's hand he, and Mary, have no choice but to follow. Shelley picks his way along a dusty ledge above the water. Gradually a white glow leavens the darkness into gloom, then – as Shelley bears his torch into an open space, and disappears – into something recognizable as day. And then they stand in a large cavern, its jagged ceiling glazed and glittering with minerals borne in the water that drips down the walls. At their feet, a goat's skeleton, with long skull and two curled horns, has been coated by that pearly water, cemented to the rock. Overhead, a grass-ringed oculus – blue sky, a twitch of passing cloud, the faintest breath of wind – shows where it fell. Poor creature: grazing innocently along the hill before the world dropped from under its feet.

"Fortune favors the bold," Shelley exults, "as Pliny once remarked." He turns to Marco and smiles disarmingly. "Certamente questa è la grotta della sibilla?"

"Sì." Marco recovers himself and smiles back. "Certamente."

Surely this is the Sibyl's Cave. It has to be, although there are no "leaves" or anything like them, only a frost of minerals and the goat's glittering skull. Yet Shelley has spotted still another path: a black vertical crack, four and a half feet high. He starts toward it, but Marco grabs his sleeve. "Questo poi, no," he says. "Short way only it goes. A hole of water in the path. No one enters there." He reaches for his torch, but Shelley, with a bright distant smile, twists away and starts for the hole. Marco stares, then turns to Mary. "Signora," he splutters, "do not let him go, he will fall into the..."

"Shelley!" Mary calls, but Shelley is gone, the torchlight dimming as he weaves into the rock. Mary smiles reassuringly at Marco and starts after her husband. She will touch him on the sleeve – like some inverse Eurydice, rescuing an Orpheus determined to press into a darkness that's thick beyond his powers to know. *A hole of water in the path* – surely his torchlight will reveal it to him before he falls. But if he falls – Up there in the world are William at play with Claire and Milly, Elise and Paolo and Elena Adelaide (*Shelley?*) trundling northward out of their lives, the crowded rooms on the Riviera di Chiaia with their view of the Royal Gardens and, beyond, the wooded hill of Posillipo and the glittering bay. Up there is the continued path through Italy that must – that *must* – lead somewhere better for them all. And here is Shelley leading Mary away from that bright and normal world. Down and down into the dark. This, she cannot allow. Not anymore.

"Shelley!" The air in her mouth is cool and sour. The tunnel bends left and Shelley's head and his uplifted arm leap black against the orange circle of torchlight. He turns to look at her. "Shelley!" she calls again. He takes a step toward her, then turns back to look into the dark. And the torch winks out.

She must have screamed, calling Marco into the tunnel-mouth to haul her out. She must have fainted. When she opens her eyes, she's level with the goat skull on the ground, staring into the pearly sparkle of its empty eye. Her skirts are tousled, her face damp with water from Shelley's flask. He's pillowed her head with his knapsack. Through the layers of her dress and stockings, the cave's stone floor is very cold. No Sibyl could have lived here for a day. Let alone seven hundred years. What story has she been chasing? Why did she ever believe it?

"I can't believe you went in there!" The words burst out of her into Shelley's shocked face. She scrambles up and beats the dust from her skirts. "What if you had fallen, if I fell after you – if William never saw us again, never knew–"

Shelley's face lights with guilt, then an odd rigidity. "Mary," he orders, "contain yourself." Shocked, she watches as his expression grows distant. In front of this Italian stranger, he's embarrassed by her fear. He has never spoken to her like this before. Never.

A rage rises in her the likes of which she has never known, stronger than the battering rage in Venice, stronger than the swelling urge to hiss into the night air *I curse you*. "How dare you?" she spits back at him. "How dare you speak to me this way?" Marco reaches for her elbow, but she shakes him off and scrambles to her feet. *BecarefulMary he'llgetan-gryand you'lllosehim andyouandWilliamwillbelost rememberhe's-donethissortofthing before* – the familiar fearful pleading starts up in her head and she ignores it. "After all that you –" Something stops her words and she lets herself believe it is the presence of Marco, hovering miserably. "After all you have done. How dare you?"

Shelley's eyebrows lift. "Be careful, Mary." His voice is cold. "Be careful what you say."

"No." By God, she will not be deterred. "No, *you* be careful. I saw the baby's name in the registry. You gave Elise's child your name. You were – out there with her in the night at Bagni. I saw you." Shelley's mouth opens but she overrides him. "Don't bother to lie. Don't bother to tell me you are *offering a poor spinster the protection of your name.* Just – don't bother. I am your wife. Leave me some dignity. At least."

Shelley starts to speak, then stops. "Damn Paolo," he sighs. "I should have known –"

"How much are you paying him? To pretend the child is his?" She doesn't wait for an answer. "So." Shelley reaches for her, but she steps back. "The child is gone. So is her mother. I do not want to hear of them again." She turns her back on Shelley and strides away, pitching her voice louder. The echoes ring from the high domed walls, a wisp of her voice escaping through the goat-killing oculus like Vesuvius's smoke. "I do not want to speak of it."

With obvious relief, Marco starts to follow her, then turns back and calls to Shelley, but Shelley doesn't move. Too bad for him. Let him rot down here in this underground grave, in his confused miserable dreams of poetry and Milordo-ship and *elsewhere* and the baby he gave his own name, now jolting away back to Bagni, never to be seen again. Mary will return to the sunlit world where their living child is waiting. She will hail her own boat back across the bay. And once back on the Riviera di Chiaia she will bolt up the stairs and scoop up William and inhale the soft bready smell of his neck and hair and never let him go. She will sit down with her writing box and when – if – *when* Shelley returns, he will find her writing as he does not seem to be able to do, even with his squirreled-away *Stanzas in Dejection* (what has *he* to be *dejected* about?) and his letters to Peacock. She will write. Something. Anything. On her own. For herself. There will be more books after *Frankenstein.* There have to be. Her future, and her boy's, depend on it. Because Shelley is not to be relied upon. And never was.

She is nearly at the cave's mouth now, with its graffitied lovers' smoke. Then she is heaving herself up into the light where the long grasses wave and the blue bay churns and Vesuvius spins its single ominous thread of smoke into the sky. At her back, a heavy protective presence treads, close behind, speaking to her in a raspy, almost-familiar voice she can almost hear. *Keep walking,* it mutters. *Don't look behind you. Save yourself.*

CHAPTER 2

Rome

ITALY MARCH 1819

Milly is out marketing and Claire is at her singing lesson and Shelley is roaming the Baths of Caracalla again under a low gray sky too heavy for a Roman spring ("my tale of Prometheus," he declares, "comes to me well, out there in the ruins") and of course William has chosen this morning to be fretful. Mary has made him scrambled eggs and for the first time in her memory he's refusing to eat. "Miss Curran is going to paint your picture," she cajoles, "don't you want to look like a handsome big boy for your picture? And handsome big boys aren't hungry because they eat their breakfasts." Appeal to who he thinks himself to be is surely basic to any creature. Even the bewilderingly mysterious package of desire and will bound up in a three-and-a-half-year-old boy.

Mary looks at her little wooden clock from Geneva. Eight a.m. and she is exhausted. But there's no help for it: in an hour, Amelia will position William on her studio chair and begin sketching and Mary will have to cajole and hold him, fighting the traitorous murmur in her brain: *forget about my son's portrait, forget about improving myself in Rome, just let me sleep.* She is carrying another child, conceived – it must have been – in the first days here in Rome, yet another city for yet another fresh start. It is quieter within her than either William or Clara was (strangely, she can hardly remember the first baby's stirrings anymore) but the weariness that drags at her is more constant. There will be no rest until William goes to sleep tonight. Maybe she can cajole him down at seven. Maybe – oh, heaven – six.

William sits throned in the rickety high chair their landlady magicked from some attic above the Via Sistina. A shallow bowl of eggs sits before him, untouched except for the single spoonful Mary has been holding expectantly for the last two minutes. It's William's own spoon, the child-sized silver spoon found in one of the secondhand shops near their flat and given him by Amelia as a gift. Again, she moves the spoon toward his face and William whines and twists away. "Come," she cajoles, "they're good!" William clamps his lips together and frowns. She touches the spoon to his mouth and he throws up his fist, sailing the spoonful of egg *splat* against the wall.

A weary red fury rises before Mary's eyes and she is lost in it. "Do you want a spanking?" Where has this voice come from? *Mustn't shout, must treat children like rational beings* – But, dammit, what child is rational? William pouts at her, his lip wet and red. Then he reaches for his plate and pushes it onto the floor. It shatters. There goes another scudi – all Italian landladies charge for broken crockery – and two fine fresh eggs brought home last week in Milly's basket. The last of the eggs, in fact, until Milly gets home with more. Oh, Milly. Out there walking serenely in the world of adults and money and reasonable trade in lettuces and grapes and brown-speckled eggs. So far away from this little room of enclosed and whining hell.

"So now I'm going to scrape this up," she announces to William and herself, "and you're going to eat it." *You little demon. Tyrant. Yes, by God, you will stay right there, bolted in, until you* – Grimly, she unearths a plate from the cabinet and scrapes the eggs off the floor and onto the plate. "There," she announces, setting the plate before him with a *thunk*. "Eat." She sits down hard in her chair and snatches the spoon. "So you won't be hungry and whining all morning while Miss Curran paints your picture." String the words together. Make an order. Order this irrational creature to see reason, to feed itself and be fed, and please, please smooth its prickles into an orderly day of play and sleep that might dispel this red mist of anger and guilt wrapping itself around her heart. What kind of mother feels this about the last remaining child of her own body, the child she says she loves? Please, God, make the boy eat.

William screeches, flings his body forward, and slaps both hands flat onto the table. They land in the fluffy mush of egg and his wrist bangs the rim of the plate. He howls, rigid and thrashing in his imprisoning chair. She shoves the plate out of reach just before he can swipe it onto the floor again. Bad plate, bad eggs, to hurt him so. No creature can learn, until it's older, that the innocent dumb things of this world are not the true source of its pain.

Of course the words will come floating in when she has no paper or pen to hand. *The minds of children are such a mystery to us! They are so blank, yet so susceptible of impression, that the point where ignorance ends and knowledge is perfected, is an enigma often impossible to solve.*[1] Enigma. That is a polite word for a three-and-a-half-year-old in the throes of a tantrum. Fever, as usual, has been general in Rome. Perhaps she should beware, perhaps she should take William to the doctor – but she mustn't be hysterical, fretting over every little thing. There is also such a thing as simple stubbornness in a child, which only strengthens the need for him to learn self-control.

Mary shoves her chair back and leaves the room. Her plants from the stalls in Campo dei Fiori and furtive cuttings in the Borghese Gardens line the wide windowsill, and she rests her eyes on their green leaves, the soil she moistens with her little watering can each day. In the corner blooms a white azalea from a vendor on the Spanish Steps, its roots clipped to accustom it to life in a pot. There in the parlor ceiling is a plaster crack, and a water stain that looks like Shakespeare's head. Shelley will be amused by that. She plants the observation in her mind like the marker for a flower buried underground to emerge the following spring: *daffodil, lily, do not forget there is indeed a future beyond this moment in which your child is driving you into a rage unhinged as old King George.* Here is the cool factual voice that never deceives her. *Your child won't always be so fractious. He'll grow on into an awkward youth who'll shy from your hand and then you'll long, too late, to embrace him. Breathe deeply. It will not always be this way.*

In the next room, William's wailing fades to sniffles and his murmurs change their pitch: "Mama? Mama!" He's beyond his fury now, blown like a little cloud into an anxious patch of need. And of course, he is hungry. "Mama!" She has pushed the food out of his reach, so he can't spoon it up even if he wants to. "Mama!"

She hurries to him. There he is, still bolted into his chair like a tiny Bedlam patient, face still red, eyelashes matted into stiff points with drying tears. He looks her directly in the eyes and lifts his arms. How has she ever been so cruel? How has she ever been trusted with such a precious – Guilt drowns her anger and she scoops him out of the chair and holds him close. "Mama!" he complains, and leans into her shoulder and sets his sticky palm against her neck. She'll warm up the eggs again, she'll feed him, she'll atone. But first, she'll hold her boy.

Thump, thump of feet up the stairs and Milly enters with two laden baskets and the smell of a fresh loaf of bread. Her eyes sweep the plate of cold eggs and the shattered bowl on the floor and the sniffling child in Mary's lap. "I'll toast him up a toast," she says, pointing her words brightly in William's direction as he lifts his face to her: *toast* is a beloved word. "Salt up the eggs and heat them back up and they'll be fine, no use them going wasted. We'll be at Miss Curran's studio in time..." Catching Mary's eye, she nods significantly. "Maybe he's got a touch of worms," she murmurs. "We'll just have to build him up, won't we?"

Mary shifts William's weight in her lap as Milly bustles into the kitchen and sets her baskets down. Amelia's portrait will capture nothing of what has just happened. And thank God for that. Only her boy's wispy golden hair, his inquisitive round eyes, set under a wide brow like his father's, his skin radiant in the studio's late-morning light. Perhaps it will also include the props Amelia likes to pose with children: a drapery disarranged to show the tender little tummy, a rose in his hand. Just out of view, Mary can coax William into the expression she loves most: the tiny incipient smile, the dawning of delight that pauses just a moment on his face before his mouth opens and he bursts into a laughter without restraint or fear, abandoning himself to delight in the world as it is in that instant, as if that instant is all there will ever be. As if he is the small son of a perfect mother. A mother who never shouts or grows angry. A mother who wakes every morning in the knowledge that with such a husband and such a child, she is, as any English matron might stitch upon a sampler, *blessed among women.* As if all these things are true. But perhaps it is sufficient for one thing to be true: she is blessed, with a fourth baby under her heart and her small boy in her arms, already forgetting his tears, already twisting to reach for the toasted bread and cheese Milly comes bearing through the door into the dining room, smiling. She is blessed. In this moment, now, right here.

The Forum is a jumble of ruins and used-to-be streets, shoals of stones that lift their backs from the sand to be polished by the feet of scholars and seekers and touts. At night, the Creature is alone here with the cats. No one can count how many there are, since no successful army shows its entire numbers at once. Despite cart-wheels and flung stones and the lanky wolves that still slink down the Appian Way by night, the cats are legion. Most are brownish-gray tabbies, blending with the dim undersides of stones. Others are orange, faded to sandy yellow by generations in this sun. Some are missing chunks of ear or tail. In the curve of a sea monster's nostril, curled around an emperor's sandaled feet, the cats loll and wait, skeptical and fierce. Of course they're courted by English ladies they ignore. They do not trust too much to sentiment. They trust the knowledge they have gained: which rusty mesh around which crumbling wreck will jerk loose a tuft of hair or snag an ear, which green plants can be nibbled and which must be avoided, how blessedly naïve are the dormice in the House of Livia, what time the wolves come round.

Now, the cats watch the Creature as he walks the Forum in the moonlight. He always seems to end up at the temple of the Vestal Virgins, a semicircle of three ruined columns on a little knoll above the path. The Vestals were priestesses in the temple here, kept secure in genteel imprisonment to pray for the city and tend the sacred fire that would ensure its survival. If a Vestal disobeyed – let the fire go out, or made love to a man – she'd be walled up deep inside this temple's cellar with a day's worth of bread and water, so that the citizens could plausibly deny they'd murdered her. Perhaps that is the prison door right there: a black square of darkness in the ground, fenced with rusty mesh by some long-dead Roman mayor to plausibly deny he'd failed to safeguard some Grand Tourist against the fatal error of falling in.

Romans, for all their love of beauty, are legalistic, practical, with that legalistic human practicality that sends the Creature into a rage he finds increasingly difficult to control. Deny you've withheld love and other kinds of food, deny you've left a hole open before someone's wandering feet, and you can plausibly deny that you have killed. Although, of course, the opposite is true. He's so tired of humans and their self-protection, their cowardice. He made a pact with Victor Frankenstein to create for him a wife like himself but Victor broke his promise and tore her to pieces in front of his eyes. And killed what would have been their child. No matter his ideals. No matter his promises. Victor is just another human. And it is always the Creature who pays for humans' folly. Even Mary cannot seem to write him into the happiness he deserves. Mary tells herself she will start another book soon. The Creature hopes that this is true. Maybe it will continue his own story. Maybe it will unwind the story she has already thrust him into, where Victor shocked him awake and, mocking, condemned him to life, stumbling through a string of days with no apparent end. From his story, he had hoped for so much more.

At the temple of the Vestals the Creature rubs his eyes and grieves for the vision only he can see: the dignified woman, head up, walking into the dark. White robe spotless. A little woven basket in her hand. A jug of water, cork fitted tight. Perhaps someone who loved her would have slipped a little paper into her hand: a powder to send her off to sleep.

Each of the impossible cities the Creature has now seen – shadowing Mary, always – bears an even greater impossibility in its heart. If Venice is a city of water and Naples a city of fire, Rome is a city of earth, ribboned by a river that soaks in the rains of winter and spring and returns them, in the summer, as fever. Death is a cyclical occurrence here, like the sunlight drawing the spiraling vines of *fagioli* up their poles and the stately rhythms of priests in their robes raising and lowering the Host below the muscular limbs of God and Adam locked forever in a painted heaven by an artist whose bones are dust. Death is a fact. And to see these humans – these men – squander the love available to them in the face of that reality, to burn one another and battle and lie and kill, is a mystery the Creature cannot pierce.

And heaven knows, he's tried. He girded himself to keep his promise to Victor Frankenstein: *I'll turn my back on your entire world if you'll just make me one woman like myself to love.* He was prepared to forfeit the sound of water under great stone bridges and the bells that warm the air with song and the tilting ears of horses as they lean into their collars and the warmth of the bread-loaf snatched from a market stall and the bits of story he catches from the careless walkers past his hiding place: *oh, Giovanni, he's such a liar, did I tell you how he... Oh, Mary. Just bring the children to me at Venice and we'll manage it with Byron.* He's been ready to forfeit the entire world for this precious thing that human beings – specifically human men – squander each and every day. And yet he's the one who's been denied it. He's the one who has been punished. While all around him this gift is wasted. Love. The precious weight of flesh against flesh, of loneliness broken-in-upon by tenderness and transformed, as a musty room turns sweet when its windows are open to a warm day. So much love is wasted, spent away into bedsheets and beatings and unheard pleadings and the plain ordinary air. So much punishment lands on those who have done nothing to deserve it.

Rome is a place where the suffering of women is meant to be beautiful. And throughout the city it's rendered so, in bodies more lovely than anything the Creature has previously imagined. Bernini's statues alone can stand for all of it: St. Teresa, her ecstasy a rebuke to all who'd call a woman's flesh incapable of speaking the divine. Blessed Ludovica Albertoni: also in an ecstasy that shades the soul toward its own little death, a heavenly obliteration. Daphne, terrified face softening into shape-shifting release, her fingers becoming trees, her thighs becoming bark, right inside

Apollo's bewildered thwarted grasp. Poor caught Persephone, Pluto's fingers bitten deep into her flesh with a verisimilitude that makes the Creature wince.

Yet how much of this awe for marble flesh in ecstasy or pain transmutes itself into care for the bodies of women right here in the world right now? Bernini had his mistress Constanza's face razor-slashed for an *unfaithfulness* that he fanned in his head to a love-destroying flame. Caravaggio painted a whore named Maddalena, as the Virgin hoisting a toddler Christ who squirms away to bless old beggars with bare, filthy feet like the Creature's own. Yet Caravaggio cut a waiter's face open with a knife, snarled and fought, let himself be mocked by beautiful, faithless boys. Poor Beatrice Cenci was raped by her father until she and her brothers rose up and killed him, inside the palace the Creature walks past in the early dawn. Shelley keeps Beatrice's portrait on his wall right now. Muse and inspiration. Beautiful dead ghost. Maybe Shelley can't see how much that portrait looks like himself, but the Creature can. And he can see how Shelley yearns toward something that partakes in the love of the real women around him but also lifts up and away from them, like a spirit leaving a body to chase what it considers higher things. But the body remains: stubborn, homely, asking to be loved. As long as it remains alive, it always will.

The Creature knows that yearning. Just like all the other mortal men the Creature's body has been made from, before his body became something that only he might wish to call *mortal* himself. And having watched Victor tear Margaret – his *wife*, she had a *name* – apart before his eyes as he shattered the window and screamed, he rages anew at that yearning in the hearts of men, and at its total folly. All these women all around. So much yearning and dignity and love. Wasted by so many men dreaming after something eternally vanishing before them inside their own heads. Even gorgeous Pauline Bonaparte is abstracted by Canova into a sage, upright, reclining Venus, wearing her elegant nudity like a sable cloak. Mary trails still, always, after Shelley, who loves her but takes her, now, for granted. He calls her, in his poetry, *cold chaste Moon*. Has Shelley any concept of how deeply she'd be hurt, if she read that line?

The Creature steals from corner to corner and wants to shake the bragging, swaggering men of Rome until their ears ring. Look at all the beauty of these women, lovely and living. Brown freckles on soft necks, firm forearms and square tanned hands, decisive steps and hair skewered with broken-toothed tortoiseshell combs, heads flung back to release laughter that ripples like a flag through the entire piazza. With all this beauty, what need is there to dream and strain away toward some ideal that could never breathe? *Love her for what she is*, he wants to shout at every Cesare and Giovanni, at every Shelley. *You goddamned fool*. Take her and hold her and just savor the presence of her actual weight, her soft shrewd flesh, her smell of grass and bread and the chamomile tea with which she washes her hair. Hold her against you and breathe her in like women put their noses in their child's hair and inhale and close their eyes, like they hold the bouquets of lilies on which they splurge for weddings or funerals, savoring the sweet breath of the flower-flesh that ushers our own flesh into and out of life, that marks the single moment that is all we can ever know and hold, that catches, like light in a high window, every way there is to speak of the beauty that stops our hearts, the beauty that if we humans (*we?* The Creature answers himself *yes*) really hearkened to would kill us from the weight of our joy. Let ourselves feel that and we'd ascend like St Teresa, bearing the weight of our joy in our flesh. And it's women who even Bernini in his jealousy knew to render as the keepers of that joy. Honor them, you fellow men, the Creature pleads. Honor them and love them. Do not waste your lives in dreams that whisper to you *ignore this ignoble world, cast off and cast away this vile forlorn earth.* Because it could so easily be otherwise. Why choose your pride and loneliness when you could have all this love?

Behind the Vestal temple comes a slither and thump of feet on stones and the Creature draws back into its shadow as the walker edges around the temple on its opposite side. It's Shelley, heedless of robbers although it's past midnight and Mary has gone to sleep in their bed in the flat at Via Sistina long since. Caring for William all day, she must long for sleep as other people long for meat. But then, of course, Shelley objects to meat on philosophical grounds. Having descended the Spanish Steps and skirted along the bottom of the Quirinal Hill through the streets around the Pantheon, he's admitted himself to the Forum, where no sane and law-abiding Roman would go at night. Yet Shelley loves ruins by moonlight. Even now, he's carrying in his pocket a fragment of some strange little story about a traveler who goes to the Colosseum on a night like this one and meets an old blind man with an ethereally beautiful, angelic young daughter. Just like Agatha, for whom the Creature had had such high hopes of sisterhood. Just like Safie, who had clung to the doorknob and screamed as Felix rushed at him and tore him away from the old blind man who would not stop repeating, uselessly, "But he's my friend! He's done nothing wrong!"

In the bright moonlight Shelley is a black figure flickering among the stones like one of the snow-blindness wraiths over the Sea of Ice in the Alps, only visible in flashes of white above his coat: his cuffs, his collar, his face under its shadowing mop of thick curls. He bends to run his hand over the large stones, then remains hunkered in the road, his back to the Creature. From the shadow of an acanthus plant a big tabby cat watches him. Shelley stretches out his hand and snaps his fingers. The cat yearns briefly toward him – surprising itself – but draws back, saving face with an elaborate nosing-around the base of the acanthus, trailing its tail along a leaf.

Why is Shelley here when his wife and his remaining child are asleep in their beds in the flat to which he has brought them, halfway around the world? Why, oh why, give away that warm weight of love and home when you could have it, simply by stretching out your hand? When in fact, as your own life is amply demonstrating did you have the self-aware-ness to recognize this, it is harder for you *not* to have these things than to simply accept them as what they are, a gift you have done nothing to earn, a gift of which – all the Shelleyan and Huntian sneering at *old-fashioned English values* be damned – you have the duty to prove yourself worthy, to care for and honor and love?

He ransacks everything like a bee, Hunt has laughed of Shelley. Except a bee stores up pollen and works it into honey to feed whole families. Not just itself. Like St. Julian, Shelley tossed his little daughter Clara's soul across that bridge to make a deal, then sauntered on. Even gave himself the saint's name in "Julian and Maddalo," a poem about himself and Byron. *What Maddalo thinks about these matters is not exactly known,* the poem says. But Shelley knows what he's done. How could he not?

The Creature begins to shake. He could leap on Shelley and hurl him to the ground and wrap his long black-nailed fingers around Shelley's throat and squeeze. It's simple. He's done it before.

After Victor tore his mate to pieces before his eyes and flung their child into the fire, the Creature had hoped to die of grief. When he woke from his black faint, he tried to catch Victor before Victor could dump the baskets of Margaret's sodden oozing arms and legs – her torso with its sideways-listing breasts, purple nipples gone slack – into the sea. But Victor had been too quick. He had escaped. Nevertheless, the Creature had waded into the surf and fished out the basket with Margaret's dismembered limbs (he *will* call her by name, he *will* call her his wife) and held her brokenness against himself. Sodden. Limp. Reeking and bleeding and lost. And he wept for her. The first of many times.

He should have killed Victor. But a father is not so easily dealt with.

Now there will be no mate for him. No love.

Does Shelley, with his sisters and his abandoned first wife Harriet and his ever-present something-more-than-sister-in-law Claire and sent-away Elise and poor longsuffering Mary whose love no treachery of his seems able to break and the eternal never-quite-here ideal woman after whom he starts like any Sussex squire after a fox (Beatrice Cenci, three hundred years dead, is only the latest), this man whose favorite words in poetry and life seem to be *inconstant* and *mutable* – has Shelley the remotest notion of the pain the Creature knows right now?

He doubts it. But he does know this: Mary is aware that Shelley is the father of Elise's child. Yet to admit this fully and let it drive her away from him would be to drop into a well of unimaginable pain, to sink into a place she must avoid for William's sake. *Man. Han. Man. Your hand in mine.* Perhaps William remembers the Creature as the Creature remembers him. Perhaps he wishes they could play again on the parlor floor while their parents shout and toss the names of dead sisters, dead wives, around and around like trapped birds in the air.

Shelley straightens and shoves both hands into the pockets of his old brown coat and rocks back on his heels, surveying the little wilderness of stone that once had been this city's heart. On a scrap of paper he's jotting lines by moonlight: *Rome has fallen, ye see it lying / Heaped in undistinguished ruin: / Nature is alone undying.*[2] He is so easy in his body. So easy in himself. So sure. The words come to his hand as easily as that cat. The world rises to him eager to be ransacked. To be seduced. It isn't fair.

There must be something I too can take. The words ring in the Creature, furious. So that the scouring depth of his sorrow will be known to the world. So it will have a life and a dignity of its own. A life apart from him, this thing of darkness that none acknowledge. *Mine.*

No, some voice within pleads. *Have mercy. There are costs, there are consequences. To the innocent. To the unseen. You know this pain too well to loose it on another.* But the Creature's blood pounds in his ears and his rage swells, blurring the shaky border between his own world and the world in which Mary and Shelley live with their last surviving boy. Unjust. But then pain does not always land on those who merit its sting. If humans want it otherwise, they should have organized their beautiful infuriating terrible world differently. Should they not?

I will be with you, he'd vowed to Victor over his wife's wrecked corpse, *in the moment of the greatest happiness you know.* Somehow his grief, his anger, will be heard.

CHAPTER 3

Protestant Cemetery

ROME JUNE 1819

The *cimitero acattolico* – a flat field, with a little hill to the east – lies behind a great gray stone pyramid that some emperor hauled in for a souvenir. A scatter of tombstones huddle near a low, partially completed brick wall. More bricks are jumbled in a heap, along with sacks of sand and buckets and mixing tools for mortar. No masons are visible. Perhaps they've gone to their lunch, Mary thinks dimly. Perhaps they'll soon return to finish the wall around William's grave.

What a mother. Traveler. Traitor. Connoisseur of burial sites for the children she endangers by trailing after the husband who flings himself around the world like some blind Orpheus, never looking back.

At least Orpheus – unlike Shelley – knew his wife was following him.

Someone has had the foresight to plant cedar trees here in a line, marching up the hill. The cemetery wall will follow their path, enclosing them. Those will become the expensive plots, up on the hill, crisscrossed by little gravel paths. An orderly place to walk and visit the orderly dead. But for now William will be buried on the flat plain behind the pyramid. Tall pine trees in the distinctive Roman umbrella shape loom over her. The trees will shade her little boy, he will not lie baking in the sun, he will not –

Suffer? A pitiless voice like Godwin's completes the sentence in her head. *Too late for that.*

In the dry grass stands a middle-aged Englishwoman in a lavender-gray dress – the color of a pigeon's breast, appropriate to every form of grief. "I am Miss Fyfield," she murmurs. Her voice, too, is soft, with a faint burr: Yorkshire, maybe. Behind Mary, two fat men in dirty trousers and fresh white smocks lift William's coffin from the wagon-bed and bear it away. "I have arranged for you." *For us to what?* Mary wonders, but then realizes Miss Fyfield's sentence is complete. Shelley, Milly, Amelia Curran, and Claire step back awkwardly and Miss Fyfield inclines her head and turns away. *I am the mother,* Mary realizes. *I am to follow first.*

The two gravediggers and a priest wait at the small rectangle of raw earth. Two spades lie rigid in the grass. "Ah, madam." The priest's voice, too, is English, also of the north. "I am Reverend Wainwright of the Anglican Church of Rome. I greet you." He nods at all the women, steps forth, and firms his lips as he shakes Shelley's hand. Thankfully Shelley does not object. No cant about atheism today. Just this moment when their son will go into the ground and they will walk away and leave him here. Just this impossible moment to be got through, with life afterwards – that impossible, bare-scorched country – on the other side.

And then at some point what Mary guesses is the service begins. Miss Fyfield retreats to a tactful distance. So do the gravediggers, folding their thick hands against the fronts of their clean smocks (like butchers: why quibble about one means of death or another, why hide the spades, why conceal what any of this is about?) Reverend Wainwright touches his cassock and unspools a fluent ribbon of words Mary doesn't bother to understand. She tightens her lips and watches Shelley nod and flounder and pretend to know what his own responses should be. *Too late,* atheos. *Should have paid attention on all those Sundays back in Sussex.* The points of the cedar trees twitch in a small, prowling wind. Claire's hand supports Mary's left elbow and Amelia's her right. As if she will fall. As if she is not already a mother experienced in grief. *This is the third, my girl.* Godwin's voice echoes in her, sardonic, terrible. *Good work.* In the distance a black-robed figure paces slowly, turning its white face toward them and then away.

At Mary's feet lies a rectangle of open earth. Feathery shadows of pines and the solid shadow of the pyramid flicker into it and out again. The larger of the two men lifts William's coffin in his arms and holds it while the second man removes one roll of white ribbon from his left pocket and one from his right and unscrolls them painstakingly on the ground in two straight lines. Long white ribbons, perfectly immaculate. For this small body's weight, ribbons, not rope, will suffice.

Sighing and shifting their feet, the gravediggers hoist the coffin between them and lower it carefully onto the ribbons. Then they lift the ends of the ribbons, hands rising with solemn inadvertent theatricality, and bear the coffin, swaying in its sling, toward the grave. Standing one on each side, they poise the small white box over the hole. Little by little, it descends. A bar of shadow slides across the lid. One fat man's hand slips and William's coffin lurches and chips the side of the grave. Grayish, pebbly soil rains down out of sight. The ribbon is smeared now, too, where it passes across the coffin wood. William is dirty now. A fresh wave of rage rises in Mary at the sight.

Reverend Wainwright has been speaking all this time but Mary has not heeded him. Nor has she heeded Shelley, who presses into the air around her like a rain cloud, felt before it's seen. Now the box is in the hole. Sighing, the two men take up their spades and begin to fill. *Swish, thump. Swish, thump.* She sees the rain of gray dirt through the light where it falls across the hole but does not watch it all the way down. The men are quick. They don't look at her. *Swish* and *thump* and then the dirt is soft and level and patted with the silver spade-backs that leave flattened shapes in it like footprints. From his pocket, Reverend Wainwright withdraws a little wooden cross painted white, her son's name inked carefully on its horizontal bar. *William Godwin Shelley, January 24, 1816 – June 7, 1819.* Solemnly he bends and plants the cross's sharp end in the dirt.

Shelley's face is still. Mary turns her back on him and stares at the sunlit tips of the cedars tossing back and forth in their private breeze. Someday this is all anyone approaching this place will see at first, just the tops of these full and graceful trees above a wall. No graves. Unless they choose to come inside this wall. Where no mother worthy of the name should ever have to set her foot.

Suddenly with a rustle of skirts a black flapping figure springs from behind Mary and snatches the white cross from the grave. Shelley whirls and shouts and the gravediggers fling down their shovels to give chase. The figure sprints away toward the pyramid, gravel flying from under its feet, black cloak billowing, hood jostled back: gray-streaked black hair scraped into a knot, a thin white neck, a thin white hand gripping William's cross. "Maledizione!" The gravediggers turn back, panting. "La madre piangente. Ancora."

The priest sighs. "Poor soul." His Northern accent curls the word like a dead leaf: *puir.* "They call her 'the weeping mother' here. She haunts this place. Her child died, no one knows how long ago, and she –" He pauses. "Well, ye see how she's fared ever since."

Mary stands rooted at the small grave, tears scorching her face. Only the dent of the cross is left: no marker, no name. As if her son has never been born. As if this infernal city has snatched his life, like some monster of Venice rose to take Clara in its jaws and plunge back to the deep. But perhaps it's only what she deserves. Venture onto the Continent with Shelley and a story in your head and this is what you reap: black hungry ghosts leaping out of rocks and cemetery walls to snatch your bread or your breath or your child's name right from your startled hand. Travel after this tall high-voiced man who has seen one wife down to death already, who has children back in England dead to him if not actually buried, and you open your naked flank to the world, baring your flesh to its spears and accidents and teeth. To risk this yourself is perhaps under-standable. To risk your children has now proven unforgivable.

Of *la madre piangente* who has raced away with William's name in her hand there is no trace, not even a footstep in the grass.

I was a mother. And I am so no longer.[1]

This is the punishment I deserve.

The dark place into which Mary sinks is a dry well, walled with uneven stones, floored with powdery sand. From somewhere above her a circle of sky bathes her with a dim light, just enough to make out the shape of a flat, open wooden box lying in the dirt. White cloth rims its interior. And above its edge is just visible the round shape of a small head, turned away.

All the thoughts that must not be admitted, all the words that must not be spoken, are waiting down here.

The first baby girl – the nameless girl, of whom Mary tries never to think – came to her in a rush of uncertainty and pain, five years ago, in the winter she was seventeen. The cold shock of water woke her near the end of February in her rented London bed and she found herself lying in a wet patch of soaked mattress. *Too soon. A seven months' baby. Too soon.* Claire's face and Fanny's face worried, hovered. Shelley's appeared and disappeared. Scissors. Steaming basins of water. Gripping, tearing pain. A howling: Mama. Mama. Someone saying *shush, your mother isn't here.* And then the tiny red plucked naked thing – shifting alarmingly in its wrinkly skin, a pulsing bloody purple knob of cord at its stomach – was laid on her breast. *Stop,* Mary started to moan, *take it away,* but then it snuffled and broke into a full open-mouthed wail. In Mary's breasts something twanged like snapping ropes, and then big warm wet spots came through her gown. "Good," said Dr. Clarke encouragingly, "here she is," and big roughened hands over Mary's positioned the red-faced bundle and dragged the neck of Mary's nightgown down and hooked that squalling maw over the nipple Mary did not recognize as her own, huge and purple, eager animal drops of white springing out of it. And the wailing ceased like a flame cupped by a candle-snuffer, leaving only the stunned relief trailing upward through Mary's blood like smoke released, like the nourishment of that pork chop gnawed in the Fleet Street gutter: *yes, yes, this is for her. This has always been for her.*

The baby slept in a drawer pulled out of the landlord's splintered bureau and laid on the floor beside the bed and padded with Shelley's old shirts because they had no money for a cradle. Every morning Mary could turn over in bed and reach down her hand. Until the morning she turned, and looked, and stopped. Curled into a half-moon, the baby's back was narrow and frail. Her eyes were closed, the lashes silver on her cheeks. She wasn't moving. And when Mary gathered herself and reached out, the baby's skin through the rough muslin gown was cold. Like the cold that lives in the heart of a stone.

It is the milk that Mary remembers now, the dumb outpouring of the dumb body that gave this baby life yet failed to keep it burning. When the dead child's blue lips brushed her breast through the thin nightgown cloth – she had not been able not to lift her – the milk came in a gush and glued the cloth against her skin. Mary burst into tears. The milk kept leaking, weeping, all afternoon, as Fanny and Claire helped Mary climb into a dress and padded the bosom and prepared some broth, some tea, as they washed the baby's body and wrapped it neatly in a white cloth. And eventually they asked where Mary would like the child to be laid to rest. "With Mama," Mary choked. Fanny nodded. "We'll see it done," she said. And her arms came against Mary's chest, shifting the baby's weight up and away. Claire set her hand on Mary's shoulder, guiding her into the shabby green chair that had scratched grooves into the floor. Together, Fanny and Claire turned away. Mary set her eyes on the holes in her stockings, peeking from under her dress – symmetrical over the big toes on both sides – so she would not have to remember anything her brain could name the last sight of her child. Footsteps crossed the floor. The door opened and closed. And against Mary's breasts the cloth was cold and wet. How could she ever make her body understand. That its milk or the blood pumped dumbly through its loyal red heart would not be needed now. Any of it.

Fanny and Mama and the baby are together now, somewhere. With William. And Clara. All killed by Mary. Five once-living beloved ones, killed by the mother who is not a mother any more.

I dread to unfold her mind, Mama wrote of Fanny, *lest it render her unfit for the world she is to inhabit –*

No worry, Mama. Her sister Mary will finish the job of killing that the world began. Then Mary will be left alone here without her husband, her children, or her mother. Because she deserves to be. Left alone here at the bottom of the well without Shelley, even without William himself. Oh, little Wilmouse with his sweet face laughing up at Amelia in her bright studio, his tantrum forgotten, frozen now on canvas, like Mama's face. Mary is left alone here with nothing but the first small baby in a bureau drawer, her face turned away into the dark.

And with words. Of course, the daughter of Godwin and Wollstonecraft is never without words. Accompanied, dogged, blasted by them, never to be left in peace. Now the words are speaking of a deposed and murdered king, Shakespeare's Richard II. Death sits inside Richard's hollow crown, laughing, applauding. *Allowing him a breath, a little scene.* Allowing us a little time upon this stage, this threshing-floor that makes us all so fierce. Allowing us to think we can control a goddamn thing. Richard realizes the truth of this, too late. *Thoughts tending to ambition, they do plot / unlikely wonders – how these vain weak nails / May tear a passage through the flinty ribs / Of this hard world, my ragged prison walls, / And, for they cannot, die in their own pride. / Thus play I in one person many people, / And none contented.* And none good. And none to be trusted with a child's life.

Tear a passage through these flinty ribs – Why must the tearing be never-ending, on and on and on? Why must the nails that do the tearing – breaking, bleeding – always be Mary's own, the ribs be the indifferent barrel-staves of the hard, hard world? Like the corset-shell that encased her mother's ribs, then Fanny's. Two dead women who would be alive if not for Mary, the upright walking body through which death tears its way into the world. Mary, the creature who kills although it howls in remorse and swears it means no harm.

In the sand at the bottom of the well Mary curls next to the wooden drawer that holds her baby. Sand covers the face of Clara on the Lido. Dirt covers William's coffin in the Cimitero Acattolico, lovingly marked but now erased by a witch who snatched his name away. *La madre piangente. Ancora.* Pregnant, again. Weeping, again. Because she has lost a child, again.

I was a mother. And am so no longer.
If she can only sleep. If she can never wake again.
A creature like herself deserves no more.

CHAPTER 4

Naples

ITALY OCTOBER 1820

The *Maria Crowther* rocks at anchor in the bay, quarantined. Its sails rustle. One soldier paces back and forth along the dock to keep the English typhus on board this English ship until it can be determined no one in in its dank hold is bearing the disease. From behind a stack of barrels the Creature watches him: a plump man ten years too old for active service, toting a musket that must have been his grandfather's. As if this city isn't already swarming with a thousand varieties of disaster: syphilis, starvation, rape, murder, fire and ash liable to rain from the sky. Still, in times of plague – when, somewhere on this earth, is it ever *not* a time of plague? – each nation needs to reassure its people that it's protecting them, offering an illusion that the people, in their need, accept. Thus a social contract of weakness becomes titanic power, since fear is the rocky ocean bed that will always bear it up. Old Mr. DeLacey taught the Creature this. Hobbes, Rousseau, the Americans, they've all wrought it into some form that suits themselves: the sovereign takes his power from the people's need to *have* a sovereign, to give themselves some imaginary bulwark against their omnipresent fear. Invaders. Wars. Famines. Plagues. The king and the *hoi polloi* are stuck with each other, hoping it will all work out. At least the people hope. The sovereign – in Hobbes, at least – has no obligation but to be his own indifferent, heartbreaking self. No sovereign, no creator, no father ever does.

Yet the Creature hasn't come here to swot up once again what he learned back there, the barest sliver of what he could have learned had stupid stone-grubbing Felix not torn him away from the old man and left him with only an empty house to burn. Mary is in Florence now with Shelley and her soon-to-be-fourth child and a novel she has at last finished, some boring Italian historical thing that doesn't include the Creature at all.[1] At the moment, she doesn't need him. But her acquaintance Mr. Keats – who's on this ship – does. Mr. Keats helped bring the Creature to life. Witnessing him now will pay a debt. Somehow.

The *Maria Crowther* is a small, bedraggled brig: two masts, one deck, dark flanks specked with barnacles, its sails salt-battered by the month-long sail from Gravesend to Naples. From end to end it can't be more than 150 feet long: so small against so large a sea. A swarm of maritime words invades the Creature's head: *topgallant sail, fore and aft, prow and stern.* Ha. Maybe one of the men whose bodies had gone to form his (his bodies, then?) had been a sailor. Two lanterns burn, one on the deck near the tiller, the other in a cabin porthole below. All the rest is dark and quiet. One rowboat is missing from its hook: surely the sailors are ashore, breaking quarantine, as the *Maria Crowther* has been here for only eight days of the required ten. But Mr. Keats knows the importance of obeying doctor's orders, no matter the sacrifice. He's staked his life on it. And his love.

City lights and distant voices flicker onshore; high up on the hills, in their expensive villas, the last nobles of the Kingdom of the Two Sicilies must be enjoying their wine. Maybe a spot of sodomy and dancing girls. To the west, Vesuvius rumbles and smokes. A reddish glow lingers around its top like the setting sun. But that isn't sunlight in this sky.

The Creature slips over the edge of the dock and hand to hand down a pillar into the bay. In four dozen strokes, he's treading water in the shadow of the ship. More than a month at sea has opened gaps in the boards; a livelier crew would spend this quarantine making repairs. But the *Maria Crowther's* passengers don't get England's best. Two meals a day and the dregs of Nelson's press-gangs are all your bargain fare will buy. At least your bed will be your own. And with consumptives on board, that's a guarantee you can't afford to skimp.

Left-hand fingers in one crevice, then the right. Right foot's toes against the boards. And the Creature's climbing, with his blessed inconvenient strength, up the side of the *Maria Crowther.* His weight keels it a little sideways in the water. In a moment he's hunkered with his feet on the ledge below the single bright porthole, looking right into a wood-beamed burrow with bunks against the wall and a table underneath a lantern swinging from a chain. Two young men and a young woman sit around it, playing cards. The woman's cheeks are red, her chest sunken underneath a kerchief stained with little brown dots. She coughs and crushes a handkerchief against her mouth. The man on the left-hand side of the table – tall and fine-boned, with a softness of expression despite his sharp nose and chin – peers at her. Flecks of blue paint are caught in the sun-whitened hairs on his forearms. "Miss Cotterell." His voice is kind. "Don't overtire yourself. We can continue this another time."

"Nonsense." Her voice is determinedly bright. "I promised Mr. Keats I'd teach him to play Skat. A brand-new game from Germany. My sister taught it me before we sailed." She struggles to swallow her cough before it bursts. "And with three players, it's perfect for us."

"Patience." The third man speaks, almost too low for the Creature to hear. "That's the game I need on board this ship, I fear." He pushes the corners of his wide mouth outward into something that can pass for a smile. His left hand – closest to the porthole and the Creature, out of Miss Cotterell's sight – moves to a sheet of letter-paper, rubs a corner between a thumb and index finger. Handwriting, upright and clear, reads *So I am about as I was. Give my love to Fanny and tell her, if I were well there is enough in this port of Naples to fill a quire of paper – but it looks like a dream – every man who can row his boat and walk and talk seems a different being from myself. I do not feel in the world.*[2] Yes. This must be Mr. Keats.

The Creature curls his fingers tighter against the boards. And something like a dream invades him: he's standing on another ship very far from here in a howling wilderness of white, looking through another porthole into another ship's cabin where a strange man – with kind eyes and a distracted brow, something of this Mr. Keats in his look – tends to Victor Frankenstein. Of course. It's Robert Walton, who pulled Victor from the frozen sea onto his own ship. And soon the Creature will cross the ice toward Walton's ship and into the cabin where Victor lies. Like a thorn the Creature feels it embedded in his flesh, this coming thing: he'll be tugged like a compass point to a magnetic north by the design of his life, the desire to drive on and on, to punish and to kill both Victor and himself. He will trek north and northward still, taunting and encouraging, and Victor will follow. Horror will precede this, horror will follow. He knows that this is true. And he knows that Mr. Keats will die.

Around him the night is black but for the red halo of Vesuvius in the west. Capri and Ischia are darker hulks against the sky. The bay beneath him is deep, and very cold.

He's close enough to Mr. Keats to hear him breathe. A liquid rustle in his throat prickles on the Creature's skin. He could stretch his hand through the porthole and touch Mr. Keats's face right now. But who wouldn't scream and leap up and overturn the table at the sight of that black-fingernailed paw reaching from beyond this cozy circle of light, a creature – literally – from another world? The sight of him, the Creature knows, can break a human mind. But maybe not every mind. Maybe on that ship in the Arctic he'll find out. He'll go through the porthole, into the cabin with Victor and Robert Walton into the last circle of human light he'll ever know before he steps off into a blank indeterminate space with no apparent end. This is his task. This is his life. This is the way the story goes.

Test yourself, Victor's voice challenges. *Interpret human contexts, human looks.* Obediently the Creature answers him. Mr. Keats won't look at Miss Cottrell because he has the same disease that's killing her and he knows it will kill him too although they've both come here to Italy in hope of life. The Creature angles his gaze at Mr. Keats' letter. *It has been unfortunate for me that one of the passengers is a young lady in a consumption – her imprudence has vexed me very much – the knowledge of her complaints – the flushings in her face, all her bad symptoms have preyed upon me – they would have done so had I been in good health.*[3] Foreshadowing, Mary would call this. But not every reader wants to know what's coming next. Mr. Keats is twenty-five. He doesn't want his disease to progress like Miss Cotterell's, although he knows it will. He doesn't want to die.

The man across the table is still trading cards with Miss Cotterell, shuffling the bright little rectangles of paper, chattering, deliberately. "It's a good time for painting, at least," he's saying. "We're held in the bay at just the right distance for a view." Mr. Keats glares at him but then his face softens: they've obviously had this argument before, about *facing reality, Joseph* versus *making the best of things, John.* "I got some rather good effects with the waves yesterday."

"The great Joseph Severn's contribution to the history of art." Keats' words are teasing, affectionate. "Painting water in watercolor, having sailed over a thousand miles of water to float for ten infernal days on still more water..."

"It's only 'cause I'm such a great artist," Severn snickers. "Passionate and uncontrollable." At Keats's smile, delighted relief swells in him like a brisk east wind. "Catullus, isn't it?" He grins. "*Sed mulier cupido quod dicit amanti / in vento et rapida scribere oportet aqua.* I'm a bad Latinist, Miss Cotterell, and perhaps no gentleman to speak of this, but you'll forgive me, they're lovely lines regardless: 'What a woman says to a passionate lover / should be written in the wind and the running water.'"

The words thud to the table like bright birds, shot. Keats's face is blank now, wiped horribly clean. *Give my love to Fanny and tell her, if I were well –*

Fanny is the girl he loves. The Creature huddles tighter to the ledge. *The girl he'll never see again.*

Severn has the grace, at least, to see what he has done. "Oh." His mouth drops open. "Oh, John. I'm such a fool –" Tears thicken in his eyes and unlike every other male human of the Creature's scattershot acquaintance he makes no attempt to hide them. "Please forgive me, I didn't –" *Just stop,* the Creature thinks. "I never thought – I mean, I –"

"I know." Keats' voice is weary. "Please don't be concerned." He gathers his pages into his hands. "I'm going up on deck."

As Keats nudges back his chair and rises, he turns his head to the left and suddenly he's staring right through the porthole into the Creature's eyes. *Damnation.* The Creature can't breathe. Thankfully Miss Cotterell and Severn have returned to their cards. Mr. Keats's gaze is clear, clinical. His eyes are an unidentifiable color: green? Brown? Gold? Beyond the initial startlement – smothered instantly to not alert the others – curiosity is waking now. A curiosity like Victor's. This man has been a scientist. No. A doctor.

And then it flashes on the Creature's sight: Keats five years ago, robust of frame and sweating in a leather apron and too-bright lantern light, scraping underneath a hundred peering eyes at something on a table.[4] A man is lying there, flattened by whiskey and opium and the grip of two blood-spattered giants as Keats cuts into his neck with a tiny silver knife delicate as a pen. Another man, wielding a sponge on a long stick, leans over him to dab away the blood. "Superficial temporal artery," drones a voice, "supplying vascularity to the temporoparietal fascia." Only the Creature can see that Keats is terrified. That in four more cuts or maybe five he will lose his composure and the knife will slip and the man will die. Cut. Cut. Dab. The giants tighten their grip. The sponger dances in and out again like a pugilist's cut-man. *I should've learned to box,* flickers some terrified dream in Keats's head, *like the Nonpareil. He makes it look so easy.* And then the final cut and with an outgush of breath Keats is reaching for the needle and the thread that will end this operation and sew up the gash of fear that's ruptured in his head before it kills his patient. He'll end his medical career before that shame can end it for him. When he sluices his hands in a basin and applause flickers through the room and Keats in his blood-stiffened apron strides out through the swinging doors, only the Creature and Keats know that he isn't coming back.

The patient on the table is insensible. A red-and-black-stitched ridge snakes from his temple to his collarbone. *Lucky bastard.* The Creature smiles bitterly. *He'll come back to life. He'll heal.* His wife will touch the scar, perhaps, tease and soothe its healing shape. And in Fanny Brawne's arms, realizing what his coughing means, Mr. Keats will weep.

But there is something more. The Creature's head throbs. Somewhere in the future there is a gravestone under tall umbrella pines. Mary knows this cemetery too. There is William's tiny gravestone in the grass (*Wilmouse, oh, Will,* the Creature pleads, *I never meant to –*) And here is a rounded stone nearby, upright in a sunny corner thronged with lavender. On it is carved a lyre with a broken string and some words that shimmer into focus as the Creature squints: *Here lies one whose name was writ in water.* A bird's shadow flickers overhead. Tiny white daisies in the grass lift their faces to a blue Roman sky. Under that gravestone, more writing curls across a stack of letters, buried down in that casket under Mr. Keats' crossed hands, large and knuckly as the boxing Nonpareil's. The words curl unreadably out of sight except for the signature: *Fanny.* The letters are unopened. In his final days Keats could not bear to read them. But he would not leave them up in the bright world while he went into the dark.

The Creature clambers down the ship's flank and starts the long swim to shore. His tears wash invisibly into the bay. At a safe distance from the *Maria Crowther* he stops and turns, treading water. There's the small silhouette of Mr. Keats, leaning against the rail. He turns his gaze to the northwest – where England is – and then back to the harbor, surveying the twinkling lights of the shops and the lavish villas and the robbers' dens, the red halo of Vesuvius. The Creature turns and raises his strong right arm to strike out for the shore. He knows, now, things he wishes that he did not. And somewhere, inside the story they both have made, Mary knows them too.

CHAPTER 5

Villa Magni

The Creature huddles in the corner of the room, unseen, as Mary writhes on her bed. She is moaning, low ragged sounds pushed out of her as her body pushes out of itself what was meant to be another child. The Creature shuts his eyes tight and hunches his shoulders against the image seared on his brain: Mary with her nightgown rucked up around her hips and her white legs tangled in bloody sheets that Claire and Jane can't seem to keep away. Her body is an open cave of blood. "For God's sake" – it's Claire's voice, angry, terrified. The Creature clamps his hands over his ears. One question beats in his loyal red heart: if Mary dies, will he die too?

Shelley has gone to the godforsaken little town of San Terenzo to fetch the doctor. Mary, mishearing the slurred accents of the Genoese, keeps calling it "San Arenzo;" it's a joke, now, to them all. But Shelley isn't so eager to laugh, here on the coast to which they've all been driven by his health, his restlessness, his galloping eagerly into that eternal Shelleyan country of *elsewhere*. The Creature could cheerfully slam him to the ground. *Look what you've done to her, you bastard!* But he has no right to defend Mary. What would be his rights – a son's? But the world sees only two of Mary's sons, one buried in the Protestant Cemetery, one bawling forgotten in his cot on the other side of this room's closed door. What right would the scholars of the Temple Bar, scratching the tips of their pens under their sheepskin wigs, accord to the Creature himself, the mute witness, the patient, sleepless eremite, the one whose love will never be named?

Once this house on the Gulf of Spezia was the home of a nobleman named Ercole Sforza, now confined to an asylum in Genoa, who instead of olive trees planted walnut and ilex and oak which have grown into stunted lush shapes on their diet of salt and rock. Housekeeping here is a trial; no soap or milk is to be had other than in San Terenzo, three miles west along the coast. The streams that trickle down the hill must be hauled back to the house in buckets for baths that can never dispel the sweat-smell from one's skin. Never is there quite enough to drink, or eat. Nevertheless, this place is now meant to be a center of literature, where Mary and Shelley and Claire and the everlasting Hunts and even Lord Byron will put together a colony of English poets, where Hunt will edit a journal called *The Liberal* and Shelley will write for it and Byron will pay for it and the Hunt children will run shrieking and finger-smearing all over a brand-new country once they arrive in two weeks' time. Here in Italy, Mary has been silently asked to stitch all the fragments of memory and hurt with the bright bruised thread of her love to make something like a wife who can walk on the golden beach and smile obediently. Limping like Byron, or the Creature himself, the marriage stumbles on. And Mary plays her role, applauding from the carriage in which she sits like a proper Englishwoman to watch the men on their afternoons shooting in the orchard, applauding as they cock their pistols and fire at silver coins wedged in the fork of a tree. Shelley saunters forth to collect his coin, crumpled by the bullet into a little Napoleonic tricorn, and drops it in Mary's hand. There are eight of them now on the windowsill. One for every year Mary and Shelley have been together. Is this intentional? The Creature cannot say.

Edward and Jane Williams, two new strangers calling themselves friends, joined the group in Pisa. They ran away from England together, just like Mary and Shelley, and live in Casa Magni with them now. "Two Eton rebels," Shelley joked to Edward as silly Jane simpered, shaking the curls she crisps with her pen-sized iron on the stove, and Mary tried to smile. Somehow, too, a man called Trelawney has magicked himself into their friendship on what seems, to the Creature, no pretext at all. Trelawney calls himself an *adventurer*, but he's really just a rogue. With thick black hair and pale blue eyes and a combed mustache, Trelawney claims he's a wandering Cornish pirate but has attached himself to Byron and Shelley with suspicious ease. Like Hunt, he'll write of them in a memoir someday, and like Hunt, he'll exaggerate; the Creature is sure of it. But, now, this patchwork colony is unraveling. Why has Trelawney been absent all week? Why is Byron holding himself so remote from all of them in his red house two towns over, the plump laird and his plump blonde mistress (*la Guccioli,* the others call her, snickering) settled into the Italian countryside as boringly as any Home Counties squire? Can't Shelley see they are flying apart, can't he see that time is running out on some invisible hourglass, can't he see he needs to *do* something –

Mary gives a single ragged gasp and the Creature's eyes shoot open. She's alive. Her face is still, eyes closed. She's unconscious. Her breath whistles horribly in and out. Claire and Jane sponge her face and her belly and her legs. Pink stains splash their petticoats and stay-fronts where they've removed their dresses in the heat. This room is stifling. Beyond the window the flat sea glares. In its bones this house feels older than anything mad Ercole Sforza could have built. More than a hundred years. Three adult generations, maybe four. Dozens of children born. Other children dead, miscarried, brought forth in these rooms until the marriage crumpled on itself like one of Shelley's Italian coins, killed by one last shot.

Outside cart wheels rumble and then male voices mutter into the house, hauling something up the stairs. The door slams open and Edward Williams backs into the room holding one end of a giant lumpy burlap sack. Shelley's bearing up the other end. The Creature's brain goes white with terror and he curls into the corner. Something has stirred his memory. The long, bulky bag, the mutter of voices and thud of feet on the stairs – But no one sees him. "Get that here!" barks Shelley, jerking his head at the tin hip-bath in the corner. Jane scurries to drag it across the floor and Edward unties the mouth of the sack. With a heave, he and Shelley upend into the tub a shower of ice. Chipped and slushy in the straw-stuffed bag, specked with dirt and sawdust and trapped bubbles of the winter night in which it hardened on some Italian pond, it's miraculous.

Crouching at the tub, Shelley paws the ice into a shallow bowl. He lunges toward the bed and bends over Mary's limp body, then pushes his arms under her shoulders and heaves her toward him. Her head rocks back. A bright spot of blood is revealed in the center of the mattress, its trail widening as he drags her up. "Get her legs!" he shouts. Claire grabs Mary's ankles and lifts her and turns her as Shelley gathers her awkwardly and they drop her carefully upright onto the bed of ice in the tub. Mary moans and tries to twist away; the ice is a shock against that cave of blood. But Shelley rearranges her nightgown around her hips and holds her in place. "No." From the pale face with its closed eyes, her voice is startling. "Too cold."

"Yes," insists Shelley, striving to master his panic. "Stay right there."

Claire hauls the last clean bucket of water over to him and carefully he sloshes it over Mary's hips, rinsing some of the blood and straw down into the depths of the tub. Mary's eyes fly open and she shoves both hands down against the lip of the tub like any woman trying to raise herself from her bath. "Stay," Shelley blurts. He pushes her gently and the ice beneath her shifts and she settles lower. A bright red thread worms from beneath her thigh. But it's nothing like the thick track of blood in the center of the mattress. Shelley's ice bath is working. *Where on earth did he find –*

Suddenly the question is gone and there's only a terrible silence that rings with unspoken thoughts. Jane: *thank God I didn't have this trouble with* my *babies.* Claire: *what if Mary dies, what then will I –* Mary: only a gray wall of pain cut by a red thread of grief: *oh, Shelley, this was meant to be another son.* Shelley, seized again by a vision he's been battling since little Allegra's death back in April: a naked child rising out of the sea with its hands clasped, its eyes fixed on him, its smile terrible.

And below this quiet babel of voices there is a silence, menacing and fathoms deep.

Death is coming here, again. The knowledge grips the Creature, shakes him. *Someone here will die very soon.*

When Mary wakes, she is alone. And so tired. In every conceivable way. She could go to sleep and not wake up. Despite the snuffling of her last child, Percy Florence, in his cradle on the floor. Her last child, in whom she can muster only a dismal throb of interest. Is she still a mother? Apparently so. By one definition of that word.

On its shelf, the hands of Mary's little Geneva clock oar forward, plowing each hour back into the soil of next day, next week, next year. There is William's portrait, painted by Amelia. Next to it are her authors' copies of her books, swollen in the ocean air. One: *Frankenstein: or, The Modern Prometheus.* Two, the novel *dug up out of fifty old books* (alas, Shelley's joking verdict was right[1] – it *is* too dutiful, too historical) during their months in Florence: *Valperga: or, The Life and Times of Castruccio, Prince of Lucca.* Three, the slim volume scrambled together in London out of her memories of the elopement and shoved into press in a vain attempt to crack the travel-writing market: *History of a Six Weeks' Tour.* Someone has eased her mother's ring off her finger and set it on top. Such a pitiful little stack, forlorn in this upside-down world where only books are damp and everything else is parched in the relentless sun.

Shelley's footsteps rouse Mary from her not-quite-sleep. Without opening her eyes she feels him bending over her, waiting. Since her miscarriage, even before, he's slept in a nest of blankets on the floor of another room, with his trunk of books and shirts and paper scraps flung open in its corner. Claire has avoided him – a deep, shocking unfriendliness darting across her face. She's bound for a governess job in Florence: "go on," Mary assured her, "I'll be fine here." She can take care of her last child on her own; given the condition of her marriage, he seems likely, indeed, to be the last.

Now, Shelley sits on the edge of her mattress and leans close. Early on the morrow he'll depart for Livorno to meet the Hunts, sailing across the Gulf of Spezia in his clumsy boat, bought from Byron at a castoff price and renamed *Ariel*, just like the Geneva skiff. He'll have some practical matters to discuss with her. She's still his wife, after all. So she opens her eyes and struggles upright against her pillows. He's staring at her with a mix of relief and tenderness and something like horror. Then he touches her shoulder, strokes her arm. In each torn nerve in her body is a thrill indistinguishable from pain. She must look frightful. Shyly, she turns her face away, realizing, too late, how Shelley will misinterpret this.

With a click, he swallows hard, tightens his hand on her arm. "Mary," he begins. "Mary. I know you are in pain – Mary, I am so sorry, Mary –" He pauses. "Mary. We can have more – There will be more children."

"It doesn't work like that." Too late, again, she realizes how disastrously his thoughts and hers are colliding, skewing away in opposite directions. "Losing a child. After all this time – you should remember. It's – not so easily cured."

He is quiet. He does not take his hand away. "We'll talk about that more when I come back," he says.

"If you come back." And here is the old fear rising again from within Mary's brain to overtake her: there is a woman on that other shore.

Shelley moves closer and drops his hands to the mattress, one on each side of her hips. She can smell his salty hair, and a ghost of his old herbal sweetness. "I know," he begins, "I know I have not always been..." He pauses. "The baby, the baby in Naples. Yes. She was..." He flounders, opening his mouth and closing it again. And he looks straight at her. In his eyes, Mary sees the truth: *She was mine.*

For an instant, she is sinking. And then he leans against her, and she holds him. His grip tightens. "Mary, I am sorry." He gulps and fights tears. "Please believe – you are my wife. You are the only one I love. You –" he struggles. "No one else. Only you, Mary. Always." His narrow back shakes; his sinewy arms are clinging to her with a strength she hasn't felt in him before. He wouldn't tell her this if he meant to move on from her and Percy Florence, to *do this sort of thing* again in some *elsewhere* country. He's telling her the truth at last because he means to come back. He loves her. And he always will. This is not another cudgeling-up of herself to follow him despite her better judgment. This is not another half-lie from which she need half-flinch, smile gamely and evade. This is the truth, which she can trust. He is her Shelley, still.

Awkwardly Shelley burrows his shoulder and hip into the mattress and tucks his long bare feet under her blanket and they hold each other for a long, silent time. Mary's nightgown is pinned in a bump beneath her hip but she ignores it. Only then does she remember a horrible dream that she overheard Shelley describing, with half-humorous abstraction, to Trelawney of all people: a naked drowned child like some Dantean cherub rising from the sea, clapping its hands, beckoning him. She remembers his words six years before, in the first *Ariel* on Lake Geneva: *Can you swim?* she'd asked him. *No more than any sailor can,* he'd laughed. "Wait." She flounders. "Shelley, do you have to go, can you not simply send Edward, can the Hunts not hire a boat..."

"The Hunts don't have a pot to piss in." This is Lordship Shelley with a dash of her own mad boy's humor. Anchor and Manager of The New English Writers' Colony in Italy. Her tired husband, his auburn hair graying now at the temples, trying to smile. "We provide the pot. And Hunt, well, its contents are one of about three things he can provide for free. Maybe four."

Mary laughs and Shelley laughs – "impecunious editorial piss?" he continues his joking list, "useless political opinions? self-serving verbosity? most annoying children in the Western world?" – and suddenly she finds herself crying. She holds him and they are kissing, then, just as they did at her mother's grave. The gentleness in Shelley's touch tears at her. For eight years, they've carried on when no one thought they could. Eight years beating in their hearts, in their laughter and their tears so closely twined. All the rented beds in inns from Dover to Chamonix to Rome, the sunset Lido beach over Clara's grave, Byron's supercilious smile, the last sight of Allegra's hand reaching from the carriage window, the bright morning on Lake Geneva when Shelley turned to look at her, grinning, his auburn curls splashing over his eyes. With all these moments flowing past and over them, it is so astonishingly easy just to hold each other now. Just to hold her husband and wish this moment would not end.

"Stay here and rest," Shelley finally says, rolling over and heaving himself to his feet. "I'll be back before you know it." He bends and kisses her. And then he's gone.

A fire is burning on the beach and Mary fights to rise above the surface of this tide that carries her between sleep and something else – that fire will consume the Villa Magni, devouring her and her last and lovely boy – but she cannot stir. Her limbs are weighted. Is she dreaming? She can't be certain. She's in a place that's not a place. Shelley is not here. She calls and Shelley does not answer. There is only the cold kiss of a bottle-mouth against her lip, pressed by some firm foreign hand ("*allora*, Signora Shelley, this will help you rest") and then the bitter taste swells on her tongue and the python from Mr. Pidcock's Emporium of Wild Beasts on Exeter 'Change back in London *(oh, why did we ever leave England, why did we ever seek this fever-land of beauty and death?)* squeezes lazily around her heart and in its eyes the demon smiles and waggles its knife in admonitory glee. *Come, now. You didn't think I'd just walk away from him, did you? I have Shelley now. All to myself. Forever.*

Mary lies cushioned in velvety mud at the bottom of a well, looking up through the murky water into the white circle of sun blazing far above, where the fire is burning on and on. Oh, God. She knows this place. The baby is here, the nameless little girl found cold in her bureau drawer. Joined now by her sister Clara and her brother William. Three dim white shapes bob around her, just out of reach. *My darlings, oh, how have you come into this dark, why did you leave your Mamma who loves you so, oh, my babies, I would do anything for you, you know that, don't you, please tell me you understand –*

A cold small voice answers her. *Oh, Mamma. It's too late for your sentiment now. Surely you can see that you're the one who brought us here.* It is William's voice. And then Clara's. *Across the mountains. Where I died, stretched across your knees, borne like the infant Christ in procession. Ironic. With such famous* atheoi *in my family line, don't you think?* There's a bitter, silvery little chuckle, a stream of bubbles drifting out of the dark. *Women can learn Greek, I have reason now to know. Not so easily in the world as it is. As our Aunt Fanny knew. At least she's here in this place to care for us.* A bright skein of laughter swirls through the dark. *And Allegra's here, of course.* A pause. *As our father is.*

As their father is – But Shelley can't be seen. Mary opens her mouth to call to him and water swirls in and stops her voice. She thrashes her head back and forth to banish the tiny bitter voices of her children and shake loose her own cry – *Shelley, my beloved, where are you, why have you gone from me* – and succeeds only in whipping her hair loose around her throat. It lashes and rises and settles again and binds her mouth in a thousand cobweb threads. *That's right, Mary.* It is a laughing voice part Trelawney, part Byron, part demon. *Let your hair down. Such beautiful hair. You are an attractive woman, in your way. But what a shame this effort comes too late. Your coldness was a pain to our Shelley, did you know that? Yes. I believe you did. To deny Shelley sympathy, your touch, the weight of you together in your bed was to starve him. And you turned from him a-purpose. Left him sleeping on the floor, all the way across the house. No way to mourn dead children, is it – to block the only means by which a man might beget himself some more? At least, beget some more on you. He did have recourse to Elise, to be sure. Ah, cold chaste Moon – you bred a line of poetry, at least.* There is a snicker and a chorus of cackles and Mary lashes out with both fists in fury but finds her arms moving in slow motion through the water, striking nothing, as the laughter fades and a terrible quiet descends.

Water swells down Mary's throat and she chokes and struggles in the mud but does not die. Of course. The woman who kills all others cannot die. The Sibyl ensconced in her Naples cave forgot to *define her terms*, as any good Godwin-trained logician must, and so will live forever, cramped and shriveled by the centuries into tight bitter dust that has no voice except the voice heard in dreams, that babble and babble with no meaning, only premonition, only fear, only dread, only grief. And soon there will be nothing left of the Sibyl but a tiny shriveled shape hunched amid the scattered leaves of paper, babbling like a madwoman in a voice no one can hear.

She is in hell. This must be hell. Or something very near.

Above Mary, the water-surface clears for an instant. A plume of black smoke rises from the beach, up there in the living world.

Oh, God, she remembers now –

Trelawney's bad, malicious Italian, splashed with his Cornish accent like mud on a travelling-coat's hem: "No women at funerals. They'll only make a fuss. The authorities agree. I have procured the iron grate for our Shelley's body myself from the blacksmith in San Terenzo, the unguents and oils to pour on the flames, oh, our Shelley would have loved them, they will make *such* a display when we commit him to the pyre like the ancient kings, returning him to the sea and the sky –" His voice, then, dreamy: "The colors against the sky at night will be quite dramatic."

Shelley is – Shelley's body is going to be – So it's true, she's not imagining, he's –

That single lantern on the single tiny boat, approaching Casa Magni across the water. Yes. It had come bearing news.

Mary turns her face into the mud and holds it there. By God, she will die too. By God, she will not let herself survive. She holds her breath and wills her heart to stop its beating. Loyal red heart, your work is done. Loyal red heart, without Shelley I have no need of you. Please understand. Release me from the bargain made before my birth. Let me go.

And then comes a woman's voice:

Mary. Oh, my dear girl. What about your boy?

I have no boy, she spits without thinking in a stream of bubbles and mud. *I have three children and a husband dead because I killed them just as I killed –*

And then her words are stilled by something outside herself and out of the murky gloom a face swims close, golden-brown eyes wide, hair drifting in a mermaid cloud. It's Mama. Mama has found her and followed her, even here. Her face is sad. *Oh, Mary. You really believe you are responsible for –*

If I'm not, who is? There is no need to shout and thrash to hurl forth the words now, for they're rising to Mama's ears on their own. *I've been nothing but a bearer of death and misery since – oh, Mama, since you bore me and died to give me life, nothing but a creature that wreaks havoc and misery and despair wherever I go, I –*

Not quite. Mama's smile turns up and twists, wry, compassionate. *You've made a creature of your own, remember?*

Percy Florence will be fine without me. Mary cannot seem to make Mama understand her despair, which stains the water dark around them now. Overhead the sky is black with smoke – oily, thick, ringing distantly with Trelawney's solemn Graeco-Celtic nonsense. *Best that I stay here. Jane Williams will –*

Oh, Mary. Mama's voice is firm now, amused. *You get your literalness from your father, bless his soul. A good man, but not always the most... imaginative. You can't leave your last son, your and Shelley's last – and despite Shelley's considerable faults he did love you, Mary – with that ordinary woman who gives herself the airs of a heroine to cover an utterly conventional heart. Really: a crimping iron at the* seaside? *And besides –* Mama cups Mary's face in her palms and leans close. Their hair swirls loose around them now, mingling, dark and light. *You are the heroine. You have made another creature still. One whose power you haven't even* begun *to guess.* Mama raises her eyebrows and smiles. *Trust me. It's* considerable. *And you'll never see it for yourself if you stay down here.*

But you hear the voices – What they accuse me of, surely you agree, I'm guilty, it is all my fault, I deserve this punishment, I'm –

These voices – Mary, they aren't real. You know that, don't you? No one believes in them but you.

But Shelley – he's dead.

Yes. Yes. I'm afraid he is.

Mary closes her eyes and weeps. Mama bends forward and slides both arms around Mary and lifts her from the muddy silt as if lifting a baby from her cradle. Her small square hand slides under Mary's hair, cupping the back of her head, holding her close. Mama's cheek is against Mary's now, just as Mary had yearned for when she played the game in her father's cold serious study, every moment she could steal. Mary holds Mama tight and feels her breathe. Mama is murmuring to her and Mary is weeping and their breath rises in a silver stream of bubbles toward the living world to join the black smoke rising from Shelley's funeral pyre. For a time beyond Mary's knowing she is simply held, beheld, by Mama at last. And then Mama gathers Mary tighter against her, with one arm around Mary's shoulders and one around her knees, and with a drift and billow of skirts Mama brings both feet under her and bends her knees and with a faint *oof* lifts off like Mr. Blanchard's Finsbury Square balloon.

Wait, Mary protests, *Shelley's down here, I must remember him, I love him, I –*

Don't worry, Mama says. She clasps Mary's hand, touching the gold ring that had once been her own. *Here are the words.* And as Mary rises from the depths in her mother's arms they murmur the words together, trailing silver bubbles from their lips into the dark below, a plainsong, a prayer: *Full fathom five thy father lies / Of his bones are coral made; / These are pearls that were his eyes: / Nothing of him that doth fade, / But doth suffer a sea-change / Into something rich and strange.....* A vision flickers: sunlight on a white marble stone in the Cimitero Acattolico, up the hill from where William lies and *la madre piangente* walks and weeps. These words are carved there, for Shelley. They will last.

But to return, and view the cheerful skies – this is the Sibyl's voice, cautioning Aeneas from her cave – *In this the task and mighty labor lies.*

The white circle of sunlight is closer now. Shelley – ah, *sola, perduta, abbandonata* – is left behind in the dark. Down in that cave. Mary flails, gasps. *I'll drown my book. I'll never write again. Without him I cannot –*

Mama's voice is firm, and sad, and suffused with infinite love. *No, Mary. You will not drown. You'll write. You'll rise.*

The light pales and the water brightens around them. Now Mary smells burning. Wood. Meat. Smoke. Salt. Sea. And the lost, sweet smell of Shelley's shirts: the herbs tucked in against him, the grassy clean smell that filled her senses the first night they kissed in the street, when the dangling man stolen by the resurrectionists jounced and beckoned into a life she couldn't have foreseen, across eight years, two continents, four children lost, five children born, books and poems and essays, laughter and words without number. Their beautiful, mad, impossible life.

Oh, Shelley, please know I love you, please know I never meant to hurt you – Mary throws out a hand into the dark water, straining back into the depths. *Please know I will not forget you, I will –*

I know. And in her ear is Shelley's voice. In her hand is Shelley's hand. *My love. I love you so. I always will.*

And with slow, unstoppable tenderness Shelley's hand slides downward from her grasp and is gone.

Mama's head breaks the surface first, and then Mary's, gasping, streaming brown stinking river-mud and water. Hefting Mary against her, Mama staggers up onto a beach shingly with pebbles and nails and broken pottery, bristling with pins and garnets and coins. Mama sets Mary on her feet and shakes out her skirts with a *slap slap* like sails in strong wind. Overhead the sun is setting, lighting the Thames in glitters of platinum and rose. "Ah." Mama's voice is satisfied. "Beautiful. Good of our city to welcome us home." On a bridge above their heads, wheels and footsteps hum like bee-wings in a hive. From the porch of a tottering tavern on stilts, high above, a trio of women peer down and raise their tankards in salute. "Better get inside, love," one calls. "It's gonna turn cold."

Mary is in London. Is it real? Where is – She turns back to Mama and finds Mama has already turned away, wading back into the river again, as on the night of the ghost tales at Diodati, the night the enormous dark eye opened in Mary's mind. "Wait," Mary blurts. She rushes forward and seizes Mama's outstretched hand. Mama's smile is fond, and sad. "I can't stay here," she says. "But my daughter – Know I love you. And know I am so proud." For a long moment, they embrace. Then, frozen on the shingle, Mary watches as Mama melts into the river and is gone.

Mary should be crying now. Instead she's smiling, lifted by fierce joy. She looks around her, but she's alone. Except for the watermen, plying their small boats between the north bank and the south. Except for the three women watching from the tavern balcony, unsurprised. Except for an extremely tall man in a ragged coat, striding away with a hitching, rapid gait toward the steps that lead up the river-wall and into the city. His feet are bare. How can he move so fast?

Mary rises into wakefulness on a hot Italian morning toward her life without Shelley, holding a scrap of knowledge in her mind:

She and Mama had not risen into the heart of their city alone. Because reaching into the Thames to pull them out had been one giant, bony, broken-nailed, impossibly strong hand.

Part Five

CHAPTER 1

English Opera House

LONDON 29 AUGUST 1823

In their brackets along the edge of the stage, the lamps flare. The violins stab the air with a single chord. The audience gasps. For there he is, reeling from the wings with his huge hands outstretched: Victor Frankenstein's dream come to life. The creature who's named, in Mary's printed program, with a single question mark.

The stage entrepreneur who's stolen her novel to bring it here – Richard Brinsley Peake, that's the name she'll write on the complaint when she takes him to law – has bent his play around it like a child making a mask out of paper strips and glue: *Presumption: or the Fate of Frankenstein.* Victor Frankenstein (some actor named Wallack), limping Byronically around the stage and clutching his hair, is not an "alchemist." Robert Walton and his letters to *MWS* (only Shelley ever noticed those initials) are nowhere to be found. Her own words remain, but mixed with Mr. Peake's: "The object of my experiments lies there *(Pointing up to the laboratory,* that was Wallack's obvious stage direction.*)* – A huge automaton in human form. Should I succeed in animating it, Life and Death would appear to me as ideal bounds, which I shall break through and pour a torrent of light into our dark world."[1] She must admit, though, that in Wallack's fine rolling baritone, they give a good effect. The sounds of a storm arise behind him on cue, some offstage hands shaking sheets of tin and hurling pebbles against glass.

And then her creature appears, in a cloud of smoke and fluttering red paper flames. Heightened with lamplight and charcoal and grease, poised like Mozart's Commendatore, he's livid as an actual corpse, embodying

315

all the decay she admits, now, she'd not troubled quite enough to imagine when writing. But what details she gave, Peake has followed. Massive height, around seven feet. Black hair stiff with an amniotic mix of sweat and dirt. Huge dark eyes blinking, mouth hardening from bewildered fear into fury. Awkward hairy body, dressed in rags, muscled and strong. They've even gotten the feet right: easily sixteen inches long, gripping the splintery boards with broken-nailed toes straight as fingers. Of course, her Creature would indeed never have known shoes. Someone offstage managing props – where the real cleverness in theatre is always to be found – has thought of that.

A shiver of conviction lifts Mary's skepticism gently off the hard floor of her mind. These are no prostheses or mere paint, but the real feet of a man used to walking. Maybe Mr. Peake recruited his actor from that Irish village where everyone is eight feet tall. Once, Godwin had gone to see one of those men, Charles Byrne, exhibited for threepence in Holborn. He had to stoop to tuck himself under the doorjamb and into a specially made chair, but he was able to converse just like anyone, willing to take your own laughably small hand in his and give it a gentlemanly shake. And in a chair in the corner sat John Hunter the anatomist, never taking his eyes from the big man's face. "Hunter," Godwin had recounted with a shiver. "Apt name. He watched that poor Giant like a cat at a mouse-hole. They say he collects these poor creatures. Keeps their bodies." She peers at her program in the dim light. Next to the question-mark for the Creature's name is the actor's: *Mr. T. P. Cooke.* But Cooke is not a particularly Irish name.

The Creature jerks into motion and reaches for Wallack, the actor playing Victor Frankenstein. And Wallack freezes. Turning to face the Creature completely, he raises both hands and stumbles backward. He isn't acting now. A dismayed, excited gasp rises from the audience. Violins quaver in a warning pitch. Recovering himself, Wallack swerves to face them – with a wholly unconvincing smile – and runs limping upstage and grabs a wooden sword from its peg on the flimsy laboratory wall and approaches the Creature. With a growl the Creature snatches the sword from his hand and snaps it in two. Wallack screams and flees. The Creature roars. The offstage breeze rises and flutters the red paper flames fiercely. With a Mozartish trio of chords from the orchestra, the curtain falls, and Act 1 – to thunderous applause – is at an end.

In his rickety chair on her right, Godwin smiles. Playing the father, entertaining his widowed daughter, successfully banishing, if only for an evening, the thoughts of her husband's body burning on an Italian beach. Sharing with her the fruits of her novel's success in London, the city every writer strives against and many fail to crack. It can do no harm to let him think so. In the space before the curtain rises again for Act II, he leans to whisper in her ear. "Of course it is not exactly a faithful adaptation," he says. "But arguably, Mr. Peake has risen to the challenge of shaping a novel so eventful into a new medium. He has managed to condense it, get to the most dramatic scene quickly, bring a touch of comedy that –"

"I can see that," Mary says. "But I still intend to take him to law."

"Of course," Godwin agrees. "You must protect your rights and those of Percy Florence. Now that Shelley is..." He looks down and resettles his spectacles on his nose. "And I'm sure you will prevail, my dear." He straightens and leans closer as the music swells and the curtains jerk, about to part. "Perhaps we should release a new edition of your novel. I could add some emendations myself. Perhaps mention this play somewhere in the prefatory matter. It could profit all concerned. Think on it."

Only from the stage can the Creature see Mary and she see him. The actor Cooke has been waiting for his cue in the wings, a vantage that reveals, to the Creature's eye, the poverty of the whole theatrical enterprise. Seen from the side, with all the actors' expressions pointed desperately toward the audience, the lights glaring into their faces at an angle that makes the Creature wince, with Bland and Keeley mugging as the Concerned Friend Clerval and Foolish Servant Fritz, the play is pitifully false. But if the Creature wants to be seen by and to see Mary, this is the only way. Falsity within falsity within his own borderless life: this alone can make him real.

So on his large bare feet, he steals to where the actor Cooke is waiting. In his green and yellow greasepaint and stiff black wig and chest smeared with stage blood, raised up on clumsy wooden pattens to something like the Creature's own height, curling and uncurling his own rope-scarred hands inside giant leather gloves stuffed with straw and painted with thick purple veins and black fingernails, mouthing something the Creature himself would have disdained as too obvious (*Where am I? Art thou my creator?*) although the script actually gives him no lines ("what a great test of your craft!" Mr. Peake must have cajoled in wooing him), Cooke awaits his cue. A square-faced and practical ex-sailor, he's, alas, this once, distracted. Easy for the Creature to snatch his throat and tap him on the head and stuff his limp body behind a coil of rope and a barrel of shredded-paper snow. Maybe he'll awaken for Act II. Meanwhile, the Creature will take the stage as if the punters – and Mary – have been waiting for him all along. Because, of course, they have.

Give actors this: deceivers themselves, they are not easy to deceive. Wallack recognizes him right away, his face alight with unfeigned fear. *Thank me,* thinks the Creature sardonically, *I've just prompted the best performance of your career.* Guilt flinches inside him as Wallack stumbles backwards: that broken leg from the stagecoach accident on the New York to Philadelphia road last year still hasn't quite healed. But Lord Byron has made limping a glamorous thing. If you're an enterprising young man of the stage, you can turn it to your advantage, as Wallack surely also capitalizes on his Byronic curls, alas, receding a little – like Byron's own – from a high white forehead. His eyes are terrified. *Don't worry,* the Creature wants to say. *You'll go on to be famous and photographed with your family as an old man in your front yard in upstate New York – birdcage and two big dogs and all.*[2] Unlike himself, even an actor can attain domestic bliss.

The script calls for Victor to snatch the sword from the wall (or, rather, the "wall") and charge the Creature. Luckily, the audience can't tell how little of this is acting on Wallack's part. The sword breaks in the Creature's grasp just as it's meant to do. As he flings the pieces at Wallack and howls – a satisfying open-throated wordless rage – he glances at the center section of the audience, ground level, five rows back, where Mary sits with the old bald man who must be her father. Now, he's all she has left. He and the boy. Peake has tried to seize her novel and the Creature himself. Byron has promised help that never came. Shelley has sailed away in his boat for good. *I'm sorry,* the Creature fires desperately at her in his head. *I should have tried—*

Yet Mary doesn't look displeased. Even in the dim reflected glow of the stage and its fake red-paper flames and smoke the Creature can see her regarding him with her usual firm-lipped, thoughtful stare: difficult, even for him, to read. She's taken more trouble this evening than usual: old blue gown brushed and laundered, Shelley's blue glass Venice earrings dangling from beneath the loops of her light auburn hair. Thoughtfully, she turns her wedding ring back and forth. She could take Mr. Peake to law for a share of the profits; any judge would hear the case, although the Creature doubts the law has kept pace with all those high-minded English words about respecting the productions of an original mind. This play's notoriety (it *will* run, the Creature is sure) might help secure her future, and his own. He seems to hear Mary now, flocked around by the press-men who'll be following her to see what she'll make of Mr. Peake. "Well, I feel somewhat like Lord Byron," she'll deflect, with her mysterious little smile. "I seem to have awoken and found myself famous."

CHAPTER 2

Field Place

SUSSEX 1824

Of course Sir Timothy Shelley keeps Mary waiting. But she doesn't expect to be welcomed here. Nothing for it but to park herself on the settee in the entrance hall where the curious parlormaid leaves her – "she's out there!" the girl is doubtless whispering to another farm-girl-brought-indoors, "young master's wife! Come from Italy!" – and conjure a faint, unbothered smile onto her face in case the parents-in-law she's never met are watching. There don't appear to be any peepholes high in the walls, no portraits with blinking cut-out eyes. This is no Gothic castle keep, although Shelley said the rear wing of the house had been built in the thirteenth century. She sits now in the main house – two stories, imposing red brick, sparkling vinegar-polished windows – that dates from the late sixteenth century. "When Queen Elizabeth was a cranky old woman," Shelley used to joke. "Just like my father."

Peacock offered to accompany her here; he's known the Shelleys since he was a boy. "No, thank you," she told him. "I must make my claim myself." Now she wonders if she'd been right. Setting both feet on the wide oak floorboards, she spreads her skirts around her. *This is me being a lady*, she thinks idiotically. *What if I were always thus –*

For an instant her mind goes slack with relief at the vision: if Shelley had continued in the track laid out for him that began and ended at this house's front door, she could have been its mistress. She could have raised all their children under this roof. Like two wells of bright water William and Clara could have flourished in this green ground, not drained away into the hot dust of Italy. Perhaps even the first baby girl could have been born here and lived, nestled into Shelley's own baby-cradle rather than a pulled-out dresser drawer. William would be the heir, walking out to visit the tenants' farms, writing treatises on cattle and poems on silver dace flickering in the summer-lit brooks. Clara would blossom as a strong young woman, romping over the fields with her brothers just as her grandmother Mary Wollstonecraft had urged (*In the name of truth and common sense, why should one young woman not admit she can take more exercise than another?*[1]) and, by the time she married, nothing would remain of her notorious grandmother's name but the honor young men would surely by then have progressed to the point of being able to confer on it. Percy Florence would be the youngest son, set for the law. This would suit her boy: he's made to move like a small star in its sweet contented course, fourth in line from the sun. Herself? *There she goes,* the Horsham villagers would say, *the author of* Frankenstein *and* Valperga. And here the vision stutters and breaks: if she'd been able to live here as ordinary Shelley's ordinary wife, would her Creature ever have come to life at all? Would she or Shelley have ever written a word, under the shadow of Sir Timothy Shelley and all the other Field Place fathers back to the reign of the Plantagenet Edward Longshanks, a world all firelight and hunks of spit-roasting mutton and good wives with their prayer-books and their babies' gravestones melting like ice into the grass?

Yet there is no denying the creeping temptation – always waiting, soft as an opium couch – of being *a woman behaving well*, of surrendering her own life to a man with a loud voice. Oh, the relief of being told what her next decision would be. Oh, the dizzying pleasant pseudo-power of despotism over upholstery patterns and roast-hen seasoning, the things he'd consider too unimportant to worry his own head about. Oh, the joy of a plump purse for clothes and laundry-soap and books, with the house around her walled and roofed with those magic words: *someone else's responsibility.* No more strained letters to Hunt, biting her pen to keep back her fury: *after all the money he gave you, you have nothing to lend back to me?* No more miserably short letters to Byron (hoping they'll reach him in Greece), unable to write the longing burned onto her brain: *remember how it was, the morning on the Lido when we buried Clara and you carried William on your shoulders? Only you and I are now left to remember that day.* No more packing and unpacking of the chipped dishes and threadbare dresses. No more rented rooms. The dream tickles her like the first blessed step over the edge of sleep each night: Sir Timothy might help. A grandson, education, legacy, the Care of a Widow – these are any self-respecting gentleman's cares. Even if he cares not one whit, personally, for the Widow herself, or for the griefs that wake her in the night, alone.

A door opens in the back of the house and Sir Timothy strides toward her, tugging the lapels of his long black coat into place. So this is her father-in-law. He's tall and a little stooped, around seventy years old, with white hair combed back in the style of thirty years before and a tall white cravat and narrow black trousers a little gone at the knees. He keeps his chin down, gaze averted, until he's ten feet away. Then he looks up. These are Shelley's eyes, Shelley's long cheeks and high forehead and his wide mouth that on Sir Timothy is haughty, and sad. His heavy eyelids dim his glance, but she can see Shelley's young face shimmering beneath the wrinkled forehead and the pouchy cheeks. Shelley's face would look much like his father's by this age. If Shelley had lived.

Stiffly, Sir Timothy nods. His mouth twitches. "Mrs. Shelley." The words obviously give him pain. "Where's the boy?"

"Good day." Mary hears her voice shake. "I thank you for meeting with me." What would a well-behaved woman say in this moment? "I... regret the circumstances of our meeting." Too vague? "Our mutual loss." No, that's too direct, too suggestive of her fear that Sir Timothy is so vindictive he mightn't have met her otherwise – Frustration flares in her. What is she to do, deny she's ever loved and married Shelley? Deny that of their five children only one now lives?

"My son is with friends, back at my lodgings." *In...?* Sir Timothy's pale eyebrows rise, but she won't say where. She and Percy Florence are sharing rooms with Jane and the two Williams children in Kentish Town, where there's a dame-school and a kite-flying field and the rent is cheap, especially for two widows and three children under six. "You've had his note of thanks for your gift? So generous." A month ago, Percy Florence had received – out of a clear sky, in care of Reverend Smith at the little church down the street, the only address she's given anyone – a gold guinea in a box, so tightly wrapped around and around in brown paper and postal frankings and seals that it took the kitchen knife to open it. He is almost five, and so he could scrawl his name laboriously across the bottom of the letter Mary had just as laboriously composed in reply, with what she hoped was a charming and touchingly vulnerable mixture of his thanks and her own. "I've put it aside for him for when he goes to school." And prayed she won't need it to buy them both food. But she won't admit that. Not yet.

"Ah." A smile flickers across Sir Timothy's lips. "Eton. Like his father." It's not a question. "Come with me." He opens the door of the drawing room across the hall and leads her inside. Why not his study? Because she's a woman, and therefore what they are transacting is not, in fact, business. No, it's only her son's inheritance. Only her own livelihood until such time as her son can support her. Only the small matter of what she and her boy will put into their mouths and on their backs and over their heads. To Sir Timothy, talk of her and Percy Florence's support is just a social call of which he'll soon dispose.

"Where are Lady Shelley? And Hellen, and Elizabeth? Bysshe so often talked of them…" This was what Godwin would call *rhetorical tactics* – starting with Bysshe, the family name Shelley hated – but it's also real curiosity, like that which must surely be spurring those hidden semi-related-to-her-now women to peek at their dead Shelley's wife. What would Shelley's blue eyes with their dreamy heavy-lidded stare look like in a woman's face? Would his sisters' hair be the same thick curling auburn as his? In childhood, he'd loved to terrify them with tales of a Great Tortoise who lived in Warnham Pond and heaved itself over the lawn at night to peer in the windows, fogging the glass with its breath, trailing the fading serpentine mark of its heavy tail. Once he'd nearly set his bedroom afire with a chemical explosion, then been banished from the house until suppertime and left to stare at his sisters through what must be this same drawing-room window. "Like the Great Tortoise," he'd said, trying to laugh. "I could see Mother's lips moving, and knew she was telling them *don't turn around.*"

"They are indisposed." Sir Timothy's voice gives Mary nothing. "I see no reason not to come to the point." He opens the lid of a cherrywood writing-desk on a nearby console-table and withdraws a single sheet of paper covered in a lawyer's neat hand. *Mrs. Mary Shelley hereby cedes the legal authority necessary for all decisions of an educational and financial nature regarding the upbringing of her son, Percy Florence Shelley, to Sir Timothy Shelley and Lady Elizabeth Shelley, being the said child's grandparents, said child hereafter to reside with them at Field Place, Sussex –*

"Sign it," Sir Timothy says. He pauses, a bit too long. "And you can still visit him."

Mary's wondering, stunned brain has not even finished reading the lawyer's words when Sir Timothy's meaning strikes. For a long moment she feels nothing. Then fury swells in her like storm clouds over an ocean, with a single panicked voice of reason stranded on the deck of a battered ship, waving its arms and shouting *Beware what you say to him.* She opens her mouth, then closes it, then folds both hands together and sets them in her lap. "I wonder, Sir Timothy," she says, "that you expect me to make so momentous a decision upon our first acquaintance." Is that light enough? Is it *reasonable?* Rising and rising, the waves of anger in her threaten to swamp that little boat. Money. *I can provide for this child.* This is how Byron had taken Allegra from Claire. This is how Allegra had become another possession to amuse La Guccioli and himself in his Venetian palazzo, then pack off to die of typhus on a narrow cot in a Bagnacavallo convent where the nuns were paid by Milordo and the Pope to wash and wrap her little body to be sent home to England for burial before Claire had ever had a chance to say goodbye. Shelley has drowned and left her with one boy. There is no one else in the world, for either of them. And, by God, she will not give him up.

Sir Timothy has the grace to look faintly abashed. "It is sudden." His voice is factual. "But consider the advantages that can be conferred by his residence here." Note the passive voice. Note the careful neutrality of *residence here.* Shelley would be furious. "Such as schooling. Eton –"

"If my son were boarding at Eton" – she cannot stop herself – "then he would hardly be in residence here, correct?" Surprise, then respect, then anger cross Sir Timothy's face. *No,* she sardonically thinks, *I'm not as sweet as Harriet.* Poor drowned Harriet, proudly twisting her turquoise ring. How long ago that was.

"No." She will be plain. "No, Sir Timothy. It is impossible that I would agree to such a thing." Why not say it all? "My husband would be furious at your proposal. You did not see how he – how he was when William died." No. Only she had seen Shelley kneeling on the floor next to William's pillow, gripping the blankets, head bowed, sobbing, the toes of his outlandish Venice riding-boots cramped heedlessly against the floor. He'd loved to swoop William up from the washing-tub after his bath and hoist him in the air and then bring his face to William's tender little tummy, still damp, and blow a big tickling splattery fart that made William shriek with joy. How he had loved their boy. Little Wilmouse. She will keep those pictures for herself. "He would not wish us to lose our last remaining child."

Sir Timothy settles and resettles the paper in his hands, then looks up at her. "How will you support him?" His eyes are cold. "My grandson. How can you pay for –"

"I am a writer. As you may have noticed" – *hurry, add a soothing clause to the end of this before it becomes insult* – "I have just published my second novel. My first novel has become a successful play." Of course, between the scandals of the stage and her own struggle to take Mr. Peake to law, this is a shaky prop, but she hurries on. "I am also preparing an edition of" – she swallows – "my husband's works, in collaboration with Mr. Hunt and Lord Byron." This is not strictly true. But, she hopes, the rich sauce of *Lord Byron* will soften the unsavory saltiness of *Hunt*. And there will be an edition of Shelley's works to come. Godwin will help her. *The Examiner*'s readers know her husband's name. Of course, here comes the inevitable *Paradise Lost* echo: *Fit audience find though few.* Well, she'll never know unless she tries.

"My son's works." Sir Timothy's voice rises. "Published. As if he hasn't done enough—"

Somewhere in this house are the marks where Shelley drove a stick through the ceiling, hunting for the hiding place of the ghost he swore haunted these rooms. Somewhere in this house are Mary's own words scratched onto a paper printed with her tears, a paper that in Italy had become a letter telling Shelley's parents that their son had drowned. Can letters bear the traces of experience as people do? Is there still a sunlit ghost of Italian grief somewhere in this house – this drawing room, Sir Timothy's study, Lady Shelley's writing-desk, tied with a ribbon grubby from being knotted and unknotted and retied for what its reader swears will be the last time now, at least today? Grief ebbs and flows in this room like a tide in a rock-pool: a lost boy, a dead son, a life gone. In Sir Timothy's eyes flickers something that wants to stretch out its hand to her, acknowledging they've both been subject to the considerable vagaries of Shelley, making a common cause, some common way – But then it's lost. And Sir Timothy's mouth is tightening.

"Words have great power." What is struggling to speak through her suddenly? Oh. Of course, her husband's Defence of Poetry. *They can be scattered throughout mankind, like ashes from a fire, to remake the world –* Or to burn it all down. Which is what will happen to this negotiation if she lets Shelley's words take over now. "Shelley had a gift." Love and longing and grief rise in her and she will not stop them. "And no one is left now to bring his words to life. Only me."

Sir Timothy looks at her. Impossible to know what he's seeing, there on his drawing-room settee with her hands clasped in her lap, hoping they aren't sweating on her old blue gown. It's started to split along the underarm seams despite all her care; this is another reason to keep her hands down. Thank God Percy Florence, not yet at school, can be dressed in rough smocks and trousers. *Valperga* is bringing in a hundred pounds next month on its royalty schedule, there are still more articles for the *Westminster Review*, maybe she can also –

"I do not consent to the publication of my son's work." His voice is flat. "I will not consent. I see, however, that you and my grandson will be in some need. As we continue to discuss these matters" – as we *continue?* – "I am prepared to offer you an annuity of two hundred pounds a year. Paid quarterly. Please let me know your banker's name." He stands, his knees crackling beneath the worn black trousers.

Fifty pounds every three months, in dribs and drabs? That will buy – well, better than nothing. And she must leave this house right now to catch the coach back to Kentish Town before she gives vent to something that will evaporate even those fifty pounds like smoke. "Thank you." She rises and offers Sir Timothy her hand for a brush of fingertips and a perfunctory bow. Mama's worn wedding ring flashes. "I will find my own way out."

When the door closes behind her and she stands blinking in the sunlight outside Field Place once again, she is tempted to turn and make a spiteful face but does not. Until she is back in her own rooms with her own boy safe in his bed, she must maintain complete control. When she has reached an assessing distance from the house, she turns and looks back. What a warm reddish-brown it glows in the afternoon sun, how stable and lovely amid its green lawns and trees. Yet to the people who live in it – to Shelley – it is surely a beloved but tiresome pile. A grandfather of a house, its rooms look as serenely smooth as an unread book to outsiders but swarm in its family's own knowledge like a remembered person, with long-held stories and resentments and known crotchets and sticky windows and mice-skittering walls and too many things in every cupboard and corner. No matter how it looks from outside: how solid and smooth its stone, how held-back the vine, how clear its many glass eyes.

Behind one of those windows (ground floor, far right) flicker three silhouettes of women: Shelley's mother and his sisters, surely, standing in his old room. Mary looks at them, long enough for her gaze to seem deliberate. Then she lifts her hand and waves. A cloud passes and hides the women from her sight.

Above the roof a skylark spirals up into the blue, hammering a string of notes as busily as a carpenter hammering nails. *Hail to thee, blithe Spirit!* Her husband saluted this little Sussex bird from Italy, a thousand miles away. *Teach me half the gladness that thy brain must know,* and then – what are the words? – *the world should listen then – as I am listening now.*[2]

She passes out the gate and continues along the road. There in the stable-yard is the big oak beneath which Shelley as a boy had pretended to play cards with Carmichael the groom. "Be I to play trumps, Master Bysshe?" he'd asked, grinning. *What a kind man*, Shelley said, *so much more patient with me than I deserved*. Shimmering just beyond the trees is the pond from which the Great Tortoise lurched to terrify the girls and delight a little boy's heart, darkening to mischief and brightening again in a rhythm unknowable even to himself.

Unknowable. When she leaves here, she'll leave the ghost of that little boy and his family to one another's care. There's no retrieving her Shelley anymore from this lovely place, from this afternoon light over the stalwart ancient trees, infinitely English-golden and infinitely sad. She is a widow now. Supporting herself by her pen. The articles and the fair-copying and the stiffening of back in chair and wrist aching against desk, every blessed day, and the prayers for her sight to stay clear. And the novel that is struggling now to be born. Is this, then, to be her life – the grim pushing onward, marshaling words, the writing only because not-writing is worse? Apparently so. Someday, she hopes, there will be a thrill again to words – a thrill like Keats's words can summon in her, for instance. Poor dead Keats. His *Lamia* is such a marvel. How could he have pinned down the precise feeling of a child turning your body out from the inside like a wet sock, of how you shivered and screamed as you shapeshifted from woman to beast? Because no doubt, he had. And at the wonder and respect of those words she feels again the intent cloud of the novel tugging at her, something to do with the Sibyl's cave in Naples, but she can't bring it clear. Only a sudden weariness all through her, dry as the Lido shells lined up on her windowsill right now, fading to chalk in the English sun.

Back home that night, once Percy Florence is asleep, she opens the trunk for the first time. Leaving Italy in that blur of grief, she'd gathered all Shelley's papers and books to her chest like a farm woman gathering wheat and dropped them in the trunk and shut the lid. But she sees it now: when you cannot write, you can organize. You can safeguard and label and preserve. You can still love the words and the man who wrote them. You can promise him: *I will publish your words, scatter them like sparks among mankind, no matter what your father says,* combing out the handwriting that Trelawney (accurately, for once) compared to *a sketch of a marsh overgrown with bulrushes, and the blots for wild ducks.*[3] And there is much that Shelley never saw in print. Like those furious poems of Peterloo and anarchy, sent to Hunt and then politely stalled and gagged and strangled. Shelley's words had come forth only in those early awkward pamphlets, *The Necessity of Atheism* ("that Oxford thing, old man") and *Queen Mab,* pirated still in London and passed hand to hand.

It is risky. You might become the Sibyl, shrieking to a careless world, your words torn and scattered like leaves. But not even trying is worse. She will put these pages in order. While her little clock ticks behind her, she will sit at her desk every day and push forward her pen. As Mama did. As Godwin does. *The world should listen then – as I am listening now.* The hope of words on a page, the hope of some responsive hand turning the leaves, reading her words and Shelley's, will move her forward. Will have to be enough.

CHAPTER 3

Kentish Town

LONDON JULY 12, 1824

At fifteen minutes till ten in the morning, Mary pushes her papers aside and stands in the window, overlooking the road. Fletcher has told her to be ready. The thin curtain twitches in the morning wind and her potted plants rustle their leaves; it's a fine day, an irony Byron himself would be first to appreciate. If only he could.

Behind her Percy Florence is settled on the sitting-room floor, pushing a charcoal pencil over her discarded pages: *I'm five, Mamma, I can write by myself.* This morning, she's had a terrible two hours in the novel that doesn't yet have a name, pushing herself to form one sentence after another, laboring as if walking through wet sand. It's just a mass of sad words, shoved from one side of the page to another like a butcher sweeping a slaughterhouse floor. Still, she must sit down each day and pick up her pen.

Last month, Hunt and his brother John published *Posthumous Poems of Percy Bysshe Shelley,* for which she wrote the preface since Hunt, increasingly averse to scandal, reneged on his promise to do so himself. Already it's sold nearly three hundred copies of the five hundred they've printed. Sir Timothy will inevitably discover it and will inevitably be furious, but maybe all the copies will sell before then, escaping like fish through his clutching fingers into the wide world's ocean. *Fit audience find though few.*

Three days ago, she'd gone to Sir Edward Knatchbull's parlor on Great George Street – all draped in black, the mirrors veiled – to see Byron back in London for the first time in eight years. The gloom hadn't concealed the tears on the faces of Fletcher and Zambelli, the laird's last servants, who'd guarded his body all the way from Greece, packed in a barrel of wine. Fletcher was stooped and warped by sun now, his cauliflower ear bright red. Mary put her arms around him. "Mrs. Shelley," he sobbed. "My lord is dead. Off in that heathen place." He gulped and sputtered. "They bled my lord to death. I tried to stop him and they threw me off and he was callin' me but then – He was just gone." He swiped his coat sleeve over his face. "They almost burned him up. Like Mr. Shel–" Jerking upright in horror, Fletcher drew away.

"No worry," Mary soothed. Two years gone, now. Her grief was familiar; Fletcher's was brand-new. She rubbed his shoulder – shrunken to an old man's, now, under a black broadcloth coat – and looked around the parlor. There in the center of the room on a bier draped with red velvet, a gleaming coffin lay, the best mahogany that someone, probably Sir Edward, could buy. Perhaps he'd been a classmate at Harrow, one of the friends who always seemed willing to step out of the mythic haze of Byron's English-schoolboy past ("and it *was* mythic," she imagined him snickering, "*epic*") whenever he needed an emissary to his ex-wife or a buyer for his ancestral home or a resting-place for a funeral. At each corner of the bier stood a tall Greek urn, each with a different scene in black on brown ground: a hunted stag leaping, a grinning Bacchus, a man reclining on a couch, two youths in one another's arms. Fletcher followed her gaze to the coffin. "We tried to put 'im in the Abbey, at Westminster," he said, "but they wouldn't let us." Something like a smile broke his tears. "'Question-able moral-ity.' That's what they said."

"Are you surprised?" Mary murmured, smiling. Fletcher started to laugh, then stopped himself. "Look out," he whispered. He inclined his head at a cluster of well-dressed men in the corner, whispering together. "Mr. Murray and Mr. Hobhouse and them. They've been asking me about my lord's papers, and –"

Suddenly, Mr. Murray turned his head and looked at Mary. He was a pale man with receding dark hair and a fastidious pointy face, as if he were perpetually pushing something unpleasant away from his nose. As Byron's publisher, no doubt he'd found that experience a familiar one. *My dear Mr. Murray,* Byron had mocked, *you're in a damn'd hurry.*[1] Yet Byron had made him a very great deal of money: *Childe Harold* in installments, *Don Juan* in installments, all those glowering Zaras and Laras and Mazeppas galloping around in their vaguely Oriental gloom. Then Mary remembered Byron's words, one night at the table in Italy: "I've got something here," he'd exulted to Shelley, waving at a heap of papers pinned under a wineglass, "that'll set them on their heels. Memoir, dear boy. My entire life. Nothing held back."

Murray bustled toward her, and Mary raised a smile to her face. Of course, he knew who she was, although he would conveniently forget that he'd rejected *Frankenstein.* "I haven't had a chance to tell you," he said, as if they were old friends, "how deep a loss your husband's death has been to the world of letters." He offered her a smiling, expectant silence and she let it fall. "Neither have I said," he continued, "how... interesting a work is your own *Frankenstein.* Such a success upon the stage." She let this coin of silence fall, too; apparently he really *had* forgotten he'd rejected it. "Should you find yourself in need of...editorial assistance," he finally said, "please do call on me. Or if you should hear of any news concerning the late Lord Byron, connected to an unfinished..."

He paused, searching. *The memoir.* Mary arranged her face into a careful blank. So: Fletcher knew of it but Murray did not, not yet. He would throw her the sop of pretended interest in her own book – her own freakish creature, good for a laugh to strut and fret its hour upon the stage (could he *really* have forgotten that he'd rejected it?) – in hopes of teasing from her some bit of information that, in fact, she didn't have. But she wouldn't give this man the satisfaction of saying so. He waited. Mary brandished her bare, polite smile. "Please excuse me," Murray finally said. And he rejoined the group of Byron's ostensible friends. They peered at her and, in unison, turned their backs. Spite rose from them like sulfur. *The scandalous Mrs. Shelley. Who'd have known that mousy little girl could write such a monstrous book.*

Good for you, Mary. It was Byron's voice, inside her head. *Don't let him at it. He'd burn it if he could. He fears the lawsuits more than loss of profit. Fletcher knows –* And then, a little breath of candle-stirring wind, a puff of some heretofore invisible dust rose from the mouth of the nearest vase, where rampant Dionysius waved his prick and grinned. *Thank you.* Had she imagined it? Probably. She was a woman, after all, and likely to be fanciful.

Along the street below her now comes the sound of wheels. It's Byron's funeral cart, open to the sky, drawn by two black horses. And it is all alone. She'd expected a procession like a prince's, outriders and footmen and an elegant carriage like the one in which he'd trundled to Waterloo, his motto in gold on the door: *Crede Byron.* But there is only the shiny mahogany coffin face-up in the wagon bed, the shadows of trees and clouds sliding over its polished surface. Fletcher and Zambelli slump on the seat up front. They are taking their lord more than a hundred miles north to Newstead Abbey by themselves, to bury him with the ghosts of the monks and the beck where the newts live and a small boy's pony can jump across without letting him fall. Behind them trots a mastiff: a giant brindle dog with black drooling lips. Of course, even now, Byron has a dog. Maybe this is the beast behind the door in Venice, battering and barking as Mary slid on Byron's own sweaty boxing muffles and beat an inanimate thing in the corner of that elegant room in the city where her daughter's body has now melted into sand.

Right underneath her window, Fletcher stops and climbs down from the wagon. He looks up at her, meets her eyes, and waves. She waves back. Then Fletcher turns and chirrups to the great dog, lets down the wagon tailgate, and pats the boards. "Come on, boy," he wheedles. The dog leaps onto the tailgate, then circles and lies down on the coffin, his claws digging long white grooves in the wood. Mary grins: so much for the elegant mahogany. She and Fletcher wave goodbye, Zambelli clucks up the horses, and the wagon lurches forward, bearing Byron and his servants and his dog the hundred miles north to Nottingham. Overhead, the trees rustle. A handful of leaves – full green, mysteriously loosed – drop through the air and swirl over Byron's coffin. The dog lifts his head and thumps his tail. The wagon winds down the street, out of sight.

Byron is gone. Shelley is gone. Even poor Keats has died, in a rented room at the Spanish Steps, just down the hill from the Roman flat in which her Wilmouse stopped breathing. Claire is a governess in Florence. Who knows where Trelawney is; who cares. Now, they are all gone.

And I alone am escaped to tell thee. These are the words of Job's servant in the Bible, and of the Mariner in Mr. Coleridge's fascinating tale. She alone is left. She is the last of them.

Percy Florence seizes one of her fallen pages and lifts it triumphantly for her to see what he has written in a language of his own. She blinks. And suddenly it's clear. The Sibyl's cave. Falling leaves, scattered, in the hope that someone will find, and read, them.

Now she sees how she will begin.

The Last Man: A Novel by Mary Shelley

Let no man seek
Henceforth to be foretold what shall befall
Him or his children.
-Milton

I visited Naples in the year 1818. On the 8th of December of that year my companion and I crossed the Bay, to visit the antiquities which are scattered on the shores of Baiae.[2]

This is how it should have been.

She and Shelley step into the cave and feel the crunch of leaves underfoot before they see them. From the accidental oculus – framing its shaggy blue circle of sky and innocent pasture overhead – light falls on the skeleton of an unlucky goat, coated in glittering dust. Slowly, their eyes adjust. A pearly mineral light reveals the ankle-deep litter of leaves and bark fragments and partially burned papers written over with languages from everywhere in time: *ancient Chaldee, and Egyptian hieroglyphics, old as the Pyramids. Stranger still, some were in modern dialects, English and Italian. We could make out little by the dim light, but they seemed to contain prophecies, detailed relations of events but lately passed; names, now well known, but of modern date; and often exclamations of exultation or woe, of victory or defeat, were traced on their thin scant pages.* Stories swirl and materialize in the air. There is Napoleon, summoning, with a snap of his fingers, an eager pageboy to stand before him so that he can prop his spyglass on the boy's shoulder and gaze to the opposite hill. There is Lord Nelson with his one eye and his empty folded sleeve, shriveling and bending double like the Sibyl himself, the dew of Lady Hamilton's young love – from right here under Vesuvius itself – having failed to plump and revive the dry heroic length of him, like salt pork kept too long in its barrel. There is the massacre at St. Petersfield in Manchester, thin horrified faces blooming In her mind's eye to match the lists of names over which Shelley had raged: *Ashworth, John. Sabered and trampled on. Fildes, an infant. Rode over by the cavalry. Partington, Martha. Thrown into a Cellar. Killed on the Spot.*[3] There are Waterloo and the fat Prince Regent and Greece's battle for independence from the Turks, in which England's most notorious poet, Lord Byron, died of fever in a tent. And there is a new thing, shouldering the words up into shape around it like the back of a whale rising from the deep: a plague. What else but a plague – a world-sweeping, unstoppable, apocalyptic plague – could remove so completely from the world everyone else but the sad owner of the sad voice that sounds so much like her own. *And I alone am escaped to tell thee.*

Crouched on the floor of the Sibyl's cave, Mary gathers the scenes of her life. In her hands the brittle pages turn warm – some are actual paper, some are fragments of bark torn from a silver-skinned tree, some are *a white filmy substance, resembling the inner part of the green hood which shelters the grain of the unripe Indian corn.* And suddenly the strange symbols swim and resolve themselves into words. Her own words. She has become the Sibyl and the Sibyl's questioner in one. Shelley hovers next to her, gathering them too – he is eager to help her – but like Orpheus she dare not turn to look at him, dare not mention his name, or he will disappear. *My companion,* she writes. *My friend.* My husband. My love. And he is gone.

O goddess-born of great Anchises' line, warns the Sibyl, *The gates of hell are open night and day; / Smooth the descent, and easy is the way: / But to return, and view the cheerful skies,/ In this the task and mighty labor lies.*

In a trunk under her bed, she keeps the shirts and breeches and coats that still smell of her husband. She dares not open that lid too frequently lest they lose their smell. All of Shelley that was solid thaws, resolves itself into a dew. Driving the scent of him – his neck, his sea-salted hair, his mouth – over the earth, the wild west wind tumbles him away. *He is become a part of all this loveliness...*[4] The words Shelley wrote for poor Keats will mourn, also, himself.

Queen Dido, lover of Aeneas, built a funeral pyre and stabbed herself with the sword he left behind, then cast her own body into the flames. Byron's body had been stuffed in a wine-cask to ship home. Shelley had been hauled from the sea and buried hastily in case of contagion (how he had hoped for such contagion in such a different mode, *scatter my words like sparks among mankind)* and then disinterred to be laid onto a fire on that beach, reducing him to one blackened scrap for which she'd battled with Trelawney. "It's his *heart,*" he'd finally shouted at her. Damn the man. "You really think it should be in *your* keeping? Like it *ever* was!" They are all gone now. Shelley and Wilmouse and Clara and the nameless baby and the not-quite-child that miscarried in San Terenzo. Fanny. Harriet. Allegra. And now Byron. Mary and Percy Florence in their rented rooms are the last alive.

And I alone am escaped to tell thee. A servant flees apocalypse, bringing Job, the man of sorrows, news he already knows.

She dips her pen. The words are here.

My labours have cheered long hours of solitude, and taken me out of a world, which has averted its once benignant face from me, to one glowing with imagination and power. Will my readers ask how I could find solace from the narration of misery and woeful change? This is one of the mysteries of our nature, which holds full sway over me, and from whose influence I cannot escape. I confess, that I have not been unmoved by the development of the tale; and that I have been depressed, nay, agonized, at some parts of the recital, which I have faithfully transcribed from my materials. Yet such is human nature, that the excitement of mind was dear to me, and that the imagination, painter of tempest and earthquake, or, worse, the stormy and ruin-fraught passions of man, softened my real sorrows and endless regrets, by clothing these fictitious ones in that ideality, which takes the mortal sting from pain.[5] Writing makes worlds. It makes a future. It makes hope.

Mary turns back to her first page and writes her novel's title: *The Last Man.* Her pen races forward to loop gently around that image the thin brown line of ink that will settle it on the page forever, neatly as Byron's mastiff crossing his contented paws. This is the language of the Sibyl's leaves as Mary has arranged them, kept them safe. Writing is how the last man – or woman – builds a stay against ruin and forgetting.

Shelley lifts one final page from the cave's floor and puts it into her hands. He turns to her and his smile is lost in a dazzle of light through the oculus that opens the Sibyl's cave to the sky. A single sunbeam fixes him perfectly as a cloud passes overhead and is gone.

The Creature climbs the steps upward from the pebbled Thames shingle where he has helped pull Mary and her mother from the water. They stand, embracing one another, as they should. He clasps his hands tightly in his pockets to preserve the ghost of their touch against his skin. He dusts one bare foot against the other. He steps into the street, and he walks. And in his wandering, he traces the map of a city that is, and a city that will be.

He is following the course of a river first noted in the time of William the Conqueror, then threaded by diligent engineers through the city gates and walls that give it its name, *Wallbrook,* and then eventually channeled underground, where it leaks through the bricks that will never contain it and runs on unstoppable as the blood in the Creature's own veins, from the north to the south and on to the sea. This is a city of footpaths, words, wanderings, all told and retold and writ in water. Roman barges sailed up the Thames and docked here; a skirmish with Boudicca's rebels took place here; a temple to the god Mithras was built here. More than a hundred human skulls lie at the bend of the river in a spot only the Creature can see, for now. Are they Romans captured by Boudicca's Britons and sacrificed to the water-god Tamesis, rival brother of the Romans' lounging Tiberinus on the Capitoline Hill? Were they slain in a battle no one named? Even the Creature can't pierce this mystery, or the power of this spell. Yet these dead voices will join all the others he cannot help but hear.

Beneath his feet, years drop away, and years accumulate. Automatons and shadows and creatures like himself – although, really, no one is just like him – rise from cobblestones and laboratory tables and the pages of books. One by one, they're born into a world they will transform. A ticking, jerking lady with wheels under her skin raises and lowers her arm, smiling fixedly at the bird upon her finger. A big metal crate with gears like Madame Diodati's music-box turning in its guts hums to itself, unstoppable. Lord Byron's abandoned daughter Ada with her whip-thin body and imperious chin paces around that metal box, watching it as Shelley watched the twitching hands of the Geneva clock. Great horseless carriages roar along twin iron rails, their bellies furious with fire; Mr. Trevithick's ten-mile-per-hour locomotive has mutated into a dragon that whisks passengers over the earth at four times that speed.

There is an order to the future emerging out of this dream in which the city as it is and the city as it will be are netted together, uneasy, rapt, inseparable. The Creature senses it is focused on that metal box around which Ada paces, scribbling her calculations, haranguing Mr. Babbage, who has the good sense to acknowledge her role in making it. That box has a name: the Difference Engine.

On its mantel, Mary's Geneva clock winds down, clicks like a swallow in Mr. Keats's boiling throat, and, for the first time in its existence, runs forward with unstoppable speed.

The Creature stands in the shadows of a comfortable French sitting-room. Two little boys are fighting with the apparatus of a magic-lantern show. They've cut out people and horses and carriages to dangle in front of the light of a candle they've magnified with mirrors on the wall. *My turn. No, I'm oldest.* Even in all their tugging and quarreling they don't upset the candle or tear their paper dolls: these brothers will outgrow their little-boy scrappiness and together they'll build something marvelous. The Creature slips into the light and when they raise their eyes he's standing there. Their faces slacken with fear but then the Creature moves his arms and legs and casts shadows on the wall. The boys grow rapt. Astonishment illuminates their faces. They applaud, helpless in their joy. Their name is such a lovely one: *Lumière.*

Somewhere in the great shambling mansion of the future with its endless rooms, with the Difference Engine in the basement churning all of life into a different atmosphere, these brothers will build a space in which the Creature will live forever. So he shows himself to them. He shuffles like a vaudevillian, windmills his arms, rolls his eyes and makes silly faces, as he did for little William, long ago. The boys laugh and clap and do not look away. Surely downstairs in their studio their parents are wondering *where are Auguste and Louis? Ah, playing with their shadows again. Just let them be.* The parents know how to cast light onto a plate and freeze it into the image of a person. Their sons will discover how to make that image move. Someday they'll capture one of those great locomotives as it roars along its tracks into a station and the people sitting rapt in a theatre before that moving image will scream and fling their arms over their heads and stampede in a panic toward the exit, unable to believe this monster bearing down on them is only light and shadow on a wall.

These engine-dragons will devour earth, devour men. They'll cut their twin shining tracks across the grassy plains of America, where Fanny's father, Mr. Imlay, once strove to make his fortune. Whooping men will lean from the windows of those rumbling carriages and fire bullets into shaggy brown buffalo who just stand blinking, never having seen such things. Those twin tracks will slice through London, too, right through the willows where Mary and Shelley lay and fell in love, driving the sad little river Fleet underground to beat like a pulse in the dark. Women and vicars and historians will save the church; *it's been here since the Normans*, they'll plead, *even before. Oldest site of Christian worship in Britain.* The engineers will sigh and twirl their watches in their fingers, but, thanks to the old gods and the new, they will yield. *We'll save the church. But this is indeed our chosen path. It can't be stopped.* A young man named Thomas Hardy will be hired to haul away the poor uprooted gravestones and instead he'll stack them reverently at the roots of a tree that will grow to surround them, making a new thing, jagged and melancholy and beautiful.[6] Thomas will try to record this beauty in a poem, but he won't find the words, not yet, even though the hesitant voice of one of those displaced dead – young Doctor Polidori, dead in his rooms on Great Pulteney Street of a prussic-acid overdose, age twenty-five – will whisper a few suggestions. Sadly, even Thomas can't hear Polidori's voice, smothered in the earth as it turns over, and turns. *I wrote a story too, a vampire story, remember my story too!*

The tall square stone with the names of Mary's parents will be spared, sinking slowly into the ground as trains rattle past it, year after year. Determined young women will write letters to Mary Wollstonecraft and fold them into tiny triangles and tuck them under the leaves of the crocuses that bloom in purple and white and gold, spring after spring.

And trains will depart that station – *St Pancras,* its name will be, just like the church – carrying earnest aunts in spectacles and families off to the Lakes and battalions of determined young men in khaki and helmets, bound for places whose names stir the Creature with unease: *The Marne. The Somme. The Western Front. Gallipoli.* Horses will twitch and fall before the roar of fire and steel, as hungry birds flicker through an afterscape of black. There's an angry droning noise whose source the Creature can't detect, coming from the sky. War and engines and the deaths of men and beasts: is this to be the future?

In this unknown year whose name has not yet changed from *18* to *19,* before the giant gear of a century catches and turns forward one more notch, in that flickering parlor candlelight, the Creature roars and dances and exults as the little boys applaud. He struts and frets his hour upon the stage over which a curtain never falls. He goes on and on and on. He is alive. And he will never die.

CHAPTER 4

Holborn

LONDON 1849

By the purest chance, Mary hears that 41 Skinner Street, her last childhood home, is being demolished to make way for a row of semi-detached houses, and so she's able to summon a cab and ride across the city, just in time. Fortunately, this is a good day, when her vision is sharp and the morning's touch of headache vanishes at the first sip of tea. Maybe what she hopes to find in that house will be long gone. Maybe water will have trickled through the window-frame and dissolved everything. Maybe there will be nothing left in her old third-floor study-room but the bitter, hopeful ghosts of words. Which, perhaps, is as it should be.

The shop – its windows with their little damn panes dim and cracked – still stands at the corner where Skinner Street runs into Snow Hill, taller and more forlorn-looking than ever, and even more obviously doomed. The sculpture of Aesop over the door is gone, hopefully to architectural salvagers rather than vandals. A painted wooden sign swings from a construction fence: *Coming Soon!* it reads. *Victoria Gardens. All Modern Conveniences.* And above a row of bright red brick houses floats a quasi-angelic figure of the Queen, extending her arms and beaming as if Skinner Street's new householders are the brown-skinned natives she dreams of conquering. Shelley would have had much to say about her Great Game, all those wars for opium and tea: *Typical English. Thrusting ourselves where we don't belong.*

Smithfield Market's blood-taint still lingers in the air as Mary pays the cabbie and asks him to wait. Luckily, no one's around to see her duck under the construction barrier and test the front door. She's still got the key, but she won't need it. The lock's been removed since her father died and this house passed back to his creditors. He's been dead for thirteen years, Mrs. Vile for eight. With Claire now a governess in Russia, refusing to return to England – *sell whatever's left and take what you can get,* her letter said, *I need no more of it* –Mary reckons herself, again, to be the last of them. To the literary journals, *them* is the fellowship of Shelley, Byron, and Keats (in her better moods, Mary dares to imagine herself included as *Shelley* too.) But *them* is also the cobbled-together family of 41 Skinner Street: three sister-ish girls (no two of whom had the same two parents) and a papa and a stepmamma and a dead mother's ghost. And now there's no more Fanny, no more Papa, no more Mrs. Vile. Mary is nearly fifty-three, the last of them. This would have made her lonely, once upon a time. Now it's just her life. She pushes open the door and enters the shop.

Percy Florence and his new wife Jane will scold Mary for sneaking into her semi-derelict childhood home, especially given what they persist in calling her *condition*. "Just think of me as a daughter," Jane pleads, "with a daughter's concern." But 41 Skinner Street can't injure Mary. Nor is being nearly fifty-three years old a *condition*, despite her weary vision, and her headaches. Spectacles help, somewhat. Last week, she stumbled on the stairs and nearly failed to catch the banister before she fell. Thankfully, Jane didn't witness that.

To Jane's credit, her concern for Mary is genuine. More importantly, her love for Percy Florence is genuine. Theirs is an odd marriage: the stoutish twenty-nine-year-old bachelor baronet and the rich youngish widow spent months eyeing each other until – surprising no one but themselves – they discovered they were in love. They bought a house called Boscombe Manor in the seaside village of Bournemouth, where Jane fitted out a lavish suite for Mary and consulted her on swatches of chair and curtain fabric, bustling about like Peggotty in the new paper-bound numbers of *David Copperfield* (why, Mary wonders, had none of *her* publishers thought of serialization like Mr. Dickens's: so simple, and so commercially sound?) "I'm designing the library," Jane breathed, "around a fitting shrine to your own and Mr. Shelley's works." And there it was: a purpose-built cabinet with mahogany ribs and glass flanks and silk-lined shelves, draped with a fringed velvet curtain to keep the sunlight off. Hiding a smile, yet touched by Jane's unfeigned delight, Mary placed on the top shelf one of the surviving three hundred copies of *Posthumous Poems* and, on the bottom shelf, the manuscript of *Alastor*. Shelley would certainly laugh: "what," he'd tease, "*The Necessity of Atheism* is too much for Bournemouth? Mary, I'm *shocked*." Mary found herself blinking back tears as she laid the pages on the shelf and fanned them to display Shelley's spiky black words, winking out like a hundred little flames as she lowered the curtain.

Shelley himself wouldn't have thought it necessary to prize these artifacts. Near any body of water, he'd seize any piece of paper, fold it into a tiny boat, and touch a spark to it when it was almost out of reach. Raptly, he'd watch as his bold handwriting ("old thoughts now overgrown by greener ones," he laughed) wicked up the water and blurred into the black edge of flame-char creeping down. "Destroyed from above *and* below, by two different elements," he muttered. Next he'd quote Milton, or say something about Prometheus. "Remarkable. And whence does the soul ascend, in all of this?" In one of his last poems, "The Triumph of Life," he'd puzzled on *Why God made irreconcilable / Good and the means of good* – Perhaps he knows that answer now, in the *elsewhere* where he is.

Happy with his wife and their Bournemouth house, Percy Florence is now thirty years old and a baronet; his father will never be either. Upon Sir Timothy's death five years ago, aged ninety-one ("boiled in spite," Shelley would exclaim, "like pickle-brine") the name and the inheritance came to Percy Florence at last. Of course, for more than a decade Shelley had eroded that inheritance with the post-obit loans that had floated himself and Harriet and Mary and Claire and the children across two continents. But Jane was unfazed. "You see," she explained, "from my papa and my late husband, I have money of my own." Percy Florence is now fitting up a room for amateur theatricals. As a student at Harrow – paid for by Mary, story after article after slender royalty check scratched out in her rented rooms above the Harrow Village water-pump five minutes' walk away, not Eton, never Eton – he discovered a passion for Shakespeare, acting in Master Lemmon's production every year. Mary had come to witness his biggest role, the First Castle Guard in *Hamlet*. A slim, brilliant boy named Ben played the melancholy Dane, and Percy Florence, aged fourteen, had watched from the wings, his face wholly, generously, alight, exactly like his father's. *Thank you*, Mary prayed into the dark air, *for kindling this spirit in my son*. Next to her, Byron's ghost had lounged, satisfied: *see, Mary, Harrow can make something of even the most unpromising young man. Myself, for instance*. Now, her shy boy has a wife and a title and a home of his own.

But Mary finds herself reluctant to leave London and join them, as Jane repeatedly pleads. How would she occupy herself in Bournemouth?

She has settled in Belgravia, in a house on Chester Square with plane trees shading a wrought-iron bench where she can sit and drink the black tea that loosens the throb and clench behind her eyes. She has published six novels and two travel books and dozens of short stories and, at last, she's received a begrudging royalty check from that theatrical thief Mr. Peake. She has the freedom to publish Shelley's poems and prose and selected letters in a complete edition with her own biographical notes. She has Mama's pewter-backed brush and comb on her bureau and Mama's wedding ring on her finger, where Shelley put it. She has a kitten named Pearlie who wedges herself, purring, between Mary's lap and the edge of the desk (who cares if others might laugh at Mary, turning into Old Dame Trot with her Comical Cat?) She has her little wooden clock that traveled all the way from Geneva through Italy and right up to now, with its hollow gold key and the fragile interior engine she winds every day to keep the minutes moving forward, tooth by tooth. Once she took it to be appraised, just out of curiosity. "Regency," the young antiques dealer breathed, as if speaking of the Dark Ages. Her youth and Shelley's and Byron's: is it now an era, with its own dusty historical name? Is she really so near to being an antique herself?

Every afternoon, when she lays down her pen and her maid, Jenny, brings the tea, Mary leans back in her desk chair and turns to look at Mama's portrait. It hangs now above her own fireplace, in which crossed logs smolder no matter the time of year. In her house, she'll never be cold. She should have the portrait cleaned – fifty years of coal smoke and dust have dimmed the creamy brightness of Mama's skin, the firm radiance of her eyes – but she can't bear to let it out of her sight. Papa must have taken respite just like this, gazing up at Mama, then pushing his pen onward under the eyes of the woman who loved him and left her daughters for him to feed and clothe. And in spite of everything, he had done his best.

The shop at 41 Skinner Street is gloomy in the late-afternoon light, all the shelves bare but for an occasional empty tin or sweet-wrapper. Apparently a grocer tried to make a go of it here after Mrs. Vile's death, and had no better luck than Papa; the ghost of retail doom can never be exorcised from a London property. But other ghosts are here. There is the counter Shelley leaned against to press Mama's *Letters from Norway* with his smuggled note into her hands. This is the creaky floor over which she wandered, tucking the slips of paper with his name into random books all over the shop. *Scatter my words like sparks among mankind...* Perhaps whoever bought Papa's unsold books was able to sell them on to boys like

Shelley and girls like herself who will open them and find the slip of paper in her writing, with her husband's name. Maybe they'll recognize it. Maybe they'll go to seek out her posthumous editions in a circulating library or a shop like this. Maybe, then, Shelley's words will stay alive.

Mary treads carefully through the rooms and up the stairs until she reaches Godwin's study. His desk and chair are gone. She kept only a few of his books: Milton, Volney, and that old copy of Byron, dog-eared at the tempting verses to Thyrza. Over the fireplace is the blank square where Mama's portrait hung. She'd been careful to supervise its removal on the day of Papa's funeral, not trusting Mrs. Vile even then despite the civility they were careful to maintain. Now, Papa's portrait is hung in her study, facing Mama's. "The principal memorandum of my corporal existence that will remain after my death," he'd called it with his usual half-infuriating starch.[1] His and Mama's authored books stand together, filling an entire shelf. Hers and Shelley's below. Amelia Curran's portraits of William and of Shelley ("it's nothing *like* me," he'd protested, "Amelia makes *everyone's* face too round.") Shelley's little telescope and his favorite pen. Her seashells from Clara's grave on the Lido, crumbling to chalk on the windowsill. And her first and only copy of *Frankenstein. I bid my hideous progeny go forth and prosper.* When she wrote those words for a new edition, eighteen years ago, she'd thought she was joking. But jokes speak more truth than their laughing tellers know.

She's almost to the top of the house, climbing carefully on the sagging but still-firm stairs. Percy Florence and Jane would be terrified. But it's *her* neck. And, anyway, houses don't entirely fall apart in a decade. Nor do gaps between plaster and baseboard entirely close.

In her old study, Mary glances at the attic trapdoor and decides not to open it: a needless danger, disturbing Queen Sophonsiba's ghost. She crosses the floor and kneels below the window, fishing in the baseboard gap with her fingers, then – unskewering a now-gray wisp from her chignon – a hairpin. She pinches the paper against the plaster and draws it forth. The folds are brittle, browned with thirty-five years of waiting through day and night and day again. It's still here, right where she left it. Her first story: *Once there were two sisters and a papa and a mama's ghost.* She had folded it up and left it here the night she eloped for the Continent with Shelley. *I'll leave this house. I'll write another story. I'll gain experience,* she had vowed. *Like Mama.* How can that girl's voice be so much a part of herself and yet so utterly strange where she stands in this tiny room, sweating in the day's trapped heat, unfolding the traces of her own words across more than forty years?

Young writers – men and, rarely, women – still make the pilgrimage to Belgravia to seek a sight of Mary and of Shelley's manuscripts, hands trembling on their teacups. "You need to find the voice of your work, first," she tells them. "There will be writing undertaken for money, that's the bulk of it. Such work can usually be done with the brain, although the heart, of course, is not unengaged." But the real work, she adds silently, ripples through you in a wave from that creature inside, turning over in its sleep, sounding at a pitch deeper than sound. A heartbeat. A presence only a mother can detect. Sheltering it, passing her own blood through its body, until it asks to come swimming through her face-up for the world to see as well. *It's time, Mama. It's time.* When it speaks, you must hearken. You must hear.

Mary pockets her first story-page and closes her eyes. Suddenly, she's fiercely tired. With longing, she thinks of Signor Farinelli's *trattoria* in Soho. Yes, that's where she'll dine. The anticipation fills her with bliss: immaculate white linens, rich red wine, the clatter of voices that loosen her own hard-won Italian, the waiter Gianni's firm question that isn't a question, *prego, signora*. She'll have a little cutlet, and the garlic-scented noodles she loves. And on the cab ride there, she'll relax and let London flow through her eyes like the Thames in its stream of eastward-flowing light from which Mama emerged and to which Mama returned in the dream she's not entirely sure was a dream. No matter how London changes, it keeps its same sky, its same river-smell, its same glimpses of known and recognized life. She has her city to soothe and summon her inward and her outward sight. She always will.

Pulling the shop door closed behind her, Mary looks up and down the street. Evening has come on rapidly while she's been indoors. There is the corner around which she ran to Shelley's carriage; there are the quadruple spires of St. Sepulchre's; there is her waiting cab. Just before she dips inside the cab and settles on her seat, she spots an unusually tall man in a long-tailed coat and top hat walking away from her, holding a little boy by the hand. The gloom is gathering. Her sight suddenly flickers. And she looks again. Something is familiar about the man's wide shoulders, the boy's upturned face. Yellow hair wisps from under his cap just as William's would if he had ever grown big enough to wear a cap. He's exclaiming something delightedly to the tall man, who is smiling back. The hand holding his small one is very large, with raw knuckles and black fingernails and a gentle grasp.

All of this is plain to Mary in an instant. She knows her son. And she knows that tall rawboned man. He has followed her for longer than she has realized, lingering just at the edge of her sight. Now that he's seen her safe in a cab, he can fade, again, from her view. It would violate his dignity, somehow, for her to ask exactly where he goes. But there's no need. After all, she created him. And, somewhere in this city, in this world, he'll always live.

THE END

Afterword

William Styron wrote, "While it may be satisfying and advantageous for historians to feast on rich archival material, the writer of historical fiction is better off when past events have left him with short rations." Although some tantalizing unknowns remain (like the exact parentage of Elena Adelaide Shelley), the lives of Mary Shelley and her circle present a feast of complexity in every direction. Therefore, in writing *Creature* (an early draft of which was 236,000 words), I've had to focus around one theme: like her brilliant mother, Mary Shelley dreams of *more* and learns to get it by trusting her art. This meant tracing a bright line of energy through that thick tangle of names, dates, and known facts while remaining faithful to the lives' known outlines. Sometimes it meant composites, compressions, omissions, or small departures from the historical record. It meant animating the births and deaths of the Shelleys' children in ways only fiction can do. It also meant re-envisioning some landmarks like the Villa Diodati "ghost story contest" while being true to every fiction writer's first responsibility: rendering reality as my protagonist understands it.

But in writing, few risks are truly new. Percy Shelley walked this path, too: "I have endeavoured as nearly as possible to represent the characters as they probably were," he wrote in his preface to his historical drama *The Cenci* (1820), "and have sought to avoid the error of making them actuated by my own conceptions of right and wrong, false or true; thus under a thin veil converting names and actions of the sixteenth century into cold impersonations of my own mind." So did Mary Shelley. While she was a rigorous researcher – Shelley teased her for "raking up" her 1823 novel

Valperga "out of fifty old books" – she also trusted her novelistic instincts: "Human nature in its leading features is the same in all ages," she wrote in her preface to *The Fortunes of Perkin Warbeck* (1830), about a real-life pretender to the fifteenth-century English throne. Writing about a writer becoming a writer is challenging but thrilling: while literary criticism (in which I was trained) dissects the fully formed creature, novelists (as I've become) love to watch it grow. Therefore, inevitably, the writers in these pages have become my own versions of people whose stories have also taken shape in other imaginations than mine.

Creature is shaped by my Ph.D. work in 19th-century British literature at the University of North Carolina at Chapel Hill and by more than twenty years of teaching *Frankenstein*, Romanticism, and writing. Since 2013, I've led a month-long study-abroad course called "In *Frankenstein's* Footsteps: The Keats-Shelley Circle in London, Geneva, and Italy;" my depictions of London, Geneva, Venice, Florence, and Rome here mingle my experiences and Mary Shelley's (I like Venice *much* more than she does, and I *did* see that fox in the alley near Ye Olde Cheshire Cheese!) I was also blessed to teach the whole spring 2019 semester in London with the Associated Colleges of the Midwest's "London and Florence: Arts in Context" program. The goal of education is expanding your capacities, becoming a self with something constructive to add to the ongoing conversations around you, and in a time when books (which build *character* in multiple ways) feel so endangered, I hope I've helped young readers in particular see how books built Mary Shelley and her Creature, as they've built me, and helped her shape a conversation that still shapes us.

Madame Diodati and her jailers, *la madre piangente* and the staff of Rome's Protestant Cemetery, Cecil (of Johnson & Hunter), Byron's stableman Giuseppe, Beauvoir the real estate agent, and the child resurrectionists at St. Sepulchre's are the only characters in this novel I've invented. Percy Shelley, Mary Shelley, and Claire Clairmont all had brothers or half-brothers, whose roles in their lives in most cases were minimal and have been elided from my narrative. Some real passages, like Shelley's description of Byron in his letter to Thomas Peacock and Keats' description of opening a man's temporal artery – as well as the real language of *Frankenstein* and *The Last Man*– will be recognizable to Romanticists, without, I hope, the burden of footnotes. I've added some anyway to prevent confusion; others should be clear from context.

While I appreciate the many literary and film adaptations of *Franken-*

stein and Mary Shelley's story, I avoided them while I was writing this book. Exceptions were Victor LaValle and Dietrich Smith's graphic novel *Destroyer* (2017) and the National Theatre's production of "Frankenstein" (2011), directed by Danny Boyle and adapted from the novel by Nick Dear, with Benedict Cumberbatch and Jonny Lee Miller alternating the roles of the Creature and Victor Frankenstein. (Like Percy Florence Shelley's classmate "Ben," Cumberbatch *did* begin his brilliant career as a Harrow School student with theatre teacher Jeremy Lemmon.)

Although I tried to avoid the overt influences of other Frankensteinians, I'm happy to acknowledge others. The "Spitalfields Life" blog, authored by someone known only as "The Gentle Author" – especially its entry of May 21, 2021, "In Search of the Wallbrook" – is a constant source of inspiration. Author Andrea di Robilant, great-great-great-great-grandson of Byron's landlady, has taught me much about Venice. The yellow roses at Elise and Paolo's sad little wedding are an homage to the same image in Shirley Hazzard's novel *The Bay of Noon* (1970), which has inspired much of the atmosphere of Naples in this book. Since I've not yet visited Naples, I'm also indebted to the novels of Elena Ferrante, the HBO series "My Brilliant Friend" based on her Neapolitan Quartet, Benjamin Taylor's *Naples Declared: A Walk Around the Bay* (2012) and Jamie James' *Pagan Light: Dreams of Freedom and Beauty in Capri* (2019). Mary Shelley's white azalea from the Spanish Steps is an homage to the short story "The White Azalea" by Elizabeth Spencer (1921-2019), originally published in 1961. Madame Diodati, her eyes "blue with age" and "wandering like a thought lost in her own mind," hearkens to Eudora Welty's pilgrim Phoenix Jackson in "A Worn Path" (1941) and to Angela Carter's *Nights at the Circus* (1984), where a beautiful house is "tucked away behind the howling of the Ratcliffe Highway, like the germ of sense left in a drunkard's mind." I stole the image of Napoleon propping his spyglass on a boy's shoulder from Leo Tolstoy's *War and Peace* (1869). John Keats shades just about everything I write, most directly his image from the Letters, about William Hazlitt – "That sentence about making a page of the feelings of a whole life stands like a whale's back in a sea of prose" – which resurfaces in my own prose here. Hilary Mantel's novel *The Giant, O'Brien* (1998) inspired a whole chapter of my dissertation, drove me and my students to seek out Charles Byrne's bones in the Hunterian Museum, and changed my writing forever. The Who, Lizzo, David Bowie, PJ Harvey, Marc Bolan, Nick Cave and the Bad Seeds, and Mozart's "Don Giovanni" were my soundtrack. As sincerely as I rail against the Internet and the world it's made, I nevertheless relied on it to research *Creature*, and I hope I've inspired readers to some creative Googling of their own.

FOR INFORMATION AND INSPIRATION:

Alderson, Brian. "'Mister Gobwin' and His 'Interesting Little Books, Adorned with Beautiful Copper-Plates.'" *The Princeton University Library Chronicle*, Vol. 59, No. 2 (Winter 1998), pp. 159-189.

Alighieri, Dante. *Inferno* (c. 1310), trans. John Ciardi. New York: Signet, 2009.

Altick, Richard. *The Shows of London*. Cambridge, MA: Belknap Press, 1978.

Boddy, Kasia. *Boxing: A Cultural History*. London: Reaktion Books, 2008.

Brooks, Mel, dir. *Young Frankenstein* (1974).

Brown, Ford K. "Notes on 41 Skinner St." *Modern Language Notes*, Vol. 54, No. 5 (May, 1939), pp. 326-332.

Byron, Lord George Gordon. *Don Juan* (1819-24). New York: Penguin, 2005.

Byron's Letters and Journals: A New Selection. Ed. Richard Lansdown. Oxford: Oxford University Press, 2007.

Campion, Jane, dir. *Bright Star* (2009).

Carter, Angela. *Nights at the Circus*. London: Viking, 1985.

Chandler, James. *England in 1819*. Chicago: University of Chicago Press, 1998.

Cocteau, Jean, dir. *Orpheus* (1950).

Crompton, Louis. *Byron and Greek Love: Homophobia in 19th-Century England*. Berkeley: University of California Press, 1985.

DeSica, Vittorio, dir. *Bicycle Thieves* (1948).

Di Robilant, Andrea. *Lucia: A Venetian Life in the Age of Napoleon*. New York: Knopf, 2008.

Egan, Pierce. *Boxiana; or, Sketches of Antient and Modern Pugilism, from the Days of the Renowned Broughton and Slack, to the Championship of Crib* London: Sherwood, Neely, and Jones, Paternoster-Row, 1818.

Fellini, Federico, dir. *Roma* (1972).

Forman, Milos, dir. *Amadeus* (1984).

Godwin, William. *An Enquiry Concerning Political Justice* (1793). Oxford: Oxford World's Classics, 2013.

Gordon, Charlotte. *Romantic Outlaws: The Extraordinary Lives of Mary*

Wollstonecraft and Her Daughter Mary Shelley. New York: Penguin, 2015.

Groom, Nick. *The Vampire: A New History*. New Haven: Yale University Press, 2018.

Hazzard, Shirley. *The Bay of Noon*. New York: Little Brown, 1970.

Hay, Daisy. *Young Romantics*. New York: Farrar Straus Giroux, 2010.

Haywood, Ian. *Romanticism and Caricature*. Cambridge: Cambridge University Press, 2013.

Hoare, Philip. *RisingTideFallingStar*. Chicago: University of Chicago Press, 2018.

Holmes, Richard. *The Age of Wonder: How the Romantic Generation Discovered the Beauty and Terror of Science*. New York: Pantheon, 2009.

Falling Upward: How We Took to the Air. New York: Pantheon, 2013.
Footsteps: Adventures of a Romantic Biographer. New York: Viking, 1985.
Shelley: The Pursuit. New York: E. P. Dutton & Co., 1975.

Hunt, Leigh. *Lord Byron and Some of His Contemporaries*. London: Henry Colburn, 1828.

Hytner, Nicholas, dir. *The Madness of King George* (1994).

James, Henry. *The Aspern Papers* (1888). In *The Aspern Papers and Other Tales*. New York: Penguin, 2014.

James, Jamie. *Pagan Light: Dreams of Freedom and Beauty in Capri*. New York: Farrar Straus Giroux, 2019.

Lawrence, William [unsigned.] "Monsters" entry in Abraham Rees, *The Cyclopaedia; or, Universal Dictionary of Arts, Sciences, and Literature. In 39 Volumes*. Vol. XXIV. London: Longman, Hurst, Rees, Orme, & Browne 1819. Referred to in *Frankenstein's Science* and other sources. Available online at archive.org/stream cyclopaediaoruni24rees#page/n9/mode/2up;digitized by University of Toronto; accessed 11/27/16.

Leigh, Mike, dir. *Peterloo* (2018).

Luckhurst, Roger. *Gothic: An Illustrated History*. Princeton: Princeton University Press, 2021.

MacCarthy, Fiona. *Byron: Life and Legend*. New York: Farrar Straus Giroux, 2002.

McCarthy, Mary. *The Stones of Florence* and *Venice Observed*. London: Penguin Modern Classics, 2006.

Milton, John. *Paradise Lost* (1667). In *The Portable Milton*, ed. Douglas Bush. New York: Viking Press, 1977.

Mantel, Hilary. *The Giant, O'Brien*. New York: Henry Holt and Co., 1998 and Pat Barker. Lecture: "Hilary Mantel and Pat Barker: Rewriting the Past (host James Naughtie) as part of the Man Booker 50 Festival, 6 July 2018.Podcast available via https://www.southbankcentre.co.uk/.

Marshall, Mrs. Julian (Florence). *The Life & Letters of Mary Wollstonecraft Shelley, in Two Volumes*. London: Richard Bentley & Son, 1889. Via Project Gutenberg (gutenberg.org.)

Mellor, Anne. *Mary Shelley: Her Life, Her Fiction, Her Monsters*. New York: Routledge, 1989.

Monson, Craig. *Divas in the Convent: Nuns, Music, and Defiance in Seventeenth-Century Italy*. Chicago: University of Chicago Press, 1995.

Motion, Andrew. *Keats: A Biography*. New York: Farrar Straus Giroux, 1998. *Salt Water*. London: Faber & Faber, 1997.

Mozart, Wolfgang Amadeus. *Don Giovanni*. https://www.youtube.com/watch?v=aL2VdxseTvE&t=40s. W.A.-

Mozart's Don Giovanni complete opera with English subtitles. Zurich 2001 production. Don Giovanni - Rodney Gilfry; Leporello - László Polgár; Donna Anna - Isabel Rey; Don Ottavio - Roberto Saccà; Donna Elvira - Cecilia Bartoli; Zerlina - Liliana Nikiteanu; Masetto - Oliver Widmer; Commendatore - Matti Salminen; Conductor - Nikolaus Harnoncourt; Director - Brian Large.

Olusoga, David. *Black and British: A Forgotten History*. London: Macmillan, 2016.

Peacock, Thomas Love. *Peacock's Memoirs of Shelley with Shelley's Letters to Peacock*, edited by H.F.B. Brett-Smith. London: Henry Frowde, 1909. Available via Internet Archive.

Peake, Richard Brinsley. *Presumption; or, The Fate of Frankenstein*. Perf. English Opera House, July 28, 2823. Available at english.unl.edu/sbehrendt/texts/Presumption/presump.htm. Also in *Seven Gothic Dramas: 1789-1825*. Ed. and introduced by Jeffrey N. Cox. Athens: Ohio University Press, 1992.

Plumly, Stanley. *Posthumous Keats*. New York: W. W. Norton, 2009.

Porter, Roy. *Flesh in the Age of Reason: The Modern Foundations of Body and Soul*. New York: W.W. Norton, 2004.

Roe, Nicholas. *Fiery Heart: The First Life of Leigh Hunt*. New York: Random House, 2005.
John Keats. New Haven: Yale University Press, 2012.
ed. *John Keats and the Medical Imagination*. London: Palgrave Macmillan, 2017.

Rossellini, Roberto, dir. *Rome: Open City* (1945).

Rowland, Ingrid. *Giordano Bruno: Philosopher / Heretic.* Chicago: University of Chicago Press, 2008.

Runciman, David. "Talking Politics: History of Ideas" podcast (https://www.talkingpoliticspodcast.com/history-of-ideas).

Sandlin, Ted. *London in Fragments: A Mudlark's Treasures.* London: Frances Lincoln, 2016.

Sekules, Kate. *The Boxer's Heart: How I Fell In Love With The Ring.* New York: Villard, 2000.

Seymour, Miranda. *In Byron's Wake: The Turbulent Lives of Lord Byron's Wife and Daughter, Annabella Milbanke and Ada Lovelace.* London: Simon & Schuster, 2018.

Mary Shelley. New York: Grove Press, 2000.

Shelley, Mary. *Frankenstein: or, The Modern Prometheus* (1818). New York: Oxford World's Classics, 2009.

Falkner (1837). Available via Project Gutenberg online.

History of a Six Weeks Tour (1817). Available via Project Gutenberg online.

The Fortunes of Perkin Warbeck (1830). Available via Project Gutenberg online.

Valperga (1823), ed. Stuart Curran. Oxford: Oxford University Press, 1998.

The Last Man (1824). Oxford: Oxford World's Classics, 2008.

The Journals of Mary Shelley, 1814-1844, ed. Paula Feldman and Diana Scott-Kilvert. Baltimore: Johns Hopkins University Press, 1987.

Selected Letters of Mary Wollstonecraft Shelley, ed. Betty T. Bennett. Baltimore: Johns Hopkins University Press, 1995.

Shelley, Percy Bysshe. "On the Devil, and Devils." Available via wikisource.org.

The Cenci. In *The Complete Poetical Works of Percy Bysshe Shelley*, ed. Thomas Hutchinson. London: Oxford University Press, 1965: 274-337.

Shelley's Poetry and Prose, ed. Donald Reiman and Sharon Powers. New York: W. W. Norton (Norton Critical Edition), 1977.

Sinclair, Iain. *Lights Out for the Territory.* London: Granta Books, 1997.

Sorrentino, Paolo, dir. *The Great Beauty* (2013).

St. Clair, William. *The Godwins and the Shelleys.* Baltimore: Johns Hopkins UP, 1991.

Sunstein, Emily. *Mary Shelley: Romance and Reality.* Baltimore: Johns Hopkins UP, 1989.

Taylor, Benjamin. *Naples Declared: A Walk Around the Bay.* New York: Penguin, 2013.

"The Gentle Author." *Spitalfields Life* Blog (https://spitalfieldslife.com/).

Todd, Janet. *Death and the Maidens: Fanny Wollstonecraft and the Shelley Circle.* New York: Counterpoint, 2007.

Mary Wollstonecraft: A Revolutionary Life. London: Weidenfeld and Nicholson, 2000.

Trelawney, Edward J. (1858). *Recollections of Shelley, Byron, and the Author.* New York: New York Review Books, 2000.

Virgil, *Aeneid,* trans. John Dryden. Available via Wikisource online. trans. Robert Fagles. New York: Penguin, 2006.

Whale, James, dir. *Frankenstein* (1931).

Wollstonecraft, Mary. *A Vindicationof the Rights of Men; A Vindication of the Rights of Woman; An Historical and Moral View of the Origin and Progress of the French Revolution*, ed. Janet Todd. Oxford: Oxford World's Classics, 2009.

Letters Written During A Short Residence in Sweden, Norway, and Denmark (1796), ed. Richard Holmes. New York: Penguin, 1987.

Wood, Gillen D'Arcy. *Tambora: The Eruption that Changed The World.* Princeton: Princeton UP, 2014.

Wroe, Anne. *Being Shelley: The Poet's Search for Himself.* New York: Pantheon, 2007.

Young, Dean. "I See a Lily On Thy Brow." *Skid.* Pittsburgh: University of Pittsburgh Press, 2002.

Young, Elizabeth. *Black Frankenstein: The Making of An American Metaphor.* NYU Press, 2008.

Youngquist, Paul. *Monstrosities: Bodies and British Romanticism.* Minneapolis: University of Minnesota Press, 2003.

Websites / databases / collections: British Library (online and in person, including 2015 exhibit on "The Gothic"), Old Operating Theatre, Houghton Library of Harvard University (in person), National Portrait Gallery (online and in person), Bodleian Library (online and around the corner from the marvelously strange Shelley Memorial at Oxford), Yale Center for British Art (online and in person), Oxford English Dictionary Online, Pforzheimer Collection of Shelley And His Circle (via NYPL), Spitalfields Life Blog, Project Gutenberg, Internet Archive, Wikipedia, Google Maps, Google Books, Google Translate, YouTube.

$$\mathcal{N}otes$$

PROLOGUE

1. William Blake homage (one of two on this page.)

1. ST. PANCRAS

1. Mary Wollstonecraft, from *A Vindication of the Rights of Woman.*
2. Godwin's description of *Letters from Norway.*
3. Wollstonecraft from *Maria; or, the Wrongs of Woman.*
4. Wollstonecraft, from *Letters from Norway.*
5. Wollstonecraft, from *A Vindication of the Rights of Woman.*
6. Milton, *Paradise Lost.*

2. HOLBORN

1. Actual primary source's words.
2. Godwin's words.

3. FIELD PLACE

1. Milton, *Paradise Lost.*
2. Ibid.
3. Percy Bysshe Shelley's actual poem, age 12. Image from the Pforzheimer Collection, NYPL. Scribed by Elizabeth Shelley, with her drawing of the cat.
4. Milton, *Paradise Lost.*

4. DUNDEE

1. Wollstonecraft, from *A Vindication of the Rights of Woman.*

6. HOLBORN

1. Ibid.
2. Ibid.
3. Godwin's own words.
4. Shakespeare, *Romeo and Juliet.*
5. Shelley's poem to Mary.
6. Shelley, *Queen Mab.*
7. Which Mary did write in her copy of *Queen Mab.*
8. Shelley's description of his marriage to Harriet, drawn from Milton's writing on divorce.
9. Godwin, *Political Justice.*
10. Mary's own words.

11. Byron, "To Thyrza."

2. LONDON

1. Wollstonecraft, *A Vindication of the Rights of Woman.*

4. GENEVA

1. "Where is my maid? Where is she?"
2. "Hello. I never thought I'd find this place."
3. Words from the scene in *Frankenstein* on which this passage is based.
4. Words from *Frankenstein.*
5. Based loosely on the relevant scene in *Frankenstein.*
6. Claire's and Mary's joking name for themselves in these years.
7. From the register in Calvin's Chapel, Geneva.
8. From Mary Shelley's diary.
9. From first draft of *Frankenstein.*
10. From first draft of *Frankenstein,* at Bodleian Library http://shelleysghost.bodleian.ox. ac.uk/explore.
11. *Frankenstein.*
12. William Lawrence's definition of "monster;" see Works Cited.
13. From *Frankenstein.*
14. Fanny Imlay's words.
15. Ibid.
16. Ibid.
17. Byron, "Darkness."
18. Shelley's words.
19. Mary's words.
20. As "Mont Blanc."
21. "Mont Blanc," again.
22. From *Frankenstein.*
23. My version of the conversation that happens between Victor and the Creature on the Sea of Ice.
24. Perhaps this paper is an early draft of "Ode to the West Wind?"
25. Blending the framing of Justine Moritz in *Frankenstein* with the suicide of Fanny Imlay.

5. BREAD STREET

1. Mary's own words.
2. Shelley's actual letter to Claire about his wedding.

6. HAMPSTEAD

1. Which, in this letter, she pointedly did.
2. And this is Hunt's original "libel" of George IV.
3. Keats' words in a letter to Charles Brown.
4. From Nicholas Roe's biography.
5. Hunt's words about Keats.
6. From the novel (as the rest of this scene is obviously not.)

7. FINSBURY SQUARE

1. Lackington's own words.
2. This was one of Shelley's editorial suggestions.
3. *Frankenstein's* actual dedication.
4. Byron's own words.

1. NEAR THE NORTH POLE

1. From *Frankenstein;* the rest of this scene is based very loosely on Walton's opening of the novel.

2. VENICE

1. Claire's own words.
2. Shelley's own words.
3. Byron's own words.
4. Byron's own words.
5. Shelley, from "Julian and Maddalo."

3. ORKNEY ISLANDS

1. From *Frankenstein;* what follows is my imagining of the scene of the female creature's destruction from the novel.

1. NAPLES

1. Homage to Shirley Hazzard's *The Bay of Noon.*

2. ROME

1. From *Falkner* (1837), MWS's last novel.
2. Shelley's words.

3. PROTESTANT CEMETERY

1. Mary's own words

4. NAPLES

1. *Valperga* (1823).
2. Keats's own words.
3. Ibid.
4. Little homage to Dean Young's "I See A Lily On Thy Brow."

5. VILLA MAGNI

1. Shelley's words.

1. ENGLISH OPERA HOUSE

1. From Peake's *Presumption: or, the Fate of Frankenstein.*
2. You can see this photo on Wikipedia.

2. FIELD PLACE

1. Wollstonecraft, from *A Vindication of the Rights of Woman.*
2. Shelley, "To a Skylark."
3. Trelawney's own words.

3. KENTISH TOWN

1. Byron, from *Don Juan.*
2. Words in italics are Mary's own, from *The Last Man.*
3. From the casualty lists of the Peterloo Massacre.
4. Shelley, *Adonais.*
5. From *The Last Man.*
6. RIP to the Hardy Tree, fallen in the fall of 2023.

4. HOLBORN

1. Godwin's words.

Acknowledgments

THANKS TO:

Mary Petiet and Anastasia Drost of Sea Crow Press.

Scholarly, translation, and writerly help and support: Jennifer Acker, Kerri Arsenault, Reid Barbour, Tim Barringer, Megan Mayhew Bergman, Taylor Brorby, Lucy Brown, Ruth Caldwell, Kristine Dalaker, Camille Dungy, Peter Geye, Bryan and Kristi Giemza, Philip Freeman, Marianne Gingher, Tim Heath and the good people of the Blake Society, the Keats-Shelley Association of America, the Byron Society, Patrick Hicks, Keith Lesmeister, Reed Johnson, Jeanne Moskal, Orçun Selçuk, Bland Simpson, Beverly Taylor, Joseph Viscomi, Tim Webb, Joe Wilkins, Elizabeth Young, and the many historians and scholars whose work, absorbed over so many years, has shaped my understanding of this period. Thanks to the staff of the British Library Rare Books and Manuscripts Reading Room.

Boxing: Mark Burford of The Ring Boxing Club in Southwark, Kate Sekules, Paul Bryers, Charles Jones, and Christina Zimber. Nick Powell of Highgate Cemetery, place of Pierce Egan and Tom Sayers, graciously scheduled me to lecture on them there in January 2023.

Study-abroad and travel: Anne Hall-Williams, guide to Harrow School (where Winston Churchill's housemaster was named "Dr. Welldon!"), Rosanna Marazzi and staff of Celtic Hotel, London, Renata Salecl, Alan Ravenscroft, Rosemary Stones, Joan Gillespie, Anita Miller, Andrew Kennedy, Maggy Wittmer, Roberto Zammattio and staff and family of Pensione Guerrato, Venice, and Stefano and Kira Loreti and staff of Hotel Oceania, Rome. Carol and Tom Birkland gave Geneva navigation and the horse's-tail image of the Staubbach Falls. David and Rachel Faldet first took me to Newstead Abbey, where kind docent Amanda Gibbons gave me a good look at the Byron Screen. Morgan Osman and Jena Lisowski are the "determined young women" leaving letters to Mary Wollstonecraft on page 337.

At Luther College: Vikki Barness, Jane Fosaaen, and Jeff Naatz of the Document Center printed multiple copies of this novel's massive drafts and cheered its progress. Edward Atwell and Emily Mineart helped with computer monitors and interlibrary loans. Anne Bulliung helped with Virgil. Alfredo Alonso Estenoz provided welcome support and conversation. Thanks to the Provost's Office and the Paideia Program Sabbatical Fund.

Thanks, as ever, to my friends, my family, and my students – especially those who've journeyed with me "in Frankenstein's footsteps." And Manchester, a model orange tabby cat, who passed away on the same day and at the same distinguished age as Prince Phillip: April 9, 2021.

About the Author

Amy Weldon is Professor of English at Luther College in Decorah, Iowa, where she teaches the study-abroad course "In *Frankenstein's* Footsteps: The Keats-Shelley Circle in London, Geneva, and Italy." Her previous books include *Advanced Fiction Writing: A Writer's Guide and Anthology; Eldorado, Iowa: A Novel; The Writer's Eye: Observation and Inspiration for Creative Writers;* and *The Hands-On Life: How to Wake Yourself Up and Save The World.* Read more at amyeweldon.com.

About the Press

Sea Crow Press is an award-winning woman-run independent book publisher based on Cape Cod in Massachusetts committed to amplifying voices that might otherwise go unheard. We publish creative nonfiction, literary fiction, and poetry. Our books celebrate our connection to each other and to the natural world with a focus on positive change and great storytelling.